BREAKNECK

NINE GRIPPING HIGH-SPEED THRILLERS

JASON CANNON, JOSLYN CHASE, JAMES DAIN, STEVE DICKINSON, TOM FOWLER, TRUDEY MARTIN, SHARON A MITCHELL, JAY TINSIANO, BEN WESTERHAM

PARAQUEL PRESS

PARAQUEL PRESS

TABLE OF CONTENTS

INTRODUCTION

THESE DAYS, TIME SEEMS shorter than ever, crammed full with work, errands, chores, activities, exercise routines, and so much more.

Our attention spans are short, conditioned by tweets, snippets, Facebook posts, text messages, and many other micro time-grabbers.

So, while novels are a fabulous way to enrich and energize your world, the savvy reader also embraces the many advantages of the short story.

After all, there's a lot to love about this marvelous form of fiction.

Like what?

The great editor, Sol Stein emphasized that stories are about "creating an emotional experience for the reader...who should be oblivious to the fact that he is seeing words on paper."

All story, short or long, targets the reader's emotions, but a short story often packs a particularly potent punch because it is, of necessity, concentrated into a smaller package.

And you know what they say about good things and small packages.

Short stories are different from novels in a number of ways. Obviously, both forms of fiction have a lot to offer, but short stories free the author to try new ideas and develop unexplored territory in ways a novel doesn't.

A benefit that passes on to the reader.

Novels are a big investment of time, for both reader and writer. Short stories allow for greater risk and the potential of a big return in story value.

Thriller author Jeffery Deaver puts it like this:

"Readers don't have the same emotional investment as in a novel. The payoff in the case of short stories isn't a roller coaster of plot reversals involving characters they've spent time learning about and loving or hating, set in places with atmosphere carefully described. Short stories are like a sniper's bullet. Fast and shocking."

A best kept hollywood secret

Because the writer of a short story must create colorful characters, in a vivid world, within a small space, the medium is a superb source for box office hits.

You may not realize that an extensive list of great movies and television shows are based on short stories.

For instance:

- Rear Window

- 2001: A Space Odyssey

- The Birds

- Minority Report

- The Secret Life of Walter Mitty

- The Shawshank Redemption

- Memento

- 3:10 To Yuma

- The Fly

- Rashomon

- The Illusionist

- Arrival

- The Curious Case of Benjamin Button

- 36 Hours

That's just the tip of the iceberg. Clearly, there's gold to be mined in short fiction.

But here's the takeaway nugget for you:

Hollywood's best kept secret can be the key to more reading treasure for you. It's often been said that the book is better than the movie—so read the stories before they hit the screen.

We hope you like our selection of thriller short stories and wish you happy reading!

GREEN STORM RISING

JOSLYN CHASE

ELUF CROUCHED INSIDE THE tiny hut, coaxing fire into the frozen twigs and bits of paper he'd tossed into the pot belly of the ancient iron stove. It slumped in the corner like an old man gone to fat, creaky with age and temperamental. At last, a few licks of flame rose and caught on the kindling with a gentle crackle, giving Eluf hope for a nice blaze by the time Betina arrived.

He turned and surveyed the pile of quilts and blankets stacked on a mattress in the opposite corner. On the other hand, the cold might drive her more quickly beneath the sheets and that suited him fine. The thought of Betina's skin beneath his fingertips, her lips, roughened by the arctic winds, moving along his collarbone and up to nip at his earlobe, made his breath come faster and he watched the vapor puff out of him like a dragon's breath.

He would be like a dragon in bed tonight.

But they had to be careful. Meeting like this, in secret and only once or twice a month, made Eluf all the hungrier for her. But it had to be like this. At least, until they could figure out what to do about Betina's husband.

Eluf plumped the pillows on the low mattress, wrinkling his nose at the smell of unwashed bedclothes that wafted up from the tangle of blankets. Ah well, nothing he could do about it now. He scooped the binoculars from the seat of an old wooden chair and stepped outside.

The midnight sky rose above him, green and magnificent, shifting lights as magical as fairy dust. Greenland, in December, always brought the Northern Lights and their brilliance allowed him to see through the binoculars. Not sharp detail, as in daylight, but he could make out the village below and see smoke rising from chimneys, the outlines of shops and houses, the church steeple and village maypole like two masts of a great ship against a heaving emerald sea.

And in the nearer distance, a dark figure moving up the hillside to meet him, her alluring curves hidden beneath layers of coats and sweaters. He looked forward to removing every one of them.

The dancing lights above him brightened and sharpened, their radiance becoming harsh in a way he'd never seen before. He shielded his eyes, but the glow intensified into a searing flame of color that tore through the sky like Thor's firebolt.

Eluf squeezed his eyes shut and sheltered his head beneath his arm. The storm of brilliant color passed with a boom he felt in his gut, though he heard nothing. The sky now was white, washed clean. He focused the binoculars downhill and was relieved to see Betina hurrying toward him.

Shifting his gaze to the village below, he stared, refocused, and stared again.

It had vanished.

Where before had stood houses and shops, a school, a church, a post office, there was now only a scattering of ash, stirred by a restless wind.

Eluf gaped for the merest moment before the binoculars bonded to his face with a suffusing heat and he and Betina turned to dust.

———

Agent Talmadge Bannerman stared at the screen on the wall above the conference table. Silence hung in the room like a heavy cloak for one and a half seconds before cacophony broke forth, everyone talking at once.

Men and women dressed in dignified military uniforms and distinguished business suits gesticulated violently enough to put out the eyes of their neighbors, who were gesticulating wildly in turn. More than one coffee cup tipped and spilled, sending hot brown liquid across the polished table. There was a sound of shattering glass and a crunch as someone rolled their chair over the resulting mess.

Tal, a newly-minted member of the Department of Homeland Security team, waved his hand for attention and cleared his throat. Beside him, his partner, Carl Wrigley, took things a step further.

"Hey!" he shouted, the pink of his scalp deepening under the stress of the situation. "Before we all go ballistic, could we get another look at that footage, Secretary Livingston?"

The room fell into a tense quiet, tinged by the smell of coffee and fear. Assistant Secretary Pete Livingston pushed a button on the remote control and replayed the satellite surveillance recording.

Tal watched the grainy image of a far-off village, shimmering under an eerie green light. The light intensified, pulling into a cone shape. There was a flash on the screen and the village disappeared. Nothing but a residue of light ash remained, gray against the snow and blowing in the wind.

Tal felt a shiver run up his back. This time, no one broke the stunned silence until the Secretary froze the image on the screen and said, "What you've just witnessed is only one instance of the phenomena. We know of at least two more."

"What is it?" a woman three notches up Tal's chain of command asked. Her coral-colored lipstick had smudged on one side, giving her mouth a lopsided appearance. "An alien attack?"

The Secretary had a face like an Easter Island rock carving. "We don't think so," he said. "Our mole in the scientific community has been tracking a troublesome development over the last several months. His team have focused their attention on a lab facility in northern Greenland."

The Secretary pushed a button and everyone's eyes swiveled back to the screen. Tal watched as the frozen wasteland of a vanished village was replaced by a frozen wasteland dotted by a fenced compound.

"We believe an astrophysicist by the name of Antonia Scylla has been developing and testing a solar weapon, powered by geomagnetic coronal emissions."

"What does that mean in English, Mr. Secretary?" asked a balding man across the table from Tal.

"The science behind it is rather complicated, as you can imagine. Put simply, she's found a way to harness the power of the Aurora Borealis."

"The Northern Lights?" someone asked.

"And presumably the Southern Lights as well. Aurora Australis."

"How is this possible, Mr. Secretary?" asked the coral-lipped woman, the boss of the boss of Tal's boss. He wished he could remember her name.

The Secretary's eyes narrowed. He turned to the man beside him. "Commander Johnson, you want to take this?"

A man in uniform rose and took control of the remote. A huge fiery ball appeared on the screen. It seemed to be covered in bright orange lava which splashed and glowed with a fierce intensity.

"The Auroras originate some ninety-three million miles away, on the surface of the sun," he began. "When massive explosions of electromagnetic matter occur—we call those CME's, Coronal Mass Ejections—they create a stream of electronically charged solar particles known as Solar Wind."

"And you're telling us we're feeling that wind from ninety-three million miles away?" Director Hawkins asked. He was Tal's immediate supervisor.

"Not feeling it," the officer explained, "but sometimes we can see its effects."

"I'll bet that village we saw disappear was feeling it," said the boss of the boss of Tal's boss.

The Secretary cleared his throat. "I'll bet that village didn't feel a thing. It all happened too fast. One second there, the next…vaporized."

The woman's face was pale. She bit her lip, transferring lipstick to her two front teeth. The officer continued his science lecture.

"Solar Winds move at extraordinary speeds, up to forty-five million miles an hour. Their energy causes a distortion in the earth's magnetic field and some of those charged particles work their way into our atmosphere around the magnetic poles, creating what we call the Auroras. Apparently, this Scylla has developed a way to focus the power of those particles into a weapon. Sources tell us she calls it a Geomagnetic Concentrator."

"Those same sources," the Secretary added, "have been calling it The Oven Cleaner, because it incinerates everything in its path without flame, leaving only ash behind."

Tal's chill of unease grew. News of this fearsome weapon was troubling in the extreme, but something he'd have expected to be way above his pay grade. Why had he and Carl been included in this conference? He didn't think he wanted to know.

But he was about to find out.

The DHS Secretary resumed control of the remote. "Thank you, Commander Johnson."

He pointed to the screen where a woman's face appeared, mid-forties with cocoa-brown skin and dark hair parted down the middle with one white stripe snaking down each side. Tal couldn't determine if the stripe was natural or artificially produced and he didn't spend more than a second on speculation. The mesmerizing eyes caught his attention and held it like a small child holds a puppy—by the neck in a suffocating grip.

"This is Antonia Scylla," Livingston said. He flashed another photo on the screen, a blonde woman, tall and sleek, near the age of fifty, but toned and elegant with glacial blue eyes. "And this," the Secretary said, "is the eminent physicist, Eudora Petrovna. We believe these two women have been neck and neck in a race to perfect a new weapon technology. It now appears that Scylla has won."

"Let me guess," said the boss of the boss of Tal's boss, gesturing to the blonde. "They call this one Charybdis."

"You pegged it, Director Miskin."

Miskin! That was it.

A new image replaced Eudora Petrovna, a jingling video showing a Christmas wonderland of a town with a gigantic statue of Santa Claus to welcome newcomers and candy cane street lamps lining the main avenues. Livingston froze the frame on a cheery sign at the town limits. It read: Welcome to North Pole, Alaska. Pop. 2103.

"Our inside man tells us Scylla has finished her preliminary testing. She now plans to make a more extensive, more public demonstration of the weapon's efficacy. She's alerted potential buyers of her intention to incinerate the town of North Pole, Alaska at the stroke of midnight on Christmas Eve."

"Letting the world know what she thinks about peace on earth and good will toward men," said the balding man across the table.

Livingston nodded. "When the demonstration concludes, she'll open the bidding and hand her Geomagnetic Concentrator over to the highest bidder. We need to stop all of that from happening."

He turned to Tal and his partner, Carl. Tal's skin prickled as if someone had just run nails across a chalkboard.

"You two," Livingston said, "are going into Scylla's base of operation to secure the weapon."

Tal stared. Carl seemed tongue-tied as well until he finally sputtered, "Why the two of us? You should be sending in a battalion!"

"Yes, we should," Livingston agreed. "But we can't risk it. Scylla's stronghold is in a wide snowfield about forty miles west of North Pole. There's no cover, no way to conceal our approach and if she sees us coming, she's liable to pull the trigger on her new toy and obliterate the target early. A couple of wildlife photographers rambling past on snowmobiles have a much better chance of getting close enough to get inside."

Tal groaned. "But why us?" he asked.

Director Hawkins fielded the question. "Both of you have experience in relevant scientific disciplines, as well as tactical training. Wrigley, you studied heliophysics as part of your doctorate program and participated in a number of field experiments."

His eyes shifted in Tal's direction. "Your work in the Epidemic Intelligence Service took you more than once into hostile territory,

Bannerman. You performed well under the rigors of war and disease in Afghanistan, Ethiopia, and the Sudan. As well as being an epidemiologist, you studied veterinary medicine for a time. That knowledge may well prove useful on this mission."

"What do you mean, boss?"

Hawkins looked at Livingston. The Secretary said, "We've had reports of strange animal behavior in the vicinity of the compound. The weapon may be sending out frequencies or in some other way interfering with the animals. Wolves, in particular."

Great. Add crazed wolves to the list of hazards.

"We'll supply you with tranquilizers and a dart gun. You'll have a better idea of the proper dosages."

Tal gulped. His pulse throbbed in his ears. "Surely you can find someone more qualified than the two of us," he said, trying to keep his voice even, his tone reasonable.

There was a brief silence, then Director Hawkins asked, "How's your cousin Amy, Bannerman?"

"Amy? How do you know about Amy? And funny you should ask. I just got a postcard from her yesterday, letting me know she's settling into her new assignment at Eielson Air Force Base in...Alaska."

"Right," Hawkins said. "Eielson." He turned to Livingston. "Where's that located?"

Secretary Livingston looked apologetic, but that didn't keep him from answering. "Less than ten miles from the town of North Pole."

Tal knew they had him. Knew they'd always had him. He raised his chin and saw Carl do the same. They were going in, side by side.

The Secretary rubbed his hands together. "Frankly, gentlemen, we don't have time to find another team. Tomorrow is Christmas Eve."

Every head in the room tilted to look at the clock above the Secretary's head. It read 12:27 am.

The Secretary checked the time on his watch. "Strike that," he said. "It's Christmas Eve already. We have less than twenty-four hours, people."

To Tal and Carl he said, "Go home, pack a bag, say goodbye to your families. Your flight leaves the airfield at Joint Base Lewis McChord in three hours."

THE WEATHER, WHEN THEY left Tacoma, had been pitch black and drizzling with rain. Four and a half hours later, when they touched down on the flightline at Eielson, the world was pitch black and pelting tiny popsicles from the sky. Tal shielded his face against the miniscule missiles as he stepped off the plane feeling groggy and disoriented. As if moving through a dream.

He wished that's all it was.

But the bite of the Alaskan wind left him in no doubt this was real. It was happening, and he didn't feel at all ready. By the look on his partner's face, Carl was processing similar sentiments.

They crossed the tarmac, slick with patches of ice, and entered the terminal, pausing to pick up a contingent of personnel assigned to assist them in preparing for the mission. As they moved through a maze of corridors, footsteps and voices echoing, Tal felt like a VIP with an entourage and gained a new empathy for folks whose lives have been derailed by public demand.

Their first stop was the canteen, where Tal and Carl were plied with a hearty breakfast, the last real meal they'd have for the foreseeable future. Tal tried to do it justice, but the lump forming in his throat made it hard to swallow. While they ate, a team of outfitters sized them up, asking questions about preferences and proficiencies.

When they finished eating, they were escorted to a large room stacked high with clothing, accessories, and equipment. By the time they left, both he and Carl had been dressed from the skin outward with layers designed to withstand cold while allowing mobility. In their guise as photographers, they didn't wear anything suggestive of the military.

On the surface.

Beneath their parkas, each wore a holstered weapon and a tactical chest rig containing extra mags, two knives, a headlamp, a Zippo fire starter, a set of wire cutters, and a multitool. The cameras they carried on straps around their necks were designed less for photo quality and more for visual reconnaissance. They incorporated smart binoculars with night vision capabilities.

They also functioned as radio communicators, creating a link between their two-man mission and base control. A burly Master Sergeant demonstrated how to operate the radio, talking them through a transmission.

"And that's all there is to it," he finished. "Unless they won't work, which is possible."

"What do you mean?" Carl asked.

The man looked suddenly uncomfortable, as if wishing he'd kept his mouth shut. "A major geomagnetic storm occurred on the sun's surface three days ago," he admitted, "creating a strong solar flare."

"So? How does that affect us now?"

"Well, that's how long it takes, sir, for the flare to reach earth. Big explosions and electrical storms on the sun can block electronic communication, foul up GPS, wipe out power grids and even push satellites out of orbit."

"Surely that kind of thing is a rarity?" Tal said hopefully.

The Master Sergeant shrugged. "I'm sure you're right."

Miskin approached, looking at her watch. "Sunup's in less than an hour. Time to move out."

Winter days in Alaska are short. As Tal and Carl piled into the back of an eight-seater van, the sky to the east glowed pink and blue like birthday frosting on a long white sheet cake.

"You've got a little less than five hours of daylight," Miskin said. "But that's just as well, Might be better to make your approach in the dark."

The van turned onto Highway 2, taking them through the town of North Pole. They passed the giant Santa Tal had seen on the video, and a visitor's center painted with red gingerbread trim and murals of holiday scenes spanning cream-colored walls. A candy-stripe maypole stood in front, next to another larger-than-life Santa with a sleigh and piles of gaily wrapped presents.

Decorated Christmas trees were everywhere, and even the golden arches of McDonalds rose on candy cane supports. The day was shaping into a fine one, clear sky stretching overhead like a blue china dome, and no snow fell but a thick blanket of white covered the ground, adding to the postcard prettiness of the town.

Despite the grimness of the situation, their driver had tuned the radio to a holiday channel and Tal heard the wistful tune of *I'll Be Home for Christmas,* played at low volume. His heart captured the moment, fraught with meaning, one of those psychic snapshots your mind takes that you never forget. Years later, you can ferret them out of your memory like an enchanted image that brings back the sights and sounds, the smell and touch.

The *feel* of the moment.

He thought of Bridget—the recent roundness of her belly, the excited sparkle in her eye, the home they'd made together.

The family they were making.

Yes, I'll be home for Christmas.

If only in my dreams.

They passed through Fairbanks, but Tal hardly got a glimpse of it. DHS Director Miskin had accompanied them on their journey and she sat on the van's bench seat, between Tal and Carl, a large tablet on her lap showing a map of the region. She began their final briefing.

"We'll drop you here," she pointed, "where you'll rent snowmobiles—Alaskans call them snowmachines, by the way—and head into this area." Her finger moved to a wide blank spot on the map. "Scylla's compound is about twenty-six miles in."

She handed each of them a GPS tracker showing Scylla's location in relation to their own.

"If things go without a hitch," Miskin said, "you can get within spitting distance in less than an hour. Even moving slow so you can stop and take pictures. Remember, you're wildlife photographers."

"While I appreciate your optimism," Tal said, "do you have any insight into the kind of 'hitches' we might expect?"

"Were you a boy scout, Agent Bannerman?"

"I get it—be prepared for anything."

"Right," she agreed, "but while we're on the subject, here's a little present for you."

Reaching under the seat, she handed Tal a hard plastic case about twelve inches square and five inches deep. It bore an adhesive label which read: Camera Accessories.

"Merry Christmas!" she said, her smile brittle.

Tal snapped the latches and opened it to find a tranquilizer dart gun nested in foam, along with a dozen disposable needled syringes with pink fringed tailpieces. The lid of the case contained several vials of zolazepam and ketamine. He hoped he remembered the dosing guidelines.

The van pulled into the parking lot of a winter sport rental facility.

"We'll wait here and see you off," Miskin said as the driver swung the door wide.

Snow crunched under Tal's feet as he and Carl crossed the parking lot to enter the building. Red and green banners fluttered from the eaves, and *Jingle Bells* emanated from a speaker mounted on a light-post. They got in line behind six happy-looking customers and waited to fill out paperwork so they could mount two rental snowmachines and set off to save Christmas.

At least, for the town of North Pole, Alaska.

Keys in hand, they returned to the van for the last of their gear and final instructions. Miskin looked at her watch. Carl looked at his watch. Tal didn't want to think about the minutes marching on. He retrieved the dart case and an insulated bag containing water bottles and power bars. Both he and Carl strapped a pair of snowshoes to their backs.

"You have approximately thirteen hours," Miskin told them. "That gives you ample time to get there, find a way in, and secure the weapon."

"Without a hitch," Tal said.

"Right."

Tal strapped the gear onto the back of his snowmobile, slid onto the seat, and fired up the engine. It started with a growl that settled into a purr and he moved off into the snow, looking back to see Carl following. Miskin and the driver stood watching them. Nobody waved.

As the machine hummed across the field, Tal was glad of his helmet, warding off cold and wind and cutting the glare. The sun was directly overhead and brilliant in the clear sky, its radiance magnified by the endless bed of white. The helmets were also fitted with headsets so he and Carl could talk to each other as long as they stayed in proximity.

"You ready for this?" Carl asked.

"Give me a hundred years and my answer would still be no. Yet here we are. Ready or not."

As they traveled the terrain, they crossed paths with other riders out for recreation, and even passed a group snowshoeing and a couple of lone cross country skiers. Soon, however, company became scarce and tracks left in the snow less frequent.

The land was mostly flat, occasionally fringed by stands of frosted pines. As they progressed toward Scylla's position, the ground became more uneven, rocky in some places and filled with undulating hills in others. At first, it was fun flying over the hillocks, taking air, and landing with a thump but it grew old fast and Tal wished it would flatten out again.

"Tal! At your ten o'clock!"

He looked ahead to the left and saw them.

Wolves.

The hair on the back of his neck rose. Wolves are nocturnal creatures. They hunt at night, and Tal found this daytime appearance disturbing. Something else about their behavior raised a warning flag. Contrary to common belief, wolves tend to hunt solo or in mated pairs. This pack of eight was moving in a solid line, flanking their position.

He cursed. Some boy scout. He should have filled some syringes and kept the dart gun at the ready.

"Tranq gun's not going to help us here," he told Carl. "I wouldn't have time to stop and dig it out before they'd be on us."

He looked down at the speedometer and saw it went up to 120 mph.

"Wolves don't act like this unless there's something wrong with them, Carl. They don't attack humans in motorized vehicles."

"Should we shoot them?"

"I think our better bet is to outrun them. They can sprint up to forty miles per hour for a short time. We can speed over a hundred. Let's go!"

Tal turned the nose of his snowmobile slightly right and gunned the engine, crouching low over the handle bars. The machine churned through the snow, sending up a spray of white matter that hit Tal's face shield like pellets of sand.

Carl kept pace beside him.

Tal twisted his head for a quick glance behind and saw the wolves still advancing but growing smaller in the distance. Just a little bit farther at this speed and they could slow down and reorient themselves.

As the thought crossed his mind, both he and Carl crested a hillock and went airborne. The earth fell away beneath them and Tal's stomach heaved with the sensation of free fall.

His ears rang with the sound of metal smashing against rock.

Tal landed on a drift of snow with a hard crack that jolted him from the seat and sent the machine skidding away on its side. It came to a rest twenty yards away and sputtered into silence.

Tal lay on his back, eyes squeezed shut against the sun's glare. He heard a groan and raised himself on an elbow, peering around to locate Carl.

"You all right?" he called.

He saw Carl's snowmobile, mangled and smoking, where it had met not snowdrift, but rock. His partner had been thrown clear of the handlebars, striking another rock rising bare from the snow. Carl lay beside it, his leg twisted. His face, protected inside the helmet, was a grimace of pain.

"No," Tal answered himself. "I can see you are not."

Tal flipped the switch on his camera that turned it into a radio, and transmitted the signal.

"Base control."

Tal gave his call sign. "We've had an accident. My partner's leg is broken. You need to send someone in to get him."

"Copy. I see your location. We can get to you in ninety minutes. Hang tight, and we'll work on getting you a replacement. Over."

"Copy that. Get here fast," Tal said.

He signed off and rose, moving his limbs, cracking his neck, shaking off dirt and snow. Kneeling beside Carl, he checked his partner's pupils and reflexes.

"Are you hurt anywhere else?"

"I don't think so. Not bodily, anyway. I think my pride's taken a hit." He frowned. "You'll have to finish this one without me, Tal."

"I'm sorry, buddy. There's no one else I'd—"

"Tal! They've caught up."

Carl pointed up to the ridge they'd recently barreled over. A line of scruffy canine heads broke the skyline. Tal reached for his holster but before he could pull his gun, a rifle shot rang out, echoing across the snow.

The wolves fled.

A low hum registered on Tal's awareness. It grew to a crescendo, then dropped as a snowmachine, unseen above them, idled. A face covered in a black balaclava stared down at them. It disappeared and the engine cut off. Tal heard the man's footsteps as he approached from a lateral angle. He kept his parka open, hand near his holster.

"Careful," Carl warned, his voice soft.

When the man appeared again, this time coming around to Tal's level, he'd removed the head covering, revealing features Tal associated with the word "eskimo." A native Alaskan.

Elderly, with white hair and a mapwork of lines and wrinkles on his face, the man greeted Tal with a hand signal. "You've had some trouble."

"Yes," Tal said. "My friend is hurt."

The Inuit said nothing for a moment as he peered up into the sky. Then he said, "A storm is coming."

Tal looked at the clear blue expanse above them. He didn't like to contradict the man, but really?

The man smiled, showing a row of crooked teeth. "You do not believe me, but that won't stop the storm from coming." He gestured to Carl. "If we splint his leg, I can take him into town on my machine."

"Help is on the way," Tal told him.

"That's good."

Again there was silence as the man surveyed the sky. In the west, Tal saw a single thin tail of cloud reaching into the blue.

Carl wriggled where he lay, as if trying for a more comfortable position. "When will this storm hit?" he asked.

The man shrugged. "Two hours, four hours. Maybe more. Best to get under shelter soon."

Tal thought about the town of North Pole, of his cousin, Amy, so close and maybe going into town for Christmas dinner or festivities. Population 2103.

He couldn't wait.

"There's something I need to do," he told the man. "Will you stay here with my friend until help comes?"

"Tal, you can't go on alone."

"And I can't spare the time waiting, Carl. Think about it."

Carl sighed. He spoke to the stranger. "I'd appreciate it if you stayed with me so my friend can go. Shouldn't be more than an hour."

"I'll stay."

Tal thanked the man and checked the GPS tracker. Righting his snowmobile, he pointed it in the proper direction and turned the key in the ignition. The engine coughed and quit.

He tried again, coaxing life into the machine. The engine ran, settling into its customary purr, and Tal pulled on his helmet. He gave his partner a thumbs up and sped away.

Once over the bluffs and out of sight, he stopped long enough to load some syringes, making the doses right for a 120 pound wolf. He packed them into his chest rig, along with extra vials and empty syringes.

He loaded a cartridge into the tranq gun and put it in a pocket of the parka. Zipping it shut, he felt more prepared.

He hoped he wouldn't encounter any crazed bears.

He continued on, figuring he must have covered nearly twenty of the twenty-six anticipated miles to the compound. The land grew flat again, wide open and clear. He was drawing closer to the destination dot on the tracker screen, but he needed to stop for a call of nature.

As he stood in the snow near his idling snowmobile, a tiny dusting of flakes, soft and feathery, fell from a sky fast filling with scudding clouds. Still, it was hard to believe they heralded something violent enough to be called a storm. He ate a power bar and drank half a liter of water. He was screwing the cap onto the bottle when he felt something strike him in the leg.

Looking down, he saw a white rabbit, fluffy as a snowball with shortened ears. An Arctic hare. As he watched, it launched itself at him again, mouth opened in a snarl. Tal's thick snowsuit and insulated boots proved impervious to the animal's attack and he shook it off, almost laughing at the absurdity of it.

Until he saw a dozen more creatures moving toward him, springing through the drifts like Santa's coursers.

Enough of them together could knock him down and though he couldn't bring himself to believe a drove of maniacal hares would be the death of him, he didn't want to stick around to find out.

Climbing back onto the snowmobile, he glided away, accelerating to 60 mph for some minutes. Hares can run as fast as wolves and he didn't want them catching up.

As he slowed, he checked the GPS tracker. The dot had vanished.

Tal knew the expanse of white could be disorienting. He could be heading a few degrees off target that would ultimately result in a total miss. Stopping the snowmobile once more, Tal got off and stood on top of a rock, holding the tracker up, turning it in different directions.

He shook the unit, tried resetting it, but the screen remained blank.

He remembered what the Master Sergeant had said about geomagnetic disturbances messing with GPS signals.

He'd have to go on memory and instinct.

As he stood atop the rock, orienting himself, he heard a cracking sound behind him and turned to see a fissure forming under the snowmachine. He'd inadvertently parked on a layer of surface ice.

The crack widened as Tal watched helplessly. The snowmobile dipped sideways, bobbed on water and slowly sank like a fat man lowering himself into the tub.

His transport was gone. His food was gone. The backup syringes and tranquilizing drugs were gone.

Tal was alone, twenty-odd miles from civilization, with darkness coming and a storm blowing in. Wild animals, driven to bizarre and dangerous acts by the side effects of a mad scientist's experiments roamed the vicinity. And the crazed woman planned to deliver her deadly weapon of mass destruction to the baddest of the bad.

But only after she'd demonstrated its usefulness on a town full of innocent and unsuspecting citizens.

On Christmas.

Somehow, in a twist he still wasn't sure he fully understood, the responsibility for stopping this from happening had fallen upon him. He had to get to her compound, wrest the weapon from her control, and render her unable to complete her plan.

Before midnight.

On foot.

Alone.

STANDING ON TOP OF the rock, wind whistling through his helmet, Tal remembered the map on Miskin's tablet. She'd pointed to a barren-looking spot, far from anything else, but he remembered seeing hot springs denoted to the north and to the east.

Hot springs could make ice dependability uncertain, unleashing warmer temperatures beneath the surface. With everything buried under a thick white blanket, he hadn't realized he'd stopped the snow-mobile on top of water.

His rock wasn't going anywhere, but was it on land—or sticking out above a lake or pond?

He still had the camera radio hanging from his neck and a pair of snowshoes strapped to his back. He activated the radio and gave the transmission signal, getting a stream of static in response. He tried again and heard only a confusion of static and garbled snippets, like scanning across the dial.

For six or seven minutes, he continued the effort, dismayed at how low the sun now hung against the horizon. His scant five hours of daylight were about to pass into night, and darkness would begin. The whistling wind took up strength, sending forth an occasional howl across the icy wilderness and the few flakes he'd seen before thickened and fell faster.

Removing his helmet, Tal sat on the rock and donned the balaclava and knit hat the outfitters had tucked into an interior pocket of his parka. He added a pair of goggles and pulled on the snowshoes, ad-justing and locking the bindings to his boots. Facing away from the fallen snowmobile, he transferred his weight onto the snowshoes and started walking, waddling like a duck.

Without poles to help his balance and aid his steps, his progress felt achingly slow and his energy waned, sapped by cold, worry, and lack of nourishment. His cover as a wildlife photographer, always dubious, was now useless but a new, more convincing one, took its place.

He was lost.

His orienteering skills had always been good and he thought he was headed in the right direction but he was going on instinct and nothing more. As he plodded on, with the lonely wind whooshing along beside him, he saw a figure in the distance. The person drew nearer and Tal saw it was a cross country skier.

They hailed each other with uplifted hands and once within hearing distance, the man shouted, "Storm coming! Where you headed?"

Tal gestured. "My buddy has a place about three miles that way, but it's slow going in these snowshoes and getting dark." He appraised the man's blue eyes behind a pair of goggles and figured it was worth a try. "You open to a trade?"

"What? My skis for your snowshoes?" He shook his head. "You'd have to sweeten the deal."

Tal tried to remember how much he had in his wallet, dreading the thought of digging down through the layers to access it. "How about fifty bucks and a Swiss Army knife?"

"Basic model or primo?"

"Primo."

"Done."

They made the trade and as he started off on the skis, Tal realized the man had gotten the better of the bargain. The skis were old, worn, the bindings loose. But he now had poles and moved more quickly across the snowfield.

The man was barely out of sight behind him when the sun fell, as if someone had snipped the string holding it up, and darkness spread over the landscape like a sinister shadow. Tal shivered and stopped. He fished the headlamp from his chest rig and adjusted it over the balaclava.

He skied.

After an exhausting length of time, he estimated he was three or four miles from Scylla's compound and hoped she'd have a few lights burning to help him find it. Gritting his teeth, he burrowed beneath protective layers to expose his wristwatch. It was an old school model, unaffected by geomagnetic interference.

It showed the time was 5:57 pm.

Six hours and counting.

He pressed forward, the sky ahead of him shimmering faintly green, reminding him of bioluminescence he'd witnessed once during a long distant sea journey. The wind, now a constant force pushing against him, hampering his progress, sounded like the roar of a pounding surf, swelling and receding, tossing him in its sway.

Tal lost two hours swishing through the snow, encountering no one. Not even a crazed and ravenous wolf. He changed direction and set off again, faring no better. He began to imagine he felt every second ticking by on the watch against his wrist. Like a drum beat of doom.

He herringboned up a hill and stood at the top, scanning with his souped-up camera for light, smoke, anything that might indicate a structure and people.

But there was nothing.

Where had he gone wrong? Direction? Distance? A single degree off course, multiplied by distance traveled, compounded the original error. Sometimes irredeemably. If he didn't find that stronghold, get inside, and stop Scylla's wicked posturing for power, thousands of people would die tonight.

Maybe millions more tomorrow.

Tal closed his eyes, prayed for guidance, prayed for peace on earth, good will toward men. Christmas was a celebration of the hope for deliverance. He needed that hope now.

He opened his eyes to see lights shifting in heaven. Glistening, shimmering emerald crossed by the nebulous gray of moving clouds, like a brilliant and mysterious green opal. He remembered that the color green, according to Christmas symbolism, represents eternal hope and renewal of life.

Embracing that hope, he strained his eyes over the expanse of darkness beneath the glowing sky and saw the compound nestled in snow. Saw it so clearly it was hard to imagine how he'd missed it before.

Sending up his heartfelt thanks, Tal switched off his headlamp and glided down the hill. The glow from the sky gave him enough light to move by and he didn't want to telegraph his arrival to anyone watching.

His skis became more of a hindrance than a help as he neared the compound. He abandoned them, realizing that without any kind of cover—no trees, only razor-wire and chain link fence surrounding the building—he'd have to crawl the last hundred yards, keeping low.

The only object that might provide him any kind of cover was a small garbage dumpster standing just inside the fence near a side door, presumably leading to the kitchen. He slithered up to the fence and laid flat behind the dumpster, catching his breath and peering beneath the dumpster's wheels.

It stank.

That was a good thing, as it turned out. Tal watched as two booted legs rounded the corner, accompanied by four black-and-brown dog paws. From his vantage point, he could only see the man from the knee down, but he saw enough of the Doberman to be glad of the stench helping to cover his scent. The wind that had pushed against him during the trek now worked in his favor—whisking scent molecules away before the dog could get a handle on them.

What now?

When dog and man had passed around the far corner of the building, continuing their rounds, Tal wriggled along the fence line far enough to give him a good look at the metal door. It was sturdy, flush with the wall, no entry keypad or card slider. Not even a keyhole. Just flat metal, unadorned.

He slinked into position behind the dumpster just as the patrol came back into view. The man paused and gave three raps on the door. It opened and a changing of the guards took place, including the dog. This time it was a German Shepherd.

Tal pulled back the layers and looked at his watch. Straight up on 11:00.

Alone, and with limited resources, the only way he could think to get inside that door was to wait until the next changing of the guard and take down the men while the door was open so their fallen bodies would prop the door open long enough for him to gain entry.

Provided no one else stood inside, waiting to drill him in the head as he crossed the threshold.

Fortunately, the cold would shorten their shifts. He bargained on their changing every half hour. It had to be. Otherwise, he'd be too late.

He spent the next thirty minutes waiting for the patrol to round the far corner and using the wire cutters to snip through the chain link fence while they traversed the opposite side of the yard.

As 11:30 approached, Tal's stomach contracted. He was shivering from laying in the snow and worried that his hands might be too numb to shoot straight. His target was less than 20 yards distant, ordinarily an easy shot for him, but the cold and wind were negative factors he had to take into account.

He readied the tranq gun for the German Shepherd, about the same size and weight as the wolf he'd planned for. With the time it would take to reload and shoot, tranquilizing the men was not an option. For them, lead.

He crouched beside the dumpster as man and dog turned the corner. He anticipated their stop at the door, the metallic rap, the bar of golden light reaching across the snow as the door opened.

It didn't happen.

The man and his German Shepherd continued past and out of sight. And again, on the next circuit. And the next.

Plan A was a bust, and there was no Plan B. Tal felt numb in the brain, unable to scramble together any kind of scheme to get him inside the concrete building before midnight. The structure featured an observatory dome on top with a raised portion down the center which Tal knew would slide open to facilitate a telescope.

Or a death ray.

Even as he watched, a mechanical hum reached him in the wind as the panel moved, creating a large opening in the side of the dome. The whole thing swiveled to point east. Toward the town of North Pole.

The only thing Tal could do was stick with Plan A and hope for a miracle.

It was Christmas, after all.

───────────

Two minutes to midnight.

Tal had his gun drawn and ready to fire. The tranquilizer dart gun held a syringe for the German Shepherd and Tal hoped he could load up another for the Doberman before it sprang on him and ripped his throat out.

The snow now was heavy enough to add visibility issues to the challenge he faced. It eddied and blew, flying against the shifting green sky while the wind moaned and shrieked an accompaniment.

One minute.

Tal firmed his jaw, willing himself to go to that place beyond fear, where resolve and determination called the shots and cold calculation won the day. He'd been there a time or two in the past, but it evaded him now.

So many lives at stake, so many obstacles to clear.

Ten seconds.

The sentry stood at the door. Three metallic knocks sounded as Tal stepped out from behind the dumpster.

He aimed.

The door opened.

He fired.

The first guard dropped.

Before the other man could return fire, Tal sent three shots into his chest. He staggered, slumping forward, and fell. Both dogs were in the yard now, barking like mad, jumping against the fence.

If they found the spot where he'd clipped through, he'd be dogmeat.

The first guard rolled and lifted onto a shoulder. He fired. The shot ricocheted off the dumpster. Tal heard it beside his ear, like an angry mosquito.

The dogs continued to launch themselves, moving closer to the weak spot. Tal shot the Doberman in the chest, the pink fringe of the dart like a party favor against the dark coat.

The dog yelped, but had time for one more leap against the fence before he drooped to the ground and went to sleep.

The downed guard reclaimed Tal's attention, firing off two more shots. One pinged off a fence post, ringing it like a bell.

The other hit Tal in the chest.

He went down.

He couldn't breathe. He'd fallen with his face right next to the fence. The German Shepherd barked furiously on the other side of it, jaws snapping inches from his nose, foamy saliva spraying against his cheek.

Tal groped blindly on the ground for the other loaded syringe, found it. Lying on his back, fighting for air, he loaded the dart gun and shot the German Shepherd at close range.

He whined as he fell.

The guard had risen to his knees. Tal saw him take aim for the death shot. But Tal's prone position made a difficult target, whereas the guard now presented a pretty decent one.

Tal fired twice.

The guard's gray parka bloomed red as he fell, face forward, and stopped moving.

Tal lay staring up into the strange green sky, flecked with emerald snowflakes. He fought to pull breath into his lungs and finally felt them expand, admitting oxygen into his bloodstream.

But it didn't matter.

It was midnight.

He'd failed.

MAJESTIC AND WONDROUS, THE aurora borealis shone forth in the northern sky. Tal watched, his brow knit in pain, waiting for the lights to brighten and coalesce, forming a cone with the power to incinerate in an instant.

When a minute passed, and then two, he pushed himself up from the bed of snow and checked his watch again.

12:05.

As he wondered if this was the Christmas miracle he'd prayed for, he remembered the dropoff point, when Miskin had checked her watch and Carl had checked his, coordinating. Tal hadn't looked at his own watch then. He hadn't wanted to acknowledge the fear that ate at him, tied to the marching of the clock.

Besides, no one really used watches anymore. Handheld electronic devices kept time for the world. He still wore his own wristwatch only because it had been his grandfather's.

And it was set to Pacific time.

Not Alaska time.

It was 11:05.

He jolted to his feet then bent over, groaning. His chest hurt, and now that he'd been given a reprieve, he paid more attention to it. He fingered the hole in his parka where the bullet had passed through and found the misshapen missile trapped in the canvas of his chest rig.

It had been deflected by the multitool, and maybe *that* was his Christmas miracle.

He zipped the bullet, a souvenir of his near-death experience, into a compartment for safekeeping and hurried to the door, still blocked open by the sentry's body. He approached cautiously, weapon drawn, but encountered no one. With all the noise of the firefight and the dogs barking, his arrival cannot have gone unnoticed.

But the halls were empty. He headed toward the other end of the building, where the dome was. Now that he'd made it inside the compound, he wondered how he'd breach the inner sanctum and secure the weapon.

He needn't have worried.

The door stood ajar.

Gooseflesh prickled along the backs of Tal's arms. Staying close to the wall, he edged to the door and craned his neck to peer inside. Antonia Scylla lay sprawled on the floor, face up, her thick dark hair with its two stripes radiating out from her head like sunbeams.

She was dead.

A tall slim blonde dressed in a royal blue jumpsuit stood beside a large bolted-down mounting device flanked by mirrors tipped at various angles. She was busy packing something into a case, but she looked up and saw Tal.

Without pausing in her work, she jutted toward him with her chin. "Al, if you don't mind," she said, her voice smooth, cultured as a debutante's pearls.

The man who'd been leaning on a counter, watching her pack, pointed a gun and fired at the doorway. But Tal had seen him first and was a better aim. When the man fell, the blonde merely sighed.

"Before you go shooting me," she warned, "you'd better hear what I have to say."

"You're Charybdis?"

She shrugged. "If you like. I learned about Scylla's accomplishment with the concentrator from my Russian friends. They want it. And if they don't get it before midnight, they're prepared to firebomb everything within a fifty mile radius of this place to ensure it doesn't fall into the wrong hands."

"Preemptive bidding, huh?"

"You could call it that. Don't bother trying to stop me."

Before he knew how it happened, she had a gun in her hand, firing off a series of shots that chewed through the doorframe and sent him hugging the wall.

Another blast of her gun and the sound of shattering glass. Then silence.

Tal risked a peek into the room. Eudora Petrovna had made her own exit.

With the weapon.

Outside, the storm had arrived in full force. Snow flew in a frenzy, as if infuriated by the howling wind, everything tinted green by the eerie lights.

Tal reloaded his gun, bunched his muscles, and leapt through the broken window, landing hard on his back. He shoulder-rolled and came up into a crouching position, gun raised and seeking a target.

Nothing.

He turned, squinting his eyes into the night, looking for a moving figure. That's when he felt the hard barrel against the nape of his neck.

"I never even knew your name."

In the instant before she pulled the trigger, a wolf howled, making both of them jump. Her gun hand jerked upward, queering the shot which grazed the back of his skull.

The howl was loud, the wolf was close. But where?

It appeared at the broken window, snarling. *Inside* the building.

Its muzzle was smeared with gore and Tal guessed it had come in the same way he had—through a hole in the fence and the open door.

Only, the wolf had stopped for a snack.

It leapt.

Charybdis screamed. She dropped the case and ran. Instead of pursuing her, the wolf went for Tal, knocking him to the ground, dislodging the gun from his hand.

Tal's layers of protective clothing impeded the wolf's fangs, but the effect would be temporary. Tal desperately felt for a loaded syringe. His fingers slid with frantic haste over the Zippo and the extra mags.

Finally, his hand closed around a tranquilizer cartridge. He didn't bother loading the pistol—simply pulled the cap off with his teeth and plunged it into the wolf's hairy hide.

The creature yelped in pain, snapping at Tal's face, but he pulled away and pushed the animal down. The wolf was weakening fast.

Tal snatched the weapon case in one hand, his gun in the other, and skidded around the corner, to the side of the building he hadn't seen before.

Charybdis was there, standing beside two parked snowmobiles. The storm was abating and Tal heard a faint rumbling overhead. He looked up.

Charybdis raised her gun and pulled the trigger.

Three times.

Four.

She'd pumped four bullets into the spare snowmobile, destroying it.

The one Tal might have used to get away with the weapon.

The smell of gasoline permeated the air as fuel streamed onto the ground through the bullet holes. The sleek scientist climbed onto the other machine and turned the key, holding Tal at bay with her gun.

"The Russians are circling," she said. "I may not have the weapon, but I've got twenty-eight minutes to get out of the blast zone, and a way to get me there."

As she sped into the night, her voice floated back on the wind.

"I still don't know your name."

As Charybdis disappeared into the night, Tal sagged against the concrete wall of the compound building. Above him, the sky continued its magnificent light display and for a moment he simply watched and allowed himself to be awed by the power and beauty of it.

How wrong that such splendor should have been used for evil, to destroy, to cheapen human life to the price a bidder would pay.

How tired he was. It seemed more effort than he could muster to lift his head anymore. He let it droop, chin reaching his chest. All his communication equipment was lost, ruined, or malfunctioning. He had no means of reaching anyone, no way to pass on any information.

At this point, the Russians represented the best case scenario.

Thinking about the ramifications of a world where such a weapon existed, Tal decided it was just as well the Russians would be blowing the incinerator sky high in—he looked at his watch—seventeen minutes.

He only wished he didn't have to go with it.

Another precious minute ticked by before Tal came to the conclusion that he wanted to do it himself.

He grabbed the weapon case and raced back, stepping over the sedated wolf to climb through the window into the observatory.

He was no rocket scientist, but a quick study of what he'd taken to be mirrors showed they were indeed some kind of reflectors. Removing the device from the case, he fastened it onto the mount as he'd seen it before Charybdis packed it away.

The weapon featured dials for setting latitude and longitude, as well as a timer. Its many smaller dials and buttons would forever remain a mystery. Tal entered the coordinates he'd seen on the GPS tracker before it fizzled out. The reflectors repositioned themselves and a beam like a laser pointer bounced off of them onto the weapon itself.

A raucous alarm sounded and red siren lights strobed across the walls. Tal set the timer, giving himself a six minute window, and pressed the button marked LAUNCH.

He ran.

Slogging through snow slowed him down. But the memory of what he'd seen on the satellite footage, the way the village in Greenland had burnt to a crisp and blown away in the wind, gave him the will to speed.

He had no idea how tight a circle the weapon drew around its target. But he was soon to find out.

The overhead green intensified to a brilliance more than he could bear. Dropping to the ground, he buried his face beneath the wing of his arm and squeezed his eyes shut. There was a *WUMP!* that Tal felt in his stomach rather than actually hearing. When he felt the light dim, he cautiously lifted his head.

The compound was gone.

Obliterated.

And the weapon with it.

He lay in the snow, weak with relief, thrilled to be alive.

The emerald shimmers continued their dance in the sky above, emanations from the sun, giver of warmth and life. In this season of joy, meant for peace on earth and good will toward men, he thought the world just might have taken one step closer to that hope.

The hum of an aircraft reached his ears, faint at first and growing louder.

It was midnight.

The hum crescendoed, beating against his eardrums as the chopper hovered over the site. Tal hugged himself and waited. Then it faded off into the distance. The Russians, it appeared, had seen the cinders and judged their efforts to be superfluous.

Now what?

Tal dragged himself to his feet, bone weary and happy. But also aware that he might not live out the night. He was freezing, hungry, alone without provisions, and in the middle of nowhere, with no way to contact help.

And there were wolves. Two of them, stalking him on the left. Not crazed or rabid. Just ordinary wolves.

But dangerous all the same.

He had only a few syringes left, a bullet or two in the gun, and then he'd be defenseless. He stumbled forward and was just thinking about trying to find where he'd ditched the skis when he heard a new sound. A low growl, rising in pitch and volume.

Turning toward it, Tal watched as a row of snowmachines crested the hill, looking cinematic against the shifting green sky. The riders wore Santa hats streaming behind them as they advanced.

And they flew the American flag.

The night was full of Christmas miracles.

MEET JOSLYN CHASE

Joslyn Chase is a prize-winning author of mysteries and thrillers. Any day where she can send readers to the edge of their seats, chewing their fingernails to the nub and prickling with suspense, is a good day in her book.

Joslyn's short stories have appeared in *Alfred Hitchcock's Mystery Magazine, Fiction River Magazine, Mystery Magazine,* and *Pulphouse Fiction Magazine,* among others.

Known for her fast-paced suspense fiction, Joslyn's books are full of surprising twists and delectable turns. You will find her riveting novels most anywhere books are sold.

Her love for travel has led Joslyn to ride camels through the Nubian desert, fend off monkeys on the Rock of Gibraltar, and hike the Bavarian Alps. But she still believes that sometimes the best adventures come in getting the words on the page and in the thrill of reading a great story.

Join the growing group of readers who've discovered the thrill of Chase! Sign up for Joslyn's readers' group at joslynchase.com and get VIP access to great bonuses—like your free copy of *No Rest: 14 Tales of Chilling Suspense*—as well as updates and first crack at new releases.

LANE DEPARTURE

TOM FOWLER

JOHN TYLER THOUGHT IT was a robbery at first.

The guy standing at the door provided the first clue. His hand clenched and unclenched like it was eager to disappear into his long black coat and pull out a weapon. Instead of a solitary suspicious man however, Tyler saw four in identical clothing milling around the front of the supermarket.

The place closed in under a half-hour. Few customers walked the aisles, and the complement of employees matched their smaller number.

Way too many guys for a simple cash grab.

Tyler turned and reached toward the back of his jacket.

"Shit," he whispered when he realized he'd left his pistol in the car. Two of the trench coat crew fanned out, one in each direction. They stopped at every aisle.

Were they looking for someone?

Tyler fished his phone out of his pocket. No signal. Even in this remote part of Maryland, there should have been coverage here. Whoever these guys were, they were jamming the comms.

He hoofed it down the aisle and grabbed a slender stock boy by the arm. Before the young man could object, Tyler said, "Something bad is about to happen. Do you have any landline phones?"

"Uh." The kid blinked a bunch of times. "There might be . . . in the manager's office."

"Good. Listen . . . five armed guys in long black coats are in your store. I don't know what they're up to yet, but I don't think it'll end well."

"Jesus." The stock boy's eyes widened, and his mouth hung open.

"Where's the manager's office?" Tyler asked.

"Um . . . up front."

"No good. What about your receiving area?"

"Yeah . . . sure."

Despite the news Tyler dumped on him, the kid held up pretty well. He led the way through two swinging doors into the back portion of the store. Wooden pallets dominated much of the floor space. Plastic shipping containers lined the walls.

Tyler spotted a phone sitting atop a desk. An old-fashioned cord connected the handset to the base.

"Call the cops first," Tyler said. "Then, page whoever's in charge to come back here."

He padded to the entrance, standing to the side of the door and peeking through one of the clear plastic panes. It offered a very limited view of the sales floor, but nothing looked amiss.

"Cops are at least ten minutes out," the kid said.

Tyler frowned. A lot of bad shit could happen in ten minutes. Even if they beat their estimate, they wouldn't rush into a probable hostage situation. They'd set up a perimeter and a command post. Try to establish contact. Negotiate.

Tyler understood—their strategy was to save innocent lives. It all took time, though, and the assholes in long coats could murder a bunch of people while the local LEOs ticked the boxes in the play-book. He used his own playbook honed from his experiences in Afghanistan.

The strategy was the same, but the tactics diverged sharply.

A pudgy man with a ruddy complexion walked in a moment later. His white button-down shirt strained to cover his stomach. "What's going on? Who are you?"

"You have five men in your store," Tyler said. "I don't know exactly why they're here, but it can't be for a good reason." He looked around the area again. "Can you move some of these by the doors to control entry?"

"I think so," the kid said.

The manager, however, frowned at Tyler. "Listen here—"

"*You* listen," Tyler said. "If these assholes start shooting, you'll be glad you took my advice." He moved toward the pass-through doors.

"You're going out there?" the stock boy asked with wide eyes.

"I am. Try to get some of those pallets lined up. If you can, get your customers back here. We want to make it hard for anyone else to storm this area."

Tyler pushed one of the swinging doors open and checked nearby aisles. A slender fellow in an expensive suit browsed canned goods. From the other end, one of the black-cloaked men scowled and headed toward him.

"Shit," Tyler muttered as he glanced around for a weapon.

A selection of cooking pans hung from slender metal pegs a few feet away in the next lane. He grabbed a durable-looking ten-inch model and hurried toward the guy giving the vegetables a once-over.

The asshole in the coat reached him first. The suited man took a step back. "Either of you tell me anything about these?" Tyler asked as he closed to within a few feet.

"Buzz off, pal," Dark Coat said, right before Tyler drew the skillet back and clobbered him in the face.

The metal clang was louder than Tyler wanted. The isolated member of the quintet dropped to the linoleum. The man in the suit cowered against the shelf.

Tyler gave a harsh whisper, "I don't know who you are, but I think it's best if you leave the store."

"Y . . . yeah," the man said.

"Let's go."

Tyler was about to step over the fallen guy when two more rounded the corner. The smaller one carried a pistol in his hand. In a panic, the well-dressed man ran toward the shooter.

Tyler ducked and scampered toward the far end as bullets slammed into the shelves near him. The larger one grabbed the mousy man's arms and led him toward the exit despite his protests.

The other kept Tyler covered with his gun as he helped his woozy comrade to his feet.

ONCE THE SHOOTER LEFT, Tyler stayed low and worked his way toward the front of the store.

The few cashiers and customers all crouched in the checkout area. In the parking lot, two men shoved another into the back of a van. A third, armed with a shotgun, kept watch.

Tyler waited for them all to pile in and zoom away before he bolted through the doors.

He fired up his Oldsmobile 442. The throaty V8 growled as he put the car in drive and gave chase. In their outlying location, the store and McDonalds's were the only signs of civilization.

The van made a left with screeching tires. Tyler followed at a reasonable distance. A full moon shone through the trees lining the two-lane road. Tyler killed his headlights and relied on the vehicle ahead of him to lead the way.

The driver kept going. He didn't stop. No evasive maneuvers. No one leaned out a window with a handgun.

Tyler's car was a beautiful dark green. The headlights would've been a giveaway. Without them, the guys in the van seemed not to notice they'd picked up a tail.

A sharp right led to another street looking exactly like the previous one. Tyler kept the van in sight but made sure not to get too close. Distance helped maintain his cover in the darkness.

The old car bounced down the road. Tyler maintained the Olds himself, and he'd made improvements over the way it rolled off the assembly line in 1972, but he might need to soften the suspension the next time he crawled under it.

Long drives or trips down bumpy roads proved too harsh. The large van's brake lights came on, and it made a left past a classic old mailbox. Tyler slowed his approach. He didn't want to follow too closely even with his beams off.

As he rolled up to the shopworn driveway, the shabby round-top tin displayed the name McVay.

When the red lights disappeared around a corner to the right, Tyler made the turn.

He maintained a slow pace to avoid the 442's engine giving him away. The battered stones of the driveway soon faded to a dirt path. It made a ninety-degree right immediately ahead.

Tyler stayed straight, driving on the grass and heading in the general direction of the trail. He steered near a small outbuilding and killed the engine when he saw the van stop outside a large, dilapidated barn.

ARNOLD MCVAY FELT AS if someone followed them. He climbed out of his van and scanned the property. No vehicle came in behind them. He couldn't see anyone or hear an engine.

Eugene Byrd sidled next to him. "What's goin' on?"

"I checked a few times for somebody behind us," McVay said. "You think the guy from the store coulda picked us up?"

"I dunno." Byrd rubbed his face. A nice bruise already started. "I kinda hope he does. Son of a bitch."

"You all right? He rang your bell pretty good there."

"I'm fine," Byrd said.

McVay stared at him. There was no give in his friend's gaze. "OK. Keep an eye on the exterior. If anyone did follow us, take care of it."

"I will."

"Get this asshole in the barn!" McVay pulled the sliding door open. Three of his friends pushed the frightened lawyer out. His feet missed the running board, and he landed face-down in the grass.

McVay put the toes of his boot under Duncan Richardson's chin and lifted his head. "You got some answering to do."

"Please, I don't know what you want!"

"It'll be clear soon enough." He jerked his head, and three sets of hands led Richardson roughly toward the barn.

McVay scanned the area again. The moon combined with the lights mounted on buildings to provide plenty of illumination. All looked clear.

McVay stomped after his friends. He pointed toward his eyes as he passed Byrd, who offered a solemn nod in reply.

TYLER HELD HIS M11 pistol on his lap.

The van's driver seemed like a cautious man. Four walked with their captive toward a large dark structure. It was one of two barns on the property; a newer model stood about a hundred yards past the first.

One man remained outside. A sentry. Maybe the driver got spooked. Maybe they always took these precautions on a kidnapping run. Regardless, Tyler would need to be careful.

He wanted to learn more about what he might be wading into, so he grabbed his phone and called his daughter.

"You're late, Dad," Lexi said.

"I know."

"Let me guess . . . something happened."

"Yeah," Tyler said. "Five guys in a van abducted a man, I followed them. They just took him into a barn."

"Tell me you called the police?"

"Do I ever? I want you to get my old work laptop. There are a few searches I'd like you to run for me."

"All right." Tyler heard Lexi pad downstairs. A moment later, she said, "It's on. What do you need?"

The laptop belonged to a company called Patriot Security, Tyler's employer after he retired from the army. When he left the private security gig, he didn't bother returning the hardware, and they hadn't come calling for it.

Some red team guys developed it, and it did things Tyler couldn't understand. Lexi proved to be a lot better with the computer stuff than he ever imagined. She'd recently begun her freshman year at the University of Maryland, and if she wanted to study technology, Tyler knew she had the brains for it.

"Let's start with a plate. Maryland . . . Romeo Bravo three eight eight five Delta."

Keystrokes clattered. "It's a van," Lexi said. "Fourteen years old. Registered to a Francis McVay of Saint Mary's County."

"Which is where I am," Tyler said. It matched the name on the mailbox. Who used their own vehicle for a snatch and grab? "Any info on the nice Mister McVay?"

"He's dead for starters. Died last year."

"Drives pretty well for a corpse, then."

"Hang on. I'm looking deeper." She typed more. "His closest surviving relative is a brother who lives out of state. He has a nephew named Arnold who lives in the same county."

Using a dead relative's van wouldn't be a smart play, either. These guys weren't professionals. The lone guard outside the barn made the point obvious enough. They'd done a fair job in the grocery store, all things considered, but this was an amateur crew. It made them unpredictable.

Tyler didn't like unpredictable. "Can you tell me anything about this Arnold?" he asked.

"Already on it," Lexi said. "The laptop is scraping his social media."

She fell silent for a few seconds while they waited for results. "Looks like's he's only on Facebook. Not too many friends. He makes lots of posts about family farms and Big Ag."

Tyler frowned. "Weird." What the hell was going on? "Thanks, kiddo. I'm going to check some things out here."

"Be careful, Dad."

"Always," Tyler said. "Don't wait up. Love you."

"Love you, too."

Tyler hung up. He opened the car door as quietly as possible, moved to the rear of the 442, and eased the trunk lid up enough to grab a bullet-resistant vest and knife. Tyler strapped it on, holstered the Sig at his left side, and the blade at his right.

He buttoned the 442 up, crouched, and used the outbuilding for cover as he took in the old barn.

"MISTER ROBINSON," ARNOLD McVAY said once the lawyer was lashed to a chair, "you have a lot to answer for."

"Please, I don't know any of you."

McVay got in his face. He could smell the cowardice on the man's breath. "You didn't know any of our families. It didn't stop you, did it?"

Robinson narrowed his eyes. "What are you talking about?"

"I know who you work for!" McVay shouted. He grabbed a clump of Robinson's hair and bent his head back. "You like being a lobbyist for a company taking people's property?"

"It's a law," Robinson said through gritted teeth. "Your legislators voted for it."

"I wonder who gave them the idea." McVay released Robinson's hair and punched him in the face. The lawyer's head snapped to the side, and he wore a pained grimace for nearly a minute.

"I was just doing my job," Robinson said.

McVay glanced at Stan Cooley, who'd stayed behind while the rest of the crew hit the store. Cooley offered a curt nod.

"We looked into you, Mister Robinson." McVay paced a ten-foot area in front of the prisoner. "We may not have the fancy investigators your firm might hire, but we did all right for a bunch of country folk. Learned where you live, where you go in your spare time, and where and when you shop. You're predictable."

Robinson didn't respond. Cooley pulled a large blanket back. The lawyer's eyes widened as saw what lay behind it.

McVay stared at it. Bags of fertilizer. Good wiring. A detonator and a timer. Plus a few components he didn't recognize, but he trusted Stan Cooley's handiwork.

He jerked his thumb toward the bomb. "Know what this is?"

Robinson nodded and swallowed hard. "Yes."

"This is an old barn. My uncle stood up a new one a few years ago. I helped. He kept this one, though, for storage. His granddaddy built it by hand years ago. It ain't so pretty anymore. My uncle thought about knocking it down, but he could never bring himself to do it."

McVay shrugged. "I ain't attached to it like he was. If it blows up with some asshole lawyer inside it, well . . . that'd be a shame, but there's a new one."

Color drained from Robinson's face. "What do you want from me?" His voice trembled like a man who understood his time was short.

"I think you know."

"Do you think I can just snap my fingers and undo everything?"

McVay gently patted the top of the timer. "I think it's in your best interests to try."

────────

Tyler studied the guard.

He'd fetched a double-barreled shotgun from the van once everyone else herded their captive into the run-down barn. The guy carried it over his shoulder like he posed for a photo. Not the best grip for bringing it to bear quickly. Another mark in the amateur column. The lookout peered around regularly, and he turned a slow 360 every minute.

When he pivoted away, Tyler moved around the outbuilding to the other side. Trees were thicker to his left. He imagined someone cut a bunch of them down and used the wood to make the old barn many decades ago.

Tyler searched the ground and found a stick large enough to throw and make noise. When the guard turned his back, Tyler padded into the forest. He crouched behind a large oak and waited for the opening.

When the sentry completed his circuit, Tyler tossed the branch toward some smaller trees about five yards away.

It produced the desired effect. The amateur swung the shotgun from his shoulder, letting it drop too far before steadying it with his other hand. He moved toward the noise. Tyler kept his back to the tree, inching around as the other man stalked toward the sound.

"Anybody there?" he challenged in a harsh whisper.

Interesting. He didn't call anyone or try to make noise. Whatever happened in the barn took priority.

The sentry stood with his back to Tyler. It made sneaking up on him easy.

Tyler pushed the muzzle of his M11 into the guard's neck. He stood at a full arm's length. Too far for a headbutt or quick back kick . . . if this guy even had such moves in his arsenal.

"Drop the shotgun."

The other man didn't respond or react. Tyler repeated his command.

"Or what?" the guy asked.

"Or a couple of your vertebrae will leave your body via your throat. Put it down."

The man raised his other hand and set the shotgun on the ground.

"Three steps to your left," Tyler ordered. The man complied.

Tyler backed off one pace. "Turn around."

The man he'd whacked with the skillet glared at him.

Tyler glared back. "What the hell are you all doing here?"

"You wouldn't understand." The accent gave him away as being born and bred in southern Maryland.

"I've never kidnapped someone in a grocery store before," Tyler said. "I suppose I wouldn't. Why don't you try to explain it to me?"

"You ain't the cops," the other sneered. "You're some jackass who likes to hit people while they ain't expecting it. Why don't you throw your gun down and see what happens?"

This guy was taller, younger, and broader than Tyler. Not a good combination on the surface, but experience tilted the scales. Still, Tyler didn't want to get into a fight in a random patch of trees in St. Mary's County.

This guy was stalling. If he couldn't stop Tyler, he wanted to keep him from interrupting whatever happened about two hundred feet away.

"Maybe some other time."

Tyler stepped forward and clobbered the guy in the head again, this time with the butt of the pistol. He was out cold before he hit the ground.

A length of rope hung from the kidnapper's belt, and after dragging him to a tree, Tyler made use of it. He turned the unconscious man face-down, put his legs around the trunk, and tied his ankles.

Even if he came to, he wouldn't be able to free himself. He could yell, however, and Tyler realized he had nothing to put over the guy's mouth. He'd deal with it if and when it happened.

Tyler inspected the discarded shotgun. It was loaded and looked to be in good repair. Two shots. Plenty of stopping power. He could take out a pair of kidnappers quickly before switching to his pistol.

Tyler carried it close to his body as he padded through the trees and approached the barn.

———

TYLER PUT HIS BACK against the wood.

Up close, he could tell the barn missed a lot of upkeep over the years. He crouched beside a window near the rear corner. The remote county location meant background noise wouldn't be a factor.

For years, Tyler had valued being quiet and listening in situations like this. In Afghanistan, he met many young soldiers who wanted to storm a building and empty the magazine. Tyler tried to teach them a smarter way. No matter what you learned from intel reports and drones, listening to your targets always paid off.

"We can't just stop it!" a desperate voice said. The captive. At least he was still alive. It changed the breach plans running through Tyler's head.

The same voice continued, "It doesn't work the way you want it to."

"You made sure of it, didn't you?" another voice said.

This one was angrier. Younger. Accented like the guy tethered to the tree. "You lawyers are always good for tricks."

"It's no trick. It's what the statute says, and it's how the process plays out."

Tyler recalled what Lexi told him. Arnold McVay posted about family farms and Big Agriculture. If those two ever appeared in the same sentence, it never turned out well for the home team.

The unmistakable sound of a solid punch pierced the silence. "Maybe you can figure out a different process. They paid you to do it a certain way. Don't it mean there are other options?"

Tyler couldn't fault the fellow's reasoning, but he also couldn't continue to stand here and listen to the debate play out. The captive was badly outnumbered, to say nothing of any weapons his abductors might have.

Tyler was about to move when a simple question made him stop.

"Do you really need a bomb?"

A MOMENT LATER, THE other male voice gleefully confirmed he did.

"Shit," Tyler whispered to the darkness.

Explosives were the great equalizer. He'd seen plenty of good soldiers maimed or killed by IEDs. Simple operations which should have gone without a hitch turned into bloodbaths.

It wouldn't take much to knock this barn down, and even a small charge would be enough to kill the poor bastard held captive inside.

Tyler thought about walking away. This wasn't his fight. Short of braining someone with a skillet and tying him to a tree, he'd stayed out of whatever the conflict was. No one knew him down here. He could drive the two hours home, say goodnight to his daughter, and get on with the rest of his life.

The hostage inside stared down terrible odds, however, and the bomb only made them worse. If Tyler left, the man trapped inside was dead.

He cursed his conscience and risked a glance through the grimy window. Probably the customer from the aisle sat strapped to a chair, his back to Tyler. Five other men stood near him.

The one doing the talking was one of the voices overheard. "Does it make you think about what you've done?" he said as he leaned closer to the other man.

"I have a family," the captive wailed in protest.

"We all had families. Didn't stop you and your rich friends from ruining everything."

Tyler ducked under the window and skulked down the length of the barn. He peeked around the front corner. The coast was clear. One of the doors remained open wide enough for someone to slip out.

Or in.

"I need a smoke," a new voice called, and a man squeezed through the opening a moment later. He fumbled with a pack of cigarettes as he headed in the opposite direction from where Tyler kept watch.

This left four inside. If these guys were going to give him an opportunity to reduce the odds, Tyler meant to take it.

He moved around the corner, saw no windows along the front of the barn, and kept going. A single step took him past the opening, and he kept going when no one shouted an alarm.

The smoker lit up a hundred feet away, about halfway to the newer barn. Lights mounted on its walls lifted the blackness. Tyler crouched and stalked closer. The guy drew in a lungful and blew out a plume of smoke. He turned a little to his right, so Tyler fanned out toward the left.

Fifty feet.

Tyler smelled the smoke as he drew closer. He'd never acquired the habit despite sharing barracks with a bunch of people who lit up. Memories of his grandfather smelling like a stale chimney were enough.

Twenty feet.

The guy looked at his watch and pivoted a quarter turn to his right. Tyler stepped to the left, but the smoker's head followed him.

Time for a change in tactics.

Tyler sprinted the remaining three steps. As he ran, he pulled the double-barreled shotgun back. Before the Marlboro Man could alert his friends, Tyler smashed him in the face with the stock. He grunted and dropped to the grass.

The lights were still on, so Tyler whacked him again. They were in the open with no trees to tie this one to. With the bomb being a factor, Tyler didn't want to waste the time it would take, anyway. He patted the prone man down and found no weapons.

Then, he moved toward the old barn.

"Set the timer."

Arnold McVay issued the command, and Stan Cooley followed it. He pushed a few buttons, and the digital display showed 10:00 in bright red numerals. One additional press would begin the countdown. Cooley's finger hovered over the small switch.

"You're going to kill us all," Robinson said.

"Just you." McVay jabbed a finger to emphasize the point.

"What will it accomplish? You kill me, and nothing changes. No one's going to listen to you with blood on your hands. You'll go to jail and lose your properties anyway."

McVay saw Harry Black frown. Was he considering the lobbyist's words? Nothing a bigshot lawyer said could be true; they were incapable of it. Something would still happen.

Something would change.

Even if he went to jail, McVay would keep all their farms out of the hands of some faceless corporation. "I'm willing to take my chances," McVay said. "We're screwed if we don't do anything. You and your asshole friends have guaranteed it. Might as well take our shot."

"Robby's been outside a while," Cooley said.

"He's smoking," McVay said without removing his eyes from the frightened lawyer. Robinson squirming in the chair made him smile, and they hadn't even started the countdown yet.

"Don't take this long."

"You worry too much."

Cooley stepped away from the bomb and started toward the barn door. "I'm gonna check on him."

He stopped after taking a single step. McVay followed his friend's gaze.

A stranger walked in, and he leveled Byrd's double-barreled shotgun at them.

EVERYONE FROZE.

Tyler stepped inside and moved moved away from the door, keeping it to his right as he covered everyone with the scattergun. The man bound to the chair indeed was the one abducted from the grocery store.

Four others all dressed in faded jeans and shirts surrounded him. They must have doffed their black coats in the van.

Tyler noticed the crude bomb right away. It sat atop a battered table. The prisoner was about five feet away. If it worked, there wouldn't be enough left of him to bury in a bucket when it went off.

The timer displayed ten minutes, but the crew hadn't started the countdown.

"I'm going to offer you an easy solution," Tyler said. "Walk away. Get back in your van and leave."

"And if we don't?" one of them said. The same voice doing the talking before. Probably McVay.

Tyler pointed the shotgun directly at him. "Then, I guess your friends will save about two hundred pounds on the escape run. Might make the van a little faster."

The fellow closest to the explosive inched toward it.

"Don't move."

Tyler swung the set of muzzles toward him. A long stride would get him there. Tyler's finger curled around the trigger.

"Do it, Stan," McVay said as he stared at Tyler. "He ain't gonna shoot."

"I can assure you I will," Tyler said.

"This don't concern you, old man. You don't understand what's going on."

"Enlighten me." Tyler never took his eyes from the one called Stan who'd moved toward the bomb.

"These men are crazy," the hostage said. "You need to stop them."

"Shut up!" McVay punched the seated man again.

Stan took it as his opportunity to lunge for the bomb. Tyler fired as soon as he registered the movement. The slugs from one barrel took the guy in the chest. He was dead before he landed on the dirty barn floor. His desperate effort paid off, though.

The countdown was on.

Tyler swung the shotgun back toward McVay. If he were smart, he would've stood behind the captive. It would take the shotgun out of the equation. Instead, he remained in the open. The other two covered their mouths.

"You only got one shot left," McVay said. "Still three of us."

"I have a Sig Sauer on my hip."

Tyler wondered if the second man he'd knocked out would join the fray at some point. If the bomb went off, he was a good hundred feet from the rundown barn. He'd probably be fine. The one in the woods was closer, but the cluster of trees would protect him.

"I shot expert twenty years running. I like my chances."

"Stay in your lane. You don't understand what's going on here."

"A bunch of you snatched this guy from a supermarket. You brought him here and rigged a bomb. The plan is either to scare him or blow him up. I'm pretty sure you've achieved the first one."

The captive nodded in confirmation. "What's your name, hostage?"

"Duncan Robinson," he said. "I'm a lawyer."

"Nobody likes lawyers," Tyler said. "You might want to leave it out the next time you get kidnapped."

"I think Mister Robinson should explain it to you," McVay said.

His two friends paced behind him. They didn't possess his level of calm. Tyler figured they would bolt before the timer got anywhere near all zeroes. Only a true believer would see it through to the end, and these guys didn't cut it.

McVay's eyes bore into him. "Just so you know what we're dealing with here."

"I . . . I represent a large agricultural company," Robinson said. "We've been looking to expand out of the southern states. There are a lot of old farms around here which have fallen on tough times. We petitioned the county to acquire them through eminent domain, and they agreed. The process is—"

"I understand how eminent domain works," Tyler broke in. "Sounds like you snatched up a bunch of farms which had been in families for generations." He glanced at the red numbers.

Seven and a half minutes remained.

"The families got paid," Robinson said. "The county got paid. The company is slated to get the land we need. Everyone wins."

"A bunch of us lost!"

McVay bent down to get in Robinson's face. "It ain't just land to us like it is to you." Robinson fell silent.

"What are you trying to accomplish?" Tyler said. "Even if you scare this guy shitless, I don't think he can undo the entire process."

"He can try."

Tyler looked at the lawyer, who shrugged as much as his restraints would allow. "I might be able to get a little more money," he said after a moment, "though I think everyone has been fairly compensated."

"You go to hell," McVay said. His two remaining compatriots continued to pace behind him. The shorter one kept looking at the bomb.

"I'll be honest," Tyler said. "I'm tempted to lock this place up and let you all sort it out. If you can't come to an arrangement in about seven minutes, I think the world will keep spinning."

"I don't wanna die," one of the men behind McVay offered.

McVay glared and turned around. "For Christ's sake, Jimmy."

"I don't. This was supposed to be easy. Grab this guy and get him to change his mind. Then, Cooley wanted to make a bomb, you went along with it, and I think we got off the rails somewhere."

"Your friend is the smart one of the bunch," Tyler said. "It's damning with faint praise, but you should listen to him." He glanced at the clock again.

Six minutes.

"I'm going to press charges," Robinson said. "I've been kidnapped, threatened, assaulted, and—"

"Shut up," everyone else said in unison.

Tyler continued, "You're not the sympathetic figure I thought you were in the store. Still, you don't deserve to get blown up. Here's what we're going to do."

"Why should we listen to you?" McVay demanded.

"Ask your friend on the ground how independent thought turned out." He pointed at Jimmy. "You're going to untie the lawyer. We're going to collect your friend outside and walk to the new barn. Once this place blows up, we call the sheriff's office, and I leave."

"What's to stop us from bolting?" McVay asked.

Tyler's only reply was a smile.

ONCE ROBINSON HAD BEEN untied, Tyler held the shotgun out toward him.

"I don't know how to use this," he said, looking at the weapon as if it were a rotten fish on his plate.

"It's not hard." Tyler gripped the gun until Robinson frowned and took it. "Point and shoot. Just like an old camera."

"Doesn't it only have one shot left?"

Tyler drew the M11 from the holster on his hip. "I can handle the rest. Let's march."

They all trudged to the new barn. McVay and Jimmy helped their friend shake off the cobwebs and get back to his feet. Once everyone was inside, Tyler told Robinson to shut the door, which he did. He then handed the lawyer a length of rope.

"I'm sure you'll find a knife or scissors around here somewhere. Tie their ankles together."

"Where's Byrd?" McVay wanted to know as he glowered at Tyler. "You kill him?"

"He's tied to a tree," Tyler said. "He's far enough away to be fine."

"What if he ain't?" Tyler shrugged in response, and McVay scowled anew.

A couple minutes later, Robinson finished turning the tables on his captors. A little over two minutes remained by Tyler's count.

"Thanks, mister," Robinson said. He held his hand out. "I don't even know your name."

Tyler stared at the hand until the lawyer withdrew it. "It doesn't matter," he told Robinson. "What's important is what you're going to do after this."

"What do you mean?"

"These men shouldn't have kidnapped you, but you work for a pack of assholes. You're going to do what you can to make things right for all the families whose farms got scooped up."

"And if I don't?" Robinson asked.

"I'll be keeping an eye on the news," Tyler said. "Remember, I know your name but not the other way around."

Robinson swallowed hard and nodded. "All right. I'll do what I can."

"Good."

Tyler figured only a few seconds remained on the countdown. Right on cue, the old barn blew up.

———

ROBINSON CALLED 9-1-1 a couple minutes later.

Tyler found him another shell for the shotgun if he needed it, but he didn't think it would matter. He got back into the 442 and headed away from the McVay farm as quickly as he could.

About a mile down the road, a trio of police cars sped toward him, sirens howling and lights flashing red and blue in the darkness. Tyler was happy to pull over and wait for them to pass.

Once he drove across the border of St. Mary's County, he called Lexi again. "I'm on my way," he said when she picked up.

"How did your situation go?"

"Fine. In the end, though, I'm relying on a lawyer to do the right thing."

"Doesn't sound like a good place to be," Lexi said.

"The sheriff and his deputies will do the heavy lifting. I only need to follow the news out of this county."

"Which means you want me to do it."

"I knew you got a scholarship for a reason," Tyler said.

Lexi yawned. "How far away are you?"

"Depends how fast I want to drive. You don't need to wait up, though."

"All right," she said. "Love you, Dad."

"Love you, too."

Tyler looked at the speedometer. Sixty-eight. A county road sign showed a speed limit of sixty.

He felt like driving a little faster, and 442 was happy to oblige.

MEET TOM FOWLER

If you've ever held your breath while reading Lee Child, walked a few gritty streets with Robert B. Parker, or marveled at Dennis Lehane's storytelling — then we're on the same page!

Let me introduce myself: I'm Tom Fowler, USA Today bestselling author of mysteries and thrillers with action, snark and flawed heroes. Just like you, I've been a longtime lover of books that keep me reading past my bedtime, turning pages obsessively, and trying to guess who's guilty.

I wrote my first "murder mystery" around age eight—a questionable addition to the genre due to a suspicious lack of an actual murder and the remarkable recovery of all injured parties. These days, you'll find no one is safe on the pages of my books, and the circumstances surrounding their demise or disappearance will always keep you on your toes.

Born and raised in Baltimore, I still live in Maryland and my home city is the setting for my novels—you could say I know all its secrets. When I'm not writing, I'm a computer security specialist, which comes in handy when C.T. Ferguson has a ransomware attack to figure out . . .

Ready to get stuck in? Make sure to grab your two FREE prequel novellas at tomfowlerwrites.com and get reading right away!

THE BODY IN THE ALLEY

JAMES DAIN

HOW THE MURDER WENT down was this.

I was an Army MP in Afghanistan, and when I finished my tour, after what happened to Christine, I was done. I mean I just didn't give a shit about nothing. So I bounced for a while at a bunch of nightclubs and bars in Philly, mostly around University City, but also over in Brewerytown and even Strawberry Mansion.

On that particular night, April 22, I was working at Minx. It was Friday night, the usual college crowd, a few drunks and arguments, nothing really out of the ordinary. The place got really crowded from nine to about one, then gradually started clearing out, leaving just the losers who couldn't find a hookup and the ones who were too drunk to care.

The victim, I guess you should call him that, wasn't a college kid but some neighborhood dude who went by the name of Little Anthony. That was supposed to be funny because this guy was fat. His real name was Anthony Silva. He was 23 years of age and occupation was construction worker and welder according to his Facebook.

When it started I wasn't even in the room. One of the bartenders, Larry Holmes, was discussing something at the end of the bar with Shawn Toomey, a hitman for the Elmwood gang, with his gold earring and his yellow plaid jacket. He liked to wear sportscoats in different loud patterns and colors. I had been with Larry around Toomey a couple of times, even rode backup on a job he ran once, and of course I was well aware of his reputation.

Toomey wasn't a big guy, but he was quick-tempered, and dangerous to anyone who crossed him or so much as looked at him the wrong way. He would kill you in a snap, like he killed the state trooper who stopped him for running a red light, or like the guy who told a joke to his wife and ended up in a landfill in New Jersey.

I personally never had any problems with Toomey, even talked 76ers with him a few times at clubs, but I definitely didn't want any problems either. Which is why I left him and Larry alone together at the bar and took that time to re-stack empties in back, until I heard the ruckus.

I ran out. Right in front of me at the pool table I saw Anthony Silva grab a pool stick and whack some poor bastard in a baseball cap right upside the ear. Out the guy went, his torso bouncing once on the table before he slid unconscious to the wet floor. His name I later found was Danny Levitt, but I didn't stop to figure out who was who. I grabbed Silva in a bear hug, pool stick and all, and half-carried, half-shoved his fat ass through the back room to the alley door.

Here's where things started to go south.

I meant to just push the prick out into the alley and slam the door, but as I boosted him out, he grabs me by the shirt and pulls. And screw me, I trip on the threshold and fall out with him.

Next thing I know I'm on the ground, the frickin' door has slammed shut on its spring, and Silva is coming at me with the pool stick.

I scrambled up enough to block his wrist, but still got smacked pretty good on the left side of my ribs. That riled me and I kind of lost my temper, I wasn't going to take any more shit from this bastard.

He was screaming, you fucker this and you fucker that, so I just came at him with a right that smashed his nose and then a left that rattled his chin and sent him to the ground, where he lay curled up and breathing hard.

I stood over him for a sec but instead of staying still he made a grab for my jeans and tried to pull me off balance. I snatched his arm and twisted it, using my knee for leverage. He screamed and squirmed and when I finally let him go, whimpered and lay still.

I relaxed. You can tell when a guy has been broke and the fight is out of him. Silva was done and wasn't going to cause any more trouble. So far as I was concerned it was over.

But now Shawn Toomey comes banging through the steel door, his sports coat flapping, intent on mayhem and who was going to stop him?

He took in the scene—the empty alley, me with my hands still clenched into fists, the guy a puddle on the ground—then pushed past me and went to work on Silva, kicking him over and over again in the gut with his pointy shoes, and then, when the guy feebly put up a hand to try to stop the onslaught, Toomey stomps him twice in the stomach and goes starting in on his face, too.

"Stop," I said, it sort of coming out of my mouth involuntarily. "You're going to kill him."

Toomey, he pulls on his gold earring and shoots me a look, an animal look. "Fuck you, man. I know that guy he hit."

That look, I'm ashamed to say, it made me freeze. I wanted to say, *Hey, the dude inside is OK.* But I just kept quiet.

He gave Silva's unconscious head a little nudge to expose the flesh of his neck, then put his shoe on Silva's neck and pressed, harder and harder until, even with the bar music seeping through the door in the background, I could hear the guy's neck snap, like a wooden stick breaking.

I bent down to see if he were still breathing.

He wasn't.

"That's Maryanne's cousin he smacked in there," said Toomey, as if it explained killing the guy. He brushed down his pant leg where it had ridden up on his ankle. "I hate these little punks."

"Jesus," I said.

"Relax, Keith," Toomey said. "Nobody saw us."

Us. That didn't sound too good. Toomey killed him, not me. I took a deep breath.

Fortunately, there was the security camera.

Toomey saw me glance.

"It's nothing," Toomey said. "Just go get the tape and we'll dump it with the body."

I didn't move. So far, I was a witness, not an accessory. Toomey killed him, not me.

"I don't think I want to get involved in this," I blurted.

Toomey's face twisted and suddenly there was a big revolver in his hand—honking big, like maybe a .44 Magnum.

"You're involved," Toomey said. "Get that tape and meet me here in five minutes. I'll bring the car around."

He was watching me closely, his brow furrowed, waiting for me to decide if I was going to cooperate or not.

"Okay," I said, holding out my hands and taking a step back. It was hard to say no to a .44 Mag.

The gun disappeared back behind his sports jacket and everything was peachy once again.

"You young guys," he said. "Grow some balls."

———

HE TURNED ONE WAY and I turned the other, my heart a lead weight in my chest. Since the back door was locked, I had to walk around the corner to get to the front, and all the way around I'm thinking, *run*. I didn't want anything to do with Toomey and his murder.

But I was an eye witness and if things turned bad, Toomey wouldn't have any trouble finding me. I'd have to get him the "tape."

Of course there wasn't any "tape," that was old school, Toomey was stuck in the '90s. But sitting on a shelf in the back room there was a black box the size of a book that recorded everything on a hard drive. Larry knew I knew where it was, and Toomey wanted it.

If I gave it to him, there'd be no proof about who actually killed Silva.

But if I didn't give it to him, I'd have to answer to Shawn Toomey.

So I had to give it to him.

I came around the front. A few guys were hanging around outside of the club, but inside the lights were up and the place nearly deserted—the real alkies finishing their beers at the bar.

Larry was mopping up where Levitt had been lying on the floor after getting hit with the pool cue, but Levitt himself was gone, and the rest of the onlookers with him.

Larry looked up at me. "Where's Shawn?" he asked.

He wore the gray bar-apron they made him wear and a blue shirt with the sleeves rolled up. He was a big guy, over six feet and pretty solid.

I heard he and Toomey had some kind of backdoor to the D. A., but I didn't really know him or his business with Toomey, so I just said, "He's getting his car."

"I saw him run out," Larry said. "What happened in back?"

"Nothing," I said.

"Okay, nothing," said Larry, and went back to mopping. "But you better clear out, the cops are on their way."

He paused and said to the mop, "You know where the recorder is, if that's what you're here for."

The tv over the bar was off, but I remembered the screen for the security system under the cash register at the counter. Larry might have seen what happened.

"You see anything on the monitor? I mean, after Toomey went out?"

"Hell no," he said. "I was busy with the guys in here."

Of course he would be, whether he was or not.

"Shawn looked pretty mad though," he added.

"Yeah," I replied sourly. "He looked pretty mad."

Clearly Larry wasn't going to be much help, even if he had witnessed the killing on the monitor. He wasn't going to cross Toomey any more than I was.

A cop car pulled up on the street, but I knew Larry would stall them. I ran to the back and ripped the recorder box from its shelf, leaving the wires dangling, and pushed outside through the steel door.

In the alley, Toomey had pulled his cherry-red Caddy right up to Silva's body, with the trunk open. He was spreading a blue tarp inside when I came out.

Funny he happened to carry a tarp.

"The cops are out front," I said.

"We'll be gone in a sec," he said.

He saw the security system box in my hand and took it, turning it this way and that. "Is the tape inside?" he said.

"The recording," I said, "Yeah, it's in there."

He threw the box onto the tarp in the trunk.

"We'll bury them together," he said, then turned to the body. "Help me lift him."

Toomey grabbed Silva's legs and waited for me to take the shoulders. Blood was coming out of the guy's ear.

"Come on," Toomey said.

The butt of the revolver was sticking out of Toomey's waist band.

I bent and grabbed Silva's feet.

God, the guy was heavy. His head lolled down and clunked on the back bumper as I tried to wrestle the dead weight into the trunk.

"Higher, you dick!" Toomey said.

I lifted the body higher and finally got Silva's ass over the edge. His shirt buttons had popped and his big white belly slopped over his belt. Together we rolled the body inside.

Toomey threw in the pool stick lying on the ground and folded the tarp over what was left of Silva. Then he checked his bumper for blood and slammed the trunk.

With the body wrapped up and in the car, I felt a hard ray of hope. If Silva simply disappeared nobody could prove he had been murdered. After all, Toomey had killed lots of people—even a cop—and he was still walking around free.

Plus when I helped him dump the body I'd know where the evidence was if it ever came down to that.

I started for the passenger door.

"Whoa, whoa, whoa," Toomey said, his hand on the handle on the other side of the car. "You're done."

"What? How are you going to get him out of there?"

"Let me worry about that. Just go home and take a hot bath, maybe not be seen around town for a while."

My hard ray of hope dimmed and drooped. "You sure you don't need my help?"

"Positive. Why? You want to see where I put him?"

"No, hell no. I just thought you might need a hand."

"I'm helping you out here. This way the guy just disappears." Toomey hunched his shoulders. "Where'd he go? You don't know. You don't know nothing. Understand?"

"Okay," I said. It wasn't a bad story, and it just might work.

"I like you, Keith. Just keep your mouth shut, and watch, it'll all blow over."

"Yeah. Sure."

"Don't tell the cops nothing," he said.

We heard Larry's voice approaching, loud from inside.

"Hit the road," Toomey commanded.

He got in the Caddy and took off. I ran up the alley and jumped behind a dumpster as Larry came outside, followed by two policemen. One of them, the fat blob cop, poked his flashlight around and fixated on something on the asphalt, apparently a spot of blood. This he discussed with the skinny-ass cop a long time, Larry still holding the door.

When they finally all disappeared inside, I rose and walked around the corner casual-like to my car. It would take a while for the cops to sort things out. I headed home to catch some sleep.

IT WAS DAWN BEFORE I could actually sleep.

I dreamt I was back in A-stan, Christine in fatigues at her desk at the compound in Gardez. I closed the flimsy door and went to her. Then she was in my arms, her lips soft on mine, her hair in my face, smelling of strawberries.

Then in the dream distant booming, coming closer and closer, and Christine suddenly lost all muscle tone and went limp, like the corpse I had wrestled into the trunk. The floor was an intricate carpet and I cradled her there but couldn't get her to wake up.

The door buzzer was rasping insistently.

I finally shook myself out of the nightmare and keyed the intercom. "Hello?"

"Is this Keith Gainey?"

"Yeah. Who's this?"

"This is Detective Siderio with the Philadelphia Police Department. I have a few questions about a disturbance last night where you work. Do you mind if I come up to talk?"

Cops already.

To keep them off my back I'd have to tell them something, but I should be safe if I stuck to the story Toomey had concocted.

I didn't want a cop in my apartment, however. He could see something, or plant something, that would get me in trouble.

"I'll be right down," I said.

Siderio was waiting on the sidewalk. He was a heavy-set guy in his mid-40s, with fat dark eyebrows and graying hair brushed back Guiney-style. He wore a gray overcoat over a gray suit with a white shirt and brown tie. A cold wind was blowing and he already looked pissed.

"Why don't we do this in my car?" he suggested, motioning to an unmarked Chevy Malibu parked nearby.

"I'm good," I said. The less comfortable he was, the sooner we'd be done.

He squinted at me, then swallowed his annoyance and said, "Okay, sure. Let's get to it then."

He pulled out a notepad. "You were the bouncer last night at a place called Minx, is that right?"

"Yeah," I said.

"We got a call on a disturbance around 1:30 a.m. involving a fight between two bar patrons. What can you tell me about that?"

"I didn't see it start but it was the usual thing. One guy went after another with a pool cue. I grabbed him and threw him out the back door."

"Then what?"

"Then I closed the door and came back to the bar. Larry had gotten rid of the guy who got hit, and then it was closing time so I went home."

"Mmm," the detective said, skeptically. "And how long did all this take?"

"I don't know, five, ten minutes."

"Did you know either of the men involved in the altercation?"

"The fight? No."

"Anthony Silva, Daniel Levitt, either of those two names ring a bell?"

"No."

"And the patron with the pool stick—that would be Anthony Silva—when you threw him out did you have any help?"

That made me squirm.

"Help?" I said. "No."

He squinted at me with his fat eyebrows again. "You're sure about that?"

"Yeah, I'm sure."

"Okay. And did Silva have any blood on him from the fight?"

"Could be. But nothing I noticed."

"And was there any altercation between you and Silva in the alley? I mean, did he try to resist you in any way, maybe throw a few punches?"

"I never went in the alley. I had him in a bear hug and tossed him out the back door. That was the last I saw him."

"What happened to the pool stick?"

"What do you mean what happened?"

"It's missing. It wasn't in the alley. What happened to it?"

"I don't know. Maybe he took it."

"What about the security system box? Did he take that, too?"

"I don't know. The security system isn't my job."

"Let me show you something," he said, pulling a piece of paper from his jacket pocket and handing it to me.

He watched as I unfolded it. Printed in smeary colored ink on a piece of copy paper was a mug shot of Shawn Toomey.

"Do you know him?"

"No," I said.

"Come on, Mr. Gainey. Everyone knows who Shawn Toomey is. He was sitting right there at the bar."

"I didn't notice."

"Witnesses said he followed you and Silva outside."

"Well, if he did, I never saw him."

"Did you know Silva didn't make it home last night?"

"No, but so what? He's probably still out drinking," I said.

"Or maybe he was murdered."

"Look, I never saw Shawn Toomey and don't know anything about Silva. The guy created a disturbance, and I did my job and threw him out, that's it."

"That makes you the last person to see him."

"Unless he's still out drinking with his buddies. Or if someone else followed him like you said."

The eyebrows went up again. "Can you hold out your hands, please?"

"Why?"

"Just hold them out."

I held them out palms up.

"The other way," he said.

My knuckles didn't have any scrapes or bruises that I could see, or Siderio either, from his disappointed look. But he dogged on.

"Where are your clothes from last night? Can I see them."

"I'm done talking. Am I free to go?"

"Look, I'm going to find out everything that happened. If Shawn Toomey was involved, just say so and maybe we can work something out, save your own ass."

"Am I free to go?" I repeated.

"Yeah, you're free to go." He handed me his business card. "Call me if you want to talk. The next time won't be so friendly."

He got in his car and drove away.

Fuck.

Silva wasn't missing 12 hours, but knowing Toomey was involved, no wonder Siderio was already treating it like a murder case—with me as a prime suspect.

But I could tell he really wanted Toomey, not me. He was already trying to get me to flip. I tried to imagine how that would work out: If I talked to Siderio and word got back to Toomey, I'd probably end up like the last witness to one of his crimes—shot through the back of her head in her own kitchen. And she was a grandma.

If Toomey wouldn't spare a grandma, he sure as shit wouldn't spare me.

I could have kicked myself for giving Toomey the security system recorder, though it's not like I had a choice. It was the one piece of evidence that could have saved my ass. But it was buried with the body somewhere.

The recorder.

If I had that, I could go to Siderio and get the protection I would need from Toomey. Otherwise, I was going to prison for a murder I didn't commit.

How I was going to do that I didn't know. But I needed a new base of operations where the cops, and Toomey, wouldn't find me.

I decided to head out to Bryn Mawr to see Lucie. I left my cell phone on the dresser so no one could track me and gathered up the clothing Siderio had mentioned to dump somewhere along the way.

LUCIE POWERS WAS AN anthropology major at Bryn Mawr College and my on-again off-again girlfriend. Lucie wasn't your average starving student. She lived in a sweet little colonial house not far from Villanova, because she had a very rich but very absent father.

As a matter of principle, I usually don't go for rich girls, but with Luce, I made an exception. She had a wild streak in her that just flat-out turned me on—and, for some reason, she felt the same about me.

When I got there, no one was home. I let myself in and fell asleep on the downstairs couch while waiting, where she prodded me awake an hour later.

"Hell, Keith, don't you think you could have called?" she said, plopping herself down in a chair opposite.

She was dressed in her ripped jeans, Bryn Mawr sweatshirt, and immaculate white sneakers. With her lithe body and flowing auburn hair, she was almost certainly the most beautiful anthropologist the college was ever going to produce.

I sat up and rubbed my eyes. "I thought I'd surprise you," I said.

"You surprised me alright. You scared me to death. When I saw you on the couch, I almost shot you."

"I thought you didn't like guns," I said. She had been less-than-happy when I dragged her out shooting for a date, and couldn't hit a 60" TV from two feet.

"Well, I would have shot you if I liked guns. Maybe I'll shoot you anyway. I still have those things from the target range. I wish you'd get them out of here."

She settled in her chair and scrutinized me more carefully. "What are you doing here?" she asked. "What do you want?"

"Come on, Luce." She was looking for more from me in the relationship than I was looking for from her.

"Don't 'come on Luce' me. We were going to find something for Bayan's wedding. Go antiquing, remember?"

Bayan was her best friend, getting married in May. I remembered the antiquing, but I purposely had forgot. I kept looking for ways to cool things down, but I was a dick and couldn't keep myself away.

"Antiquing. That's why I'm here."

"Come on, Keith, cut the bullshit."

"Look, I need a place to stay for a few days. Do you want me here or not?"

My irritated tone agitated her. "You can't just parachute in here anytime you want," she said.

Lucie said she had fallen for me because I was a free spirit, but she didn't like my free-spirited ways.

"I'm sorry," I said. "But something came up and I can't go home just now."

"So, you're not here to see me, you just need a place to flop?" she said, anger creeping into her voice.

"No, are you kidding? Of course, I want to see you. There's no one I want to see more right now. That's why I'm here." I reached out and touched her hand. "Really, Luce. I need you."

She shifted in her chair, but she didn't take her hand away.

"What's going on?"

I hadn't meant to draw her in but suddenly I found myself blurting out the whole damned story, from the moment I dragged Silva out the door, to Toomey's Caddy driving away with the body in the trunk, to Siderio's implied threats. She listened—first with skepticism, but then aghast, before finally getting up and sitting beside me quietly on the couch.

I brought her to me, brushing her hair from her face, then put my lips to hers.

At first, she pushed me away, not very hard, then wrapped her hand around my arm, then embraced me fully and passionately. When she ran her fingers up under my shirt and lightly brushed my stomach, I gave up on any idea of cooling it and tugged off her sweatshirt to reveal her perfect, and bra-free, breasts.

When we finished, she lay atop me on the couch.

"You've got to go to the police," she said.

"And get my head blasted off by Toomey?"

"They'll put you into some kind of witness program. Protect you."

"Protect me, right," I said. "You don't know these guys. If Toomey finds out I'm talking to the cops, I won't last ten minutes."

"So—what?—you're just going to let them arrest you for murder?" she said.

"Not if I can help it."

"But, prison, Keith. I couldn't take that," she said flatly. She got up and began pulling on her clothes, biting her lip. I could tell there was something else.

"Do you remember Grayson Rhyne?" she asked.

"The golf team kid?" She had dragged me to a charity event, Ponies for People.

"He's not a kid, and he's very nice."

"Very rich, anyway."

She turned her back to me as she slipped on her sweatshirt. "He asked if we could get engaged, and I accepted."

Part of me felt relieved, part of me was struck hollow.

When she turned back, I said, "Congratulations."

"Is that all you've got to say?"

"What do you want me to say? He proposed, you accepted. I hope you're happy."

"Oh, Keith, don't be like that. How long have we been seeing each other?"

"I don't know. Since I got back from A-stan."

"Over two years. And I'm supposed to go to Thailand next fall to start my fieldwork."

"So you're saying, what, I had my chance? You told me you never wanted to get married."

"No. I said I'd rather be single than end up like my mother."

Her father was the philandering, never-home CFO of an international liquified natural gas company, and her socialite mother a 20-year therapy patient.

"I'm not Grayson Rhyne," I reminded her. "Bouncers don't make much."

"But you liked the idea of Thailand, and living among the hill tribes."

"Doesn't Grayson?"

"There's no golfing in Thailand," she said, not sounding very happy. She held up her left hand. "What do you see?"

"I see a very beautiful hand."

"Not very observant," she said. She wiggled a finger. "No ring. Grayson gave me one, but I'm not wearing it yet."

"So, you're not really engaged."

"No. We are." She smiled a tight little smile. "But..."

"You don't want to live among the hill tribes alone."

"Don't say it that way," she said.

She was being vulnerable, and I could see that I had hurt her. But marriage wasn't in my plans, not after Christine. Plus, I didn't want to get tied down, have to get a real job, have a mortgage, whatever.

And with her money she'd probably put me on an allowance, cut my balls off.

But damn she was too fine to lose, especially to an asshole like Grayson Rhyne. Beautiful and rich, yes, but independent, smart and willing to call me on my shit.

"Just think about it, okay?"

"Okay," I said. And I would think about it, if Shawn Toomey didn't kill me.

As if reading my mind, she said, "But first we have to keep you out of jail," she said. "I'll call Dad's lawyer."

Her sun-streaked hair cascaded in flowing curls over her shoulders. I reached out a naked arm to pull her to me, but she danced back.

"I have another class," she said. "We can talk tonight over dinner. I'll make you that shrimp pesto pasta."

She gathered her books and left.

THE ROOM SUDDENLY SEEMED very quiet and empty. I wondered about the hill tribes of Thailand, what they did and whether we would hunt and live in a grass hut, or what.

Escape to Thailand sounded great, but what I really needed was to recover that hard drive—what Toomey stupidly called "the tape"—from the body.

Assuming, that is, that he really did bury it with the body like he said, because if he hadn't I was truly screwed.

So, find the body. That wasn't going to be easy. But it had taken two of us to get the body into the trunk. Toomey wasn't going to mess up his nice sports jacket man-handling a body by himself, so he must have gotten some help burying the fat fuck.

For that he'd probably call in some young muscle from the Elmwood gang. Someone related to someone he knew and could be trusted to keep his mouth shut. There were lots of guys like that floating around, guys who would help out with a robbery or would run across the river to Camden to pick up some guns.

Elmwood plus local toughs made me think of Pronto's, an Italian restaurant over on South 65th Street owned by Pete Mattia, who along with Shawn Toomey controlled a lot of the local scams, particularly out at Philly airport.

Rudy Delgadillo, who used to bounce with me, worked there now as a manager. If anyone would know about Toomey getting help for a job, it would be Rudy.

And he owed me a favor.

I drove over and went inside. It was only a little after five but the tables along the wall were already almost full—neighborhood men getting off work, some girls who looked like Catholic high schoolers, and a table with four guys talking low over a beer pitcher. They looked up at me suspiciously when I came in.

Rudy, in a white shirt, was ringing up a customer at the register, his meaty hands barely able to hit the keys. When he turned and saw me his eyes went wide.

"Keith. What are you doing here?"

There was a waiter, a young guy like the ones drinking at the table, pulling some cannolis from a glass case nearby.

"I was driving by and thought I'd come in, say hello," I said.

He turned to the waiter and said, "Watch the front for a minute." Then he lifted a hinged section of the counter and motioned me into his office in the back.

There he took a seat on a swivel chair behind a cluttered desk, leaving me to sit in a folding chair against the file cabinet opposite.

"You're crazy for coming here," he said. "The cops have already been in asking about you and Shawn."

"What did you tell them?"

"Get real. What do you think?"

Meaning, nothing.

"Listen," I said, getting right to the point. "I'm in a jam and you might be able to help. I need to find something."

"Like what?" he said.

"Something that Shawn Toomey might have buried last night."

He rubbed the back of his head. His arm was the size of my leg. But when he dropped his hand to the table, he did not look happy.

"I don't know anything about Shawn," he said.

Right, I thought. No one ever did.

"I'm not asking about him," I said. "But whatever he did last night, he was going to need some help."

"Okay."

"And I thought you might have heard something."

"You shouldn't have came in here," he said. "I can't tell you nothing. Those guys outside, they saw you."

"Those guys at the table? Was it one of them?"

"I can't say anything," he said. "It'd be like pissing in Shawn's face. He'd know. Shawn's in here all the time."

"Like last night?" I pressed.

"Don't ask me that," he said. "I've got a wife and a kid."

It was his kid Mike, 13 years old, that I hid from the cops when he and an older boy tried to rob a bar I was working.

"How's Mike doing?" I asked.

Rudy rubbed the back of his head again. "Better," he finally said. "He made the wrestling team."

"That's good," I said, and waited.

"Okay," Rudy said. "But you didn't hear this from me, understood?"

I nodded.

"Shawn came by late last night, maybe 3 a.m., right as we were closing. There was a guy here, Aldo, with some buddies. Shawn talked to him and left. And then a few minutes later Aldo also left. That's all I seen and all I know."

"Aldo," I said. "Do you know his last name?"

Rudy shook his head no. "But I've seen him around. He works at Keystone Beverage."

"What's that? A beer distributor?"

"Yeah, over on Elmwood. He's a Hispanic guy, husky, with a scraggle-ass beard and glasses."

"Thanks," I said. "Now I owe you one."

"You don't owe me nothing," he said. "Just keep my name out of it." He opened the office door and pointed toward the kitchen. "Better go out the back."

I SMILED TO MYSELF as I walked back to the car, feeling like I was finally getting somewhere. If Aldo had helped Toomey the night before, he would have to know where the body was. The only problem was going to be, getting him to tell me.

Keystone Beverage was a one-story stand-alone building butting up against a row of brick townhouses. Sandwich board signs on the sidewalk proclaimed "OPEN" and "BUDWEISER SPECIAL," with the walls and windows plastered with ads for other bargains for Miller Lite, Dab and Yuengling. They sold cigarettes, too, and lottery tickets, for convenient one-stop shopping.

The parking lot held five spaces but I passed it by, circled around, and parked on the other side of the street. I wasn't going to just waltz in there blind. I wanted to see this Aldo, figure out my approach.

I sat for a while, watching cars pull in and out of the lot and wishing I still smoked. This was Pennsylvania with its tight liquor laws, and beer distributors like Keystone only sold beer by the case. Some buyers would carry out their own, but others needed help.

Pretty soon a customer came out, some old geezer missing half his hair. Behind him was a guy carrying a full-size keg on his shoulder. It was a sure bet that the keg guy was Aldo. He was early 20s, about two hundred pounds and pretty well-built. I could see he had a scraggly beard like Rudy said, and cheap, black-rimmed glasses.

It had to be him.

He quite handily set the keg in the pickup's bed, then, as the geezer drove off, sauntered back into the building.

Right off, I could see this wasn't going to be easy. Aldo didn't know me from Adam, and for sure he had enough street smarts to know to keep his mouth shut about what he did with Toomey.

I decided my best chance was the direct approach—try to scare him a little, appeal to his self-interest, maybe suggest I could keep him out of jail.

When Aldo emerged to hoist a keg into the back of another customer's pickup, I pulled up beside and waited.

"Aldo, hey," I said from the car when he came past. "Got a minute?"

"Who are you?"

"Someone you need to talk to," I said. "Hop in."

He eyed me suspiciously. "I'm working. Talk about what?"

"Last night," I said, and when he needed a further nudge, "That spade work with Toomey."

His eyes narrowed behind his glasses, and he leaned down to look at me more closely. Then, with a glance at the store where the lights had just come on, he walked around and climbed into the passenger seat.

"What do you want?" he said, in not-too-friendly a tone.

"The fat dude from the back of the caddy. Where'd you plant the body?"

He crossed his arms. "I don't know about no body."

"Yeah, you do. I was the other guy that helped Toomey. I put the body *in* the trunk."

I had his attention. He shifted uncomfortably.

"And you and me," I continued, "we're in big trouble. The cops are right on my ass. Which means they're on your ass, too. We helped Toomey put away that dude and you know what that means?"

"What?"

"In the eyes of the law we're just as guilty as he is. It's called aiding and abetting. We're accessories. They could send us to jail for a long time."

He chewed on that a minute.

"You're a young guy," I pressed. "Do you really want to spend the rest of your life in Allenwood to cover up for Toomey?"

Mentioning Toomey was the wrong strategy. He shuddered and reached for the door handle. "I'll take my chances," he said.

"Those chances are pretty bad, dude. The cops already have your name."

That got his attention. He let go of the door handle and eased back into his seat.

"Look, Aldo, the cops don't want us, they want Toomey, and they'll squeeze us hard to get at him. But there's evidence with that body that will prove we had nothing to do with it."

"Like what?" he asked

"A video," I said, "that shows exactly what happened. The cops will arrest Toomey and we can make a deal with the D.A. A get-out-of-jail-free kind of deal. We turn state's evidence and get off with a wrist slap."

"So you're saying we squeal against Shawn in court? No thanks." He opened the car door and said, "Don't come around here again. And if I was you, I'd watch my mouth."

He slammed the door with a bang and tromped back into the store.

Shit. That got me nowhere. There was no doubt he knew where the body was, but he wasn't talking. Plus, if he took what I said to Toomey I'd be a dead man.

I had Siderio's card in my pocket. Maybe I should go to him, tell him my story. The cops could lean on Aldo and if they found the body with the recording, they'd have to believe me.

Except Aldo might not talk and they might never find the body. Toomey had gotten pretty good over the years at disposing of things.

If I was lucky I had scared Aldo just enough to keep him from running to Toomey. I'd have to work on him again, in a different way.

Suddenly I was very hungry, and I remembered the dinner Lucie was making.

It was after nine when I pulled onto Lucie's street. I was late and knew she would be pissed, but I wasn't expecting to find the house looking dark and deserted.

I let myself in to the vague smell of basil and flipped on some lights. Maybe she was upstairs sleeping?

"Lucie?"

No answer.

The dining room table was set with some silver-rimmed plates, wine glasses and a vase of pink flowers. In the kitchen I found a sauce pan full of basil pesto, cold to the touch, and, in the sink, a colander piled with thin white noodles, also cold. I didn't see any shrimp. On the counter was a stainless steel bowl containing wilted salad and a note:

Enjoy your dinner. Out with Grayson. Don't wait up.

I crumpled the note and held it in my fist. Didn't she understand what I was up against? Couldn't she see how the walls were closing in on me? There wouldn't be any dinners together if I didn't clear my name.

And Grayson. They were probably out at some expensive restaurant near the college. Or worse, hanging out together at his house in his jetted hot tub.

"Don't wait up." Screw her.

I hated women who played power games. I wasn't going to be rushed into any lifelong decisions because of Grayson or anyone.

I threw the note on the counter, then microwaved myself a plate of noodles and ate it in front of the tv in the living room.

———

TWENTY MINUTES LATER CAME a god-awful knock on the door:

"Police, warrant, open up!" screamed a gruff voice.

Electrified, I sat up, knowing immediately I was about to be arrested for Silva's murder.

I could turn myself in and hope everything came out all right, or I could make a run for it and try to get the evidence I would need to prove I was innocent.

I decided to run.

They probably had men covering the back, so instead of banging through the kitchen door I slid open the dining room window and quietly let myself down into the narrow alley between the houses.

I swung up over the side fence and landed in the neighbor's walkway, then made a beeline for the backyard and freedom.

There I came face on with a cop in combat stance, both hands pointing his nasty-looking handgun straight at me.

"Stop right there!" he screamed.

I skidded to a halt and froze, knowing that he had me zeroed. I looked desperately towards the alley beyond him, but there was just no way out.

"Hands up!" he said. "Now!"

The cop was young, barely out of his teens. But he held the gun rock steady and now, out of the corner of my eye, I glimpsed reinforcements running his way.

I put up my hands.

"Lie down on the ground," he commanded. "Put your hands behind your back."

I knew the drill from my M.P. work. I bowed to the inevitable, put my face in the grass, and let the cop cuff me.

Kneeling on my back he screamed, "I got him, I got him!"

A second later I was swarmed by three beefy officers and hauled to my feet.

Trembling and totally out-of-gas, I let myself be searched and then dragged from the back yard out to the front, barely hearing the young cop, still high on his adrenaline rush, stumbling his way through my Miranda rights.

My body kept wanting to go limp. It was all I could do to hold myself upright as they dragged me up Lucie's walk and stuffed me into the back of a police cruiser.

DEPRESSED AND EXHAUSTED, I spent a restless night lying on a wall-mounted ledge in the local lockup, waiting to find out what would happen next.

Charged with murder.

Now I was really in for it. I drew a blank trying to think what evidence Siderio might have found linking me directly to the crime. Whatever he had, it was enough to get a judge to issue a warrant for my arrest.

The only thing I could think was a witness. But if there *was* a witness, Siderio would know that Toomey killed Silva, not me.

I sat up on the ledge with my head in my hands, paralyzed with uncertainty. Everything was happening a lot faster than I had thought. If they didn't even have a body, how could they charge me with murder?

Siderio, I decided, had given up on trying to implicate Toomey. And—even with his fucking warrant—he probably didn't have enough evidence to convict me.

Shit! I suddenly thought. He was probably trying to panic me into a confession.

But I had nothing to confess. I just had to keep my mouth shut. That would save my ass from the law *and* from Toomey.

But what if Siderio really *did* have enough evidence, even weak evidence, to convince some lame jury? I'd be spending the rest of my life in a tiny cold cell like this one.

No. No way I was going to let that happen. Siderio had me right where he wanted me, and I could only think of one way out.

Squeal.

I tried to think how Toomey would come at me if I testified against him. He'd have to kill me before we got in court. So, for sure, they'd surround me with marshals and keep me under wraps. Which meant I'd have to leave my jobs, not contact any of my friends, not see Lucie.

And after, even if—especially if—they managed to put Toomey away, he wasn't going to just forget it. I'd have to say goodbye to my mom and exit Philly for good, start a new life somewhere far out of the way, maybe Thailand with Lucie, maybe back to Afghanistan on a contract with SOSi, which I knew was still hiring after the disaster at Bagram.

But even A-stan was better than life in prison. If I was going to save my ass, I was going to have to roll over on Toomey.

I was ready, even anxious, to talk to Siderio.

I just hoped to God he believed me.

———

THE NEXT MORNING, I prepared to spill my guts. I told the cop who brought breakfast I was ready to talk and around nine was led out of the holding cell to a small stuffy room with a steel door.

I sat at the table for about fifteen minutes, going over my story in my mind and waiting for Siderio.

Finally he arrived, wearing the same gray suit jacket and white shirt as before, but no tie and carrying two cups of coffee from Starbucks.

"Here, I brought you something," he said, handing me a container. "I hope you like black."

"Thanks," I said. I knew he was just buttering me up, but the coffee was delicious.

He sat down across from me, looking not menacing but tired and sad.

"They treating you right? Everything okay?"

"Yeah, except you arrested the wrong man."

"Look, I'm just trying to get to the bottom of this mess. They told me you had some information for me."

"I sure as hell do. Toomey..."

"Shawn Toomey?"

"Who else?"

"Hold on a minute before you start talking, we've got some paperwork to get out of the way." He pulled a business card from his pocket. "Miranda rights," he said. "I know they read it to you last night, but I've got to read it to you again." He shrugged apologetically. "Regulations."

He read me my rights in a bored tone, the familiar words from tv, "*You have the right to remain silent; anything you say can and will be used against you in a court of law...*"

He stopped with the legalese and looked over at me. "Did you finish high school?"

"Did I finish high school? Of course I finished high school," I said.

"No offense, just that some of the guys I deal with aren't too bright."

He passed the card over to me, along with a pen.

"There's some questions on the back for you. Just circle them yes or no and sign it anywhere."

He leaned back and waited, looking at me over the lid of his coffee.

I examined the back of the card:

1. Have you read or had read to you the warnings as to your rights? Yes/No

2. Do you understand these rights? Yes/No

3. Do you wish to answer any questions? Yes/No

4. Are you willing to answer questions without an attorney present? Yes/No

So basically I was giving up all my legal rights.

How stupid.

But it was either squeal on Toomey and get some protection, or face life in prison, and I had already made up my mind.

Yes/Yes/Yes, I circled but I paused at number four. Maybe it would be best to have a lawyer present, even if just a public defender? Maybe I should wait?

Just then, the door opened and the cop that had escorted me into the room poked his head in and motioned for Siderio to join him outside.

An annoyed look crossed Siderio's face.

"Finished with that?" he said, motioning to me for the card.

"I'm thinking," I said.

"Thinking about what? You said you wanted to talk."

"Joe," said the cop at the door insistently.

Siderio stood.

"Just finish with the card," he said. "I'll be right back."

He went out, leaving me alone with the card.

What the fuck, I thought. Either I trusted him to get me out of this jam or I didn't.

I circled the final *Yes* and signed the card.

The door opened and Siderio entered, followed by a stout, gray-haired guy in a dark suit and red tie. They weren't talking, and Siderio looked pissed.

Siderio took his old seat across from me, while the new guy sat at the table end, catty-corner from me.

"Dave Wachtel," he said, shaking my hand. "I'm here to represent you."

I sat there shocked. Lucie must have found out about my arrest and sent him. She said she was going to talk to her father's lawyer and she had. Not many women would have done that.

"You didn't tell me you had an attorney," Siderio said to me.

"He's not required to tell you anything," Wachtel said. He turned to me and asked, "What have you said so far?"

"Nothing," I said. "We were just getting started."

"Good," he said.

He saw the card in front of me and picked it up.

"Oh, no, no, no, no, no," he said, ripping the card up and pocketing the pieces. "My client's not waiving any of his rights. This interview is over."

"Really?" said Siderio. "Are you sure that's the way you want to play it? Because Keith here had something he wanted to tell me..."

"I said no, absolutely not, we're done," Wachtel said. He sat back and crossed his arms. "And please leave us for a few minutes so that my client and I can talk."

Fuming, Siderio stood up and left without a word.

Having steeled myself to squeal, my resolve blew out of me like a deflating balloon. It was reassuring to have Lucie's lawyer beside me, but I didn't see how he changed the situation any. I was still going to have to snitch on Toomey.

Unless this guy Wachtel had some other ideas?

I was definitely willing to listen.

He glanced around the room to satisfy himself there weren't any cameras, then turned and said to me, "What the hell did you think you were doing? Never, ever, never talk to a cop."

"Okay, but what am I supposed to do?" I said.

"Don't worry, I've handled a thousand cases like this. We're going to take care of you, I guarantee it."

He seemed awfully confident. In the back of my mind, though, I thought to wonder why an attorney for a gas company executive would be so involved in criminal law.

"How long have you been working for Mr. Powers?" I asked.

"Powers? Who's that?"

"Lucie's dad. Isn't that who sent you?"

"Oh yeah," he said. "Lucie Powers. Your girlfriend, right? The broad from the college."

Broad.

Wachtel saw the look on my face. He leaned in and whispered, "Relax, so long as she doesn't testify, Shawn will take care of her, too."

My heart froze. Wachtel wasn't the attorney Lucie sent; he was the attorney *Toomey* sent.

No doubt to keep tabs on me, and make sure I kept my mouth shut.

Suddenly my hands were clammy, and I could hardly breath. I'd have to appear to cooperate, find out what Toomey's game was.

Then thread the needle and keep myself alive.

"Okay," I said. "That's good about Lucie. Tell, ah, Shawn I appreciate it."

"Keep your voice down," Wachtel said, "Don't mention his name."

"Okay," I said. "Sure. Whatever he wants."

Wachtel sat back and looked at me appraisingly. "That's good to hear you say that. I know you're in a rough place. But I assume you want to do what's best for everyone."

"I'm not a rat, if that's what you're getting at," I lied.

Wachtel smiled. "That's the attitude we like to see. He said you were a smart kid, and let me tell you right now, we're going to take care of you no matter what.

"First of all, this case, it's garbage. There's no body and all they got against you right now is a single witness, who may or may not have seen something on the security monitor."

The witness who saw the security monitor would have to be Larry Holmes, the bartender. But Larry would never talk to the cops. Unless...

Of course.

Toomey wanted him to.

Which meant I was being set up. Somebody had to go down for the murder and it wasn't going to be Toomey.

Wachtel continued: "So I think we can plea bargain this down to involuntary manslaughter, ten years at most. And even if they convict you for third degree murder, we'll fix it so you're comfortable—maybe get you into Mahanoy, which is more like a country-club than a pen, make sure you have a cushy job, plenty of spending cash and friends. You understand what I'm saying?"

"Yeah. Yeah, I understand perfectly."

"Good, that's all settled then. I'm going to enter you a not-guilty plea at the preliminary. You don't have to say anything—I'll do all the talking."

"What about bail?" I asked.

Wachtel grew evasive. "I'll see what I can do," he said. "You got any money?"

I thought about it. "I could scrape together a couple of thousand."

"A couple thousand, huh? Let me talk to our friend and we'll see."

THAT AFTERNOON, I WAS transported to the Criminal Justice Center in downtown Philly, where the preliminary arraignment went off swimmingly—for Toomey.

I sat numbly as the charges were read: second degree murder, resisting arrest, tampering with evidence and a host of other infractions. Bail, after a whispered conference between the magistrate and my "attorney," was set at $500,000.

Afterwards, they issued me an orange jumpsuit and stuck me in a new cell, smaller and darker than my old cell. If Wachtel got his way, I was going to be enjoying the hospitality of cells like this for at least the next ten years, while Toomey ran around in loud sports jackets free as a beagle off-leash.

I was still alive, but I was back to square one.

Or actually, worse than square one—square zero. Because now I was stuck in a cell and the only way I could even hope to beat the murder charge was to find the body and retrieve that hard drive.

Aldo could lead me to it. I knew where to find him, and this time I'd go with my Glock, force him to take me where I wanted to go.

But before I could get to Aldo, I had to make bail, which meant I needed $50,000 for the bondsman.

Wachtel wasn't going to arrange it; he was taking care of Toomey, not me, and the last thing Toomey wanted was me on the outside.

There was only one person I could turn to who had that kind of money.

I was going to have to go begging hat-in-hand to Lucie.

But damn. Just the thought of having to ask her made my guts squirm. I mean, you don't go hit a girl up for fifty K and think she won't expect something in return. There were a lot of things Lucie wanted to change in me and this might give her just the leverage she'd been waiting for.

However...

Using the phone card Wachtel had provided to contact him, I dialed Lucie's number.

"Hello?" Lucie said.

"*You are receiving a call from 'Keith Gainey' at the Philadelphia Detention Center,*" came a recording. "*Press 1 to accept the call, press 2 to hang up and block the caller...*"

"Keith?" I heard Lucie's voice say.

"Press 1," I said.

"Keith, is that you?"

The recorded message began to repeat, and I realized she couldn't hear me. Still, I said "Press 1" again, more loudly, and held my breath.

I heard a tone as Lucie accepted the call.

"Keith?" she said, a third time.

"Yeah, it's me. Thanks for picking up."

Silence dripped from the other end.

"Lucie?" I said.

"I should have blocked you," she said.

"Don't say that. I'm in trouble."

"I was wondering what your car was doing here. I thought maybe you had found some other girl to use as a hotel."

"Lucie, when I got back to your place last night, they arrested me."

"For what?"

"For murder."

"For murder?"

"Yes, for murder," I said. "That and a couple other things."

"Oh, Keith," she said, a hint of compassion finally softening her voice.

"Lucie, listen. I need...I need to borrow some money."

The hardness snapped back. "Well, no surprise there."

"For bail," I explained. "So, I can get out and prove I'm innocent."

There was a moment of silence. "You are such a screw-up, Keith," she said, suddenly sounding tearful. "You ruin everything. Why did you get mixed up in this?"

I didn't get mixed up in it. It got mixed up with me.

"Lucie," I said, "I promise I'll pay you back. Every cent."

"How? Your bouncer salary?"

"You know I'm good for it. Listen—Toomey's setting me up to take the rap for the murder. If I don't get out of here, they'll put me away for years. For years, Luce, no lie."

"Why are you only calling me now? I was worried sick about you."

"This is the first chance I got. And we can only talk for fifteen minutes."

"I hate you," Lucie said, not meaning it, calming down a little. "How much do you need?"

"$50,000."

"Get real, Keith, I'm not a fucking bank."

That sounded more like her.

"I told you, I'll pay you back." Man, she was making me sweat.

"Keith, it's not that and you know it," she said.

Here it comes.

"Why are you calling me?" she asked.

"I told you, I need to make bail so that..."

"No, Keith. Why are you calling *me*? *Me*, get it? And don't say I'm the only person you know who can lend you $50,000."

That was exactly what I was going to say, so I didn't say anything.

She snorted.

"You're calling me, asshole, because I'm the only person you know that actually cares about you. More than cares about you. Loves you. And you know that."

I made some sort of guttural sound.

"And you're grunting because you're too emotionally blocked off to accept that simple truth. Even though you love me too. You date all those party girls and yet you hold me at arms-length why? Because you won't accept real love. Because of what happened with Christine."

Christine.

Lieutenant Christine Hernandez had been my girl in Afghanistan for both of my deployments. She built wells, schools, and clinics with civil affairs. And our own affair was the talk of the town—what with her being an officer and me just a grunt.

Of course, all that ended that night at the hotel, when she died in my arms.

We were supposed to get married as soon as our deployments ended.

She was the love of my life.

"Let's leave Christine out of this," I said.

"How can we? Do you think Christine would be proud of you, in prison for murder?"

"She would have at least understood. And I said leave her out of this."

"I'm not leaving her out of it because she's still in it. She's still in you. Look, I know I'm not Christine and never will be. But you need to move on with your life. If not with me, then with someone else."

Push, push, push. She could never let anything rest.

"Keith, are you there?"

"Yeah," I said.

"You're too good a man to drift through life the way you've been doing. And if Christine could be here, that's exactly what she would say and you know it."

It wasn't the first time she had laid it on me like that. She just didn't, couldn't, understand what Christine and I had going. What the hell was I supposed to say?

"It's okay," she said, hearing my hesitation. "Just think about it. We can talk more when I see you."

"Does that mean you're going to bail me out?" I blurted.

She snorted. "Don't I always?"

Four hours later, Lucie pulled up to the detention center parking lot in her Volvo S90, the car of the moment at Bryn Mawr.

"How are you feeling?" she asked, as soon as I got in.

"A lot better now than this morning," I said.

She was dressed in a different baggy sweatshirt from the last time I saw her. She looked tired, but more beautiful even than I remembered.

"Thank you," I said, leaning over to give her a kiss.

She turned her cheek and accepted the kiss passionlessly. "You smell," she said.

"You do, too," I joked. "But good."

That got a smile. She punched the accelerator and off we went.

"What are your plans?" she said.

My stomach knotted and I went into defensive mode. "Well, ah...ah, I don't know," I said. "I need more time to think."

She gave me an exasperated look, then laughed. "Not about *us*," she said. "Where am I taking you? Back to my place?"

My car was there, and the handguns we had used at the practice range.

"Yeah, that would be good. But we're not going to be able to stay. Toomey knows who you are."

"So what?"

"Look, Toomey has connections. For sure he already knows you bailed me out. If he wants to find me, your house is the first place he'll look. And to get at me, he's liable to do something to you. So we have to go somewhere else."

"I've got classes," she said. "I can't go anywhere."

"Lucie, you're going. Toomey kills people at the drop of a hat."

"But I'm not a part of it."

"Yes you are, Luce. Because you're with me."

She glanced over sharply, for a moment looking—what?—surprised?

"What are you saying?" she asked.

"I'm saying for once you've got to listen, or we could both end up dead."

She slipped back into annoyance. "Right, like Bonnie and Clyde."

"Exactly. And last time I checked, they died in a hail of bullets."

That seemed to get through to her.

"All right," she said at last. "Bayan's family has a place in Bucks County where we could stay. I can drive to my classes."

"You can't go to those either."

"For how long?"

"A few days, maybe," I said. "Or a few weeks."

"A few weeks! Finals are coming."

"Finals can be made up, Luce, but dead is dead. Like it or not, we have to hide."

"This is ridiculous. We've got to get you to Dad's lawyer."

"I have a lawyer," I said. I explained the situation with the attorney Toomey had sent.

Lucie listened, appalled. "Are you kidding?" she said. "You have to fire that guy."

"No. Toomey has to think I'm playing along. At least until I resolve the situation."

She snorted. "And without a real lawyer, how are you going to do that?"

I was going to shove a 9 mm up Aldo's nose and make him take me to that body.

But I only said: "I got to go see someone."

———

A FEW HOURS LATER, we reached Lucie's friend's place in Upper Bucks—she driving her Volvo, me following behind in my own car. We would be staying in a renovated carriage house behind the enormous colonial farmhouse that belonged to Bayan's parents.

Lucie was already in a foul mood by the time we arrived, irked at having to pack so quickly and go into sudden hiding. There were two bedrooms in the carriage house, and she made clear, as she wheeled in her enormous suitcase, that we would each be sleeping separately.

I had only the clothes on my back and the canvas bag from Lucie's place that I had stuffed with the pistols from the range. The guns were spread on my bed and I was loading a clip when Lucie pushed open my door holding a blanket.

She stopped dead in her tracks.

"Are you out of your mind?" she said. "What are you doing, Keith?"

"I told you," I said. "I have to see someone."

"With a gun?"

"I might need it. For protection."

"Who? Who are you going to see? Toomey? You said yourself he'd kill you!"

"Not Toomey. The other guy I told you about, Aldo. He knows where the body is buried."

"Absolutely not. No. Put that thing away."

We had been under the same roof for less than 15 minutes and she was already telling me what to do. Slowly, methodically, I packed the Ruger with its ammo back into the canvas bag and put it beside my nightstand on the floor. Then I slid the clip in the Glock and slipped it into my waistband, where it was invisible under my jacket.

Tears sprang into Lucie's eyes. "Why, Keith? Why are you doing this? At least wait until tomorrow when we can talk to Dad's lawyer."

"We can talk to the lawyer after I get that video," I said.

"What good's a fucking video if you're dead!" she screamed, throwing the folded blanket at me.

She was blocking the doorway.

"Please, Luce. I have to go. I don't want to, but I *have* to. We can argue later."

She turned and ran into her room, slamming the door with a bang.

Her stifled sobbing as I left tore my heart out. But I needed to see Aldo if I was ever going to get the evidence I needed to stay free.

IT WAS ALMOST NINE when I got to Keystone Beverage. It was Tuesday, a slow night, with only a few customers pulling in, and I drove by twice before I caught sight of Aldo loading a keg into someone's car. The alley behind was devoid of parked vehicles, so his car, I figured, must be on the street somewhere. The plan was to waylay him when he went to get it.

I parked in a spot a half-block away, but I had no idea when the store closed or what time Aldo would be getting off. I'd just have to wait and watch.

After about an hour, the air grew still and specks of drizzle appeared on my windshield. The drizzle came and went and eventually stayed, gradually wetting the streets and becoming rain.

At one point, Aldo exited the store and stood under the awning at the entryway, smoking a cigarette, aimlessly looking up and down the street. When he glanced in my direction, I slid a little further into the seat. He seemed to take no special notice, but merely stomped his cigarette and went back inside.

Twenty minutes later a Philly police cruiser rolled past, wipers going, and after another twenty minutes a black Escalade. The parking lot at Keystone Beverage was now totally deserted. At 10:45, Aldo came out and began folding up the advertising signs, carrying them inside.

It wouldn't be long now. I started the car and pulled it to the alley in the back, around the corner from the shop's front door.

As soon as I parked my heart started racing. I checked my gun to see that a round was chambered and the safety was off. I'd have to be real careful but also real quick. The cops might cruise by another time, and Aldo might have a gun of his own. After our last encounter, I didn't think I could talk him into my vehicle again. If he saw me and ran, I'd either have to chase after him or open fire—attracting the cops and the neighbors and maybe getting someone killed. I'd have to get the drop on him real clean, and use the Glock to make sure he didn't resist as I hustled him to the car.

The idea scared me. As an M.P., I'd never actually had to use my weapon, unless you count that one time when I unsnapped my holster flap to show an aggressive asshole I was serious. But to purposely point a gun at someone to force compliance—never.

I was becoming scum like Toomey.

I pushed the feeling down. Fight fire with fire. That was the wicked way of the world. I wasn't going to jail so Toomey could roam free.

I got out of the car and crept in the drizzle to the corner of the building, crouching down between the neighbor's garbage cans, but with my head up high enough that I could see the door.

The Glock was gripped tight in my hand and now I really felt like a criminal. But the only thing that was going to keep my ass in one piece was to keep focused. I needed that hard drive to have a chance against Toomey, and come hell or high water, Aldo was leading me to it.

The store lights went out and suddenly there he was, coming out of the building, dressed now in a cloth jacket against the rain. But in focusing on Aldo, I had forgotten about the store manager, a big round man who emerged a second later.

"Pull the gate," I heard the manager say.

Aldo turned and walked in my direction; I froze in the shadows, but after a few feet, he grabbed the store's scissor gate and began dragging it away from me noisily across the store's facade, where the manager locked it with a huge shiny padlock.

"Okay, see you tomorrow," the manager said. "You need a ride?"

"No, I'm good," Aldo said. "I'm waiting for someone."

"Don't forget, inventory tomorrow," the manager said. He wrestled open a small collapsible umbrella, walked around the corner and was gone.

Aldo stood under the store canopy, looking around calmly, waiting.

It's now or never, I thought, worried that the someone Aldo was waiting for might suddenly show up.

When his back was toward me I rushed him, grabbing him by the hair and jabbing the Glock behind his ear.

He felt the gun and froze, his glasses flashing in the streetlight.

"Whoa, whoa, whoa!" he said.

"Remember me, mother fucker?" I said, pressing the barrel in harder.

"Yeah, yeah, I remember. Cool it, man. What do you want?"

I jerked him around by his hair, got him pointed toward the alley.

"You see my car over there? We're going to get in it and you're taking me to that body. Now march."

I shoved him with my knee, and we started to move toward my car in awkward unison.

Then a blinding flash of pain ripped through my head and I fell to the ground and blacked out.

———

THE BRITS ARE GIVING a Valentine's Day party at a hotel in Kandahar. It is very late. I am very drunk.

Christine is across the room talking to her friend Marie Noelle from one of the French NGOs. The room is jammed with aid workers from all over, and the pounding music from the DJ is keeping me upright and awake. Outside, through the big plate glass windows, there is a flash of lightning; it is threatening to rain.

Christine, in her black dress, so beautiful, smiles at me and I rise and pull her away from her friend and across the dance floor to the garden outside.

Then we are sitting, both together, in a deep rattan chair, in the shadows away from the hotel's outdoor bar. Toward the airport, the black clouds roil with branching streaks of light. We sit close, using our jackets like blankets against the January cold, and we say nothing but simply sit, the dub-dub-dub of the music carrying us far away from the war.

And now we are on the roof deck, 11 stories high. A distant lightning strike illumines the sprawl of Kandahar, briefly silhouetting the commercial buildings near the hotel.

Suddenly, a detonating flash—definitely not lightning this time.

Artillery fire, and from a street nearby. The Taliban, who had recently captured a battery of D-30s from the Afghan army, were firing on the hotel— deliberately attacking the gathering of Western aid workers.

I grab Christine hard by the hand and start running for our room.

Down, down, down the concrete steps we go, with the flashes and booms growing brighter and nearer at each landing's window.

Closer and closer now, the explosions reverberate through the building.

We reach the room. I yank the mattress from the bed and start to pull it over us as we huddle on the floor.

A blinding explosion.

Christine is torn from me as we go flying, flying, flying.

I come awake.

Dust in my mouth. The wall of the room is sheared off, open to the yellow lights of the city beyond. The artillery barrage suddenly ceases.

Christine is a broken puppet in the corner, against the wall.

I crawl to her. Her dress is half burned-off and her bloody back peppered with shards of glass.

"Christine."

She is dead.

Her body has shielded me.

A moan wells up direct from my soul.

———

I SWAM BACK TO consciousness, desperately trying to drive away the memory of Christine's mangled body. My face was pressed into the window of a car, which was jolting down a dirt road surrounded by dense woods.

Rain streaked the window and the leaves of the passing trees glistened in the vehicle's lights.

My right temple throbbed where I had been hit.

I was in the back seat of a big SUV, my hands bound in front of me with a zip tie. Aldo sat against the opposite door, a gun in his hand, pointing it at me. At the wheel, gold earring gleaming in the reflected dashboard lights, sat Shawn Toomey.

The grogginess turned to fear.

"He's awake," Aldo said.

Toomey didn't even bother to glance around. "Just keep him covered," he said.

Beyond the windshield was darkness and rain. We were in some rural area far outside of Philly.

Driving, undoubtably, to my death.

The gun in Aldo's hand, I saw, was mine. I felt my pants pocket with my wrist and remembered my cell phone was back at my apartment. I had nothing else on me, not even a pen knife.

They had me good.

"Where are we going?" I asked, unable to keep the quaver out of my voice.

Toomey snickered. "Someplace you've been working hard to find, asshole," he said.

A rendezvous, then, with the body from the alley. Undoubtably we were heading to the place Toomey liked to bury his victims.

I was lucky I wasn't already dead. I probably would be, except that Toomey didn't want to chance messing up the leather seats on his Escalade. I had to get away, and fast, before we got to where we were going.

My hands were bound, but I could maybe whack Aldo in the face, if I timed it right. But if I didn't, I'd get shot in the gut at point blank range.

The only other alternative was the chrome door lever. The big Cadillac was moving slowly down the rough dirt road; if I was fast enough, I could throw the door open and be out of the car and into the trees before Aldo could react.

I inched my hands closer to the door lever and waited. Aldo still had the gun pointed at me. A tree branch brushed by and momentarily distracted him.

I reached for the lever and pulled, simultaneously throwing the weight of my entire body against the door.

It didn't budge. It was locked from up front.

Aldo, after his momentary lapse of attention, suddenly sat up—tense, his eyes angry, the Glock pointed directly at my heart.

"Not in the fucking car," Toomey snapped at him from the front seat. And to me, in a calmer voice: "Stay put, smart boy. We're almost there."

Defeated, I slumped back. Wherever we were almost to, I didn't want to be there.

I'd have to make a run for it as soon as they let me out of the car.

———

A MINUTE LATER, THE road took a bend and the trees thinned out and then completely disappeared. We were in some sort of clearing—a farmer's field, I saw, with the dirt turned over in neat rows.

We bumped along the edge of the field for what seemed like forever and finally stopped, Toomey cutting the ignition. Up ahead in the headlights and rain sat a beaten-down, abandoned farm tractor, with the tires missing and the '50s style grill rusting off the front. Tall weeds had sprouted up around the hulk—except for an area to the left where the ground had recently been dug up to form a muddied mound.

"This what you was looking for?" Toomey said with a grin, and I realized the mounded earth was Anthony Silva's grave.

"Why'd you kill him?" I asked.

"Because I felt like it," Toomey said. "He got what he had coming."

"It was just a bar fight," I said.

Suddenly the .44 Mag was in his hand, pointed at my head.

"Shut up," he snapped, his face rigid. "I've had about enough of you."

I sat stock still, my heart thumping. He looked like he was ready to pull the trigger then and there. Only the nice clean upholstery of his Escalade held him back.

"Get him outside," he finally said to Aldo. And to me, still pointing the gun: "One move and you're dead."

He released the locks from up front, and Aldo exited and came around to my side, pulling open my door and taking a step back to better cover me with his weapon.

"Get out," said Toomey.

This was my moment to run.

I put one foot outside and strained to find footing. The mud was slippery as hell, and the tree line a good fifty feet away.

It's funny. I always figured if I got cornered, I'd make a run for it no matter what. But here, now—those guns shamed me. All I wanted to do was stay alive, even if it was just for a few more seconds.

And there was no way I could sprint to the safety of the trees on such wet ground—not with two guns pointing at me.

No matter how fast I ran, I'd never make it.

In despair, I got out and stood in the cold April rain beside the car. My options were dwindling moment by moment. The air was pungent with the ammonia smell of fertilizer. Aldo stood like a silent statue pointing my Glock at me from some ten feet off—too far to try to jump him.

My mind was working furiously, trying to figure some way to escape, some way to get out of there.

Toomey exited the driver's door and walked around toward the back of the vehicle. The hair on the back of my neck scraped up against my shirt collar. *Fuck*. Was he going to shoot me from behind?

I tried to run but my feet were paralyzed, glued to the mud.

But then Toomey popped open the back of the Escalade and pulled out a shovel. He came around and threw it at my feet.

"Pick it up," he said. "You wanted that tape, and now you're going to get it."

The relief I felt over still being alive flooded my body like a breath of air after a drowning. The "tape," of course, was the hard drive from the security camera that Toomey had buried with Silva's body. Aldo must have told Toomey that I was looking for it.

And now that Toomey realized his mistake, he wanted to destroy the evidence. My execution would apparently be delayed until I dug up the box.

Of course I would be digging my own grave too.

But I would also be buying time. And the more time I could buy, the greater the chance I could make something happen that would give me an edge on Aldo and Toomey.

Buy time and look for my chance. That would have to be my strategy. They had the guns; I had nothing.

"Pick up the shovel, I said," Toomey repeated.

I bent and picked up the shovel, holding it awkwardly in my bound hands.

At five feet long with a metal blade, it would make an excellent weapon—if I could get close enough to Toomey to use it.

I held out my wrists to show him the plastic zip tie. "If you want me to dig," I said, "you're going to have to cut this thing off."

Toomey merely laughed. "No way. You think I was born yesterday? Start digging."

"My hands..."

"You'll figure it out," he said, then smiled. "Right, Aldo?"

He looked at Aldo, who nodded minimally, keeping the Glock on me center mass.

"Dig," said Toomey.

My legs leaden, I walked to the muddied mound and started to dig. The cold rain continued to fall, and the headlights cast razor-sharp shadows over the disturbed earth. The ground was heavily saturated but turned over easily. Toomey and Aldo stood off to one side, between me and the woods, half-lost in the darkness beyond the cone of the headlights.

Aldo's weapon, however, stood out bright and clear in the harsh light, pointing at me steadily.

I dug, moving as slowly as I dared. Toomey lit a cigarette and watched. Outwardly, he seemed calm. But his eyes were narrow and never came off me.

Buy time. Wait for my chance.

"You know, Toomey, killing me is only going to bring the cops down on you harder. Just let me go and I'll disappear."

Toomey said nothing, but simply glared at me the way a man might glare at a pathetic insect he was about to squash.

"This doesn't have to happen," I continued. "I was getting ready to leave the country anyway, go back to the Middle East on contract."

"Too bad you didn't," said Toomey.

"It's not too late," I said. "I can be out of here tomorrow. The cops will think because I skipped I must have done it. And you can get Aldo there to testify against me."

"You fuck with me, you pay the price," Toomey said. "Keep digging."

Aldo still had the weapon on me so I had no choice. Numbly, I dug down a foot, then two, the cold rain running down my back and forming puddles in the sucking mud. I didn't know how far down I would have to dig, but every inch was an inch closer to that security camera evidence—and my death.

A nauseating smell developed in the hole, and then my shovel hit something soft and yielding. Silva's corpse, wrapped in the tarp. And there, peeking out of the plastic beside the broken pool stick, was the black box that would prove my innocence.

If anyone ever saw it.

For a fraction of a second, I froze—and Aldo picked up on my hesitation.

"He's found it," Aldo said.

Suddenly, Toomey's Mag was back in his hand.

"Pick it up," he said.

I bent and picked up the recorder box.

"Throw it over here," he said.

I threw it toward him.

"Now get out of that hole," he said.

His gun was pointing right at me, and reluctantly I complied—dragging with me the shovel, which now seemed to weigh a thousand pounds, as my only weapon.

He seemed to be reading my mind. "Throw the spade in the hole," he said. "Do it!"

He was too far away to use it anyway.

I threw the shovel in the hole.

"Get down on your knees," he said.

Buy time. Wait for my chance. Yeah, great plan. Except now I was out of time and out of chances. This was the way it was going to end—a shot to the head by some Mick gangster in the rain.

I thought then of Lucie—so smart, so giving, so alive and willing.

What the hell had I been waiting for?

What I had with Christine had been beautiful, but that was all in the past. Lucie was here and now—and I had pissed it all away.

What an idiot.

"On your knees," Toomey repeated,

Suddenly, I'd had enough. It wasn't that the fear actually left me, but it was swallowed up in a preternatural calm which swept through my body like a cleansing breeze.

"You know," I said, "you are one sick motherfucker."

Toomey cocked the revolver for emphasis and waited for me to fold.

I glared at him. If I was going to die, let me die like a man.

But my lip began to quiver.

Toomey smiled and I swear I saw his finger begin to squeeze the trigger.

Then time stopped and everything happened at once.

A hail of shots rang out. Aldo grabbed his stomach and said *oouf* once, then dropped like a stone.

Toomey turned as the gun in his hand went off with a deafening *bang!* The bullet seared past my left ear, with powder from the explosion peppering my face as I stood there, frozen and confused.

More shots—a wild barrage of bullets—with slugs hitting the Escalade, the tractor, and all points in between.

Toomey slipped as he turned and suddenly, I was on his back and we were both falling, my bound hands controlling the gun in his grip.

We wrestled fiercely in a tangle on the ground near the grave. Toomey bucked me off, rolling on top of me and trying to bring the revolver around to shoot me in the face.

More shots hitting the earth nearby; then I grabbed Toomey's gun hand with both of mine and twisted hard. The weapon went off, blowing a hole in his chest.

Toomey's mouth opened in surprise as his grip relaxed and I finally wrested the revolver, wet with blood, from his hand.

Toomey's body convulsed a few times and then stopped moving, dead weight atop me.

Time rushed back and everything was suddenly quiet, the only sound a light drumming of rain on the sodden ground.

"Keith?" I heard a voice call from the distance.

No way, I thought. *It can't be.*

"Lucie?" I ventured.

"I'm over here," she yelled, from somewhere in the darkness by the trees.

I started to get up, but suddenly her gun went off and a bullet smacked into the mud a few yards from my foot. I instinctively dropped to the ground again, finding myself lying right on top of the security system box.

"Stop shooting, Luce. They're both dead."

"Sorry," she called meekly. "I thought it was on safety."

I finally stood as she walked toward me, watching as she tried to work the action of the gun. "Actually," she said, "I think it's out of bullets."

She came up and stopped, the empty gun dangling loosely from her right hand. I took it and tossed it aside, then slipped my still-bound arms awkwardly around her shaking body. We clung together there under the drizzling rain, locked in a silent embrace.

"What are you doing here?" I said at last. "How did you find me?"

"I followed you. From the carriage house."

"You *followed* me?"

"And when I saw him hit you and stick you in that car"—she shuddered—"I followed *him*, and called the police."

"You've got to be kidding," I said.

She slumped down from my arms and sat in the mud. "I didn't want to shoot. But I had to."

I sat in the mud with her. "You did good, Luce. You saved my life."

"You and your fucking guns," she said, but with a weak smile.

That's when everything changed for me.

I think it was that smile that did it. Or maybe the fact that Lucie had just saved my worthless ass. Either way, all the uncertainty I'd had about her vanished. The worry about getting trapped and controlled.

And most importantly, all the fears that losing Christine had walled up within me. Where else on earth was I going to find a girl like Lucie? She was one of a kind.

I leaned over and kissed her, just as the cops arrived.

MEET JAMES DAIN

Enjoy this story? If you like fast-paced action thrillers with intriguing settings and quick-thinking characters, check out James Dain's Hard Knock series.

Can a Man Stand By When his Brother is Murdered?

It's a dog-eat-dog world in rustbelt Youngstown, Ohio--but MJ Shea, a small-time cocaine runner, is making out just fine, thank you.

Until his crack-addicted brother turns up on the street, his brains blown all over the pavement.

With his own life on the line, MJ must fight his way through the lies and hidden dangers of the mean city streets to get justice for his dead brother.

And what he finds will change everything, forever.

Prepare to stay up late reading this gritty, fast-paced novel by best-selling thriller writer James Dain.

Visit https://www.jamesdain.com to get started.

EXTRACTION DAY

JAY TINSIANO

DANIELLA MAVRIDES HAD CIRCLED the block between 5th Avenue and Madison Avenue in the historic Carnegie Hill neighborhood several times before parking up the street. She scanned for anything or anyone that seemed out of place. ***

Smoke from vents hit the cold air and drifted across the tree-lined street. The trees had begun to shed their auburn leaves as winter beckoned. The elegant Brownstone, redbrick and terracotta buildings loomed overhead but one in particular, converted into condos, earned her attention.

She caught sight of her face in the mirror, dark hair tied back into a ponytail and ever-deepening wrinkles, and tutted out loud before taking a swig of coffee from her flask. Then, she pulled out her mobile phone and typed a message to the asset in waiting on the encrypted Icarus app:

'Snowcat to dark tag. Stay in place until I complete a risk assessment.'

After sending the message, Mavrides watched anyone walking near the building as part of her counter-measures routine.

An elderly woman walking her poodle paused at the Italian restaurant window, looking over the menu before moving around the corner. A black Ford Transit pulled in further up the avenue. A man in a long black trench coat walked past, and in the rear-view, she watched him pass the restaurant before disappearing into the store on the street corner.

She needed to be sure it was all clear before getting him out.

Her app dinged. *'Received...want to come in for coffee?'* came the reply.

She frowned and glanced up at the five-story redbrick townhouse where the asset, Troy Rhodes, waited in the top apartment. Either he was very relaxed about the situation or didn't realize the stakes here.

Troy, she knew, was a unique character.

His father, John Rhodes, had founded the Liberatus global freedom movement. John's brother, Michael, created the Goya Tech Corporation that now dominated modern life with its gadgets and communications devices, not to mention the secret Government projects they didn't advertise.

Troy had created the encrypted Icarus comms app for the sole purpose of Liberatus, yet he had worked for his uncle's Corporation too. Before, the old guy had been jettisoned out of the airlock by his own board.

Liberatus had sent out an encrypted message for volunteers across their network. Troy was a potential target by agents of the deep state intel and covert ops apparatus, Ghost 13. They were looking to either extract some critical information he held or take him out of the picture altogether.

Daniella Mavrides took up the call.

Mavrides needed to get him out and away to a safe house, fast but quietly. Straightforward enough, except his would-be assassins or kidnappers could already be en route or in the area, according to the intel.

She peered down the street at the Ford Transit. No one had stepped out of the vehicle yet. Her opponents could be inside that truck, waiting, watching, assessing.

Troy needed to be extracted, and she couldn't have him just walk out the door. Her fingers rapidly typed into Icarus with instructions to stay put and to await her signal. Then she asked if there were any other exits besides the front.

The reply beeped on her phone.

'The back leads to small courtyards. Otherwise, only roof access?'

Mavrides turned her head, looked at the restaurant and up along the rooftops to Troy's building. She checked her small backpack, pulled out a fake NYPD badge, and looked at the photo, her younger face staring back, before stuffing it inside her jacket.

Just before she opened her door, two men dressed in blue overalls exited the van, clutching black trainer bags and proceeded to cross the street with determined purpose. One glanced up at Troy's building as they beelined towards it, leaving Mavrides in no doubt there were enemies in the field.

Mavrides brushed her hand over the Glock G26 inside its chest holder as she got out and walked casually across the street towards the restaurant. The smell of cooking wafted towards her.

Who were they? Contractors? Another alphabet agency? The lines were blurring, and it was hard to know.

She pushed open the door and flashed the badge at the waitress she saw.

"Lieutenant Fitzroy. I need access to the rear of the building right now."

Initially startled, the girl seemed to compose herself and led Mavrides down a narrow walkway. The lunch rush had long passed, but a few stranglers remained. In the rear kitchen, a male chef stepped out of a storeroom and stared at Mavrides with a confused look.

"This is Lieutenant—" the waitress began to explain.

Mavrides pulled out the badge again. "—Fitzroy. Lieutenant Fitzroy. Roof access if you please? It's an emergency." She rolled the words off with an air of authority.

"Roof access? Right, okay," the chef said and gestured to a rear exit door. Outside in the trash area, the chef pointed at a fire ladder.

"Thanks. Nothing to worry about, but if you could carry on your business as normal, okay?"

"Sure," the chef nodded and looked at her, intrigued.

Mavrides pulled down the retractable ladder, climbed past caged balconies until the top and then hauled herself onto the flat townhouse rooftop. She moved past vent boxes and jumped across several neighbouring buildings until she got to Troy's building.

Then, she sent another message before descending on the fire escape ladder until she was level with the top floor window. After a minute, it opened, and the face of a young man with long floppy blond hair and stubble appeared.

"Hey, there," he said with a lopsided grin. He didn't look older than twenty-five.

Mavrides glared and jutted her head. "Let me inside, quickly."

Troy pulled up the window, and the agent climbed inside his apartment hallway.

"They're here, out front. We need to move quickly! Back out this way."

"I need to get stuff. It's important," Troy said and immediately disappeared into the spacious, modern apartment before Mavrides could stop him.

She followed him into the main room, with an open plan feel, but felt cluttered with art posters on the walls, plants scattered everywhere, a guitar lay on the couch, and computer screens stood on a line of desks.

In one corner, a giant TV screen had some kind of shoot-up game on pause. Had he actually been gaming while waiting for her?

"Hey. We don't have time for this," she said, a feeling of frustration and concern rising.

At that moment, an ear-piercing fire alarm went off throughout the building.

Were they flushing everyone out of the building?

Troy ignored the alarm, pushed a leather chair aside, and pulled up a rug.

"That's them. We haven't time—" Mavrides repeated, louder this time.

"If I don't get this shit, we lose the whole reason you're here, the whole reason I need to be saved," he said over the din.

He produced a claw hammer from a drawer and began removing nails from the floorboard. Mavrides moved through the apartment to the front and shifted along the wall to the main window, which had the blinds drawn.

She peeked down through them onto the front street. The van was still in place, and a few residents from the building gathered outside.

Yes, they were clearing the building.

She moved back to the rear of the apartment and saw Troy had the floorboard aside and was pulling out a small backpack. He stood up and threw it over his shoulders.

"Ready!" he announced.

Just then, there was a hissing sound, and the sprinkler built into the ceiling began spewing water across the room.

"Come on!"

From the corner of her eye, Mavrides caught sight of a shadow moving under the apartment door to the hallway.

They were outside now.

Troy and Mavrides got to the window just as a loud bang shook the apartment.

Mavrides pushed Troy out first.

"Get to the roof deck," she ordered.

When he disappeared up the ladder, she got out and aimed her Glock through the window towards the door, still smouldering from the explosive. She fired a couple of rounds to warn them off.

A *clunk, clunk* and a canister rolled inside, spewing dense smoke.

Mavrides holstered her weapon and hauled herself upwards. She clambered onto the roof, rolled and retrieved her pistol, aiming it at the top of the ladder as she moved away. She glanced over towards Troy, who was jogging across the rooftops.

She thought she would have more time and realized that route wouldn't work. They could pick them off easily as they descended the ladder.

"Troy!" He stopped and turned.

She jabbed a finger at the door access point on the roof of the neighboring building. They both headed toward it. The door was locked with a padlock.

Mavrides took a stance, aimed the weapon and fired. The lock shattered, and a hard smack with her boot punched it open.

"Go!"

Troy ran inside and down the interior steps. Mavrides turned and raised her weapon just as a head popped up and then disappeared again. A hand with a gun popped up and fired in her general direction, hitting the doorframe.

Mavrides followed Troy down the steps. At the bottom of the stairwell, a wooden door blocked their entrance inside, and he banged his fist on it, then immediately began slamming his boot against it. Mavrides grabbed a fire extinguisher set into one of the walls and handed it to Troy.

"Try this, and focus on that." She pointed just below the handle and lock. "I'll hold them off."

As Troy began smashing the metal cylinder against the door with rhythmic thuds, Mavrides cautiously reclimbed the steps, weapon raised.

At the top, the entrance to the rooftop swung to and fro with an eerie creak, buffeted by a gust of wind, revealing a darkening sky. Mavrides stooped as she reached the top and focused on the wall where the gunman was last sighted, but there was no sign of him. Loud smashes continued behind her as Troy continued to beat at the door.

She was about to leap up and pull the door shut when a volley of bullets peppered the door panels and the stairwell ceiling behind her with holes. She dived and rolled and began to crabwalk back down the steps backwards as the firing ceased.

"Door?" she shouted.

Troy had managed to mangle and splinter the door panels, but there was still no way through.

Mavrides drop-kicked the stubborn door, felt movement, and heard a crack. She grabbed the fire extinguisher and backed up before swinging the end and cracking it hard in the same place. The lock caved, and they pushed it open. Troy went through first out into the interior hallway.

Another volley of gunfire burst the plasterboard on the wall, ripping it to shreds as they both fell into the hallway. Mavrides, on her back, aimed up the stairs and fired before rolling out of sight. She leapt to her feet and ran after Troy down the staircase.

A woman peeked through her apartment door.

"Stay inside, Ma'am. It's not safe. Get back inside," Mavrides commanded as she rushed past.

The woman did as asked and slammed the door shut.

As they got to the ground floor, Mavrides checked her six, aiming upwards. No one seemed to be following.

"Wait," she said to Troy as he got to the front door. "We need to be careful."

She went in front of him, unlocked the door latch and lowered to her haunches, then edged the door open a sliver. She could see her vehicle just across the street. A noise came from the floor above them.

"See the blue Chevrolet? That's us. Come on."

Mavrides took out her key fob, and as they both ran down the front steps, she pointed it at her vehicle and the taillights flashed once.

Once inside, she fired the engine, pulled out and accelerated along the avenue with a screech of tires. In her rear-view, she caught a glimpse of a figure in a blue maintenance uniform coming out of the house and running back toward their van.

Still coming.

There was a whooping of sirens a few blocks away. Clearly, someone had finally called the real cops about all the gunfire.

Mavrides headed north up Park Avenue and caught sight of the black Transit. She should be able to lose it, no problem. She planned to head North via Randall's Island and the East Side and hopefully ditch them on the way.

At the next block, she swung the Chevrolet, then switched right along one of the East Streets, cutting across East Harlem.

She checked her rear-view and couldn't see the truck.

"I hope you're worth it," she muttered.

Troy snorted a laugh. "So do I."

Troy turned to look out the rear window and then turned to her. "Any idea who they were?" he asked.

"Contractors...some kind of kill squad. Ghost 13? Although they weren't too subtle, so hired thugs most likely. How many enemies do you have nowadays?"

Troy gestured with a hand. "Pretty much everyone, man." He laughed but without humor.

"Seriously though," he continued, "People like me, my father, and well, all of us, are enemies of the State and the dark fucking world they want to impose right under the nose of the people."

There was a hard edge to his voice now.

Mayrides chimed in. "It's why I ex-filed the entire shit show," she agreed. "That new shake-up across all the alphabet agencies and the emergence of the new super agency, Ghost 13, was the final straw."

Another check in the mirror, the familiar black Ford van on the far lane.

"You can tell me to take a hike, but what's in the bag?" she asked, her eyes still on the mirror.

"I'll have to tell you to take a hike," Troy replied with a smile.

"Fair enough."

"Although, I can say it's related to the tech that might save us when things go south."

"Any tips for a friend?"

She took a sharp right turn towards Lexington Avenue, picked up the speed as much as possible under the speed limit, and checked her rear-view. No sign this time.

Troy blew out slowly.

"Ah, now you're asking. It could be anything, really. I mean, the Cabal are hell-bent on enslaving their populations."

Troy spoke fast. She had triggered a favorite subject.

"They've successfully infiltrated every level of Government and Society," he continued, "and that gives them the power they need. They want to engineer a major crisis to usher in their plans, right? This we know. This is what they always do. Problem. Reaction. Solution."

Mayrides glanced at him, saw the frustration she heard in his voice echoed in his expression.

"My Dad always bet on either the current threat of war with Russia and China," Troy gestured with his hands, "or the global food crisis after huge catastrophic droughts in Asia."

He shifted in his seat. "Then there's financial collapse and the threat of rogue viruses. Those horses of the Apocalypse are riding hard right now, but our intel recently picked up on October 31st as a key date for a big event. They like certain dates, kinda' using numerology to communicate in plain sight."

"Halloween? That's in a few days," Mavrides said. "You're saying a big shit storm could happen in a few days?"

Troy gave a non-committal shrug.

As they headed towards Harlem River via a couple of sharp turns, Mavrides could see that black van again. Still hanging back, but weaving lanes.

"Shit. Can't seem to lose them."

"They still on us?" Troy asked.

"Yeah, it's them, all right."

Mavrides drove the vehicle several blocks, switching lanes with un-predictable swerves, before heading up 1st Avenue towards Wills Av-enue Bridge, edging through the traffic. Their pursuers did the same.

"What's the plan?" Troy asked.

"Hoping I can lose them around the Bronx."

As they reached the bridge, crossing the gray Harlem River, Mavrides kept in the middle lane to give herself some options. The traffic thinned out, and she pushed on the gas heading to the redbrick blocks on the far side.

Their friends in the black van did the same, and she noted they were gaining fast. Two large trucks blocked her way, and then the van speeded right up behind them and shunted in their rear bumper, jolting them in their seats.

"Hang on," she said with a grunt of effort.

Mavrides swung the wheel, taking them into the far-right lane and causing a pickup truck to brake hard as she did so. A blast of their horn soon followed.

The van was directly alongside their left flank now, the tinted win-dows giving no clue to the occupants. It swerved nearer to them, forcing them to scrape against the road barrier.

"Goddamn it," Mavrides muttered.

The lanes ahead split, and they were stuck on the exit to Bruckner Blvd.

Mavrides glanced in her rear-view. Some of the cars behind were slowing, giving them a wide berth, except a couple of big trucks who drew close behind the van.

"Hold tight!"

She hit the brakes hard, sending a screech through the air, then swung a hard left, bringing her Chevrolet right behind the van and across the lanes onto the right exit, narrowly missing another barrier where the road split.

"Shit!" Troy shouted.

A car screeched to a halt as they cut it up—another angry horn blast.

Their pursuing vehicle hit the brakes, but it was too late. They were heading down the exit road with trucks right on their rear.

"Adios, assholes," Mavrides said with satisfaction.

"Nice," Troy said nervously.

She kept an eye on the van as it disappeared along the bending road.

"They can still catch us. Keep your eyes open."

Mavrides kept going through Mott Haven and South Bronx, her eyes darting from the rear-view to the side mirrors and interlinking streets.

They kept going north along the freeway until the landscape gradually changed from urban blocks to tree-lined suburbia.

"I think we're good," she muttered, more to herself than Troy. She took some loops off course to play it safe, then headed to their destination.

The safe house was situated in Connecticut, just inland from the coast at Old Greenwich, isolated and tucked away in a cluster of woodlands bordering a golf course.

They stepped inside the small family house from the garage. They gravitated towards the large open-plan kitchen with an island in the middle, above which hung a collection of saucepans and cooking utensils.

Troy checked that the window blinds were shut before switching on a side lamp.

Mavrides, standing on the far side of the kitchen island, had a weapon aimed directly at Troy.

"What—" he said, his eyes staring at the barrel of the weapon, "—the fuck are you doing?"

"The bag, take it off and place it there." Mavrides motioned to the kitchen counter with her pistol.

Troy glared at her. He did as she asked and slung the bag down.

"Didn't take you as a traitor," he said evenly.

She ignored the comment.

"Now, open it. Slowly and carefully, spread out the contents. Let's see what you've got."

Mavrides felt calm but alert. This was the culmination of years working undercover for Ghost 13, coming over to Liberatus as a disgruntled CIA agent and gaining their trust.

Troy pulled out a couple of USB sticks, a military-grade laptop, and a larger black plastic box.

"Is that it?" she asked, eyeing the box.

"Is that what?"

"No games, please. The method of uploading your code onto the satellite network."

"I've no idea what—"

"We know you installed Trojan horse code on the Quantum satellite system," Mavrides said, cutting him off, "which helps you leverage it for your own comms. Isn't that right, Troy?"

His face didn't give anything away, but Mavrides knew he had. That's what she was here for.

To fix the problem.

She knew the basics. The Quantum tech was next level. That all communications were on flecks of light and electron particles, and the 'Quantum Zeno' effect was used for the teleportation of particles of information, known as 'qubits.'

It was top-level secure quantum cryptography, and all this Quantum computing and tech would revolutionize the entire world. Naturally, the world hierarchy would use it solely for their own benefit. The satellite system communicated with base stations, but Liberatus had piggybacked onto the system, thanks to Troy's involvement and access in Goya Tech.

"Why did you bring me all the way here before doing this?" Troy asked with a questioning frown.

"We had visitors, remember? Besides, I wanted to be in safe surroundings because I will make you remotely remove that code."

"I wouldn't count on that," Troy said cryptically.

"Count on what? I'll cut your fingers off one by one until you do it," she said, her voice laden with menace.

"No. I wouldn't count on being safe."

She caught something in his eyes. It was like a switch turning on total confidence and assurance—complete control of the situation.

There was the slightest movement. A reflection in a hanging saucepan, and even before Mavrides heard the click behind her, she dropped her body behind the counter and began to swing her weapon around in an arc.

Two well-built men in black combat gear, one bearded, one with cropped blond hair, stood on either side of the kitchen door, aiming weapons at her head.

"Don't—" the blond man began to say, but she fired, clipping him in the shoulder.

She hadn't counted on two of them.

A bullet ripped into her chest in reply. Then, the bearded gunman was on her with lightning speed, moving around the counter.

He fired again into her shoulder, which forced her to drop her Glock G26. She slumped onto the floor.

It was over.

The looming gunman took a step closer, kicked the pistol away from her, and then began searching her for other weapons.

Troy appeared in her vision.

"You didn't have to do that," he said with genuine disappointment.

Mavrides clutched her chest wound, the blood reddening her whole hand and blossoming fast across her shirt. Pain spread over her body in waves. She wasn't going to make it.

"I thought our pursuers were foreign intel," she whispered, "wanting the same thing. I guess not?"

Blood appeared from her mouth, drenching her teeth.

"Quick. She needs medical attention," Troy shouted over his shoulder.

He stooped down onto his hunches, checking her wounds and wincing.

A woman with tied-back dreadlocks appeared and leaned over Mavrides, checking her vitals. She cut open her shirt and pressed a bandage on the chest wound.

Mavrides looked at Troy.

"Tell me," she said, barely audible.

"My friends, the ones chasing us? Exactly that, friends," Troy said with a smile.

"We were never in any real danger," he continued. "It was dangerous, of course, but we knew there was a traitor. There always is, but we thought putting this job out on Icarus might hook in some interest. We're always casting the net out and you're the fish that came in."

Mavrides coughed, causing more blood to splatter from her mouth.

"Happy Halloween," she managed to croak.

Troy frowned at the comment before turning to the woman treating Mavrides.

"Will she live?" he asked.

Together, they watched as the light faded from the wounded woman's eyes.

"That's a negative."

Mavride's body was hauled into a zip-up bag, removed from the house, placed in a van outside, and taken away. Others proceeded to deep clean the kitchen area.

One of the shooters who had come in to save him approached Troy.

"Now, at least we know what they know." He paused, squinting, then asked, "Are we good?"

A long moment of silence passed while Troy considered. Finally, he nodded.

"Yeah, we're good."

MEET JAY TINSIANO

USA Today and Amazon best-selling author Jay Tinsiano was born in Ireland but grew up on the flat plains of Lincolnshire before moving to the city of Bristol in the UK, where he is currently based.

Jay is an avid reader and writer of fiction, specifically thriller, apocalyptic, and speculative, and interweaves his experiences into his fiction writing. He is currently working on a thriller / post-apocalyptic series called Dark Paradigm in collaboration with Jay Newton and spin-offs in the same universe.

Join the Reading Group newsletter for updates, reports and goodies PLUS a free starter library featuring 3 Thriller shorts.

Don't hesitate and head straight to: https://jaytinsiano.com/new sletter/

THE MAN FROM THE CAUCASUS

BEN WESTERHAM

I HAD THE UNEXPECTED and unsettling sensation of being in a darkened space. Sound was as absent as light, and my senses teetered on the verge of being overwhelmed by the void.

Equally unnerving was the realisation that I could not recall how on earth I had come to be there; wherever there was.

The situation remained so, for how long I could not say, until a thin, soft strip of light began to open on the horizon. If that was, indeed, what I was looking towards.

It widened steadily, all the while growing in intensity, until I found the brightness difficult to cope with. Shapes, blurred as if seen through a distorted lens, began to form and I struggled to bring proper focus to them.

I found then that my mouth was filled with a thick, sickly taste and my head began to throb most disagreeably, sensations that coaxed from me some recollection of recent events.

For an unhappy few moments, I revisited the preceding twenty-four hours.

———

THE PREVIOUS YEAR I had done some little service for my country, entirely as an amateur, in helping put an end to a monstrous scheme that sought to undermine the safety and security of the British Isles and its Empire.

As a result, I had been persuaded to try my hand at the role of the professional spy, working for His Majesty's secret intelligence service, a change in circumstance that I still found rather extraordinary.

As part of my training just the previous week, I had been assigned a simple task considered most suitable for someone lacking experience. Of course, I was eager to set about the business and had departed London for Vienna on the express train, filled with the enthusiasm of youth.

It was the spring of 1913 and the general view amongst my colleagues in London was that war with Germany would follow within another eighteen months or so. During this time, it was our intention to do two things to the very best of our abilities.

One was to defeat German efforts to obtain intelligence information from the British Isles. The other was to accumulate as much information as possible about the dispositions and plans of the German army and navy.

It was with the latter activity in mind that I was to visit Vienna, where I was to collect from one of our Austrian agents a set of plans showing the design of the latest destroyers being built by the Kaiser's Navy.

It really ought to have been the simplest of tasks, something even a relative novice such as I could accomplish with a little care and preparation.

As these recollections filtered through my sluggish mind, the fog in my vision almost entirely abated and, with a degree of discomfort, I was able to focus on my legs, for I found my head was tilted forward on to my chest.

I attempted to raise a hand to draw it across my sweaty face, but found I was bound to a substantial oak chair. Instead, I lifted my head and, waiting a moment for a little grogginess to pass, took a look around me.

The scene that greeted me was not a promising one.

I was in a high-ceilinged room decorated with indifferent examples of late-Victorian furniture and a pair of landscape paintings on the wall to my right. I could not make out the setting of either.

Heavy curtains were drawn across tall windows, so what little light there was came from a pair of standard lamps either side of closed double-doors. But somewhat more of a concern was the brooding figure of a stocky, dark-haired man who stood in silence between the two windows.

He stared at me dispassionately, his eyes unblinking, his arms folded across the front of an ill-fitting brown woollen jacket.

What was it, exactly, that had put me in such an unwelcome position? I settled my head against the back of the chair, closed my eyes and returned to reflecting on recent events.

ONCE IN VIENNA, I had made my way to the British Embassy, where I was further briefed on my task.

I was informed I was to meet with our agent, Michael Massing, at a popular cafe in the centre of the city, where I was to take possession of the plans.

Busy locations, I am told, are ideal for such exchanges.

I found Massing to be a nervous man, his hands always on the move and his eyes perpetually on the lookout for any sign of trouble. That, in turn, left me feeling distinctly unsettled.

My attempts to engage him in anything more than the most cursory of conversations were met with curt replies and he could not force into my hands quickly enough the leather-bound copy of Shakespeare's Midsummer Night's Dream, into which the naval plans had been stitched.

With that task completed, he turned and marched off without another word.

It was then that I realised all was not well.

Even a novice such as I was able to spot two unfriendly-looking men begin to follow Massing the moment he left the cafe. He, too, saw them and immediately took to his heels, running towards a narrow street a little way on from the cafe.

His pursuers wasted no time in setting off after him.

My nerves were at once on edge, my muscles tensing at the prospect of needing to affect an escape. I looked around me in search of menacing figures with their gaze fixed on me.

In the hubbub of noise and confusion of a busy cafe it was difficult to quickly and accurately assess the throng of people around me. Once

I stepped off the pavement and began to cross the street, I could watch the reflection in the window of the tobacconist opposite and observe another two men of large and unfriendly disposition get up from a table and begin to follow me.

I have never considered myself the bravest of fellows and am certainly no hero, despite my recent adventures in Scotland, but I felt unexpectedly confident of my chances of evading capture.

My training had provided guidance on how to respond should I find myself in such an unwelcome situation and I knew I was in fine physical condition, likely to be able to outrun all but the most able of men.

The only serious disadvantage I foresaw was my very limited knowledge of the streets of the Austrian capital, though I knew I was but a half-mile or thereabouts from the embassy. Clear thinking, swift movement and keen observation should leave me well positioned to evade capture.

This confidence was, I suppose, born of ignorance of the reality one is faced with in such situations. In truth, I blundered more than once and made it all too easy for my pursuers to reach me.

I made the mistake of leaving the busy streets almost at once, turning down a narrow side-road, where I encountered only one other person, an elderly man letting himself into his home. From there, I made another turn and another, by now running as fast as my feet would carry me, all the while my ears picking up the sound of running boots on the cobbled street behind me.

Lost and in the first stages of a panic, my head became a confused jumble of thoughts. I stopped at one point and tried to open one of several doors on a deserted, tree-lined street.

The last thing I can recall is turning to find the light disappearing behind me as my pursuers fell upon me. Some piece of damp, odd-smelling material was forced against my face as my arms were locked in pain behind my back.

Of what happened after that, I have no recollection.

THUS, HAD I COME to find myself a prisoner.

Of the naval plans there was no sign, nor was there any of Massing. I rather hoped he had managed to evade his own pursuers, not least since that would allow him to alert the embassy to my own dangerous predicament.

My mouth had begun to feel uncomfortably dry, so I turned my head towards the guard and, in a rasping voice, asked for water, but my efforts elicited not so much as a single glance. Whether it was because the man could speak no English or he had been instructed to exchange no words with me, I could only guess.

At least my head had by now cleared enough for me to think freely and the last of the fog had lifted from my eyes. It did little to help affect an escape as things stood, but I was now in a position to make the best of any subsequent opportunity that might come my way.

One other thing I would have liked to know was the time, for I had no idea how long I had been unconscious. Were my fellow country-men yet engaged in efforts to locate me, or was it too soon for them to have become sufficiently concerned?

To think it was the former would provide me with at least a little solace.

Barely had this thought passed through my mind when the two heavy doors swung open, their hinges complaining at the effort with a dull groan that seemed to match my own darkened mood.

The figure that strode through the doorway was at once wholly out of place in that dim, gaudy and silent room; a strutting peacock that would have enlivened the most gloomy of situations.

The peculiar thing was that, despite never having met the man before, I was almost certain I knew who he was.

"Ah, Alexander Templeman, as I live and breathe."

The words tumbled from his lips with a good degree of amusement as he came to a stop directly in front of me.

"Such a shame we meet for the first time under such unfriendly circumstances."

His eyes sparkled under a pair of thick, dark eyebrows and there was more than a hint of an eastern European accent in his rich, lively voice.

I straightened my posture as best I could and made an effort to sound unconcerned as I replied. "Gregor Lomidze, if I am not mistaken."

"So, you know all about me."

He grinned, then turned towards two looming figures that had followed him into the room.

"You hear that, Masha? He knows who Gregor Lomidze is. My fame has travelled as far as London. Only good things, I hope," he added, in amusement, turning back towards me.

"Not entirely," I replied, recalling that Lomidze had been considered largely responsible for the murder of one of our agents in Libya the previous year. Though his men had not pulled the trigger themselves, Lomidze had provided information that had led to the murder.

"Ah, but what is there about Gregor that could bring anyone to think badly of him?"

His yellowed teeth showed through his thick beard as he laughed and waved a hand in the air in a rather theatrical manner. It seemed this must be a show and the leading part was his to enjoy to the full.

"I really could do with some water, if you don't mind," I prompted.

"Water? Yes, of course. My men have not the wit to realise these things unprompted."

He nodded at one of his fellows, who hurried off. As we waited, Lomidze had a chair placed directly in front of me so he could lighten the load of his not inconsiderable bulk on his feet.

As I swallowed sips of the pleasingly cool water brought for me, I hurriedly tried to recall what little information I had been provided with about this enigmatic and dangerous man that sat patiently before me. Although it was not much, there could be something that might help me in my predicament.

He was believed to be of Georgian birth, though there was a good deal of uncertainty about this, especially as he himself seemed rather keen to keep his ancestry and family background as little known as possible.

He had, on various occasions, claimed descent from at least four different ethnic groupings. Even his age was a matter of speculation, though he was generally considered to have been born somewhere between 1865 and 1870.

He laid claim to having fought with the Greeks in their brief war with the Ottomans in 1897. If this was true, he did well to avoid death, given the Greeks' disastrous showing.

What is without doubt is that at some point after this he began to devote his energies to building for himself a considerable fortune. Much of this, it is believed, is the result of providing arms and munitions to the various groups that have fought for independence from the Ottomans over the last twenty years, most especially the Albanians.

Without doubt, he had also added to his coffers through the trading of information to whomsoever has been willing to pay for it.

However, more to the point, there were two things I recalled that had a bearing on my unfortunate situation. One was the character of the man.

There were very few members of the British armed forces or diplomatic corps who had met him, but those who had described an extravagant, outrageously confident and very determined individual, though one afflicted with a somewhat erratic temperament.

Of more significance, however, was his role in the murder of our agent in Libya.

It seemed I would do well to adopt a cautious approach towards a man whose view of the world was driven largely by money and who had little concern about offending the British Empire.

Perhaps the one chink in his armour that I could exploit was his over-confidence and, I imagined, a tendency to succumb to flattery. He had, after all, secured the Austrian naval plans and so had, I imagined, little to gain from causing an incident by treating me roughly.

"You are refreshed, yes?"

"Yes, thank you," I replied, handing back the glass.

"So, you know all there is to know about Gregor, my friend? It is all good, no?"

He laughed, his entire body shaking, and his men at once joined in.

"It is true that you are well known to the British Government and its diplomats," I ventured by way of flattery. "Your activities have left their mark on the world."

He stood up and stepped close enough to me that I could smell the garlic heavy on his breath and see more clearly the lines and pockmarks in the skin of his face where it was not covered by his beard.

"That is good. Gregor is pleased to hear even the mighty British Empire knows of his presence in this world." There was another hearty laugh.

"Your English is very good," I added, as his laughing subsided.

"Ah, I speak several languages most well. It is necessary for my business dealings. Many people are too ignorant to speak anything but their own tongue and business would be hard if we could not talk to one another."

"I speak a little French myself, but that is my limit," I admitted.

"Tres bon, Templeman. My French is not so good. I try hard to make it better but there remains much work to be done."

He planted his large hands on his hips and tilted his head a little to one side.

"Now then, what are we to do with you, my friend? We have the plans of the German boats, which you had hidden with such skill in that book you were carrying. I am sure my friends in Germany will pay most generously for those plans."

He stroked his beard in thoughtful manner as he continued speaking.

"But here you are, a British spy, in my possession. It would be giving up a fine opportunity to let you go home to your masters in London without you first paying for your freedom. Do you not agree?"

I said nothing and endeavoured not to show any signs of the discomfort his words gave me. My attempts at flattery seemed to have fallen on deaf ears.

"You don't wish to have your freedom?" he prompted.

"My freedom would be most welcome," I replied after a brief pause. "Though, given my circumstances, I cannot see how I am in a position to pay you for it."

"Ah, but that is where you do not see things like a businessman, my friend. Like Gregor. You are blind to such an opportunity."

His yellow teeth showed again as he warmed to his subject.

"Gregor, he sees opportunities wherever he goes. Every day, in the street, at the market, in conversations overheard in the cafes. Always there are opportunities. It takes only practice to learn how to benefit from them. And I have been a very good student. One of the best."

As he spoke his light-hearted tone was replaced with a far more serious one and he wagged a finger in the air as if to underline his words. I began to feel warm, the first traces of sweat developing in my armpits.

"You expect my government to pay for my return, I take it? I'm a very small fish in their pond, so they are unlikely to offer very much for me."

"It is true, the British Government may pay for your return. But that is not how I make the most money from you, Alexander Templeman, spy and wanted man."

His eyes narrowed a little. "No, you have information which is of much value to many governments. It is this which will buy your life."

I fear that I was unable to stop a flicker of concern showing in my eyes. It seemed my career as a British secret agent was to be a very short one indeed, for there was no possibility of me betraying any secrets that might aid an unfriendly government and if the only alternative was death, then I was soon to meet my maker.

I could only hope I did so in a manner that left me a degree of dignity and no shame for my family.

"I fear you may have excessive expectations as to my role," I ventured. "I am new to this game and know very little indeed about anything other than my mission here. Even if I was to speak, which I won't, it wouldn't provide you with much of value."

"You British, always so willing to die for your country. But you will be useless to me dead, Templeman. No, if we cannot make you talk, then we will sell you to the highest bidder and let others have their turn at making your tongue loose. Gregor is no beast, but I cannot promise that of others."

I said nothing by way of a reply. There seemed little I could say that might assist my situation and I wasn't altogether keen on the idea of upsetting my captor, at least not without a purpose in mind.

It may be that time was my friend. Time spent on observation might allow me to fashion some sort of plan of escape. It would certainly be better to die making a bid for freedom than to do so under torture.

"You do not wish to help Gregor," my host prompted, with a wrinkle of his nose.

"I cannot see how I can," I replied. "I possess no secrets that you could sell and even if I did, you must know that I would not disclose them."

"Ah, Gregor understands you must make him wait. But you must also understand, Templeman, my patience it does not come from a well without a bottom. It is best you help me to buy your freedom, but if you will not, then I will sell you to the highest bidder, even if they are barbarians. And then I will not sleep for one night, wondering what they do to you."

"Maybe some food would help me to think more clearly," I suggested. It seemed a reasonable way of buying myself a little more time. "I believe it has been quite some time since I last ate."

"Yes, we give you food. It is poor man's food, not fine eating for the King of England, but it will fill your belly. Then you sleep and Gregor come back tomorrow to hear you sing like the blackbird."

He laughed again at his own attempt at humour, his large shoulders heaving up and down.

"Thank you," I replied.

"Now, I must speak to my German friends and tell them how much they must add to Gregor's riches if they are to have their plans back. They will complain at the price, I know, but then they will pay and tell Gregor he is a hard man and so much a friend of the Kaiser. Then we drink together, and Gregor tries to get information from them he can sell to the Russians. Remember, Templeman, opportunity is everywhere, if you are looking for it."

I had to admire the man's audacity in the way he went about his business. It seemed to me that if he had chosen to follow a legitimate course of business he would by now have been known for good reasons throughout much of Europe and, perhaps, beyond.

He turned to the two men behind him and seemed, from his tone of voice, to be issuing orders, though I understood not a word of them. One of the men left the room as soon as Lomidze had finished speaking.

"Now then," declared my captor, turning back towards me. "I must leave you. You tell me tomorrow if my men are bad to you and I make them lick the street clean with their tongue. We speak again tomorrow, Templeman."

I watched him strut out of the room in the same manner he had arrived, with the exaggerated confidence of some minor monarch keen to impress an audience, although I suspected that few such monarchs would have the charisma and intelligence of this man.

I had been treated to an audience that few of my contemporaries had enjoyed and, should I make it safely home, I imagined my story would need retelling a good many times.

THE MEAL I WAS brought some little while later consisted of rye bread and a hard, strongly flavoured cheese that I knew the Austrians to be fond of. This was washed down with a thin, tasteless beer that was welcome all the same.

As I devoured this meal, my gaolers dragged into the room a battered chaise longue which one of them pointed at and then held his hands up against his face to indicate it was for me to sleep on. Luxurious it was not, but it was at least better than the floor.

Not long after this an interesting thing occurred. One of my guards escorted me to a bathroom at the end of the corridor off which my cell was located. As we returned, I saw another man, bound as I was, being bundled into a room a little further along the corridor.

I thought for a moment that it might be Massing, but the blonde hair and tall height of the man told me otherwise. However, it left me pondering as to the possibility I was in some sort of centre of operations where Lomidze kept anyone he thought might have a saleable value.

It was a disturbing if interesting thought.

I had no idea whatsoever as to what time it was and had to assume, therefore, that when one of the guards undid the bonds that tied me to the chair and pointed towards my bed it must be night. In truth, it made little difference, and I welcomed the prospect of sleep if not the arrival of the new day when Lomidze would return.

My guard had no intention of allowing me a comfortable night's sleep and, ignoring my protestations, set about retying my hands and feet before I settled down on to the chaise longue. As he did so, a considerable commotion erupted in the corridor.

I could not make out what was happening but there were several voices raised in anger and the sound of crashing objects, perhaps furniture. My guard's attention was attracted by all this activity and, having finished tying me up, he left the room to investigate.

Even before he had poked his head out of the door, I had noticed his error, for he had failed to tighten the bonds around my wrists sufficiently and, with a little discomfort, I was rather easily able to slip them off. I felt at once elated, the prospect of freedom driving adrenalin through my body.

It was but a moment's effort to untie the ropes binding my legs, leaving me now entirely free. I took a deep breath, then allowed the air to escape from my lungs in a slow, deliberate manner as I attempted to calm myself. Decisions made in haste were all too easily then regretted, I reminded myself.

The effort brought immediate reward as my first course of action came to me almost at once. I took the longer section of binding at my disposal and used it to tie round the door handles. I couldn't be certain how long it would hold but any amount of delay to the expected pursuit would be welcome.

The windows were my next port of call, but when I pulled back the curtains on each in turn I found the windows strongly locked, with no effort on my part able to shift them so much as an inch.

For a brief moment I felt my pulse quicken as I feared the worst. But at the back of the room was another door and I strode over to it in a determined manner.

It was, of course, locked but the mechanism was far inferior to that on the main doors, and I had a degree of confidence that I could break it. The fireplace offered up a hefty iron poker and I soon set about forcing it between the door and the frame just below the lock.

The frame began to splinter and crack in an encouraging manner until it reached a point where a well-placed blow from the heel of my shoe caused the door to crash open in a shower of broken timber.

I found myself in a second, smaller room. It was, perhaps, some form of antechamber for when the main room might once have been a bedroom. A single, large, partitioned window ran from floor to ceiling on the wall to my right and an empty fireplace faced me across the room. What there was not, I quickly saw, was another doorway.

It was a dead end, of sorts.

I hastened over to the window and my temper turned ill when I found it too was locked. But being less of a beast than the lock in the door, it proved no match for my trusty poker and soon lay in pieces on the bare wooden floor.

After a minor bout of resistance, the window gave in to my attempts to open it and creaked outwards in complaint. I must admit that a smile crept on to my face.

That smile soon left my face, however, as the noise of shouting reached my ears from the corridor. The handles to the doors turned and turned again, followed by the heavy clump of shoulders impacting on the wood.

There was no time to waste.

I leaned out of the open window, into the darkness of the night, to find myself looking down on an open courtyard from what appeared to be the first floor of the building. The drop was not a dangerous one, but it did run the risk that I might injure myself.

As the noise levels from the hallway rose ever louder, I let myself out of the window with great care, feet first, until I was hanging fully stretched out, with my hands clinging to the stone window ledge. A light breeze played across the back of my exposed neck and from somewhere far off came the faint sound of a ship's horn.

Trusting to little more than blind luck, I let my fingers slip away from the cold, hard stone and felt myself falling through the air. It was an oddly thrilling experience.

I landed on the cobbled ground and allowed myself to fall to one side, lessening some of the impact by rolling away. Though my knees and elbows complained, the trick did the job and I was up on my feet in an instant, running my eye over a high stone wall that held out the promise of being the outer enclosure of my prison.

The double doors set in the middle of this wall refused to yield to my efforts at opening them. This was unquestionably one lock I was not going to be able to force.

With little other choice, I placed one foot on the hefty iron lock and, scrabbling at the pitted face of the wooden doors, launched myself upwards, grappling for a hold on the top of the wall.

It was heavy work dragging myself up and I would have liked to stop a moment to catch my breath. But I had barely sat upright when angry shouts burst out into the night sky from the open window.

I looked back and up at two bearded faces, filled with menace, and was tempted to taunt them, until a hand emerged, pointing a revolver in my direction. As I slipped promptly over the outer edge of the wall, two shots shattered the still of the night and shards of stone exploded above my falling figure.

It was an uncomfortably close thing and, as I climbed once more to my feet, I could feel my heart racing so rapidly it was a wonder it didn't break.

I had landed in a wide street, dimly lit by gas lamps. Houses of the sort I had just vacated faced on to the thoroughfare, each one enclosed by its own imposing stone wall.

Not one of them showed so much as a single light.

There was no time to spend attempting to gain access to any of these houses, especially as I had no way of knowing whether or not my pleas for assistance would be favourably received.

That left me two choices: to go left or right along the street. I had once heard it said by a man better educated than me that, in such circumstances, most people choose to go left, so I went right, at once running as fast as I was able.

Threatening voices echoed into the darkness from the yard I had left behind, from which I surmised that my captors had already got men outside the house.

During my school days, I had always put on a respectable show when competing in cross-country running, my greatest strength being an ability to maintain a steady if not spectacular pace, while others tailed off as the miles passed.

However, running across open countryside or even through woodland was one thing, while negotiating the streets of an unfamiliar city was another. My confidence at evading recapture was a slender thing.

I shortly found myself at a crossroads and, thinking it the better option to avoid using the larger streets, I turned right down a narrower one, flanked by a mixture of domestic and commercial premises.

This way took me up on to higher ground and, as my head began to clear and my nerves recovered, it occurred to me I would be wise to get a better idea as to my whereabouts and had here an opportunity to do precisely that.

At the top of the rising ground, the street angled away to the right and on the outside of the bend stood a small stone church, dedicated to St Margaret. What caught my attention, however, was the fine-looking tower at the front of the building.

I found the door to the church open, as should be the case in any Christian establishment, and having taken a little trouble to ensure I was there alone, I climbed the steps of the tower steadily until I found myself amongst the bells at the top, their heavy imposing presence somehow reassuring in my time of trouble.

My reward was a welcome, if rather limited, view across a range of rooftops that rose and fell like a mad set of stairs all around me. I could pick out several other church buildings, but the lingering darkness made it impossible for me to get a clear enough view of my surroundings to identify where I was.

It also made it all but impossible to lay out some sort of clear escape route.

As the wind picked up, I buttoned my jacket and pushed my hands into its pockets. I had a decision to make. Either I could continue my flight, seeking to put as much distance as possible between myself and my, no doubt, still active pursuers before the morning arrived.

Or I could lay low until dawn, then seek help from whatever manner of authority I could find.

In my deliberations I had to make allowance for the fact that I was in some unfamiliar town or city, aware that I may have been transported away from Vienna during the time I was unconscious. What's more, even if I was still in the Austrian capital, I had no understanding of its streets and would, therefore, be fleeing who knew where.

From my lofty perch I watched two men, their voices low in conversation, walk down the street I had just travelled. From the look of their attire, I judged they were heading for work at a bakery, where they would, no doubt, be setting about the task of making bread and pastries for the town's population to start a new day. The thought of warm, fresh loaves made my stomach growl.

As they disappeared into the darkness, my mind was made up. I was going to seek to put as much distance as possible between myself and my former prison. While I stayed close by, there remained the distinct possibility of being found, especially as I had no certainty of finding a reliable hiding place.

I retraced my steps down the winding tower and walked out on to the street, keeping hard to the shadow of the church. But I had barely taken a single step when the sound of running boots on the cobbled street and men's voices, three or four at the very least, echoed up towards me.

I pictured my pursuers interrogating the startled bakers and hoped perhaps their denials of having seen a stranger lurking in the shadows might send them in another direction. The odds were likely little more than even and I wasted no time in stealing away before I was noticed.

It was an unexpected and unwelcome sensation to find that, though I was undoubtedly in some large town or city, there were so few opportunities to conceal my presence. Everywhere doors and windows were closed or shuttered and barely a light was visible, leaving little prospect of finding a warm welcome should I take a risk and hammer on a door. Even my shoes seemed set on betraying me, the studded heals clipping on the cobbles with an unwelcome echo that made me wince.

It was only when I stopped for a moment to assess a narrow alleyway and then looked up at the crescent moon that I made the unnerving discovery that my route was doing nothing more than taking me in a tidy curve around the part of town from which I wished to distance myself.

I may have travelled perhaps half a mile but was quite likely no further away from my former prison. I cursed silently and took a second look at the alleyway. It would do, if for no other reason than it most definitely led away from the dreaded house.

I bolted into the darkness without another moment's hesitation.

Having climbed a short set of stone steps, I then made my way along between tall brick buildings that seemed to lean over me like menacing frozen giants. It was a relief to be disgorged on to a much wider street, lined on either side with mature beech trees, their leaves rising and falling in the stiff breeze.

Almost at once a loud, threatening challenge from away to my left shattered the silence, leaving me briefly startled.

My pursuers had spotted me.

There was nothing for it. I raced away to my right, all but consumed by blind panic.

I made no attempt to look back, too afraid of what I might find, and instead focused as best I could on searching out some opportunity to throw off my pursuers. Little offered itself as I hurtled by a row of sleeping shops, their large windows blacked out by substantial blinds. Two or three sported what I took to be names, but I could make nothing of them other than they appeared to be German.

Worryingly, my breathing had already become somewhat laboured and my legs a little heavy and I guessed that my highly nervous state was helping to drain away my stamina faster than would normally be the case.

The street opened up into a modest-sized marketplace, in the centre of which stood a looming bronze statue of some hero from the town's past, though I never got close enough to read the name plaque. It was here that I found, at last, an opportunity to throw the chasing pack off my scent.

There were at least half a dozen streets and alleyways leading off the marketplace. But which of these would be best for my purposes I had, of course, no way of knowing. After a brief consideration, I ran into an alleyway in the far left corner and I was only just in time, for I had hardly entered its dark confines when voices and the sound of running feet tumbled into the marketplace behind me.

Once more conscious of the noise my shoes made on the cobbles, I stopped running and looked around me. There was a dark, recessed entrance to a dwelling on my left. I ducked into it silently.

As I did so, I stubbed the toe of one shoe on something hard and looking down, saw a single brick, one end heavily chipped. I bent down and picked it up, feeling the welcome weight in my hand. Any kind of weapon was better than nothing at all.

As voices once again filled the night air, I pressed my back against the wall in the deepest part of the shadows and gripped the brick a little more tightly. As I waited, I began to wonder how many men Lomidze might have at his disposal, conscious that it was entirely possible he might be able to cast a very wide net indeed, leaving me little chance of escape.

The sound of footsteps entering the alleyway echoed off the walls. I held my breath and listened intently. Whoever it was, they were alone.

As fresh air flooded my lungs, I pressed my back ever harder against the wall, hoping, perhaps, it might wrap itself around me.

I was so tense the muscles in my right leg began to quiver and it took a considerable effort to relax them. As I did so, the steady crunch of footsteps closed on me until, in the gloom of the unlit alleyway, a dark figure appeared opposite me, then stopped.

In his right hand I could clearly see the man held a revolver.

The next moments are something of a blur, since they happened so very quickly. I remember the man's head began to turn towards me and, fearing discovery, I stepped forward at once, swinging my right arm out in a fast, wide arc. The brick slammed into the side of the man's head with a sickening thump.

The man tottered, then slumped to the ground. It was good there was no time for me to think, for the idea that I had in all likelihood killed him would have left me feeling sick in the extreme.

As it was, I picked up the discarded revolver, feeling instead an instant sense of relief, and turned towards the alley's entrance to ascertain whether or not I had attracted any further unwelcome attention.

As I did so, a shot rang out, the bullet ricocheting off the wall behind me. Something sharp sliced across the back of my left hand and I glanced down to see blood already showing.

Struggling to stop myself from shaking, I raised my own newly acquired weapon and let loose two shots at the dark, shadowy figure running towards me. The man stopped, dropped his weapon, then slipped to the ground, groaning with pain.

There seemed little chance of making my way back out into the square, so I turned tail and fled along the alleyway, which felt as if it was closing in on me with every step I took. I stopped for a moment in the shadow of an empty cart, so I could assess the situation.

There was no sign of pursuit, which left me a little puzzled, but the relief, temporary though it might be, was welcome and I took the opportunity to see how many bullets were left in my revolver.

My hands were shaking as I did so and my nerves were not helped when I found I had only the one bullet left. I had better be sure to use it wisely.

Few men are, I believe, as brave as they would like to think they are and I must admit, as I stood there staring at that single bullet, I wondered what on earth had possessed me to accept the offer of employment from our secret service organisation.

Playing the unsought part of the hero on a lonely, fog-bound Scottish hillside was one thing, but to make a profession of such a precarious activity was another matter altogether. I suppose you never truly consider it will be your own life that is lost in some great adventure in the service of king and country. Surely it must always be the villain of the piece that pays the ultimate price?

And, to top it all, I now also had a wife to add to my considerations. I had to wonder at my own sanity. If I managed to come out of this scrap with my life, perhaps it might be time to bring an early end to my career as a government agent.

My ruminations were brought to an abrupt end by the now familiar shouts and hollers of male voices. But they weren't coming from the alleyway. They were, instead, closing in on me from both sides, attempting to catch me in a pincer movement.

Once again, I found my next move decided for me and made off quickly along the street ahead feeling increasingly uneasy at the thought a net was being drawn tightly about me.

I was almost at once on a wide, open thoroughfare with imposing stone buildings all around me and, at about a hundred yards distant, a door was open, with light spilling out on to the street. My earlier reticence to seek help from strangers left me and, at the risk of involving others in my life and death struggle, I set off towards the light, thinking I could at the very least get a locked door between myself and the chasing pack.

But I had gone barely twenty yards when another barrage of angry shouts was followed by an explosion of fragments all around me as bullets crashed into the ground. I was adjacent to a narrow side road and, firing off my one remaining shot at my pursuers, I threw myself into it as more bullets hit the walls and ground around me.

In an instant, my situation had come to feel very exposed indeed. Had I perhaps now entered whatever trap it was they had set for me?

I prayed it was not so.

The road made a sharp turn to the right after fifty yards or so, which took me out of sight of my pursuers. As I negotiated this turn, I looked up to see, a short way ahead, light angling upwards from an open cellar hatch.

As soon as I reached this, I all but fell through it in my eagerness to escape a bullet in the back.

I landed on a hard, stone floor, but there was no time for fussing about the resulting aches and pains and I was quickly back on my feet, pulling the cellar hatch closed and sliding the lock into place with angry voices shouting down at me almost as soon as I was finished.

I rubbed at my right thigh, which ached considerably, as I turned to take in my new surroundings. It was the cellar of an inn, barrels of beer and bags of oats in neat clusters, as their familiar and delightful aromas reached my nostrils.

As I wondered on my next move, feet began to kick and stamp against the cellar hatch.

I turned towards the open doorway on the other side of the room, then stopped when I saw it was filled with the figure of a tall, well-built man of perhaps forty years, wearing a heavily stained apron. His hands were large and his features less than welcoming.

What he originally intended to say or do, I shall never know since, before he could speak, my pursuers began to fire bullets at the cellar hatch. At once the innkeeper's expression changed to one of alarm and he gestured to me to follow him out of the cellar.

We passed along a short, narrow corridor, then made our way at something close to a trot through a warm, high-ceilinged room that housed the inn's own brewing facilities. The aromas were, even in my haste to flee, delightful and tempting. Indeed, I must have slowed a little, for the innkeeper pulled at my arm as we headed towards another door.

We were now in the public area of the inn, where my eyes struggled to adjust to the darkness. I suppose the innkeeper knew full well where he was going in what was such a familiar place to him, but I struggled to keep up, while avoiding the obstacles presented by the sea of tables and chairs.

It took what seemed like an age for him to open the bolts and the large single lock on the big oak door that led on to the street but, as he did so, a thought occurred to me.

As the innkeeper swung open the door, I pointed at the ground and asked, "Vienna?"

After a moment's thought, he nodded and replied, "Vienna, ja."

The weight I had been carrying around with me lightened at once. That I was still in the Austrian capital filled me with hope of completing my escape and even made realistic the possibility that my fellow Englishmen might find me before I succeeded in working my way to the embassy.

My accomplice could see the relief on my face, and he grinned broadly as he slapped a heavy hand on my shoulder.

Sounds of violence echoed from the rear of the premises and I was on the point of departing when it occurred to me that it would greatly help me in locating the British Embassy if the innkeeper could point me in the right direction. Frustratingly, however, I could not get the man to understand me, so I tried a different tack.

"Opera?" I asked, drawing the shape of a building in the air, before breaking out into a short rendition of The Marriage of Figaro.

The Austrian guffawed and shook his head, before leading me outside. His efforts to describe the route I should take were beyond my understanding of the language, but he made it clear I was to head what seemed to be due north.

I thanked the man greatly, though I doubt he understood what I said, and we shook hands firmly before I disappeared into the gloom.

As I ran, the first traces of the dawn to come began to appear over the rooftops to my right and I noticed there were ever more lights showing in the buildings I passed, though there were but few people as yet on the streets.

For the first time since I had escaped my prison, I began to feel a degree of certainty that I would remain a free man. My mood had lightened considerably and, though I was very tired indeed, I slowed my pace and walked on briskly in good cheer, content in the knowledge that I had put quite some distance between myself and my pursuers, who now faced relocating me in the maze of streets and alleyways.

After a while, I found myself in a commercial area of the city, where a range of different sized and aged buildings were occupied by numerous professions and trades. I passed two chemists, a bookbinder, a draper's and, on one corner of a small crossroads, a tobacconist's, at which I could not resist stopping to survey the wares on display. It reminded me of a tobacconist's near my home in London and, for a brief moment, I felt a little homesick.

"Templeman." The shout was both loud and threatening and, most worrying of all, it came from close by.

The shock was immediate and, I suppose, all the greater for my having slipped into a more relaxed and confident mood. My muscles tensed for action as I looked around.

There, running down the street along which I had just travelled were three men, one of whom was quite clearly Gregor Lomidze, who moved with surprising swiftness for a large man.

I had this time at least the advantage that I was able to disappear down the adjacent side street and, for the moment, get out of sight of my pursuers. My stamina, however, was beginning to desert me and, in particular, the muscles in my legs were complaining most insistently at the demands being made on them.

I began to wonder how much longer I could keep up my flight.

As I turned another corner, I found myself looking on at an abandoned house, it's windows and doors knocked out and a general air of decay hanging over the place. If I was not able to keep running for much longer then the only sensible alternative, I decided, would be to find somewhere to hide.

Perhaps this was as good an opportunity as I was likely to find. First glancing over my shoulder to make sure Lomidze and his men had not yet rounded the last bend, I left the street and disappeared into the dark and chilly embrace of the derelict property.

As a young boy, I spent a weeks' holiday one summer staying with a cousin and his family, who lived in a large, well-appointed house in the countryside a few miles outside of Bath. The main entertainment that week for us and two of my cousin's friends was to explore and play games on an abandoned farm that had already been much swallowed by encroaching nature.

One of our favourite games was hide and seek, since the possibilities for hiding seemed to be endless. One of the lessons we learned that week was that the best way to remain undetected was to stay on the move and, better still, to follow along behind those who were searching for you.

The difficult part of this approach was avoiding detection in the early stages of the search so that you had an opportunity to move from your initial hiding place, but if you could successfully do so then it proved so much more difficult for the others to find you.

Where then, in this sad, empty shell of a house, was I to make my first hiding place?

The sound of approaching voices in the street outside forced my hand and, perhaps subconsciously drawing on my childhood experiences, I walked to the back of the short hallway and stepped into a room I found to be the kitchen, though it wasn't fit for any such purpose now.

By placing myself behind the open door, I had a sheltered view of the hallway and the entrance to the house. My heart was already racing from the physical exertion of running and now I felt my palms growing clammy.

It was possible I might not leave this unloved and empty house with my life still intact.

It was Lomidze who walked in through the open doorway first, his two men following close behind. All three of them clasped a revolver in their right hand.

After a short moment of assessment by Lomidze, whispered words were exchanged by the three of them and I watched with some satisfaction as Lomidze and one other made their way up the creaking stairs, from which the runner had long since been stripped. That left me with just one of them to avoid, a challenge I felt confident about meeting.

The sole member of the hunting pack left on the ground floor was a short, wiry fellow with large ears that jutted out from beneath a head of curly dark hair. He did not immediately strike me as the type someone like Lomidze would employ to rough up his opponents, but I was not about to make any assumptions as to his suitability for such a role, especially as he was armed, and I was not.

He stole with care into the room to his left, revolver raised in front of his chest. I had no idea what might be in the room, but it felt as if a full minute had passed by the time he reappeared. Indeed, it was so long that I felt a sudden unease that there might be another corridor on the ground floor.

As he crept into the second front room, I took another look around me, for a new plan was forming in my head; one, I hoped, that would provide me with a good deal more security than I currently enjoyed.

What I found suited my purpose ideally. Towards the rear of the room a section of the kitchen had been walled off with its own doorway. I took this to be the pantry and knew that my pursuer would have no choice other than to take a look in this prospective hiding place.

That would allow me the time I needed to position myself to best effect.

The room opposite the kitchen, which I supposed was the dining room, was immediately adjacent to the doorway from which my wiry hunter now emerged and it was, therefore, only natural that he should make that his next port of call, which he duly did.

Now was my opportunity. Having first taken a deep, steadying breath, I slipped both quickly and, I prayed, silently from my hiding place and made for the room Lomidze's man had just vacated.

Every step ratcheted up the terrifying prospect of discovery and recapture and I struggled to hold back a sigh of relief as I entered what I found to be a rather small room where the smell of damp was almost overwhelming.

I took up a position behind the door, where I could see through the gap between it and the frame. From directly above me, I heard the soft groaning complaint of a loose floorboard that had just been stepped upon and whatever minor sense of relief I had felt at reaching my new hiding place left me at once.

For the second time it felt as though an eternity passed before the large-eared henchman reappeared in the hallway. Although I could not be certain in the poor light, he appeared to be smiling, in a manner, as if hopeful the one remaining room on the ground floor would yield up his quarry.

What was certain was that he checked his weapon and reset himself before proceeding to enter the kitchen.

I immediately left my hiding place and, all but tiptoeing, made my way across the hallway to a shallow recess in the opposite wall, where I imagined there would once have been an occasional table with, perhaps, a vase of flowers.

I had already noticed leaning against the wall there two lengths of solid timber, perhaps the remnants of some broken up piece of furniture. I picked up the longer one of the two, which was nearly the length of a man's arm, and felt its pleasing weight in my hand.

Then I waited, very quickly feeling myself to have become a bag of tense, nervous energy.

My opponent wandered back into the hallway in a distinctly nonchalant manner, his arms down by his sides, while he muttered something unintelligible. He turned to climb the stairs, a short distance from me, and it was then that I struck.

Striding out from the shadows, the length of timber already raised above my head, I was upon him almost before he had noticed. He tried to swivel towards me, so as to bring his revolver to bear, but I struck home a heavy blow with a sickening thud before he could complete his manoeuvre.

Under other circumstance, I might have felt pleased with my efforts to obtain for myself a weapon, but almost as soon as I landed my blow the near silence of the empty house was shattered by the eruption of a single shot from the man's revolver as his finger closed hopelessly on the trigger.

It startled me into temporary inaction, my ears ringing and my brain a fog, unable to do anything more than watch my opponent slump to the floor. It was only the sound of raised voices from the upper floor that brought me back to my senses and I promptly bent down and pulled the revolver from out of the hand of the unconscious or, perhaps, dead, man.

Lomidze and his one remaining man must have been at the rear of the house when the gun went off, for I managed to flee through the open doorway and into the street before they reappeared at the head of the stairs. But I knew they would not be far behind and that I still faced the disadvantage of not knowing the streets of the city in which we were playing out our game of cat and mouse.

At least I now had the benefit of possessing a gun.

I set off to my right, towards a cluster of buildings that were set back a little way from the street. But, almost at once, I stumbled and fell, the revolver slipping from my grasp.

With a curse worthy of a docker, I climbed back to my feet and retrieved my weapon. The delay proved crucial, for my pursuers had reached the open doorway and a shot rang out, the bullet ripping past my ear so close I could feel the air move.

Running across the road with all the vigour I could muster as another shot rang out, I plunged down a short stretch of cobbled street and promptly found myself entering a small, enclosed courtyard. I had not time to make a proper assessment of my options, but there seemed to be little obvious way out, other than by working my way through one of the brick and timber two-storey buildings that stood on all sides of me.

Hearing running feet behind me, I made at once for the building at the rear of the courtyard, the loose-fitting double-doors looking the most likely to succumb to an attempt at forcing them. I kicked at the flimsy lock with the heal of my shoe, as hard as I could, and was rewarded with the satisfying sound of splitting timber. But the lock still held.

As I raised my foot to strike a second time, a pair of shots echoed in the enclosed space and bullets thumped into the wooden door. My heart now beating so fast it seemed impossible to sustain, I struck out with my foot and fragments of timber broke away from the lock, but still it held.

I was sure that a third strike would have the door open, but there was no time.

I looked round to see Lomidze and his man standing in the entrance to the courtyard, their weapons directed at me. Perhaps Lomidze expected me to accept my situation was now hopeless and to return meekly to my former prison.

But I had no such intention and quickly fired off two shots in their direction as I lunged for cover behind a cart.

It offered me only limited protection but would suffice for my purpose. My opponents would not have things all their way if they were to persist in their attempts to recapture me. Maybe I could even manage to put one of them down before I was either killed or forced to concede.

Lomidze might have been best served simply waiting things out while more of his men found their way to him, as they no doubt eventually would. But I judged he had not the luxury of such time, since the city's authorities would by now be aware of the running gun battle that had occupied half the night and must be on the search for the cause of the trouble.

His was the next move and he wasted little time in making it, calling out to me in a voice that hinted at understanding and forgiveness.

"Templeman, you have made a fine effort, my friend, but you must see it is now hopeless for you. We have you in a trap and many of my men will follow. Why not end all this trouble and keep your life."

I took a look down the side of the cart. Lomidze was positioned behind a cluster of barrels almost directly opposite me and his man was a little to my left, peering round the corner of a wall. They had positioned themselves well.

"I'll take my chances, if you don't mind," I replied, through uncomfortably dry lips.

"But it would be such waste to see you dead. Come quietly now. I show you I am man of my word. I say you live then you live. Let us stop this silly game before you die."

I had no intention of taking Lomidze's word about anything, least of all his assurances about my life.

"This game is not run yet and I fancy my chances of staying alive until day break, when the city will come to life. I've shaken you off several times already and I can do so again."

There was a pause before Lomidze spoke again and this time there was a little menace to his words.

"Ah, but you have killed two of my men, Templeman. They were good men and their fellows have not taken their loss well. If any of them should catch you when I am not there to hold them back, then I fear they would tear you into a thousand pieces and feed you to the crows. It would be better that you come with me now and I can protect you from their anger."

"I'm afraid not. I'd rather take my chances. I seem to have done a pretty decent job of things so far."

"It is true, you have been a good opponent. Many would not have got so far. You deserve a man's respect. But surely Alexander Templeman is no fool. You must understand that you cannot escape me when I have so many men at my disposal. Let us reach an honourable agreement. I will promise to spare your life. I think that is very fair. You are in a difficult place."

I couldn't tell if the man was being honest or amusing himself at my expense. I supposed he had his reputation to consider, something that would suffer a dent of sorts should I complete my escape.

But was I really worth so much trouble when there was so little information that might be prized out of me? It seemed to me that by far the more likely outcome was a bullet to the head, in which case I might as well suffer that fate while continuing to affect an escape as by handing myself over meekly.

"My mind is quite made up. It's freedom or nothing for me."

There was a moment of silence, then, as Lomidze let off a short volley, a sudden movement to my left as his man scurried from one position of cover to a new one, a little further to my left. Almost at once he fired several shots in my direction as Lomidze made a matching move to my right. They were seeking to outflank me in an eminently sensible move.

Concentrating on the man to my left, I ignored Lomidze's next volley and took careful aim at the spot where I knew his man to be hiding. Sure enough, hoping to take advantage of the covering fire, he ducked out into the open.

I fired two shots into his body and watched with a degree of satisfaction as he fell to the ground. If I was right, and I was sure that I was, that left just Lomidze and myself on the battlefield.

The sensible thing to do would have been for him to wait, since it was only a matter of time until reinforcements. But I had an inkling that was not Lomidze's style. In a one-on-one fight I suspected he felt confident of his chances.

Almost at once he proved me right, slipping further to my right under cover of another short volley. I fired back in a vain attempt to put him down. With the ground to my left exposed and the cover to my right under the view of Lomidze's gun, my room for manoeuvre was heavily restricted.

Looking behind me again, I decided the building to which I had attempted to force an entry was a stables. That door, now clinging to the frame by a thread, was perhaps my last chance of escape.

Two more shots rang out and this time Lomidze had a much wider open piece of ground to cover as he raced further to outflank me. It was my best opportunity to put him down before he got to a point where he would have a clear line of fire on my position.

I took aim and pulled the trigger just before he reached cover. All I heard by return was a sickening metallic click.

I was out of bullets.

But had Lomidze noticed? Perhaps he had been too focused on reaching his next objective to have heard the empty sounding click.

"Ah, Templeman, you are out of bullets."

He stood up from behind the barrels that had been his latest shelter. I aimed once more and pulled the trigger again, with the same stomach-wrenching result.

"A brave effort, my friend. Your fellow countrymen will still have respect for you. But it is time now for you to put an end to this silly game and come with me."

He grinned as before but now there was a difference in his voice, only a slight one, but it had an edge of frustration and perhaps anger.

"I am no monster. Take no notice of those stories you have doubtless heard from my Ottoman enemies, who rail with frustration at their hopeless efforts to catch me whenever I pay them back a little for their past crimes. My only revenge will come from the price I get for selling your secrets. Come now, let us end this like proper British gentlemen."

I glanced again at the stable doors. A solid impact might prove enough. What had I to lose?

Without wasting my breath in a response to Lomidze, I launched myself at those doors with all my might and felt them part in a shattering cacophony of breaking timber that sent pain searing through my right shoulder.

I scrambled inside as bullets thudded into the door above me.

As I rolled away to one side, clear of the doorway, another sound reached my ears. There were four gated stalls down the opposite side of the building and in the first of these was a nut-brown horse, now kicking and whinnying in alarm.

Under other circumstances, I would have felt sorry for the beast, but I had no time for such emotions right now.

I realised that, above all else, I needed some sort of serviceable weapon or else I was done for. But as my eyes swept the rest of the stable, I found the only such thing, a vicious-looking pitch-fork, was propped against the far wall and to make an attempt at reaching it would leave me entirely exposed should Lomidze enter the building at that point.

It was fortunate that I did not give into the temptation, for at that very moment the sound of timber splintering under a heavy foot told me that Lomidze had now reached the doorway, though he remained out of sight. He was, no doubt, assessing the situation as best he could before making his next move.

I had not a moment to spare. To my side was a narrow set of wooden stairs that led up to an open loft space. With seemingly nowhere else to go, I bolted up the stairs and crouched down behind a pair of horse saddles and a tangled web of ancient tack, my calves so tense and fatigued I could feel cramp beginning to creep into them.

The doorway was now out of sight, but a sudden flurry of noise and movement told me that my adversary had entered the stables. I pictured him finding some sort of cover from which to survey the inside of the building before making his next move, since he wouldn't want to give away his advantage carelessly.

I could say that my nerves grew ever more stretched but, in truth, every muscle in my body was by now as tense as I could believe was possible and my whole body felt as if it was covered with a film of sweat. My life was in the balance, and I was not well placed to protect it.

There was the faint sound of movement from directly beneath me and the horse whinnied nervously. My senses shut off the outside world, bringing their entire focus into the stable building and my ears strained, unsuccessfully, to pick out any tiny sound that would tell me which way Lomidze was moving.

I then flinched as my adversary crept out into the open directly beneath me, his revolver sweeping the room ahead. He hesitated, looking towards the empty horse stalls and, as he did so, an idea formed in my head.

I placed my now trembling hands on the two saddles, took a deep breath then pushed as hard as I could. The saddles were heavier than I was expecting but that didn't stop them from plunging over the side of the open loft. There was a half-formed shout of alarm from below, then a heavy double thud as the projectiles hit their target.

Without pausing to assess the effectiveness of my attack, I bounded down the stairs to follow it home with my bare hands, driven on by the base animal instinct for survival. Lomidze was a little dazed, but already halfway back to his feet and, worst of all, he still had a firm grip on the revolver.

Rushing up to him, I struck out with one foot and kicked the weapon from his hand, sending it flying against the nearest stall.

Lomidze let out a deep, bear-like growl then threw himself at me, landing a heavy blow to my midriff that left me gasping for air. I staggered backwards and, for a moment, we sized each other up.

Blood ran from a deep gash on his right cheek, but he seemed not to notice it, his dark, intent eyes fixed on me from under thick eyebrows. Oddly, his hands seemed now to be twice the size of mine and I wondered why I hadn't noticed such a thing before.

All in all, he was a large, powerful man and I felt uncomfortably mismatched.

We began to circle each other, Lomidze twice feigning a lunge towards me. Then, with a speed and agility I would not have thought possible of the man, he side-stepped to his left before dropping down and sweeping out a leg in one swift movement.

I was flat on my face in the dust and dirt before I could even think of taking avoiding action.

I expected him to be on me at once, but instead he ran straight past me, and I knew immediately where he was going. I rolled over and up on to my feet just as he reached the revolver.

He brought it halfway round as I fell upon him.

We grappled madly, he attempting to bring the gun to bear on me, while I sought to force it from his grasp.

Sweat trickled into my eyes, stinging and half blinding me, but I clung on desperately, every sinew stretched and strained close to breaking point. But my opponent had the better of me and he must have realised it for he let go one hand and drove a vicious punch into my stomach.

Pain surged through me, and my head began to spin. I must have let go of my grasp on Lomidze, for I found myself dropped to my knees, doubled over and struggling for breath.

"You have caused me much trouble, Templeman. More than I can accept, and you were right, you are not worth me keeping alive."

I looked up through a haze of pain to see Lomidze take a step back before bringing the revolver up in front of him.

It was all over.

I had got so far, kept myself out of the man's clutches for so long, but I hadn't been good enough to last the course, to keep myself alive until the welcome embrace of dawn. Still, at least I had made the man pay for his crimes. His private army was a little thinner than it had been.

I had nothing to say and certainly no intention of pleading for my life. I lifted my chin and began to say a prayer to myself as he took aim.

But the next sound to reach my ears was not that of the revolver being fired.

Instead, the stabled horse, still terrified by the violence so close to it, kicked out wildly at the door of the stall. One blow left it broken and dangling loosely on the top hinge, then a second sent it flying through the air.

Lomidze turned just in time to avoid being hit, but in so doing, lost balance and fell to the ground, losing his grip on the revolver which tumbled away to one side.

I struggled to my feet and, as Lomidze tried to do likewise, I swung back a leg and kicked out at the side of his face with all the energy I could summon. The blow hit home with a thud and Lomidze dropped back to the ground at once.

I steeled myself to strike again, still struggling to hold myself upright because of the pain in my stomach. But Lomidze remained motionless, flat on his stomach, his arms out to the sides.

I let out a deep, painful breath and rested against the damaged stall as the horse stepped nervously out. If I could have let it know how grateful I was for its intervention, I would have done so at once.

After I had recovered somewhat from my injuries, my first thought had been simply to leave Lomidze there, lying on the floor of the stables. Perhaps I could have tied him up first in order to give myself more time to complete my escape.

But as I was about to walk away something Lomidze had said when we first met came back to me.

"Remember, Templeman, opportunity is everywhere, if you are looking for it."

It was sound advice, indeed, and here I was looking down at a fine example of opportunity.

I dragged Lomidze to the small cart outside the stables and, using as much strength as I was now able to summon up, pulled him up on to the back of it before binding his arms and legs, as well as fitting a gag. I then covered him with a woollen blanket I found in one of the empty horseboxes.

Harnessing the horse took quite some effort, since it was a job I had done only a few times in my life, but with that complete, I climbed on to the driver's seat. We were soon making our way towards the city centre, along streets increasingly busy with human life as dawn rose in all its glory.

Of Lomidze's men, there were no more sightings.

I WAS WELCOMED AT the British Embassy as someone who had been lost, presumed dead, in the deepest, darkest African jungle for years.

They had, of course, assumed the worst when neither I nor Massing could be found after our rendezvous and strenuous efforts had been made all the preceding afternoon and on through the night to track us down.

The news of Massing was bad, his heavily beaten body having been fished from the Danube only an hour or so before I reappeared. There was no way of knowing if it was Lomidze's men or the Austrians who were responsible for Massing's death, though we were at least now in a position to ask my former captor himself about that.

Indeed, the delight evidenced at the gift I delivered to the ambassador was considerable.

There was every expectation Lomidze would be shipped back to Britain, where he could choose to either help our secret service and diplomatic corps with his own vast bank of information and contacts or, if he preferred, he could be handed over to the Turks, as a gesture of good-will on our part.

He was unlikely to find the latter an appealing prospect.

IT WAS THOUGHT WISE that I return to London without delay, since remaining in Vienna ran the risk of having to answer some very awkward questions posed by the Austrian police.

Though disappointed not to have the opportunity to explore the architecture and culture of the Austrian capital before returning home, I could only agree it was the sensible thing to do. Thus, I found myself stepping off a train carriage at Victoria Station in London little more than thirty-six hours later. Unexpectedly, there was a man from the secret service waiting to greet me.

He had news and it was not especially good.

The people at our embassy in Vienna had wasted no time in following up on the information I had provided to them. Whilst it was rather incomplete and somewhat of a jumble, they had been helped by Lomidze when it was made clear to him this would in all likelihood make a good impression on the people in London who would decide his fate.

The house where I had been held captive was quickly located, but Lomidze's men had been well trained, for the place had been emptied of anything useful. There was also no sign of any other captives, though there was a rather solid-sounding rumour that the Turks were missing an army officer.

The worst of the news, however, concerned Lomidze himself.

Our ambassador received instructions to despatch the enigmatic eastern European to the north Italian coast, where arrangements would be put in place for our captive to be transferred to a Royal Navy vessel that would carry him onwards to Plymouth.

There was a great deal of excitement in London at the prospect of benefitting from the vast library of information Lomidze possessed, as well as the network of contacts he had built up across the continent. It was felt sure that when faced with the choice of either cooperating in such a manner or being handed over to the Turks, he was likely to prefer the former.

However, he never made it as far as the rendezvous point in Italy. Somewhere on the railway journey south, the two guards who accompanied him were overpowered and Lomidze was spirited away into the night. It was a heavy blow and the head of the Service had already demanded an investigation into how such a thing could have happened.

I have to admit that, although disappointed, I was not altogether surprised at the news of Lomidze's escape. Though I had not known him for long, he was clearly a man of much resourcefulness and great determination. Such talents would, after all, have been needed for him to achieve the levels of success and wealth he had amassed.

That, I had assumed, was to be the end of the matter. But it was not so.

Three days after my return to London, I arrived home in the early evening feeling a little deflated after an uninspiring afternoon spent listening to a rather poorly-delivered lecture on recent developments in the use of ciphers.

Lying on the floor inside my front door was a postcard, on the front of which was a photograph of the opera house in Vienna. On the back was a brief message, written in a flourishing hand. It congratulated me on my safe return to London and hoped I would not leave it long before returning to the Austrian capital.

It was signed Gregor Lomidze.

I smiled. It would have been hard not to.

Whilst it seemed most unlikely I would be sent on a further assignment to Vienna, I did have an almost certain feeling that Gregor Lomidze and I would one day cross paths again.

MEET BEN WESTERHAM

BEN WRITES CRIME, MYSTERY and thriller stories right across the piece, from classic murder mysteries set in 1960s Banbury in Oxford-shire, to Buchan style spy thrillers that range across the globe and humour-laced hard boiled crime stories set in 1980s London.

His writing places a big emphasis on developing engaging characters and often comes with a streak of humour, although he also has a dark and sometimes disturbing side.

If you'd like to check out some of Ben's writing completely free of charge, you'll find there's always a story from his Shorts in the Dark crime series available at benwesterham.com, where you can also sign up for his newsletter, which delivers you a free copy of the novel *Good Investigations* as a welcome gift.

The Man from the Caucasus features Alexander Templeman, who appears in a novel for the first time in *The House of Spies,* available at all the usual outlets from November 30th 2022.

GRAVEYARD GIFT

JASON CANNON

"GRAVEYARD GIFT"

Noun.

A bouquet of flowers stolen from a graveyard, traditionally given to the director or leading lady after the closing performance of a theatrical production.

The macabre superstition symbolizes the death of the show and the transient nature of theatre, and puts the play to rest. Also it butters up the director, from whom you may be hoping for another gig when the next batch of auditions roll round.

Practically speaking, theatre is not a profitable profession. Actors back in the day rarely had the funds to buy bouquets fresh. But cemeteries overflow with free flowers.

And while you'll often see flowers arrive in a dressing room *before* a performance, that is actually *bad* luck. Don't do it.

The performer hasn't earned them yet.

THEY WERE COMING.

Gideon Price crouched near the fridge in the dark. Dark boots, dark pants, and a dark long-sleeve T wrapped his lean, six-one frame in shadow. His sparsely furnished one-bedroom apartment was still, as though holding its breath.

The front door was around the kitchen's corner, so Gideon couldn't see it. No matter. What he could see was the bedroom, same as anyone standing at the front door. The digital bedside clock tracked Monday's infancy with sleepy red numbers. Clouds and blinds conspired to throw distorted stripes of moonlight across the rumpled bed. The body-shaped lump—rolled-up towels and balled-up shirts—looked convincing enough. Gideon needed only a couple seconds distraction.

They were coming. Definitely two, maybe three. Muscle hired through an intermediary. Two layers of plausible deniability for Gideon to peel back from his ultimate target. Plan was simple. Incapacitate Layer Two and use them to unmask Layer One—probably the Producer's Agent, maybe the Producer's Assistant—and use Layer One to bring the Producer down as publicly and painfully as possible.

Gideon rolled one shoulder, then the other, easing tension. He box-breathed. Four count in, four count hold, four count out, four count hold.

They were coming.

He adjusted his grip on the 1200 lumen high-intensity discharge arc lamp, the newest toy from resident Troupe genius Adler. It had arrived by courier that very morning. Right after Gideon signed for it and the delivery lady drove away, his sunglasses on the tiny workstation desk buzzed. Could only mean one thing.

Gideon slipped them on.

"What's up, Adler?" The innocent-looking sunglasses were in fact a virtual reality, night-vision, GPS-enabled communication system. The exquisitely calibrated microphone in the bridge paired with the bone conduction speakers nestled in the temple tips enabled hyper-encrypted yet crystal clear conversation.

Gideon still had no idea how Adler had engineered much less manufactured them. Adler with his wild hair and Buddy Holly glasses and stained, ubiquitous bathrobe and ironclad metabolism.

"Hey there, Giddy-gid. You get my present?" Adler, as always, spoke with his mouth full of something stomach-churning.

"Haven't even had a chance to open it."

"Be sure to read the instructions super close and deploy with caution. Oh, and wear your shades, too. The infrared filter should keep your corneas from turning to goo."

Adler munched as Gideon opened the box, found the instructions. He pulled the arc lamp from its form-fitting foam bedding. It felt coiled and dangerous in his hands. His molars clenched.

"Adler?"

A burp. "Yeah?"

Gideon coaxed his jaw loose. "Thank you. I mean, I know you're breaking protocol here. But thank you."

"While it may be entirely my pleasure, Mr. Gideon Pee-rice, you are not wrong. You owe me big big biggie time. When're you baiting the hook?"

"Tonight. At the closing cast party."

"Break a leg, dude. Just remember I can't be on coms for you. You're s'posed to be on sabbatical. And no one knows I've been helping you out."

Gideon was surprised. "Rheia hasn't figured it out?"

"Nope. And I'd like to keep it that way. If she or Stan knew I'd fed you intel, much less a weapon?? Egads!"

Gideon set the arc lamp on the kitchen counter, opened the instructions, skimmed and fiddled. "This flashlight packs a wallop, huh?"

Adler huffed with offended outrage. "It's the *Eye Melter*, Giddy. Flashlight, my ass."

They bickered a bit. Gideon asked a couple arc lamp operation questions. Then Adler heaved a sigh.

"Dude. Be careful, ok? You're on your own. Don't be calling me up all crying cuz you mucked up your jam."

"Will do. I'll need an assist on my exit—"

"UUUUUUGH!! Fine."

"If it's such a bother then why are you helping me? You don't have to."

Gideon heard Adler's breathing speed up. "The shit this producer asshat has done?"

"Yeah?"

"Something similar happened to me. Long time ago. But scars are forever."

Gideon's heart tightened. He understood scars. "Yeah. I'm sorry."

Adler raspberried his lips. "Stuff your sorry. Just teach this jerk the lesson of his life. That's why the Troupe be doin' what we do, right?"

The Troupe. Yes. Gideon again wondered how the hell he'd ended up working undercover with this secretive team of vigilantes and their vast resources. Using theatre, spy craft, and precision violence to bring down bullies of all sorts and inspire the common civilian to friggin' stand up David-to-Goliath style. He was an actor, and a damn good one, but he'd never imagined a role like this.

"Break a leg, Giddy."

"You know it."

Gideon slipped off his shades and ran a finger along Eye Melter's trigger. The night couldn't fall fast enough.

THEY WERE COMING.

Time passed on tiptoe. Gideon breathed. Fought back impatience. Fought back frustration.

But most of all, he fought back eagerness. If the *feeling* got too delicious, he'd undo all the work of the last couple months. "Sabbatical" may have been Adler's delicately put term, but "forced leave of absence" was more like it.

"Dammit, Rheia, I'm fine. No drinking, best shape of my life, I'm ready to perform."

Rheia. Her large slate eyes and shaved head and unyielding will. She had approached him in the basement gym mid-workout with the unwelcome news.

"Gid. Think about what you've gone through the last few months. Spearhead. Five Points. You watched a man bleed out at your feet in the Pit."

"All part of the gig, right? The Troupe travels to dark places."

"You come from the theatre world, Gid. You've got a lot more training and un-learning to do. And what Stan saw in you up on that mountain—"

"So this is Stan's idea? Bench me just when I'm getting hot?"

And that was when Stan had appeared, implacable as granite, his massive bulk filling the stairway, ducking his head to avoid whacking it against the ceiling.

"Hot's the problem, Price."

"Come again?"

"You need a break. You're liking it too much."

"Liking what too much?"

"Vengeance. You're burning hot. We need you cold."

Rheia piled on. "Justice is cold, Gid. Impartial. You may not be drinking, but that doesn't mean you aren't still addicted."

It got ugly. A real spat. But there was nothing to negotiate. Everything had been arranged, and Gideon was left choiceless. So he'd been shipped off to play the lead in a show at a mid-sized theatre company in the middle of midwestern nowhere.

"It's summer stock, Gid," Rheia said. "Just a few weeks."

"Clear your head," Stan said. "And keep it down."

"Yeah!" Adler chimed in. "No fisticuffs, throwdowns, or rumbles!"

Gideon opened his mouth to protest, but Rheia held up her hand.

"Enjoy rehearsal. Focus on the show. Hang with your folk. No people like show people, yeah?"

Gideon had grumbled. But he'd found being in rehearsal and back on stage in front of audiences invigorating and cleansing. The wrathful intoxication suffusing his blood waned.

Stan and Rheia had been right. He'd needed a break. A chance to re-balance and find perspective on this new life he was pursuing.

And it didn't hurt that the show was a hit. Rave reviews. Full houses. The final week began. Gideon realized he was going to miss the cast, the structure of eight-show weeks, the applause. He'd be glad to get back to the Troupe, hanging with Adler in the Rehearsal Room

HQ, combat training with Stan, going out on missions with Rheia. But he wasn't necessarily eager. He was content. Grounded. Cool.

But then, on the Friday of the last weekend of the production, the Producer showed up.

THEY WERE HERE.

The deadbolt slid open with a whispered click. So, they had a key. Whoever hired them had access to Company Management.

No surprise. Simply confirmation that it was probably the Agent, maybe the Assistant.

The door snicked open. Two large men pushed through, paused, then made a slow, stealthy beeline for the bedroom. No button hook or clearing of rooms; the body-shaped lump had done its job.

They moved forward. Gideon stayed put. And ended up behind them.

Gideon named them "Tall" and "Thick." A lesson from Rheia. Assign descriptive, de-humanizing names. You can tactically track more accurately while staying detached. Violence always costs, but you can haggle the price.

Tall carried a crowbar. Thick carried a bat. Gideon hefted Eye Melter. He stepped around the kitchen counter.

"Hey fellas."

Two heads turned. One finger flipped a trigger.

Light strobed supernova, pulsing at a disorientating 19 hertz. The two turned heads snapped back and four eyes screamed as two mouths gasped and four arms flailed.

Gideon took a split moment to marvel. Even with Adler's shades compensating, he could feel the light bludgeoning like a cudgel. He knew a single flash at 500 lumens created blind spots that lingered for several minutes, and here he had 1200 lumens flashing 19 times per second. He imagined Adler cackling.

The crowbar and bat clattered to the carpet as four hands scrabbled at two twitching faces.

Gideon flicked Eye Melter off, set it reverently down, and charged. Lowered his shoulder into Tall's sternum. Textbook tackle. Drove Tall into the wall and imagined stopping his shoulder a foot past the stud, same as pulling a jab three inches past your target's nose.

Gideon's mass and the unforgiving wall smooshed Tall like a burger bleeding grease between spatula and grill. Breath and eyesight gone, Tall tumbled to the floor.

Gideon pivoted and saw Thick clawing at his face, as though he could wipe the blindness from his eyes. Gideon stepped forward and swung his leg. Family jewels no match for a well-aimed shin bone. Sixty-yard field goal, uprights split.

Thick squeaked and collapsed.

And so Layer Two was laid out. They were mercenaries. Wouldn't take long to get the name of Layer One from them. Probably the Agent, maybe the Assistant. Whichever one, make them spill.

Bring the curtains down on the Producer.

———

THE ENERGY OF GIDEON'S co-star in the performance that final Friday was off.

Way off.

She dropped lines. Gideon covered. She missed an entrance. Gideon improvised until the Assistant Stage Manager tracked her down and flung her onstage, even though she was in the wrong costume.

After curtain call, she sprinted for her dressing room, slammed and locked the door.

And it wasn't just her. The actor playing Gideon's nephew, an electric young lad with star potential written all over him, zombie-walked through the show.

He hit his marks, but with no zest. He said his lines, but they were devoid of feeling, robotic. After curtain call, he shuffled in a catatonic daze to the dressing room he shared with Gideon, sat down at his station, and stared at himself in the mirror.

And it wasn't just them. The entire cast and crew were vibrating. The curtain closed and the buzzing fever pitched. Gideon grabbed the Assistant Stage Manager.

"What the hell's going on, Gene? Sasha's a wreck. Miles was practically sleepwalking. Everyone's out of sync."

Gene was wrung out and sweaty. He'd barely kept the show on the rails.

"Hey, Gideon. Best I can figure, it's the Producer."

"Who?"

Gene said a name, but Gideon wasn't quite listening. He was tracking the chaos backstage as Sasha ran and Miles shuffled and everyone else pin-balled between urgent, whispered conversations.

"He bankrolled the show," Gene was saying. "New big-time donor, underwrote the entire season. This is the third show he's popped up on closing weekend. Makes everyone real nervous. Board. Production team. Cast."

"Kiss the king's ring, huh?"

Gene shrugged and mopped his brow. "Yeah. It sucks, but that's show biz. Friggin' patronage."

"Don't I know it," Gideon said.

"Hey, thanks for keeping your shit together tonight. Show would've collapsed otherwise."

Gideon shook his head. "Team effort, Gene. You had all our backs. Rockstar."

Gideon went to his dressing room. Sat next to Miles, who stared and stared at his made-up face. The eyeliner, blush, and powder—which under stage lights looked flawless—in the real-world looked garish. Gideon applied cold cream to wipe off his own painted mask.

"You ok, Miles?"

Miles stared and stared.

"Hey. Miles. We got through it."

Miles shuddered. Silently stripped off his costume, pulled on his clothes. As Miles was changing, Gideon noticed a bandage on his chest. Blood-specked gauze taped over his heart.

"Miles?"

Miles finally looked at Gideon. His eyes were haunted hollows. "I sucked tonight."

"No, hey, Miles, don't worry about it. But what happened to your—"

"I gotta go."

Miles grabbed his sling and scurried out. Gideon quickly finished cleaning his face, got into his street clothes, stepped out and tapped lightly on Sasha's door.

"Not now! Go away!"

"Sasha, it's Gideon."

A sniffle. "Oh. Hang on." The lock clicked. The door cracked an inch.

"Hi, Gideon. I thought you were—" And she said the Producer's name. Gideon's lizard brain stirred. "About the show, Gideon, I'm so sorry—"

"No no, no worries."

"—I missed those lines and then that entrance, I totally hung you out to dry, I just—"

"Sasha." He said her name firmly but gently. She met his gaze. Haunted hollows, same as Miles. "Can I come in?"

She let him in. They sat. It took a little while, but she told him.

He waited outside her door as she put herself together. He walked her back to company housing, a few blocks from the theater. He made sure she got into her room safely. And alone.

He went to Miles' room. Knocked. No answer.

He went to his room. He closed the door and pressed against it. It got hot.

He gulped air to cool down, but he was so hot. He stalked the sparsely furnished one-bedroom apartment. Cranked the a/c. He couldn't cool off. He wanted a drink. Something stiff.

He gritted his teeth as Stan and Rheia gazed at him from every shadow. He poured soda over ice and squeezed in lime. He forced himself to sip. To breathe. To think.

To cool.

He knew some, but not all. He should leave it. He knew the more he learned, the hotter he would get.

He finished his soda and lime. He set the glass down on the counter. Too hard. It cracked. His palm bled. He blanched it with a paper towel.

"Screw this."

He put on his shades and pinged Adler.

SOMEONE ELSE WAS COMING.

Gideon had just pulled zip-ties from his pocket and was deciding whether to leverage Thick against Tall or vice versa when he heard furtive steps approaching down the hall.

Well, there ya go. Fellow number three, hanging back as a lookout. "Lookout." Good name. Lookout's head and torso appeared in the doorway.

But wouldn't you know it. Lookout was actually the Producer's Assistant, Pritchard, wearing his trademark garish bow tie. Tagging along to ensure a proper job.

Gideon would've put good money on the Agent being the Producer's "fixer." He wouldn't've bet the whole farm, but maybe a pasture or two.

No matter. This made it easier. Cleaner. Layers One and Two had arrived together.

"What's going on?" Pritchard hissed. "What's taking you two so long?"

Gideon snatched up Eye Melter and clobbered the Assistant with lumens. As the Assistant staggered, Gideon grabbed the ludicrous bow tie. Yanked hard forward and down.

Pritchard splattered face-first on the floor.

Gideon moved quick. Ankles and wrists zip-tied tight. Mouths slathered with duct tape. But no blindfolds. Not with Eye Melter around.

Gideon checked the hall, slowed his breathing, listened hard.

Had the ruckus gotten anyone else out of bed? Any heads poking out of doors or 911 warnings to worry about?

No. The building was still.

He closed the door. Turned back to Tall, Thick, and Pritchard all writhing on the carpet. He pulled up a kitchen chair.

Sat. Watched. Waited.

Stan had taught him how to wait. Stan, that mountain of retired Green Beret who had drilled sense and patience and cunning into Gideon's bones. Waiting was a weapon. The readiness is all.

Breathe and embrace the creeping passage of time.

As Gideon stared at Pritchard's increasingly frantic face, he went back over all the history Adler had dug up. It had taken a little prodding, but luckily, he'd caught Adler bored and jonesing for some deep-dive hacking.

When the first background search came up zip, Adler asked, "What's this guy's name again? Maybe I misspelled."

Gideon spelled out the Producer's name. Adler worked his magic.

"Well, no wonder. He changed his name. That's why I missed him first time around. He tried to scrub it, but alas, I am a golden god and the google is my pool boy. Hold on to your butt, here we go."

The Producer had started out as the Founder and Artistic Director of a little storefront theatre company in Chicago. Quickly gained a following for putting up edgy and provocative plays. Critical darling. Swelling subscriber base.

The storefront became a studio. More seats. Bigger shows with longer runs. A training program for up-and-coming actors. Awards. Grants. Big checks from heavy hitters.

Plans for a new performing arts center. Millions fundraised. About to break ground. The Founding Artistic Director of the little storefront theatre was building an empire. He would leave such a mark.

He turned his eye toward taking shows to Broadway.

But his eye also kept turning to the young actors and students desperate for his blessing. His guidance. His wisdom. Boy, girl, didn't matter.

They looked at him with adoration and hope, and those that smelled sweetest of desperation he would discreetly take under his wing. A late-night one-on-one class. Visits to dressing rooms, door locked.

An invitation to his glittering tenth floor condo looking out over Lake Michigan, ostensibly to run lines or get in-depth direction on a difficult scene. The eyes of these young actors gleamed less and less. Hope rotted. Promising careers withered away.

And everyone knew, but no one said. To speak out was to ensure your opportunities with the company evaporated. The Artistic Director took what and who he wanted, used them up, tossed them aside.

And still the accolades and audiences came.

But then the private ministrations spilled into public settings: a dressing down in the lobby after a shaky performance, notes screamed in faces after a not-quite-perfect dress rehearsal, coffee mugs and clipboards thrown at actors during call-backs.

The dam burst when one terrorized actor confided in a Stage Manager, who had worked at the company long enough to know to go straight to the Board President.

At the next board meeting, when confronted, the Artistic Director flipped a table. The Board demanded his immediate resignation. He took the Secretary's laptop and used it to smash every framed poster in the conference room, all the shows upon which he'd built his empire.

Police were called and led him away in disgrace. The board quickly deliberated and declined to press charges in favor of washing hands that swept under rugs. The Founding Artistic Director never showed his face in Chicago again.

The board initiated a national search for a replacement. There were still millions fundraised. It would be shaky going, but with transparency and accountability, the company could survive.

An offer was made to an excellent candidate. They accepted. The Treasurer sent the new Artistic Director their first salary check.

It bounced.

The panicked investigation revealed that the millions fundraised, and the endowment, and the company's checking account, and even the petty cash, were all gone. The Founding Artistic Director had left the cupboard bare.

The company folded. And everyone in the community did their best to forget, and to absolve themselves of their years of complicity.

Two years later, in the middle of midwestern nowhere, a new Producer started throwing money around at mid-sized theatre companies.

"And this Producer is that same Artistic Director from Chicago?" Gideon had asked.

"It took some hardcore back-dooring, but I cracked it," Adler answered in a crunchy voice that meant Cheetos were for dinner. "This predatory buttmunch went all out. New identity, new chin and cheeks, new hairline. He wears colored contact lenses. Passport, driver's license, he even forged diplomas and a social media history. So what's he doin' there, Giddylicious? Why isn't he trying to crank out Broadway hits?"

Gideon thought about it. Realized immediately that of course the Producer, after his epic fall from grace, would adjust his approach. His ego would demand it.

It was not artistic success that drove this man. It was power. It was toying with the hopes and dreams of young actors who worshipped him.

"He can indulge his big fish appetites by devouring controllable small ponds," Gideon said. "Why even bother making the art when he has millions fundraised to buy unfettered access to that which he truly desires?"

"Whoa. That is some serious character analysis jujitsu right there. Who says acting school is a waste?"

Gideon clenched his fist, causing his palm to bleed again. "Adler. You have to help me take him down."

"Ummmm, no can do, buckeroo. I've already done way more than I should've. And I can hear it in your voice, Giddy-gid."

"What's that?"

"You're hot, as Stan would say."

No sense denying it. "Boiling."

"And therein lieth the problem."

Gideon clenched and clenched and clenched. He sucked blood from his palm.

"Gideon?"

"I'm here."

"You're gonna go after him. Aren't you?"

"Isn't it better if I say nothing?"

They both said nothing for a bit.

Then Adler said, "Tomorrow's Saturday."

"Yep."

"You close Sunday."

"Mm-hmm."

"You're on the road back to us first thing Monday."

"Uh-huh."

"So you've got two days to... not do this thing."

"You are a math genius, Adler."

Adler muttered, "This guy does seem like low-hanging rotten fruit."

Gideon waited. Sucked blood from his palm.

"OK fine!" Adler said. "I'm sending you... an item. Doesn't leave a mark. Self-defense only. You can't tell anyone."

"Understood."

"I can't help you any more than that."

"I can handle it. What I can't handle is where certain millions and info get sent."

Adler brightened. "Well now, you're talking to the right whizkid! And I wouldn't reeeeeally be helping you in an actual Troupe performance, soooo..." Cheetos crunched in earnest. "How you wanna play it?"

"Wipe him out. Show closes Sunday. Wait till midnight. Then have him donate a big chunk to the theatre; they're gonna need help once this blows up. And spread the rest around to all the actors he hurt."

"Oh, I shall spread that laundered wealth, my man."

"And then, first thing start of business Monday, drop the truth bomb. Press. Law enforcement. Every theatre geek with a blog. No two-year reappearance this time."

"Lovely plan. Just one thing."

"Name it."

"Everything I've dug up is circumstantial."

"So let's get a smoking gun."

"If you could wrangle me up a phone, tablet, or laptop, I would be happy to oblige. One of the Producer's would be best, but his fixer's should do it."

"Fixer?"

"Well, he ain't getting his own hands dirty again. Look around. Someone there is doing his heavy lifting."

Gideon considered. Probably the Agent, since procuring young talent was the main thing. But could be the Assistant. Easy to find out.

Just set a trap with irresistible bait.

NOBODY ELSE WAS COMING.

Gideon was sure. So he waited.

Everything costs something, and waiting is simply a way to spend time. Waiting buys you power. Waiting buys suspense and anxiety. Waiting allows the minds of your captives to percolate and fester with stories and suspicions.

By not telling them what you want right away, they fill in that gap with spectacularly creative inventions, which you can observe, then leverage.

Now the two hired hands splayed on the floor before him, even with mouths duct-taped, were telling fantastical tales to each other with grunts and straining muscles and panicked eyes. They spared not a glance for the Assistant. Instructive.

"You. Pritchard. You paid these goons their balance yet?"

Pritchard shook his head.

"I'm guessing final payment required pictorial proof of them having roughed me up?"

Pritchard nodded sheepishly.

"You two." He nudged the nearer, Thick, with his boot. "This is nothing personal, right? You don't know me, don't care who I am or why this moron hired you?"

Tall and Thick shook their heads.

"So I get him to top off your PayPal accounts or whatever, you'll head on out and not look back. No harm, no foul. Sound good?"

Tall and Thick nodded vigorously.

"Cool. Think about finding a different line of work. I see you again, I won't be near as gentle."

There was no question in there, but Tall and Thick both thought a response was appropriate. So Tall half nodded while Thick sorta shrugged.

Pritchard squirmed.

"All right then." Gideon grabbed Pritchard and shoved him to sitting, back against the couch. He'd confiscated everything from all their pockets, inventoried the haul on the coffee table. He placed Pritchard's phone in his zip-tied hands, sat on the couch above and behind him.

"Go ahead, Pritchard. Pay 'em off. Just know I can see everything you're doing to that screen."

He pressed Eye Melter against the side of Pritchard's head. "No texts, no calls, no social media SOS. Nothing but funds transfer. Go on now."

A few flicks of Pritchard's thumbs swelled Tall and Thick's bank balances. Gideon raised his eyebrows.

"Damn. Nice work if you can get it."

He pulled the phone from Pritchard's fingers, ensured it was still unlocked, placed it back on the coffee table. Cut the zip-ties from Tall and Thick's ankles.

They stood, wobbled as blood rushed back through their legs, held out their wrists. Gideon shook his head.

"Nah. Here's your car keys." He slid them into Thick's hand. "I'm keeping everything else."

He waved at their phones and wallets, the bat and crowbar. "You both look imminently trustworthy, but, y'know, leverage."

Tall and Thick looked at each other. Gideon sighed and lifted the arc lamp.

"Happy trails, friends."

Tall and Thick hurried out the door, down the hall, not looking back.

"Just you and me now, Pritchard."

The Assistant thrashed.

"I know, I know. You won't tell me anything. But you don't need to. All I needed was your phone. And you've already unlocked it for me."

The fight drained out of Pritchard. He whimpered behind the duct tape.

Gideon attached one of Adler's specially designed dongles to the Assistant's phone. Its light blinked red, red, then green. And immediately his skull vibrated with Adler's voice.

"Oh, Giddy, for meeee? You shouldn't have. Gimme a couple minutes to perform some digital dissection. Hey! How'd Eye Melter do??"

Gideon confirmed Eye Melter had done great. But then Adler started humming Motown hits—"It's a Shame" was first up—which meant he was locked in to his work.

So Gideon didn't tell him about how on Saturday he'd made sure he, Miles, and Sasha were all eating together in her dressing room during dinner break between the 2pm matinee and the 8pm evening show. Didn't tell him how the Producer had breezed in and come up short, surprised.

"I didn't expect you'd have company."

Sasha giggled nervously. Miles stared down at the plate on his lap.

"I don't believe we've met," the Producer said. He stuck his hand out toward Gideon. "I recognize you from the show, Mr. Price. I'm—" And the Producer said his name.

Gideon ignored the offered hand, shoveled a forkful of chicken salad into his mouth.

It got awkward.

The Producer turned on his megawatt smile and said, "I truly enjoyed your performance. You're an exquisite actor."

Gideon glanced up. Spoke with his mouth full. "So?"

It got tense.

The kind of tense that everyone senses when two predators square off. The Producer's smile still shone. His entire face gleamed, actually, but not from sweat. His skin was simply tight and shiny.

Gideon chewed loudly. The Producer finally withdrew his hand.

"I didn't mean to interrupt your meal," the Producer said. "Break a leg tonight."

"OK," Gideon said.

The Producer left. Sasha and Miles exhaled. Gideon ate chicken salad.

"It's a Shame" gave way to "Baby Love," so Gideon continued to not tell Adler how he'd walked Sasha and Miles home that night and repeated the protective detail routine all through Sunday.

And he didn't tell Adler about the closing night party late Sunday, down at the karaoke bar on the main drag. How the Director of the show had warbled through Billy Joel's "A Matter of Trust"—ironic considering the circumstances, Gideon thought—and then called the Producer up on stage to thunderously forced applause.

A speech crammed with every cliché—*couldn't do it without you, commitment to the art, generous support, continued relationship*—and the Director presented the Producer with a large bouquet of half-wilted flowers.

"Ah yes," the Producer said. "I am aware of the tradition. I trust you didn't actually steal these from a nearby headstone?"

Polite laughter.

"I aged them myself," the Director said, beaming.

"Thank you," the Producer said, and then took over the mic for a speech of his own.

"I am overwhelmed by all your talent and generosity. I know you all want to get back to singing and celebrating, so I'll keep this brief.

"The two strongest muscles in the human body are the heart and the tongue. I think that is simply a gorgeous metaphor for the actor, for what you all do. Actors have the biggest hearts and the most sensitive voices. The stage and your craft demand it. Whatever my small role in helping you tell these stories this summer, know that I am the one who is honored and humbled."

More applause. The Producer made his way to his table, shaking every hand and squeezing every shoulder. A filled pitcher was summoned. He put his flowers in water.

"Baby Love" cross-faded into "Ain't Too Proud to Beg," so Gideon didn't tell Adler how he'd walked to the Producer's table and plucked a faded bloom from the bouquet.

"Ah, Mr. Price," the Producer said, his eyes already narrowed. "Allow me to introduce you to my Agent."

He gestured at a thin-faced woman sitting next to him. She puffed non-stop on a vape. Smoke curled out of her mouth as she gave the merest impetuous nod.

"And my Assistant." The other side. A round-faced hedgehog of a man wearing a blaringly loud bow tie.

Gideon ripped off a petal and flicked it at the Agent. "Minion." Ripped another and flicked it at the Assistant. "Lapdog."

The two offended parties blustered, but the Producer shushed them.

"Happy closing, Mr. Price."

"I want to talk to you about something."

"And what would that be?"

"Wrigley. Soldier Field. Michael Jordan."

The Agent and the Assistant blinked in confusion, but the Producer's shiny smile widened.

"Anything else?"

"Roger Ebert. Deep-dish pizza. Lake breezes and windy winters."

"Sounds like my kind of town."

"It won't let you down."

"What do you want, Mr. Price?"

"What any actor wants." Gideon ripped the head off the flower and crushed it in his hand. "Art don't pay." He scattered the creased and crumpled petals across the table, into their laps. "But you will. If you want me to keep quiet."

The Producer plucked a petal from where it had landed on his plate of celebratory cake. "Do you have a number in mind?"

"Swing by my apartment later. I'll show you what I've got. You can decide how much you think it's all worth."

Gideon walked away. He knew a few hours later they would be coming.

———

No one else came.

Gideon used the time to pack. Then Adler's breath caught and "Mercy Mercy Me" choked off mid-chorus.

"Holy mother of shitballs."

"What is it, Adler?"

"This phone got me into the Producer's private server, and there's some photos here, and... um..."

Gideon was stunned. He'd never heard Adler not snarky, much less vulnerable.

"What did you find, Adler?"

"So we already knew he forced all these actors and students into sexual favors. But..."

"But?"

Adler's voice was shaky. "He marked them. With a razor blade."

"*Marked* them?"

Pritchard made a noise. He'd overheard. Gideon looked over, and the glint in his eye caused Pritchard to make another noise.

"Scars. X's. On their chest, above their hearts. And... and also on their tongues."

"There's pictures of this?"

"Giddy, I can't—"

"Tell me."

Gideon stepped toward Pritchard. Pritchard scrabbled backward on his backside until he thunked into the wall. Gideon kept coming until he had one foot on either side of the Assistant's quivering, bound body.

The *feeling* flowed through him. A tiny part of him wondered if this was how the Producer must feel when he had a young actor cringing before him. That was an uncomfortable thought.

"OK. Um. So there's pics of the fresh cuts. Even of the blade actually—" Adler sounded on the verge of tears. "So much blood. And then more pictures. Like time lapse. Like... like he'd circle back and take another picture month after month to see how the wounds had scarred."

A tidal wave of righteous fury washed all discomfort away. Gideon pressed the sole of his boot into Pritchard's chest, pinning him to the wall.

Pritchard made noise after noise. Gideon pressed. He heard Adler blow his nose and clear his throat.

"Well, this is patently awful." Adler's snark was back, if forced. "But good news is you got me the phone and with one phone I can unlock the world and we got everything we need to bury the bastard. So you can get outta Dodge."

Gideon pressed. Pritchard writhed.

"Giddy, y'hear me? Chop chop."

Gideon pressed. A rib cracked. Pritchard made a horrible noise, made more horrible for being muffled.

"OK, dude, I just pulled up livestream from your shades, and you gotta stop what you're doin'. Like, now. Let the authorities take it from here. Self-defense is one thing, but if you take this fight up the ladder—"

Gideon pressed. Another rib cracked. Tears and snot streamed down Pritchard's face.

"Holy shit, Gideon!"

But Gideon had taken off his shades.

He didn't want Adler watching what was coming next.

HE WAS COMING.

Gideon made Pritchard comfortable on the couch. Well, as comfortable as one can be with zip-tied ankles and wrists and two broken ribs. He finished packing, including Tall and Thick's stuff. Wiped his prints off Pritchard's phone and left it on the kitchen counter.

"See you on the news."

He locked the door on the sniveling Assistant, threw all his stuff into his car, and marched a few blocks, straight to the Producer's door. The swankiest room in the swankiest hotel in town, of course.

Wasn't saying much. The carpet was patchy, the pool murky, the continental breakfast probably stale. But it wasn't a chain joint and Gideon knew enough about the Producer at this point to understand only the best would do. Best being relative in the middle of midwestern nowhere.

Gideon arrived at the door, stood against the wall to the side, out of sight of the peephole. Took a 4-4-4-4 breath. Tried to cool down. Managed maybe a degree or two. Knocked lightly but urgently.

The Producer's whisper came quick. He wasn't asleep. He was awaiting the report. "Pritchard?"

Gideon covered his mouth with his arm and did his best impression of the Assistant's reedy voice. "Yes, sir."

The barest hesitation.

"What are you doing here? I told you to call me when it was done."

"I know, sir, yes, I'm sorry, sir, but I thought you'd want to see his evidence right away."

Gideon knew his ruse was running thin, but the prospect of getting his hands on anything incriminating tempted the Producer just enough. The deadbolt clicked.

"And those two gentlemen you hired are taking care of Price?"

The latch depressed.

"Yes, *sir*," Gideon spat, and slammed his shoulder into the door. The "in case of emergency" map that hangs on the back of every hotel door in every hotel room in the world smashed into the Producer's face. Gideon kept driving into the room as the Producer staggered back.

Gideon's lizard brain hissed. Countless hours sparring with Stan and Rheia had hardwired a new alarm into his situational awareness programming: *incoming*.

So Gideon's body came to an abrupt stop before his mind even knew to issue the command. Which was good, because the Producer, even while tumbling, had enough of his own self-preservation instinct intact to slash with the razor blade secreted in his hand.

The keen edge sliced a gash through Gideon's shirt. Gideon sensed a couple of his chest hairs drifting into the air, shaved stubble tight.

The Producer stumbled another two steps back. Gideon followed, straining to stay cold. His hand reached out and snatched at the first item it found on the entry table. An acrylic vase, cut to mimic crystal, proudly displaying the graveyard gift.

Another wild, defensive slash.

Gideon crisply parried with the vase. Wilted flowers scattered.

The Producer found his footing. Wiped blood from his broken nose. Pulled a second knife from his pocket, flicked it open. Pointed instead of bladed.

The Producer snarled, "I hope you like scars. I'm gonna—"

"Shut up."

The Producer blinked. Gideon stepped forward with his acrylic vase. The Producer, despite his two knives, backed up.

"Don't threaten. Don't bargain. Don't plead. You are over."

The Producer breathed in to give his reply, but Gideon took another step forward.

The Producer backed up and waved his blade, held up his point.

"I've emptied all your accounts. Your assets are mine. And every-thing you've done is going front page. Both your names. Both your faces. I'm gonna chum you to the sharks."

The Producer blinked again. Gulped. Then forced a chuckle.

"Bullshit. You're an actor. You're nothing."

"Whatever you say. Pritchard'll be going down with you. Is that a comfort?"

"Pritchard. Where is he? What've you done with him?"

Gideon smiled.

"He's already over."

And then Gideon waited. It was inevitable what would happen next.

The Producer would launch a last-ditch, desperate attack. His ego demanded it. Gideon watched the Producer's face scrunch, then open, then sharpen. Tale as old as time. Talking himself into believing he still could snatch glorious victory from obvious defeat.

Gideon glanced at the Producer's feet, which were shifting as the story in the Producer's head took shape. The feet settled.

He glanced at the Producer's hips balancing just so, then at his shoulders as they wound like a winch. Easy now to see the future. Big, theatrical, advancing slashes with the blade. Three of them—fore-hand, backhand, forehand—none intended to land, but rather to set up the finale: a Cyrano-esque thrust of the point to Gideon's heart.

As it was foreseen, so did it come to pass. The blade swished by three times, Gideon retreating step for step for step. The Producer's other arm reared back but never moved forward because Gideon executed a thrust of his own.

No rearing back, no wasted time or motion.

He speared the vase two-handed at the Producer's mouth. Even if the Producer had thrusted simultaneously, it wouldn't have mattered.

The vase was a good eight inches longer than the knife. The Producer would never understand that he never stood a chance.

Math and physics, plain and simple.

Acrylic shattered. The Producer's jaw dislocated with a squishy *pop* and several teeth cracked. Gideon didn't pull his strike this time. He followed through deep, and so the sharded vase tore bloody gashes into cheeks, chin, and nose. All that plastic surgery, instantly shredded.

Knives dropped forgotten to the floor. The Producer held his face as though it were falling apart. Which, frankly, it was.

Gideon stepped forward before the Producer could shriek. A sharp elbow to the temple and Gideon was left the only conscious being in the swankiest room in the swankiest hotel in town.

He looked down at the crumpled, bleeding Producer. Eager rage raced the pulsing tracks of his veins. And that felt good. So so good.

He leaned over, hands on knees. He box breathed. He tried to talk sense to his thudding heart. He tried to go cold. He really did. But midwestern summer is muggy. It's oppressive.

And it's really goddamn hot.

———

SOMEONE WAS HERE.

The Producer awoke, hoping he was alone, knowing he wasn't. He tried to reach for his throbbing face, but his hands were bound. He tried to scream for help, but his mouth was gagged and taped. He tried to stand and escape, but his body and feet were tied to a chair.

But more ominous than all that was the weight and pressure on his head. Like a heavy hat or tight visor.

"You didn't believe me earlier."

A tablet screen floated into view. Scrolled through screen shots of bank statements and investment records.

"Every cent. Poof."

The screen shots had to be doctored. HAD to be. The Producer strained, to no avail.

"Don't worry. All going to good causes."

The Producer growled deep in his throat. He wanted to thrash his head, stomp his feet. But he couldn't. This nobody, this *actor*, had left him not an inch of wiggle room. The tablet floated away.

"How about a little experiment?"

The Producer saw an arm cross his vision. Felt fingers fiddling with the weight on his head. And then suddenly it got very bright. The Producer blinked. Tried to turn away. But the flashing light followed. It was everywhere. He felt nauseous.

Nineteen hertz will do that to most people.

"There have yet to be any documented cases of permanent blindness caused by tactical lights. But we've got a couple hours to kill here together. So let's see if we can make some history. Don't take it personally if I stay to the side here. Don't want to flash myself. Need to make sure I can see what I'm doing."

The actor chuckled. The Producer snarled. The flashing light got brighter.

The Producer squeezed his eyes closed. The light was fists pounding on the doors of his eyelids.

"That's fine. We're only at two hundred. I can go to twelve. Step at a time."

The fists became battering rams. The Producer grunted wordless pleas for mercy. But a whisper breathed hot in his ear: "This is nothing compared to what you did to them."

The battering rams became axe strikes.

"Silly me. I still have it strobing. Let's just leave it on full, shall we?"

The Producer gasped as the strikes melded into one... unrelenting... *push*.

"Strap in."

The Producer felt the actor's fingers prying his eyelids up.

Hours later, media and police received the same email tip with an info dump attached.

Pritchard and the Producer were plastered all over live coverage, evening coverage, and days of follow-up coverage. Trial dates would fast approach and keep them in the public eye for months. Tall and Thick never surfaced.

The Agent was grilled hard, but ultimately let go; she'd been totally in the dark and was aghast. She quit showbiz and got a job with a dispensary.

Gideon was questioned, too—along with the entire cast and company—but records showed he had checked out of housing hours before what the Producer's harried public defender called the "unprovoked attack."

A few traffic cams even caught Gideon driving away from town prior to the time he was, according to Pritchard and the Producer, allegedly administering them torture. Adler could juggle timestamps with his eyes closed.

The mountain of evidence against Pritchard and the Producer was so damning, and the public outcry so deafening, no one put all that much effort into figuring out how they both ended up bound and bloody. Any of several dozen victims would've had motive.

"Unprovoked"? Not so much.

Sasha didn't question the windfall in her checking account. She used the money to move to L.A. and start her own production company.

Miles did question the good fortune, sent a few queries here and there, but then got a text from an unknown number. *You won the lottery, kid. Let it be. Your heart and voice belong to you and only you.*

Miles donated every penny to a variety of shelters and abuse prevention programs, and two years later won his first Tony.

Pritchard caved, took a plea deal, buried the Producer even deeper, got himself out in a few years with good behavior. He never went near a theatre or wore a bow tie again.

The Producer, broke and incarcerated, endured several surgeries at the state's expense—some ocular, some reconstructive—and retained a modicum of blurred, spotted eyesight.

But a deep-seated migraine, a dagger of the mind stabbing and ever stabbing, stayed with him for years. A scar to match those on his ravaged face. He raged in his cell and rotted away.

Like flowers on a grave.

MEET JASON CANNON

Jason Cannon is a best-selling author and publisher, as well as an award-winning actor, director, improviser, playwright, and teacher. He has an MFA in Directing, a Master's in Drama, and a quarter-century in the professional theatre.

As an actor, Jason has portrayed everything from a rapping dinosaur to a robot and from a hitman to Hamlet. He has written plays about Stevie Wonder and J. R. R. Tolkien, directed plays about hiccuping dragons and foul-mouthed puppets, and once while improvising he was attacked by a stage light.

He lives in Florida just a holler from the Gulf with his partner Rebecca and their two silly pups, Gaia and Odin. He makes a killer key lime pie and runs lots of 10Ks and half-marathons.

Jason believes storytelling in all its forms—whether seen on the stage or read on the page—has the power not only to entertain but also to comfort, provoke, and inspire us to be better humans.

Want more thrilling TROUPE stories? Grab your free e-copy of THE UNDERSTUDY by joining IBIS BOOKS at ibis-books.com. Your e-copy will also include a free extended preview of GHOST LIGHT, the first novel in the thrilling TROUPE series

A brutal dog-fighting ring up in the Georgia mountains. A secret team of vigilantes with vast resources. An undercover operation that goes sideways.

It's time to let THE UNDERSTUDY off the leash.

If you like Lee Child, James Rollins, Dan Brown, Randy Wayne White, *Criminal Minds*, or Broadway plays—yes, seriously!—then the TROUPE is for you.

Jason is also available as a workshop leader, story coach, editor, teacher, speaker, emcee, and even wedding officiant.

Learn more about Jason at jason-cannon.com and check out his other books at ibis-books.com.

LOST PROPERTY

TRUDEY MARTIN

FRIDAY

I BIT MY LIP and gripped my passport to my chest as we shuffled forward in the queue. Glancing sideways at Sam, I couldn't help but contrast his relaxed and happy attitude with John's tense demeanour in these circumstances.

We'd been gradually moving ever closer to the check in gate for what seemed like an eternity. I glanced up at Sam once again; his black eyes taking in everything around him. He ran a hand across the shaved dark skin on his head and looked down at me and smiled.

"Hey, you," he said, with a grin that filled his face. "Ready to relax and holiday?"

I nodded, and stared at my feet. Going on holiday with a man who wasn't my husband was a weird experience. Everything had seemed straightforward when, after a couple of glasses of wine, Sam suggested that we cement our new relationship with a long weekend away. I'd been giddy on the alcohol and the atmosphere of a gala award dinner that my friend Keith had organised.

"Oh my God, yes!" I'd said, and we had spent the following two weeks trying to come up with somewhere that, on the one hand we both wanted to visit, and on the other hand at least one of us hadn't been to with a previous partner. Our options were limited by those parameters.

My husband, John, and I had travelled frequently during his life. We hadn't been restricted by children or other commitments. And Sam had travelled with past girlfriends.

Eventually we had settled on southern Spain. Robert and Keith had recommended Torremolinos as a destination that they loved so we'd taken the plunge and booked it.

Now, I took another couple of steps towards boarding the plane and hoped that I wouldn't regret the decision.

The autumn heat hit me as we exited the airport, still wearing our England-weather clothes, and we followed Robert's instructions on how to get the train.

It turned out to be relatively easy and less than half an hour after leaving the arrivals hall we were heading out of the train station into Nogalera Square, in the heart of the town centre. The apartment we'd booked was a five minute walk away, the concierge obviously expecting us as he greeted us by name.

"Mrs Spencer?" he asked as we approached the desk.

"Err, yes," I said, flicking my eyes towards Sam.

We followed the uniformed man to the lift and up to the fifth floor, where he showed us into our one bedroom apartment, told us how to operate all the appliances, and opened the door on to the balcony to reveal a stunning view down the cliff to the sea below. The paseo that led along the sea front was busy with walkers, runners and cyclists, and I stood for a moment taking in the sea air.

"Look," I said as Sam came out to join me, having tipped the concierge and sent him happily back to reception. "The sea, the pool, the mountains. It's got the lot."

He leant down and kissed me on the side of my head and placed his arm around my shoulder. "I think I'll be giving the pool a miss," he said. "It's warm, but not that warm."

After unpacking we decided to head out for a drink and something to eat. As we shut the heavy wooden front door a couple of men emerged from the apartment opposite.

"Hola," I said, trying out my limited Spanish for the first time.

"Buenos días," the taller of the two replied. "I'm Jaime," he carried on, clearly sensing that we were foreigners. He pointed to his partner. "And this is Mark."

"Hey," Mark said, the transatlantic twang clear in his voice. "Did you just arrive this afternoon?"

Both Sam and I nodded.

"Well, you're really welcome to join us, if you'd like," he ran his hand through his thick dark-blond hair, then rested it lightly on his hip. "We're just heading out for a drink to one of our favourite local bars."

"Sure," I said, shrugging, "That would be great." And we headed off towards the lift.

"Are you guys on holiday too?" I asked as we descended.

"No," Mark replied. "We live here. We bought this apartment a couple of years ago, when we moved to Spain."

We emerged out into the daylight and Jaime led us out of the complex and across a couple of small roads.

"We used to live in New York; we got married over there, but came back here for Jaime's work," Mark continued as we walked. "Jaime's got family in Málaga so we thought this was close, but a safe enough distance." He laughed.

We walked down a little alley and emerged into a charming little square, the bright white buildings reflecting the last of the evening sun. Water tinkled down a fountain in the centre, although the sound was almost drowned out by the buzz of people on the restaurant terraces.

On one corner a cute bar, with a rainbow flag flying above its door, teemed with customers. We found a table and sat down on the little wooden chairs.

"It's a gay bar, but they welcome everyone," Jaime explained. I hadn't actually noticed that most of the clientele were male.

He carried on, "Torremolinos is the gay capital of Spain."

I nodded; no wonder Robert and Keith liked it so much.

We chatted over our drinks, Jaime and Mark giving us a few tips of places to see, bars to try out and restaurants where the food was worth sampling.

After a while, Mark said, "So, Verity, what do you do?"

"Oh, um...well, I do investigations for people."

"Oh wow, exciting."

"Well, most of the time it's not, you know, I chase after people's husbands and photograph them," I said, not wanting to bring up my latest investigation into a child murder. "Sam's job is much more exciting. He's a detective inspector in the Met," I said, deflecting the attention elsewhere.

Sam looked at me with one eyebrow raised. He knew what I was doing. He kept quiet.

"Gosh," Mark said, raising his hands. And his carefully coiffed eyebrows. "I feel so boring."

Jaime patted him on the knee. "Well, you're doing really well at the moment. There's clearly a high demand for telemarketing consultants right now."

After another round of drinks I was beginning to feel a little light-headed. The measures were a good deal larger than I was used to back home.

So, Sam and I went off to try one of Jaime's restaurant recommendations, and we left him and Mark chatting to a group of gentlemen, most of whom were clad head to toe in leather.

After dinner, we wandered back to the apartment. We seemed to be out of kilter with most of the Spanish people out on the streets, many of whom were just entering the restaurants ready to eat.

I glanced at my watch; it was almost eleven and I'd been up for almost eighteen hours. I yawned and Sam turned to me and laughed.

"Come on," he said, taking my hand, "let's get you home."

"Jesus," Sam said, after we'd both finished cleaning our teeth and getting ready for bed. "I see why you were yawning. I'm shattered. Travelling really takes it out of you."

"Yeah," I said, pulling back the bed clothes. "That and eating all that lovely food."

"It was good," Sam said. "That fish was amazing." He sat down on the bed next to me. "What with a full belly and getting up at silly-o-clock this morning, I think I might drop straight off to sleep."

I glanced over at him, then I put my hand on his chest and pushed him backwards onto the bed. "Yeah, right," I said. "You lay back and try."

Afterwards we lay curled together on the bed, the bedclothes tangled round our legs, Sam's arm around my shoulder.

"So," I said, sleepily, snuggling into his chest. "What do you fancy doing tomorrow?"

"This," he said, and kissed me lightly on the top of the head.

"All day?"

He laughed. "Well, maybe we could pause for lunch, yeah?"

"Okay!" I said. "We'll hold off on the sightseeing, shall we?"

There was no reply. I glanced up at him, his jaw slack, his eyes closed tight and I gently moved his arm and shifted across the bed.

I lay back, gazing at the ceiling as I slipped into a fitful sleep, my thoughts flitting unbidden from past holidays with John, to recent outings with Sam, to conversations with Robert, to my old job at the college teaching teenagers.

SATURDAY

THE BRIGHT LIGHT STREAMING in through the bedroom window woke me the following morning, although I'd slept well and it wasn't early.

I found Sam sitting on the balcony, a book in one hand and a cup of tea in the other. I joined him for a while, until hunger got the better of me and we decided to go in search of something to eat.

The apartment block we were staying in had its own lift down to the sea front, so we took that and wandered along the paseo, pausing to look back at the apartment block perched at the top of the cliff to figure out which was our balcony.

The headland pushed out into the sea like a ship setting sail into the morning sun. We meandered along, talking to the stray cats that lived at the foot of the cliff as we went.

The light sparkled across the sea as the sun rose high above the waves, causing ripples and flashes of light to bounce off the clear blue water.

"Oh, look at that," said Sam.

As we rounded the corner, what looked like a film crew filled a large stretch of the beach. Two jeeps stood at jaunty angles on the edge of the sand; a couple of men dragged long fluffy microphones out of the boot of one, whilst someone else heaved a camera onto their shoulder from the back of the other.

Another man was walking around, gesticulating at various points in the sand, shouting commands that drifted away across the sea. In response, a bevy of young men and women scuttled about positioning chairs, moving them, repositioning, then moving them back.

A young lady with a high ponytail unfolded a stack of blankets and lay them haphazardly on a spot in the centre of the beach.

To one side, a bank of chairs was filled with what I assumed were actors. Make-up artists and hairdressers fussed about them like a swarm of bees.

We found some seats in a café, set a few feet back from the paseo, and ordered coffee and pitufos.

"¿Qué hacen?" What are they doing? I asked the waitress when she returned with our breakfast, and I pointed out at the beach.

"Van a grabar una pelicula," she replied. "They make a film. They were here two days already, recording. Se llama Propiedad Perdida. Es sobre los traficantes de drogas. Pues, eso lo creo."

Sam looked at me as she left, his eyebrows raised in query.

"I think she said it's called Lost Property and it's about drug dealers," I said, frowning in self-doubt. I'd tried to polish up my Spanish a little before we'd arrived but, if I'm honest, it was still fairly basic.

It was fascinating watching them, and we sat there through another round of coffees or two, some toasted sandwiches, and eventually a beer and a glass of wine.

The guy doing the pointing I assumed was the director. He would strut about convening huddles of actors, then walk away circling a pen in the air. Every time he circled his pen the clipper board man clicked his board and the cameras started filming the action.

We were too far away to hear any of the dialogue but it looked like it was going to be an exciting film.

The director spoke briefly into a walkie talkie, then waved his arms towards the sea, running forward and shouting "Vamos, vamos!" The words drifted across the sand, loud enough to hear. "Viene el bote! Venga!"

The camera operators ran towards the sea, their cameras pointing at the water from different angles. The people holding the microphones followed closely behind and seconds later a massive grey inflatable boat appeared from around the headland, three enormous engines powering it towards the shore.

The cameras continued filming as the boat neared the beach. One of the cameramen, a pony-tail bouncing against his back, knelt down and filmed upwards towards the actors as they jumped off the boat, splashing through the shallow waves and onto the sand. Then he stood up and waded towards the boat, holding his camera up high and pointing it into the boat.

On the boat, a black actor with an afro was dragging to his feet a shaven headed actor whose hands were secured behind his back. Afro guy threw shaven headed guy out of the boat and into the shallow water, then jumped down and pulled him along, sea water dripping from his face and clothes.

The cameraman followed closely as shaven headed guy was dragged, struggling and shouting, to the area with the blankets, where Afro guy pushed him to his knees.

The cameras drew closer now, recording the action from various positions, pointing at the shaven headed actor, then at Afro guy and taking in the extras who were forming a circle around the blankets.

The actors shouted at each other, the extras oohed and aahed. They fell into silence as Afro guy produced a gun and shaven headed guy began to plead.

Fake blood arched across the beach as Afro guy shot shaven headed guy directly in his forehead from about six feet away. He picked up one of the blankets and threw it over the actor playing dead on the ground.

The director waved his hands in the air and the cameramen, actors and all the others relaxed, laughing and shaking hands. Some began to light up cigarettes.

The director ran over and peered into the camera that had taken the close ups, then turned and gave the thumbs up. Everyone, extras and bystanders included, began to clap.

The director leant down and, with a flourish, pulled the blanket off the shaven headed actor, who jumped up, shook hands with several other actors, and ran off to claim one of the chairs.

"Hasta lunes!" the director shouted, and everyone began to pack away.

We signalled the waitress and asked for the bill.

"They finish," she said as she placed the bill on the table. "Terminan."

"Hasta lunes?" I asked. "Until...? Lunes? Is that Monday?"

Sí, sí. Lunes regresan. They come back Monday."

We walked home, chatting about what we'd just seen and promising that when the film was released we'd be sitting on a sofa together watching and reminiscing about seeing it being filmed.

We spent a lazy couple of hours taking in the afternoon sun on the balcony, watching people coming and going along the paseo and spotting ships on the horizon.

"Fancy a siesta?" Sam asked after a lengthy silence.

"Well, we are in Spain. And it is the done thing."

As we moved back into the apartment a hammering on the door made me jump.

Then again, another bout of frantic bashing on the door.

"Sam, Verity! Are you in there?" It sounded like Jaime.

Bash, bash, bash!

Sam rushed over to the door. "Hold on, hold on!" he shouted.

I think he was fearful that Jaime would actually knock the door off its hinges.

As Sam opened the door, Jaime practically fell into the apartment, breathless and gasping.

"He's gone, he's gone! You have to help me, he's gone."

"What?" I asked. "Jaime, what are you saying?

¿Qué dices? Who's gone?"

"Mark. Mark has gone. He's gone and I don't know what to do."

He threw himself on the sofa, pushed a cushion over his face and began to sob.

I knelt down next to him and rested a hand on his heaving shoulder. "Jaime, slow down. Tell us what's happened."

He stayed where he was, crying into the cushion.

I patted his back. "Come on, come on. We need you to tell us what's happened. Or how can we help you?"

He pulled the corner of the cushion off one eye, glancing at us both in turn. He gave a sigh, put the cushion on his knee and rested his hands on it.

"He's gone," he whispered, almost too quietly to hear. Then, his voice rising and cracking as he spoke, he added, "You're both detectives. You have to help me!"

Sam moved closer, standing at my back. "Start at the beginning and tell us what's happened."

Jaime ran his hands through his hair and leant his forehead down onto the cushion before looking back up at us. He drew in a deep breath and blew it out through pursed lips.

"I go out after lunch to do the shopping. Mark stay at home to tidy and do the washing."

He pulled at the edge of the cushion and gave another sigh. "Well, you know, the everyday chores." He paused. "I was halfway round

Mercadona when my phone vibrated. It was a message from Mark. I think he is texting to remind me to get something, then I look and I don't believe what I am reading."

He pulled his phone from his pocket, tapped at the screen a few times, then held it up.

I took it from him, standing up to read the message and holding the phone so that Sam could read it over my shoulder.

I've done something stupid. I think I'm about to pay for it. I just saw them coming.

"What does he mean? What has he done?" Sam asked.

Jaime glanced up and over my shoulder at Sam. "I don't know." He shook his head. "I don't know."

"Who did he see coming?" I added.

Jaime looked back at me, holding his hands palm up at his side. "I don't know," he said again.

"Did you reply?" I asked.

Jaime nodded and indicated with his finger to scroll down the phone.

What's going on? What did u do? Nothing will matter we can sort it. Love you Jx

I kept scrolling.

It's too late. There's no way out. I'm sorry xx

Call me. We'll sort it. Jxx

"Is that it?" I asked. "Did he call you?"

Jaime fished into his pocket and brought out an iPhone. "This was on the floor," he said, gasping in air with every word. "He never goes anywhere without his phone."

Jaime shook his head from side to side and started to sob once again, his face contorting with the effort of crying. He clutched at the cushion and squeezed it in his arms.

"What does he mean, 'I saw them coming'?" Sam asked him.

Between fitful breaths Jaime said, "I think he must have seen someone. I don't know who, but you can see the car park from our apartment."

"Can we have a look?" Sam asked.

Jaime nodded and got to his feet, dumping the cushion as he stood up. We followed him across the hall and through his open front door.

I stood open mouthed as I took in the smashed coffee table, the overturned chairs and the floor covered in pieces of glass. We picked our way across the floor and Jaime pointed to the door that led to the balcony. Sam opened it and led the way outside.

The view was stunning. The mountains glistened in the light of the sun, the crystal blue of the shoreline curving past the city of Málaga and away into the distance. Jaime came out and pointed over the railings.

"Down below, you see. That's the car park for our building. I think he must have seen somebody coming round to the entrance."

He pointed around the side of the building. "He must have known who they were. He must have known what they wanted."

"It looks like there was a struggle," Sam said pointing to the debris. "Is there anything missing?"

Jaime shook his head. "I don't think so, no."

"Have any of the other rooms been touched?" Jaime gesticulated for us to have a look around.

The apartment was larger than ours so Sam took one bedroom and I looked in the other. We met back out in the entrance hall.

I shook my head. "No sign of anything in there."

"Nothing in that one either."

We walked back to the living room and surveyed the damage.

"Have you called the police?" I asked.

Jaime nodded.

"As soon as I got here. As soon as I saw what had happened. But they were not too interested. 'Perhaps he's gone for a walk', they say. 'Perhaps he broke the coffee table by falling and he's gone to buy glue.'"

He looked around, his shoulders rising in disbelief. "They make a report, but they don't really take it seriously. They say go back in twenty-four hours if he hasn't come home."

He shrugged, turning down the corners of his mouth. "Maybe they will look into it then."

He fell to the floor, on his knees and held his hands out, indicating the broken furniture. "But what if I don't have twenty-four hours. What will I do?"

He lifted his face to the ceiling, tears streaming down his cheeks. He looked over at us, standing there watching him.

"What will I do?" he asked again. "What will I do?"

Can we look around?" Sam asked.

Jaime nodded, then sat back on his heels and started to rock gently. I knelt down next to him.

"Jaime," I said, and he looked up at me. "If we're going to find Mark we need you to help us. I know it's stressful. I know it's worrying, but you need to get up and help us."

He stared at me, a blank expression on his face.

"We need you to tell us what he's been doing, where he keeps his things, where we might find a clue as to what he's been doing. He said he'd done something stupid. Do you have any idea what he was referring to?'

Jaime shook his head. "I don't, not any idea."

"There must be something," Sam said. "Think about the last few months. Has there been anything odd, anything suspicious? Has he been away?"

Jaime carried on shaking his head, his brow furrowed as if he was trying to conjure up a memory.

"Has he met anyone new? Started going to a new bar or café? Started a hobby that he's never done before? Come into money?"

At that, Jaime stopped. He looked up at Sam, his mouth opening, his eyes widening.

"Sí. Yes. He make money. He is, how do you say it, a consultant. Since, I don't know, the last three or four months, he's been doing well. Before that, business was not good. But then things improve and he starts to make money."

"Do you know how that happened?" Sam asked.

"I think a new client."

"What do you know about the new client?" I pitched in.

Jaime shook his head. "I don't know nothing," he said.

"Did he go out to meet the new client?" I stood up and moved across the room.

"Yes, yes he did."

"Do you know when?" I asked.

"No. I can't remember."

"Where are his things?" Sam said as he moved out into the entrance hall. "Where does he keep stuff ? His clothes, personal items, anything."

Jaime stood up and led us through to one of the bedrooms. It had the appearance of a spare room, there was little that was very personal in it.

"His clothes are in that wardrobe. We have too many for our room, so he keeps his in there."

He pointed at the chest of drawers. "There's some stuff in there too. Then in the bedside table in our room. There might be things in there."

He looked around, as if trying to weigh up if he'd forgotten anything.

"Oh, and obviously, there's his personal stuff in the bathroom." He indicated over his shoulder.

"Okay," Sam said to me. "You take the drawers and the bathroom and I'll start on the wardrobe."

I headed over to the drawers. I looked back at Jaime, biting the skin on the side of his thumb, his forehead wrinkled in concern.

"Has he left anything else behind that's unusual?" I asked. "His wallet, maybe?"

Jaime went off to see if he could find it anywhere in the apartment, and Sam and I started to go through his possessions.

I rummaged through Mark's underwear and socks as Sam poked around in the wardrobe. I glanced over at him, hoping he was having more luck, but his mouth turned downwards as he shook his head.

I moved on and into the bathroom, pulling open the cabinet under the sink and sifting through razors, hair products, and medicine. Several bottles of tablets lined the edge of one of the shelves and I picked them up in turn, shaking them to see if there were pills inside. As I shook the third, or maybe fourth, bottle there was no familiar rattling of the contents.

I unscrewed the top, and wedged inside was a roll of bank notes. I pulled at the notes, struggling to remove them they were so tightly packed.

The roll was made up exclusively of fifty-euro notes. There must have been several thousand euros there.

Clutching the wad of money, I had started to move back towards the living room when Jaime came running in, an old fashioned little mobile in his hand.

"This is not Mark's phone!" he shouted as he ran between Sam and me, brandishing the phone in front of him as if it might suddenly explode. "What is this doing here?"

I said nothing, just held up the roll of fifty-euro notes.

We all exchanged glances.

I took the phone off Jaime and flipped it open. There was no need for a passcode, it just sprang into life. Sam moved behind me, placing his hand against the small of my back as he looked at the phone over my right shoulder.

I clicked on the 'calls' icon. The last call had been made a week ago, at half past two in the morning. I held the phone up to Jaime, who responded by crinkling his forehead into a deep furrow.

"I remember something," he said, his voice soft and slow. "I woke up. He was on the balcony and I could hear him speaking, but I could not hear what he is saying. He sound...how do you say?" and he pulled his brows down even more as he fought to locate the right word. "Angustiado...preocupado..."

"Worried?" I ventured. "Agitated?"

Jaime clicked his finger and pointed at me. "Agitated, yes. He sound agitated. He was speaking, five, ten minutes. Then, a while after he came back inside and I ask him 'what is wrong?' 'Nothing,' he say. He say he is asking a neighbour to turn down the music. At that time, I am thinking this sounded strange, but his phone is by the bed."

Jaime heaved his shoulders in a great shrug and held out his up-turned palms.

I said nothing. I went back to the phone and looked at the messages, starting with the most recent and reading them in reverse. They were all to and from the same number, and were all received three days ago, apart from the top message. This had been sent by Mark just yesterday, in the afternoon.

I started with the last message, scrolling down and reading the story backwards.

I got it. Where shall I meet you?

U done it now. U crossed a line. Keep an eye on ur back.

I don't have it. I gave it to your man.

U got 2 days 2 get me my dough

No!

You f 'in double crossed me

I gave it to your guy!

You hand my dough to some random candyman?

I was! I just met him.

My guy says u not there

No! I just met your guy

Lying bastard u double crossed me

I'm where you said

Where the fuck are u?

I glanced at Jaime, then Sam, then back to Jaime. "What on earth has he got caught up in?" I read the messages again, this time starting at the beginning.

Jaime threw himself face down on the sofa and once again began to cry.

Sam walked over to him and laid a hand on his quivering back. "Jaime, you need to take this to the police."

Jaime remained where he was, motionless except for the rapid rise and fall of his shoulders.

"Jaime, this sounds like Mark's got involved in something and got out of his depth. It sounds like drugs to me." He paused. "Could Mark have got involved with drug dealers?"

At that, Jaime looked up, shaking his head as he gazed at Sam.

"These messages came three days ago," Sam carried on. "Then the last one saying he'd got it. Has he been worried over the last couple of days?"

Slowly Jaime began to nod. "Yes," he said, and he stood up, nodding faster now. "Yes, he has. He was, how do you say? Preoccupied. He was all the time pacing and biting his nails. He keep going out. I ask him what is wrong but he don't tell me."

Jaime walked right up to Sam, wagging his finger as the memory came back, becoming more animated as the words tumbled out of his mouth.

"But then, just before you come," he pointed towards our apartment, "he suddenly was cheerful again. He went out for coffee and when he come back, he is all relaxed and happy."

"He certainly seemed fine last night when we went out for drinks," I said.

Sam took the phone from me and scrolled through the messages again. "This last message," he said, looking up at Jaime. "It was sent yesterday morning. That's when you said he cheered up?"

Jaime nodded.

"It says 'I got it'." I said, looking over Sam's arm.

"I wonder if he means money? Could he have borrowed money from someone?"

Jaime wrinkled his brow and moved his hand back and forth.

"We do have some friends with money," he said, dipping his head. "He could have borrowed some, yes."

"Okay." Sam moved his finger across the screen as he once again read the messages. "It sounds like he's sold drugs, or something dodgy, for someone."

Jaime gasped, his mouth flapping as if he was fighting for something to say. His face crinkled as he let out a long wail.

"Hang on, hang on," Sam said, raising his arm, "Sit down and listen to me."

He pointed at the sofa and Jaime obediently sat down. "You need to listen to me, if you want to find Mark, you need to listen."

Jaime said nothing, just blinked up at Sam expectantly.

"So," Sam carried on. "It seems that he has sold some drugs or something. Who knows why?" He shrugged. "Maybe someone told him it would be a quick way to make some money. It happens; then people get sucked in."

He coughed and paused. "Anyway, it seems that either Mark has given the money to the wrong guy, or he gave it to the right guy who then told his boss that Mark didn't pay up."

I paced across the room, then back the other way. Turning towards Jaime I said, "The police told you to go back again if he hadn't turned up by tomorrow?"

"Yeah," Jaime said and pulled at his hands. "Well, maybe we can do stuff while we wait."

Sam interjected. "I wonder if the police will take more notice now we have the texts? They took a report, maybe these will spur them on to take it more seriously."

"I'm not sure they prove much," I said. "And the last one actually says, 'where shall I meet you?' Personally, I think they'll take that as proof that he's just gone off somewhere for a few hours."

"Hmmm," Sam pondered. "You're probably right."

"So," I turned to Jaime. "Ring all your friends and see if you can find out where Mark has got the money from."

I picked up the roll of cash and counted it out on the coffee table in front of Jaime and Sam. There was five thousand euros.

"And ask everyone you know if they've seen him, if he's said anything out of the ordinary, behaved at all out of character. Anything," Sam added. "No matter how small. Anything at all."

Jaime whistled through his teeth. He looked up at the ceiling and said, "Oh, Mark my darling, what have you done?"

As we headed back to our apartment, we left Jaime sitting on the sofa hunched over his phone. He promised to let us know the minute he had any news.

We wandered out onto our balcony and took in the view for a few minutes, standing in silence as we contemplated the strange turn of events that afternoon. The sun was dipping down behind the mountains to the west, casting a pink glow across the garden, the pool and out over the sea.

I took in a deep breath and closed my eyes, letting the breath escape slowly through my lips. The weight of Sam's hands on my shoulders prompted me to reopen my eyes.

"You okay?" he asked.

"Yeah," I said, sighing and closing my eyes again. "This just wasn't quite the relaxing afternoon we'd planned."

Sam moved behind me and began to massage my shoulders. I leaned back against his kneading hands.

"Hmmm, that's nice," I said. "I do feel sorry for Jaime, and the overturned coffee table is a worry, but if it's all a misunderstanding I'm sure they'll sort it out."

Sam spun me round so that I was facing him. I looked up into his dark brown eyes and leant up to kiss him on the lips, then I rested my head against his shoulder as he encircled me with his arms.

"Let's pick up on the relaxation now," he said. "There's nothing we can do at the moment, and we need to eat."

I nodded in agreement. My grumbling tummy was reminding me that I hadn't eaten since breakfast. "Good plan," I said.

"That's why they pay me the big bucks," he said, laughing as he led me back into the apartment by my hand.

After quickly sprucing ourselves up we went out to find some dinner, pausing for a quick drink at the bar we'd been sitting at with Jaime and Mark less than twenty-four hours previously.

"I'm going to try harder with my Spanish," I said gazing at the fountain as we sipped our drinks. "When we get home I might sign up for a class, or a course or something."

"Is that before or after the self-defence course and the advanced driving course?"

"Yes, well," I said, looking back towards him. I was just trying to conjure up a good excuse as to why I still hadn't taken the self-defence course I kept promising, when my phone pinged.

"Ha! Saved by the bell," Sam said, winking.

I raised my eyebrows at him, but said nothing.

It was a message from Robert, my good friend who was caring for my newly acquired cat while I was away.

Peggy fed and watered. She wasn't too pleased when we left her again, though.

The message was accompanied by a picture of Peggy, gazing up at the camera as if imploring them not to leave her.

Aw...I think she's missing me!

Peggy had only been living with me for a few weeks but we'd got into a good routine with each other, and she loved curling up on my knee in the evening.

I took a photo of the little square with the fountain and sent it off to Robert. A message soon came pinging back.

One of our favourite spots! Enjoy, say hi to Sam, and see you soon x

After much deliberation and a quick discussion with the owner of the bar, we headed towards a little restaurant nearby and ordered. Sam chose local- caught fish and I had the gambas pil pil.

As we ate, we watched people coming and going, bustling about the busy street creating a hum of noise as conversations became louder and laughter peeled out into the night.

Despite the late hour every restaurant spilled over with people; families, couples, singles. A beautifully made-up drag queen on roller skates whizzed by, presumably on her way to perform in one of the clubs. She was soon followed by two men dressed in skimpy leather shorts and boots carrying a flag around the town advertising one of the bars.

There was little need for conversation, just watching was entertaining enough.

I wiped round my dish with the last bit of bread, soaking up the spicy juices and savouring the final mouthful. Just as I was leaning back in my chair, a message pinged through on my phone.

"It's Jaime," I said, sitting upright and holding up my phone so it would recognise my face. "Let's hope it's some good news."

I held up the phone and read the message out loud. "Have rang all in my phone and Mark's. Nothing useful so far. Have left messages with some. What now?"

I glanced over at Sam and raised my eyebrows. "What can we do at this time of night?"

Sam looked at his watch. "Nothing. To be honest, there's probably nothing much we can do tomorrow either, but that won't be the message he wants to hear."

I sighed. "Well, maybe I'll suggest we meet in the morning to touch base and see if anyone has come up with anything useful. Then we can decide what's best. It'll be almost twenty-four hours by then so at least the police should take it a little more seriously."

Sam huffed and raised one eyebrow. "Not that I think it will actually do much good. The more I think about it, the less I think they'll be able to do."

I typed out a message suggesting we discussed things over coffee in the morning, but I got no response.

After having a final drink in the restaurant, and a little glass of limoncello that the waiter brought with the bill, we sauntered back to our apartment through the still crowded streets.

"It is weird, though, don't you think?" I mused as we waited for the lift. "Those messages, and all the money. I can't stop my brain from mulling it over."

Sam nodded and ran his finger along his jaw. "I certainly don't think he's just gone for a walk. Or fallen on the coffee table, that's for sure."

Tiptoeing past Jaime's front door so as not to alert him to our return, we carefully turned the key in the lock and inched the front door closed.

Then we tumbled into bed and, tangled in Sam's arms, I fell into an exhausted sleep.

SUNDAY

———

THE SHRILL RING OF the alarm on my phone pierced through my sleep.

As I snapped awake, my dreams dissipated before I could catch hold of them, leaving only the memory of a fire bell sounding from the end of a long, dark corridor.

I leapt up to turn the alarm off, flopping back onto the bed before realising that Sam was no longer occupying his space in it.

"Ugh," I said to the empty room. "Whose idea was it to get up this early on a Sunday?"

I shuffled across the room and pulled back the curtains. Sam sat on the balcony, his ankles resting on the railings in front of him, his head leaning back, and his hands clasped together across his chest. Earbuds protruded from his ears and his right foot tapped rhythmically against the railing.

I threw on some shorts and a vest and wandered out, trying to make a little noise as I went so I didn't startle him as I approached.

"Good morning, sleepyhead," he said, removing his earphones as I approached.

He brought his legs down off the railings, and pulled me by the hand onto his lap. We sat in silence, looking out across the sea at the rising sun and watching the people sauntering, jogging and cycling around the headland.

After a few minutes I jumped up. "We better go and see how Jaime's getting on."

After knocking for some time, Jaime's door crept open and his head appeared through the gap. He stood, head bowed, and rubbed his hands through his dishevelled hair. He glanced up, blinking at us through eyes encircled by dark shadows, but he remained silent.

"C'mon," I said, taking his arm. "Let's go and find you some coffee."

We wandered over to Nogalera Square, which nestled in the centre of town, surrounded by little cafes, bars, and restaurants. We weaved our way through the tables past a mixture of locals having a swift coffee before work and tourists having a leisurely breakfast before heading to the beach.

After a few sips of coffee, the caffeine seemed to reanimate Jaime a little and he filled us in on what he'd learned from talking to his and Mark's friends. Not that much really, except it had become obvious that during the last week Mark had been anxious about something. A couple of friends had told Jaime that Mark had rung them but not really said much.

"One of our friends, Jack," Jaime continued, "said that Mark had called him around a week ago. Jack says he was, how you say, not his self?"

"Not himself, yes," I said.

"Jack tells me that Mark did not want to talk to him about anything, but did not want to end the phone call either. He say he did not think much at the time, just that it was a little raro, a little strange. Only when I call him to ask him does he think, yes that was not right, Mark was appearing to be worried about something. Like he wanted to say something but couldn't say it."

"And other friends have said the same, you said?" Sam asked.

Jaime nodded.

"But nobody has said anything about lending him any money?" I added.

"No." Jaime glanced down at his phone. "But I still have some people that did not ring me back yet."

Sam and I tried our best to distract Jaime a little, asking questions about the neighbourhood, the buildings, tourism, and anything else we could think of to try to keep his mind occupied. Jaime would engage for a few, brief, sentences but every few minutes he'd peer at his phone, his brow knotted in concern, then return to a glum silence.

After fifteen minutes that felt like an hour, Jaime's phone rang and he leapt up to answer it, moving away from the terrace of the café and into the shade of a nearby shop doorway. He paced up and down, moving into the glare of the sun, then back into the shade of the doorway, throwing his free arm into the air every now and again before running his hand back and forth through his hair.

"I hope it's good news," I said to Sam, unsure whether I wanted that more for Jaime or for myself.

Sam drank down the last remains of his coffee and glanced over in Jaime's direction.

"He's coming back," Sam said in a low whisper. "You'll find out soon."

Jaime threw himself into his chair and slumped down. Not so good news, then.

"This was a friend, José," Jaime said, pointing to his phone. "He lends Mark the money."

"He leant Mark five thousand euros?" I asked.

Jaime nodded. "He say Mark collected it Friday morning, early."

"Did Mark say what he needed it for?"

"He ring José last week sometime and say he need money. He tell José he is in some trouble with business and need money, that he will pay back as soon as he can."

The news did nothing to lift Jaime's mood and he slumped over his coffee, his shoulders drooping and his back bent almost double. I glanced at Sam and raised my eyebrows.

"Perhaps it's time you reported it to the police," Sam suggested to the top of Jaime's sagging head.

Jaime nodded but didn't move.

I rested my hand on his shoulder. "C'mon Jaime. We need to be active and even if there's not much for the police to go on, at least if they're aware he's missing, Mark will be on their radar."

He took in a huge breath, his shoulders moving up and down. Without lifting his head, he stood up.

"I'll go now," he said, stuffing his hands into the pockets of his shorts and shuffling across the square without another word.

I threw myself back in my chair and ran both hands through my hair. "I think I need another coffee," I said, laughing.

We sat in silence, attempting to relax, and sipped at our coffees while we watched people coming and going across the square. After a while, we paid and wandered off to Calle San Miguel, the main shopping street.

We sauntered along, hand in hand, glancing in the shop windows and zigzagging backwards and forwards across the narrow pedestrianised street. As we pottered down the street, we stopped to pick up a shoe, or hold out a T-shirt, but we weren't really interested in buying, it was just nice to see what was available.

At the bottom, the street opened out into a little square with a cute church to one side. The sun bounced off the bright white walls as the two bells overhead began to ring out, calling the faithful to worship.

The large church doors hung open and a little gaggle of smart-ly-dressed people hovered nearby, bibles in hand, looking as if they were waiting for the morning service to begin. I peered into the austere interior where a few more worshippers sat on stark wooden benches, their heads bowed in obeisance. Effigies of the Virgin Mary and Jesus gazed down on them, their hands spread wide in supplication.

Back in the sunlight, tourists in shorts and flip flops filled the shops, cafes and bars that lined the street and the square, a jarring contrast of two different worlds. I glanced about at the milling crowds as Sam and I passed the church and headed to the cliff-hugging slope that wound its way down to the sea front.

We passed the first few shops and bars, lingering in front of one of the restaurants to peruse the menu. People brushed past us, most of them heading towards the sharp right hand turn to continue their journey down to the beach, but a few headed up towards the town centre.

I finished reading the menu ahead of Sam and glanced around the restaurant inside, mentally adding it to my list of potentials. Through the windows at the other end of the dining room, the stunning view of the coast rolled out into the distance, the crystal blue of the sea glistening in the sunlight.

I took Sam's hand with the intention of hurrying him along, when a reflection caught my eye. In amongst the slow-moving holiday makers, a head bobbed, hurrying along. It was a head that I recognised, but it took my brain a second to comprehend where I had seen it before.

I whipped round, scanning the crowd for the bobbing head. There it was.

"Mark!" I shouted, into the mass of people, several of whom turned round, their faces crinkled in curiosity at what the shouting was about. The head stopped bobbing, turning to see who had shouted its name.

Mark's face came clearly into view, almost at the sharp right-hand corner below.

I snatched at Sam's hand, and threw a quick glance up at him, his face wrinkled in confusion. I turned back and shouted out again. "Mark!"

Sam and I pushed our way through the people milling about across the little street, nudging a few of them out of the way in our haste to get to Mark.

Mark's face was still, his head not moving. He opened his mouth, but nothing came out.

He stared in our direction, transfixed. I hurtled down towards him, my legs going faster than I could cope with and I almost tumbled into the tourists heading up in the opposite direction.

Then, as suddenly as his face had appeared, it was no longer there. I stopped, scanning the slope ahead of me.

"There," Sam shouted, pointing ahead.

To the left of the imminent right-hand bend in the slope a set of stairs headed straight down in front of a row townhouses. Halfway down the stairs and away from the crowd, a tall, long-haired man had his hands firmly clasped on Mark's arms. He was a good few inches taller than Mark and several inches wider.

"Mark!" I shouted again as we reached the top of the steps.

As Mark began to turn his head towards us, the long-haired man let go of one Mark's arms and pushed his face back in the opposite direction. Sam and I raced down the stairs in pursuit.

I was out of breath. The steps stretched out ahead of me, too many to take in. They were getting ahead of me.

Sam crashed past me, leaping down the steps two at a time, catching up on the pair ahead of us. The long-haired man looked over his shoulder as Sam advanced towards them, and he dragged Mark down the steps with a renewed urgency.

A rush of familiarity passed through me as I caught a brief glance at the long-haired man's face, but where would I have seen him before?

Mark and Mr long-hair reached the bottom of the steps, disappearing around a wall at the end with Sam in fast pursuit. He must have reached the wall barely two or three seconds after the others.

I ran with a new vigour, spurred on by the thought of catching up with Mark, but as fast as Sam disappeared behind the wall, he reappeared a look of bemusement filling his face.

As I ran up to join him, he shrugged and pointed ahead of him. Then, resting his hands on his knees to catch his breath he said, "I don't understand it. They were right here."

"C'mon," I said grabbing his arm. "They can't be far away."

The steep steps we had just run down re-joined the more gentle slope that meandered down the cliff a little lower down on its journey.

People poured up and down, pausing to catch their breath, fanning themselves, and looking at the wares displayed outside the trinket shops that lined both sides of the slope.

Sam and I scanned the heads of the crowd, weaving our way through the mass of people. At that time of day the main traffic headed down towards the beach, and we were pushing against the flow.

"Look!" I shouted. I spotted the back of the long-haired man, pushing Mark along, against the flow of the crowds.

"Mark!" I screamed at the top of my voice, ignoring the stares from those around me.

I shoved my way through, stumbling over the shallow steps in a desperate attempt to reach him. Stretching out a hand to steady myself against the wall, I picked up my pace and hurtled up to the slope.

Mr long hair was leaning against a narrow, wrought iron gate that nestled between two shops, pushing it open. He dragged Mark behind him.

Momentarily, the light bounced off a nearby window and caught something ahead, the glistening hitting my eye, and for the first time I noticed the handcuffs around Mark's wrists.

He was being dragged along, the long-haired man holding tight to the chain between Mark's wrists and yanking him through the gate. I was yards away, scrambling on legs so shaky they would barely hold me up, desperate to get to the gate.

As he disappeared into the alleyway ahead, Mark turned towards me, his face wet with tears, his lip trembling.

He shouted to me as he disappeared, "Tell Jaime I lo–"

The gate slammed.

I ran the last couple of yards and grabbed the wrought iron bars, shaking the little gate but it was firmly locked. The tiny alleyway beyond had a couple of miniature-looking doors that appeared to lead directly into the cliff face, but there was no sign of Mark or the long-haired man.

Sam joined me, and we leant against the wall snatching at breaths and clutching at our chests.

"It's way too hot to be running up and down stairs," I said, gasping in as much air as I could.

Sam brushed the sweat off his forehead with his hand, then turned to examine the gate.

The bars were close together and vertical, with decorative twists along their length. There were no horizontal bars, so no chance of a foothold. In any case the gaps at the top and bottom were small enough that a mouse would struggle to get through.

"I swear I've seen him before, Sam. The guy with Mark."

Sam turned to look at me, his right eyebrow raised in query.

I shook my head and shrugged. "I have absolutely no idea."

"Did you see where they went?" Sam asked.

"By the time I reached the gate, they'd disappeared. They must have gone in one of these little doors, here."

I glanced around me at the shops and the bustling crowds. You could walk past the dark, narrow alleyway without ever noticing it was there.

"There's no way of knowing where they lead," Sam said, craning his head back to look up. "I don't think they're any kind of dwelling. Look at where they must go."

He pointed to the wall above the doors, formed from the cliff that the slope clung to as it made its way down to the beach.

"And if you look at the configuration above that shop," he indicated a leather bag shop that was the other side of the tiny alleyway, "they clearly don't belong to that. You can see the doorway to the flat above, look."

I followed his gaze, and he was right. There was a door the other side of the shop that had a couple of names next to doorbells. I looked back down the alleyway again and peered at the little doors, shaking my head.

"Maybe they're just little store cupboards or something?"

Sam stood, hands on hips, peering through the gate. He ran his hand across his shaved head. "I think they must lead somewhere, but I can't imagine where."

He leant back against the gate and sighed. "Shall we have a beer while we think about it?"

"I think we deserve one," I said.

Sam took my hand and we carried on down the winding slope as far as the beach. We sauntered along the promenade, passing a few bars until we found one that took our fancy.

We made our way through and found a table on the terrace at the back, overlooking the sea. A rainbow flag hung limply overhead, flapping every now and again in the light breeze.

Holiday makers stretched out on sunbeds under umbrellas on the sand; a few families, but the majority were occupied by male couples.

"I see why Keith and Robert enjoy coming here," I said.

An hour or so later a waiter brought fresh drinks to the table.

"Gracias," I said as he laid them on the linen tablecloth.

"De nada," he replied, bowing his head slightly as he moved away from the table.

"Have you found anything yet?" Sam asked, and he hunched over the table to peer at my phone, shielding his eyes from the glare of the sun.

"Not yet," I said. "I'll keep looking. I'm running out of search terms."

Sam leant back in his seat and looked at his watch. "I wonder how Jaime's getting on with the police. He's been a while."

I didn't respond. Something on my phone had caught my eye, and I scanned quickly down through a travel article I'd found from some archive. I had no idea how I'd come across it, I'd been clicking from one article to another to another. I looked up at Sam.

"What?" He leant forward, placed his elbow on the table and rested his chin in his hand. With his free hand, he stroked my arm. "Have you found something?"

I glanced back down at my phone. "I think so," I said, tapping my cheek with my finger. "This article is from the eighties." I pointed at my phone. "But it is suggesting that there may be, or that there were then, some old tunnels in the cliffs here. Old tunnels that were used to smuggle goods from the beach into the town."

I looked up at him. "If there are tunnels in the cliffs, then maybe that explains the tiny door that Mark disappeared through."

Sam sat up in his chair glancing around him, as if Mark was about to appear in front of us.

"And if they lead down to the beach, then..."

His enthusiastic tone died off. He held his hands out, palms up.

"They could lead anywhere," he admitted, indicating the stretch of beach in front of us. "We have no idea where they might end up."

He looked across the road at the shops, apartment blocks and houses. "They might even lead into a building." He slumped back in his chair. "We are, actually, no further forward."

"I guess the only thing we know that we didn't before, is that Mark is probably not being held up there on the slope behind one of those little doors."

Sam ran his hand over his face. "I'm not sure if that's progress. It means we have absolutely no clue where Mark is now."

"Great," I said. "I'm really looking forward to passing on that piece of news to Jaime."

We sat back and, as if we'd coordinated it, we both picked up our drinks, took a sip, then placed the glasses back down on the table. Sam scoffed. He reached over and took my hands in his.

"So were your holidays with John this much fun?"

He glanced down at our hands, clasped together. "I'm sorry." He shook his head. "I shouldn't have said that."

"No," I agreed. "You shouldn't."

I placed one of my hands on top of his. "But it's okay. We all say things we shouldn't, and I know it's been a thing."

I glanced over towards the beach and watched a woman in a burka sitting on one of the sunbeds by the water's edge, towelling down her toddler and getting him dressed. I looked back at Sam; his deep, dark brown eyes full of something. Sorrow maybe, or regret.

"It's hard, Sam. I still miss John. But when I said I was ready to make new memories, I was right. I meant it."

He reached over and stroked my cheek with his thumb.

"I know." He nodded, and took in a deep breath. "I know. And actually, I want to hear about some of those old memories. I'd like to understand a bit more, get to know a little bit about your history."

"Ha! Well–"

The ring tone of my phone cut me off. I pulled my hands away from Sam's to answer it.

"Jaime. How did you get on?"

It turned out that the police were more interested in Mark's disappearance than they had initially appeared to be.

The officer who'd taken the report had apparently spoken to his detective colleagues and there had been another couple of mysterious disappearances which, according to Jaime, bore a striking resemblance to what had happened to Mark.

When we filled Jaime in on what we'd seen that morning, he insisted on us showing him the alleyway with the little doors behind.

We walked up and down the slope several times trying to find it. The sun was dropping down in the sky, soon to disappear behind the buildings beyond, but the heat still radiated from the stone steps.

"It was next to a leather bag shop," I said, looking around and realising that this didn't really narrow it down much as every third shop seemed to be selling leather bags.

As we rounded one of the sharp bends for the umpteenth time, I spotted it.

"There," I shouted, pointing.

It did us no good. Jaime had no idea that there might even have been tunnels in the cliffs, and even less idea where they might lead.

"Tell me one more time, what he said when you saw him," Jaime said as he plonked himself down on one of the steps and rested his chin in his hands. His initial euphoria at hearing that Mark was both still alive, and still in Torremolinos, had dissipated just as fast when he realised that Mark was still, clearly, in danger. He looked up at me, his eyes imploring to hear the words again.

I leant down and touched him on the shoulder. I looked straight into his eyes.

"He said that he loved you, Jaime. C'mon," I said, pulling him up by his elbows. "You need to rest, you look terrible. And we need to eat, we're starving."

Sam leant down and helped hoist Jaime to his feet.

"Let's meet in the morning," he said. "You really need to go home and try to sleep."

Jaime plodded off, up the steps. As he approached the bend ahead, he looked back and lifted his arm in a half-hearted waved.

"See you in the morning," he spluttered as he turned to slope off up the rest of the steep hill.

Sam looked at me and pointed both ways. "Up or down," he said.

"Let's go down," I said. "At least we can get the lift back up to the complex when we're done."

We ate locally caught fish, sitting in a restaurant on the edge of the beach, staring out at the dark sea and sipping our wine in silence.

The almost-full moon, rising in the sky above the black ocean, cast a silver glow on the water like a path leading out to the horizon. Its pull was almost palpable, calling you to walk across the sea towards it. I stared out, mesmerised.

A tap on my arm interrupted my thoughts.

"You're not listening, are you?" Sam said, and he leant back in his chair and laughed.

"I'm sorry," I said. "I'm so tired. Let's go home and go to bed."

"Now, there's an invitation I can't refuse," he said, a broad smile spreading across his face.

MONDAY

I REACHED OUT MY hand to turn off the trilling alarm that was calling out from my phone.

"Urgh," I said, trying desperately to remember why I'd thought it was a good idea to put on an alarm. A haze filled memory of sitting on the balcony drinking gin nudged its way into my brain but I couldn't, for the life of me, remember turning on an alarm.

I glanced at the phone. Nine o'clock! I threw my head back onto the pillow cursing my drunk self from last night.

Still, it was our last day here before flying home and I wanted to wander down to the beach at some point and watch the crew filming

Lost Property. So maybe being up early wasn't such a bad thing. It meant we had more time to try and catch up on a bit of sight-seeing.

After some considerable prodding I managed to wake Sam up and we pottered about for a while, eating fruit for breakfast, and preparing to go out.

"Did we agree to meet Jaime for coffee?" I asked Sam, still struggling with my gin hindered memory.

"Yeah, coffee late morning," he replied glancing at his watch. "We could head out soon and find somewhere."

We left the apartment and found a spot in Nogalera Square, under the shade of an umbrella, and ordered our drinks. The square was busy with people coming and going; locals scuttling along to their next appointments, overweight tourists sweating in their shorts and flip-flops, children running and shouting in excitement and we sat in silence taking it all in.

About halfway through our drinks, a guy with an impressive moustache came along and plonked his heavy bag down just in front of the café on the opposite side of the square. He ran his hand over his receding black hair, and began to unpack a variety of glittery cloths, some hats and gloves, and a folding table.

"It looks like we're going to get a magic show," I said as he pulled a magic wand out of his bag and laid it on the now folded-out table.

"I can see why you make such a good investigator," Sam said, glancing across at me and raising his eyebrow.

I said nothing. Across the square the magician was donning a red cape and a top hat. He spread his arms out wide and nodded to the people seated at the various bars in the vicinity, then he took his magic wand and tapped it against the side of his hat.

He lifted the hat from his head to reveal a bunch of flowers which he took and placed on the table beside him. Everyone applauded and the magician gave a deep bow. He placed the hat back on his head, tapped it again and this time lifted it up to reveal a glittering golden ball, which he set down on the table next to the flowers. The audience gave a louder applause, with several murmurs of approval rippling around the tables.

Over the next few minutes, the magician pulled a variety of objects from the seemingly empty hat, and the table was filling with balls, silk scarves, a garden gnome, and various other sundry items. Each time the applause was louder as the audience became more in awe of what the magic hat concealed.

Then, the magician took one of the balls and, after dramatically circling it above his head and around his body, he threw it high into the air, where it vanished to gasps of astonishment from the onlookers.

One by one he threw the balls in the air until they had all disappeared. The magician bowed once again, turning to the various cafes to accept the appreciation.

Next, it was the scarves' turn. The magician picked them up one at a time, flapping and shaking them before scrunching them between his hands. His mouth opened wide in mock-astonishment as he spread out his hands to reveal that the scarves had been replaced by a bunch of artificial flowers.

As he geared up towards his finale, the magician took a large silk cloth from the table and let it flow in the light breeze, twisting it this way and that to show that it was just a normal piece of cloth. He twirled round in the sunshine, dramatically holding the cloth aloft.

Then, he stood facing the square and, grasping the cloth by two corners, he held it up so that he was hidden from view. After several seconds, he threw the cloth into the air...and disappeared.

Along with everyone else, Sam and I gasped as the cloth floated to the ground, the man who had been holding it only seconds before completely vanished.

And then, to our astonishment, he started walking through the café, his hands aloft in triumph as people began to stand up, clap, and debate how he had managed to transport himself instantly a good twenty yards away.

I stood up, but not in appreciation of the magic.

"Sam, we have to go," I said as the magician began to offer his empty hat to the onlookers.

Sam looked up, his forehead crinkled in puzzlement.

"We need to pay," he said.

"Just leave some money on the table," I yelled, pulling at his arm. "I know where Mark is and we need to get to him, now!"

I sprinted off, away from the square, heading towards Calle San Miguel and the slope that would take me down to the beach. As I glanced over my shoulder, Sam was scrabbling to get to his feet. He tucked some money under his saucer and ran after me, soon catching me up.

"You call the police," I shouted at him as he ran alongside me, "and I'll call Jaime."

I fumbled in my bag for my phone without breaking my stride, leaping down the shallow steps of the slope and trying not to barge into people taking the descent a good deal more slowly.

"And tell them what?" Sam shouted at my back as he careered along behind me.

"To meet us down at the beach. We have to get to Mark."

I jerked to a halt as Sam grabbed hold of my elbow and pulled me round to face him.

"What are you basing this on? The magic tricks?"

"I know he's there, Sam," I panted, taking the opportunity to regain my breath.

"Verity, they're not going to take you seriously if we say, 'Verity saw a magic show and it gave her an idea'."

"Fine," I snapped, snatching my arm from his grip.

I flew round to face away from him, my cheeks stinging as they coloured up and I continued my run down the slope. I stabbed at my phone, calling Jaime as I hurtled towards the sea front and shouted at him to meet us by the beach.

I quickened my step, heaving for breath as I sprinted round the tight corners, finally emerging onto the road.

Without looking round to see where Sam was, I kept up the pace and ran along the sea front. By the time I reached the headland my legs were leaden, but I ploughed on regardless willing them to keep propelling me forward.

As I rounded the headland, the film set loomed ahead.

The crew were in full swing; large fluffy microphones circling the action, dancing with the cameras as they changed places to record from different angles. A massive grey boat, dragged onto the shore, bobbed in the background as it was buoyed by the waves lapping at its bows.

The director stood to one side, gesticulating silent orders to the crew and the extras as he stepped first to one side and then the other, then crouched down as he looked from a different angle at the main actors.

I ran onto the sand as a firm hand grabbed my arm, and Sam's voice bellowed against the sound of the waves. "Verity!"

I yanked my arm free and bolted across the beach before he had the chance to try to stop me, horrified by what was playing out before me.

I had to get to them, quick.

Cameras pointed in my direction as the clearly confused crew thought, perhaps, that I was part of the action. One of the camera operators moved in my direction, crouching down to get a good angle as I sprinted across the beach towards them.

The director's mouth dropped open as he threw his clipboard onto the sand and flapped his arms above his head. No one seemed to notice his frenzied gesticulations as he watched me hurtle towards him.

Behind the director a pony-tailed cameraman was pointing his camera at the same actor I'd seen the other day, the afro haircut of the actor outlined against the clear blue of the sky. I almost stalled.

The cameraman!

The long-haired man who had dragged Mark down the tiny alley-way was here, aiming a camera at the action. And I had to stop the action.

Afro guy once again held a gun outstretched in front of him, Once again it pointed directly at someone's forehead. Once again, a man knelt in front of him on a pile of blankets, pleading for his life, his hands handcuffed behind his back.

Only this time, the man was Mark.

I ran towards Afro guy, screaming as I ran. "Stop! Stop!"

Afro guy swung the gun towards me aiming it at my face and I came to a standstill, holding up my hands, palms towards him.

All the cameras had followed the commotion, maybe hoping to catch some unscripted action. I inched forwards, my hands still above my shoulders. Afro guy squeezed one eye shut and peered down the barrel towards me.

Footsteps pounded in the sand behind me, and Afro guy swung the gun towards Sam as he barrelled across the beach.

Sam stopped, spreading his arms wide to show he was weapon free. As the gun moved in Sam's direction I took a few steps forwards, but the barrel of the gun moved back towards me.

Sam and I made tentative steps, the gun vacillating between us, until I took the plunge and barged my shoulder into Afro guy with as much force as I could muster.

He stumbled onto the sand, the gun flying from his hands and twisting in the air before it landed on the blankets, six feet or so in front of Mark. Afro guy attempted to stand up, but Sam charged in and thrust his foot into Afro guy's chest, forcing him back onto the sand.

The long-haired cameraman threw his camera to one side and rushed to Afro guy's aid, just as the director ran onto the blankets and pulled at Mark's hair, dragging him to his feet. Several of the extras slipped away across the beach as the camera man swooped in and grabbed the gun, aiming it towards Sam who was attempting to wrestle Afro guy onto his front.

Both Sam and Afro guy ignored the pointed gun and the cameraman whipped round, about to point it at me, but he was apparently distracted by distant shouts, ever louder and coming closer at a fast pace.

"Mark! Mark!" Jaime was sprinting towards us, stumbling as he ran across the sand. A crowd was gathering on the paseo behind him, heads bobbing as people peered around each other to get a view of the action.

"What the fuck..." the director shouted in perfect English as he tightened his grip on Mark's hair. He pointed at the cameraman who was holding the gun, then at Mark.

"Mátalo," he shouted, throwing Mark down onto the blankets. "Kill him."

At that, the blankets moved, wriggling slowly at first, but then more frenetically as arms, legs, then the body of an actor appeared, his clothes a carbon copy of Mark's. His brow furrowed as he thrust his hands into the air.

"¡Espera!" he shouted. "Wait!" He scrambled out of the way, clutching handfuls of sand in his haste to get clear.

Sam's mouth flapped open. "But..." he started to say, then, without finishing his sentence he straddled Afro guy's back and pinned him to the ground.

"Mark!" Jaime shouted again as he neared his stricken boyfriend, but his words were drowned out by the shrill whirr of approaching sirens.

Jaime dragged Mark to his feet, as the camera crew and microphone operators abandoned their equipment, scattering in different directions. Sam sat astride Afro guy as he fought to escape, pushing his face sideways into the sand.

The director and the actor dressed like Mark hurtled across the beach to the boat, leaping on board and throttling up the engine. They'd not made it off the sand when a police boat rounded the headland, and the droop of the director's shoulders said that he knew the game was up.

We sat outside the bar in the little square with the fountain, the rainbow flag flapping gently in the wind. Mark took a sip of his wine, as Jaime gently stroked his knee, gazing across at him.

"I can't believe how close I came to losing you," he said, a tear bubbling in the corner of his eye, not for the first time that evening.

"How did you figure out what was going on?" Mark asked.

Sam put his arm around my shoulder. "Verity had a moment," he said. He turned to look at me, a grin plastered across his face.

I glanced down at my lap and pulled in my lips, then looked up at the two guys who had been strangers only a few days ago.

"It was the magician, disappearing and then reappearing," I said. "It made me think about things not being what they look like, and how easy it is to distract the human eye. How we make sense of what we see, because we see what we expect. I realised that the blanket they'd used to cover up the man they shot the other day was not the same as the one they pulled off the actor who was pretending to be him."

I paused. "I wonder what they did with the body?" I said, more to myself than anyone else.

"Everyone assumed it was the same chap," Sam continued. "Because it was a movie, right? The guy was only acting being dead."

"I can't believe how fast that police officer was," Jaime interjected. "Did you see him run after the cameraman?"

"It was the director's face that got me," I said. "As the police boat approached. It was defeat and anger and a little bit of 'can I make a run for it' all mixed in."

"What about that guy with the beach umbrella?" Sam asked. "Just walking down for a day of sunbathing. He felled that crew member like he was chopping down a tree!"

"Then his rather large wife sat on top of him," Jaime added.

"I think one or two of them did actually get away," I said. "But there was so much abandoned equipment they must have loads of fingerprints and stuff."

"The detective inspector told me they'd been hunting these drug dealers for months," Sam said. But it was only recently they'd escalated to murder. Of course, they thought Mark had crossed them..." He trailed off, not needing to say what would have happened if we hadn't arrived when we did.

"Cheers!" Mark said and raised his glass. "To Verity and Sam."

"Cheers," we all said as we clinked glasses.

"Drinks are on me, all night," Mark announced. "And whenever you two come back to Torremolinos, drinks will always be on me."

"Cheers to that," I said. "I hope we make it back very soon."

MEET TRUDEY MARTIN

Trudey Martin is from Lincoln, England a beautiful city that provides the stunning backdrop for her novels. She has worked in social care for many years and likes to incorporate this experience into her writing. Trudey has previously written and directed plays and several academic articles but hadn't until recently published a novel. Her first, No Deadly Medicine, introduces Verity Spencer as the protagonist. It is set in Lincoln and London and delves into the world of child trafficking. Trudey has always enjoyed reading suspense, crime and mystery thrillers and wanted to create a resourceful heroine, who she says contains elements of herself, but is "much more confident and resilient than I would ever be!"

Find out more about Trudey at trudeymartin.co.uk, where you can download the free story Even Money and sign up to her readers' group to receive news, gifts, enter competitions and get advance notice of forthcoming releases.

THE HOUSE OF TERROR

STEVE DICKINSON

THE NORTH-WESTERLY GATHERED PACE across the snow-capped Austrian alps, whipped along the Danube and cut through Budapest like a knife.

On Vaci Street, Zsigmond Horvath dodged a spinning maelstrom of cigarette packets, newspapers, and discarded posters. He raised the collar of his green woollen greatcoat and tugged on the peak of his flat cap until his eyes were barely visible.

Fearful of being recognised, he scurried past the surging crowd outside Nyugati station. It took him twelve minutes to reach the headquarters of the AVH Secret Police, where he entered through the side door and lit a cigarette.

The armed sentry locked and bolted the door behind him.

60 Stalin Street, or the House of Terror as it was known, would be the last place on earth most Hungarians would go to seek refuge in 1956. For Horvath, it was his only chance of safety, until the madness died down, and the government restored order.

Every evening this week, after his work in the basement was done, he had stood with colleagues on the roof terrace and observed the demonstrations play out on the streets below. Crazy workers and students had overturned the giant statue of Stalin and shouted, "Ruskies go home."

Some even climbed the union building opposite the statue and hauled down the huge red star from its roof.

Horvath said to the sentry, a man in his forties, twice his own age, "When Gero orders the crackdown, our basement will be overloaded. We'll be paid more overtime than we can dream of."

The sentry was unimpressed. Instead, he looked grim-faced. "Why are you here? Most have fled. The rumour is, we are their next target."

Horvath turned and walked away. He swallowed hard. The place seemed eerily quiet. The sound of his own boots echoed throughout the atrium.

When he passed through the lobby, a brick crashed through a pane of glass and landed at his feet. Angry faces glared at him.

One shouted, "Hey, you with the green coat. Open up, you bastard, and come out with your hands in the air!"

Horvath stood rooted to the spot, open-mouthed, weighing up his diminishing options. It seemed he now had two choices. He could be the first the enraged mob laid their hands on, or he could run, and they could try to find him.

But where would be the safest place?

Back in the atrium, he scanned the landings of the upper floors. He was certain other AVH staff and officers were holed up there, armed and ready to shoot anyone who came their way. He could be mistaken for a rioter.

His mind was made-up.

He turned and bolted down the flights of worn stone steps that led to the basement; steps he had trodden hundreds of times. Today the stench was familiar, but the normal soundtrack of torture was absent.

His call was tentative. "Hey, who's on duty?"

Only groans greeted him.

Horvath removed the key ring from his belt. He unlocked the barred gate to the compound and entered warily, leaving the gate unlocked behind him.

Each day, at the start of shift, Horvath received orders from the duty officer. Their daily mantra was: 'Don't only guard them, hate them!'

Some prisoners were detained here for days, others for weeks or even months. They were fed only once a day, with their ration of one cupful of bean soup and one hundred and fifty grams of bread.

Some died here. Some were released, so they could spread the word of fear back to their family and neighbours. In every cell, twenty-four hours every day, seven days a week, a lightbulb shone brightly. For the prisoners, there were no days or nights, no days of the week. Just endless torment, and sleep depravation.

When time had been destroyed, the rest came easily.

Each day, Horvath would be ordered to 'look after' several of the prisoners, who were known to him and the other guards only by their numbers. He could decide in which order he would deal with them, and use whichever technique took his fancy.

It was not his role to carry out interrogations. His job was merely to soften up the prisoners for the inspectors upstairs to do their work.

Horvath favoured water. He and another guard would lay their prisoner face up on a board, where they would be bound around their wrists and ankles. The board would then be inclined, with the head tilted downward.

After covering their face with a cloth, Horvath would pour buckets of water over the cloth. Invariably, water would be inhaled, resulting in gagging and total panic.

Afterwards, he would take his prisoners to a special cell, point to a line of steel-cored hoses on the wall and say, "Choose the one you want." Then, taking the chosen weapon, he would beat the man senseless.

No records were kept of the treatments handed out. If a prisoner died in their hands, no one in the outside world would ever know.

In the distance, he could hear raised voices. Horvath tried to stay calm. He went to the duty officer's room, unlocked the safe cupboard, and took the bunch of keys. Next, he unlocked one of the cells and entered.

In the corner lay a pile of filthy sack cloths, and next to them stood an overflowing bucket of excrement. He yanked away the sacks.

Cowering beneath them was a battered body, covered from head-to-toe with open wounds, bruises and dried blood. A pair of pale blue eyes stared up at Horvath. The eyes belonged to a young Catholic priest who had been arrested on charges of treason. Now, huddled in a foetal position, stripped bare of his sacks, the man shivered.

Little was known about him, for despite the treatment he had received from Horvath and the other guards, the priest had never spoken a single word. The guards believed him to be mute.

Horvath removed his green greatcoat and quickly stripped out of the rest of his clothes, placing them upon on the sacks. With a cold October wind blowing through the tiny, barred window, the cell felt like a refrigerator. Goosebumps covered his newly naked body from head to toe. The slimy, ice-cold concrete floor felt disgusting under the soles of his bare feet.

Horvath placed his hands under the prisoner's arms and hauled him into a seated position.

Prisoner 2387 squirmed. His reluctance to be manhandled once again came as no surprise, but Horvath had a job to do and little time.

"Let me help you into these clothes," he said.

Horvath dressed the prisoner with the clothes he himself had arrived in. Finally, he hauled the man to his feet and hung the green greatcoat over his shoulders like a cape. The weight of the coat was too much for the prisoner's frail and damaged body, and he slumped to the floor like a sack of potatoes.

Both men had wiry frames, but Horvath had not been starved and tortured, so was by far the stronger of the two. He hauled the prisoner out of his cell and across the corridor to the duty officer's room, where he propped him up in the only chair.

There was a small sink inside the room. Horvath filled a bowl with water and washed as much of the filth and blood from the prisoner's face as possible.

"That's better," he said. "Stay there. Someone will be along soon, and you'll be home before you know it."

The distant crack of gunfire rang out.

Horvath felt the urge to explain. "My duty is to protect our government from its fascist, capitalist, and reactionary enemies, including the Catholic church. There's nothing personal. Do you understand?"

The prisoner said nothing, but his blue eyes flickered with some sort of recognition, and the ends of his lips turned slightly upwards.

Horvath left the prisoner propped in the chair and returned to the now vacant cell. He poured the contents of the excrement bucket onto the floor. Bracing himself, he rolled around in the puddle before pouring what remained in the bucket over his blonde hair.

Grabbing a piece of sackcloth, he wiped the worst of it from his eyes. Then he pulled the remaining sacks over his filthy, shivering body and sat leaning against the wall.

A gang of armed men burst into the basement. Through his half-open cell door, Horvath watched the moving shadows. He listened to the men shouting, as they discovered the appalling conditions and, one by one, came across the incarcerated prisoners.

He listened expectantly, waiting for them to discover the man in a green greatcoat, seated in the duty officer's chair. That moment would surely be announced with gunshots, and Horvath would be free.

When two of the men entered Horvath's cell, he played his role. Slowly, they helped him to his feet. One of his rescuers removed his own coat and placed it around Horvath's filthy body. Using the men as crutches, he hobbled to the cell door and peered out.

He could hardly believe his eyes. For there was 2387, still wearing the green greatcoat, held in the embrace of one of the armed men.

Horvath's heart sank.

As their hug unfolded, the priest turned his head and fixed his gaze on the shit-covered wretch that Horvath had become.

The priest's battered face somehow looked serene. He addressed Horvath in a cracked yet calm voice.

"May God go with you, brother. The torture you have received has been the greatest inflicted on any of us. Everyone deserves a second chance. Take yours and find a better life."

Horvath was shocked, hardly able to believe his ears. For forty days and forty nights, he and the other guards had tortured this man to within an inch of his life. In all that time, the prisoner had not uttered a single word.

"Am I free to go?" Horvath mumbled.

The priest nodded.

Horvath had never seen humanity such as this. He grabbed hold of the priest's cold hands and squeezed them. "I shall forever be in your debt."

The priest's pale blue eyes fixed upon his gaze. "Until we meet again."

Horvath's overwhelming emotion was one of relief.

His two rescuers led him up the stone steps. Horvath was taken home in the back of a delivery van.

FOR THE FOLLOWING DAYS, he went into hiding. Later, he heard some AVH men were clubbed to death. A few others tried to run but were caught and killed. Some of the dead were strung up by their heels.

The next week, the city was besieged by the Russian onslaught. Four thousand Soviet tanks and upwards of 140,000 troops swept into Budapest and quashed the revolt.

When Horvath was certain the Russians had recaptured the city and established a new communist government, he reported back for duty at the House of Terror. He was shocked to hear the AVH had been disbanded, but a communist official took him to one side and explained that a new special police group was being formed.

Given his record within the AVH, the official said Horvath would be appointed as an officer. "You'll have a car. Your job will be just about the same, but this time you'll wear a blue uniform, and we're going to call you *R Troops*."

For a moment, Horvath remembered the prisoner-turned-judge. "Did the Russians round up many Catholic priests?"

"They shot hundreds and jailed many more. There will be a ban on church services and publishing religious books and pamphlets."

Horvath smiled. His relief was complete.

He and prisoner 2387 would surely never meet again. Thanks to communism, order in his world had been restored.

He thought, how good it was to be on the winning side of history.

———

ACKNOWLEDGEMENTS:

To the brave men and women who provided eyewitness accounts to the peerless James A. Michener, which he wrote about in his book, The Bridge at Andau. Originally published in 1957 by Random House.

And to my friend, Julianna Lancaster, who was shot at from the Parliament Building in Budapest in October 1956, before she and her family escaped to London in 1957.

———

MEET STEVE DICKINSON

Steve Dickinson was born in 1957 in Liverpool, England, just too late to become the fifth Beatle. Now a recovering international businessman turned author, Steve says, "Ultimately, stories are the only way to change the world, which makes writers very powerful people."

He lives with his wife in the beautiful English county of North Yorkshire, and is a proud father and grandfather. When he's not writing, Steve is a keen foil fencer and tennis player. He keeps himself fit for his sports by working out in the gym and doing Pilates.

Set in Budapest, Hungary, a city he has worked and explored extensively, *Confession* is Steve's first novel.

Visit Steve at stevedickinsonbooks.com and sign up for your own free copy of the gripping thriller *Confession*, the first novel in the Detective Erika Kelemen series.

WHEN A PLAN COMES TOGETHER

SHARON A MITCHELL

UPSCALE TRASH - A bar for those wealthy enough to indulge in slumming, without the risk of running into *those* kinds of people. A haven where people with money could let down their hair, don those stylishly ripped jeans and t-shirts that cost more than a week's salary for an average Joe.

"I gotta go, Jackson. The old ball and chain invited her parents for dinner. I skipped out the last time but can't afford to do that again. Gotta keep on daddy's good side."

Paul pushed his high stool back from their polished, round table and stood, buttoning his coat.

"Ah, Paul, the bill's not paid."

Paul clapped his old roommate on the shoulder. "Your turn, mate."

Jackson shook his head. "No can do."

They'd been drinking steadily since they arrived here after work. Twice, the waitress had cleared the empty glasses from their table. With each drink costing 20 bucks, the tab built up.

"Man, you're not broke again, are you?"

HUMBLE ROOTS WERE ONE way to describe Jackson's upbringing. They got by, barely.

His dad ran a sewing machine in a shoe factory; his mother cleaned offices on weekends. They believed they instilled values in their only child, values of honesty and hard work.

Of those, only the hard part stuck. He wanted no part of hard.

Smart enough to win a partial scholarship to Vassar, Jackson got his foot in the door. Sadly, that full ride was beyond his abilities, which meant taking fewer classes and working part-time just to eat.

The free tuition and books, plus his own job in Vassar's Gordon Commons Cafe, allowed him to pay the rent on the rat-hole, one-room apartment he rented off campus.

He lied on his job application, and no one checked to ensure he had the cooking experience he claimed. He'd never even made a grilled cheese sandwich at home.

YouTube was a wondrous thing, and he learned enough to pass. Although there were other jobs on campus, cooking kept him behind the scenes where he wouldn't run into any classmates, classmates who never gave a thought to where money came from. It was just always there, with parents who kept the old bank account topped up.

Bad karma, or just plain bad luck, prevented Jackson from being born into such households.

Bursting with pride at their valedictorian son, his parents had expected Jackson to go to college, but the local state college. That way he could live at home and keep his part-time job at the supermarket.

How would *that* look on his resume?

Jackson had a pretty good idea, and for the career streams he had in mind, he needed a school with some prestige.

In those endless hours researching colleges, Vassar kept coming to the top of his list.

He also needed money.

His parents obliged unwillingly, though. A car accident ended both their lives—and Jackson's money woes—making dreams possible.

Vassar was Ivy League. Maybe not the best, but respectable.

It was known for being a woman's college—not exclusively, but many young women from well-to-do families headed there. Perfect!

A wealthy heiress was exactly what he needed.

PAUL WAS ON HIS phone.

"Meggsy, I'm sorry, honey, but I'm going to have to miss dinner." He lowered his voice. "I got a buddy here who is in a bad way. I've tried to get away, but I can't leave him alone this evening. He's had a tough breakup, and you never know what he'll do."

He listened.

"No, not everyone has a marriage like ours. Give my love and regrets to your parents. I'll make it up to them."

Weird noises came through the tiny speaker. Paul rolled his eyes at Jackson. "Yeah, love you too, Snookums."

"Snookums?" Jackson asked.

"Ya do what ya gotta do," Paul said. He sat back down. "Thanks, buddy. Your state of near suicidal grief gave me a legitimate excuse to avoid spending hours with my in-laws."

"So next time I see Meg, she'll grill me about my supposed break-up?"

"Wouldn't be surprised. Make it good, will ya?"

They'd covered for each other so often over the years; it was second nature, perfecting their woeful faces, and pity-inducing stories.

"Enough, man. This has gone on long enough." Paul put his arm around Jackson's shoulders. "We need a plan to get you hitched and hitched well." He raised his arm, signaling the waitress. "Two rusty nails on the rocks and keep them coming."

"Paul, I can't pay."

"Neither can I. But Daddy-O can. Business expense, entertaining clients. Pays to marry the boss's daughter." The two men clinked glasses.

"Now, let's see about getting you hitched."

ELIZABETH BRUSHED HER LIPS with the damask napkin. She folder her hands in her lap to keep them still, waiting for just the right opportunity.

"Mother, Daddy," she said when she judged the moment was right. "It came."

"What's that, dear?" Melody, her mother, asked.

"My acceptance letter came. From Vassar."

Her father frowned. "I thought we had talked about this."

That meant *he* had voiced his opinion. No one disagreed with Winston Abberly.

"Yes, Daddy, we did."

Thankfully, because of her mother's training, her voice remained steady. A lady did not allow her emotions to take control. "I know you'd prefer I attended Princeton, but I really want to go to Vassar."

"Vassar isn't renowned for its business training; Princeton is."

"True, Daddy."

Now was not the time to broach her dream of interior design, rather than entering the family business. One thing at a time; this was her only opportunity to get away.

"I'm confident your acceptance letter from Princeton will arrive any day. Perhaps I'll have a chat with the Dean this week to speed that up."

He held his knife poised over his chateaubriand. "You can send Vassar a polite note declining their offer."

This was it—a first for Elizabeth. "No, Daddy."

Melody sucked in a breath. No one—but no one—said no to Winston Abberly the Third.

"I'm sorry, but I'm going to Vassar." She hastened to add. "I could go to Princeton for grad school."

Not if she could help it, but that promise might appease Daddy.

"Excuse me." Winston centered his knife and fork in the exact radius of his plate. "I find this conversation distasteful." He rose and left the room.

"Now see what you've done?" Melody turned to her daughter. "You've upset your father."

Their world revolved around not rocking the boat, and certainly never going against Winston Abberly's wishes.

"Mother, I don't wish to upset you or Daddy. I'm eighteen now and get to choose what I want to do with my life. Vassar is where I want to attend college."

"But you can't live at home if you go there."

Exactly.

She stifled that disloyal thought. She loved her parents, she truly did, and owed them so much, but did she owe them her life?

———

As THE LONE CHICK in the nest, there were times when Elizabeth Abberly found life stifling. Immediately, whenever those feelings surfaced, she stuffed them down where they belonged.

After all, it was her fault her parents now had only one child.

After all the heartache they'd endured, she owed it to Winston and Melody Abberly to not rock the boat.

Peace was the rule in their household. On those rare occasions when dissent arose, they handled quietly it, with refinement.

One sentence from her mother halted any objection or independent thought Elizabeth harbored. "Your father wouldn't like that, would he?"

Life within the walls of their estate revolved around keeping Daddy happy. Why not? It was his due; Winston provided for them and provided well.

The third generation of Abberlys, Winston never rested on the laurels of his ancestors, but increased their real estate empire. It was a given that Elizabeth would follow in his footsteps, taking a role—but not a dominant role—in his business.

She was a girl, after all.

THERE WERE A LOT of "Elizabeth, this is not like you"s over the next month.

True, it wasn't like her. Usually, she'd roll over at the least sign of displeasure from either of her parents. After the grief she'd caused them, she just could not pile on more.

Until now.

Once the notion of getting out of this house, out from under her parents' exacting expectations took hold, it wouldn't shake loose.

So now she'd done it—lived through those icy meals the three of them shared in the formal dining room of her parents' mansion when she would not bow to their will.

MOVE IN DAY.

While both parents accompanied some students, just Melody came with Elizabeth. Meetings in Europe prevented Daddy's presence, although Elizabeth suspected if not those meetings, something else would have stood in the way. Daddy arranged for his private plane to take her and her mother to Newburgh, less than 20 miles from Vassar, and for a waiting limousine to drive them to the campus.

Even if the plan was not his, Winston Abberly must have his hand in it.

"Your father is not going to like this."

Melody was right.

Elizabeth ignored her mother's presence as she hung up clothes in the tiny closet and emptied her suitcase into the one set of drawers. "At least I have a private room."

"Private? You call this private when there are 20 other people with you on this floor, and you all share the same bathroom?" She shattered.

"It's fine, mother. It'll be a good way to get to know my fellow students."

"Do you *want* to know them? We don't know where they come from, or if they're the sort you should associate with. You know, we've always been so careful about your friends growing up."

Too true. Only children of those in the right social circle were allowed over to play. There was no blanket invitation to socialize with just any of the students attending her private school.

Now, her social circle could broaden. With it costing over $60k a year in tuition alone, it's not like riffraff weren't already weeded out, as her father said. Initially, Winston had threatened to not pay her college expenses if she didn't attend the school of her choice.

Luckily, Elizabeth's maternal grandmother had left her a sizeable trust—hers to control as of her 18th birthday. When Elizabeth spoke with the family attorney to see about accessing funds to pay for Vassar, the lawyer contacted Winston to let him know about Elizabeth's plans.

Winston stepped in, and the two men convinced Elizabeth it was in her best interests to sign agreements tying her grandmother's inheritance into a trust with only a yearly annuity.

She'd ruffled feathers enough this year. Signing wasn't a big deal. Daddy would pay for her degree. After that, she'd be making her own money. Independence was in sight.

She'd be free of a man controlling her life.

"You're a bit of a lost cause." Paul was definite.

"It's got to be the right woman. If you screw up too often, and end up with a slew of divorces, it gets harder to convince the next chick to take a chance on you." Jackson eyed his friend. "Isn't that what you've found?"

"Yeah. Two divorces, and I only came out richer from one of them. Damned pre-nups. With number two, she made more than me, so I could claim alimony, but they were fighting me on it. Her daddy wanted me to go away, so he gave me a settlement. It helped."

"Enough?"

"Not for the way I like to live. Now I'm back to living off my wage."

"Sucks, doesn't it? I plan on marrying so it sticks. That's why I'm choosy."

"What's to choose from, apart from she has to be rich?"

"Looks. If you're going to be tied to a woman, you at least have to be able to stand looking at her and not be ashamed to have her hanging on your arm."

"Tied on paper, anyway," Paul said.

"Wasn't that the cause of your first divorce?"

"I hadn't learned how to be discreet then. I'm wiser now."

"I have standards," said Jackson. "I couldn't stand to be around an airhead either, no matter how pretty she was."

"Hanging out at Vassar, you don't come across many imbeciles."

"True. I've got my eye on a woman I think might fit my needs..."

———

"ELIZABETH! ELIZABETH ABBERLY, IS that you?"

Heads turned. Yelling across the commons at Vassar wasn't done, but Jackson couldn't risk missing the woman he'd been searching for.

Elizabeth turned to see who hailed her. She colored as the man ran up to her. They'd dated two years ago, and she'd thought it might lead to something.

That was until Mother and Daddy met him.

"Isn't he rather common?" Melody had asked.

"Make him wait," Winston said. "See if he's after more than your money. See what he makes of himself." How could they not believe that a man would want her for herself?

"I've never told him my net worth," she defended. "Nor has he any idea who my family is."

"You're an Abberly," Winston said. "Doesn't take much work to research our name."

"Jackson wouldn't do that. He's not like that. He's keen on getting his MBA and making a career for himself."

"I could tell he was keen."

Winston only used sarcasm when it looked like someone wasn't immediately falling in with his line of thinking.

In the end, Jackson did her a favor by turning his attentions elsewhere. That had hurt. But it stiffened her resolve to go her own way.

While her parents' disapproval of her attending Vassar instead of a university of their choice had dimmed over the last three years, Elizabeth's next plan would raise even more objections.

To Winston, no major was acceptable except for business. Frivolously studying art history was not for Abberlys.

"Maybe if your brother was here to take over, you could indulge yourself. As it is...."

Winston let the rest trail off. Rarely did he or Melody mention their lost son, the true heir.

It was Easter dinner at home, nearing the end of the five-course meal. Elizabeth held in reserve her one bargaining chip.

"What I want is to specialize in interior design. I think I could be an asset to your real estate holdings, rather than you having to outsource that type of work."

There was a pause while Melody looked to her husband to see how he'd take this news. It wasn't *his* idea, so you never knew.

Winston finished chewing his roasted duck. "That could work. We'll think about it."

In her father's words, that 'we' meant 'he'. She took a big breath and called on her inner strength, refusing to allow any tremors to enter her voice.

"I have thought about it, Daddy." She swallowed. "I have a plan."

Four raised eyebrows met her impertinence.

Elizabeth rushed on. "The only Ivy League school offering a major in interior design is Cornell and the waiting list to get in is years long."

"Don't worry about it. Let me see who I know and what we can do about this. I can pull whatever strings are needed."

"Thank you, Daddy, but you don't need to go to that effort. I have an alternative."

This was the hard part. "Vassar has a reciprocal agreement with the Glasgow School of Art. It's a year-long study abroad program. They only take in a few foreign students each year." She searched her parents' faces. "I applied, and they accepted me. I leave in May."

Silence.

Winston carefully placed his fork and knife perfectly centered on his plate. He pushed back from his place, laced his hands together, and leaned forward.

"I'm not sure I understand. This is the first time you've mentioned an interest in interior design."

"Yes, Daddy. I've been thinking about it for some time but haven't been here to discuss it with you."

"They don't have phones or email at Vassar?"

It was never good when sarcasm entered his speech. She'd handled this all wrong.

"Now, Winston, don't upset yourself. I'm sure Elizabeth is simply throwing around some ideas."

"Melody, I don't get upset—"

"No, Mother. I've been accepted—"

"When exactly were you going to tell us that my daughter planned to flit across the ocean?"

"I'm not flitting, Daddy. I'm going with a purpose. Booked a plane ticket."

At the look on her mother's face, she added, "First class, of course." She rushed on. "I'll be in school there for 15 months, then return to Vassar for my final year. Combined with what I'll take at Glasgow, and the classes I've taken at Vassar, I'll end up with a Bachelor of Science in Interior Design, on top of my B.A. in Art History."

Elizabeth looked between her parents, silently pleading for them to see that this was a good thing, to support her in what she was doing.

Nope.

It wasn't Daddy's idea, nor had she discussed her thoughts before acting on them. In their micromanaged household, nothing happened without Daddy's knowledge and consent.

Well, that needed to change.

'Twas meant to be, he conceded.

Jackson had searched every feasible way to find Elizabeth this past year, all to no avail. No one on campus had seen her, not that she socialized much.

Nothing in the society pages to show where she was. Often, among the wealthy, that meant a discreet stay in some posh rehab facility, but that didn't fit with the Elizabeth he'd known.

Known and lost. His fault.

Yeah, he got that. He'd had her—the hook set—and just as he carefully reeled her in, something shiny flew by, distracting him. Something with shiny, red hair, a figure to turn any red-blooded man's head, and clothes leaving little to the imagination.

Far more fun than the demure, wait-until-marriage Elizabeth Abberly.

Fun? Yes. A good time? Oh, for sure. A loaded Daddy? Nope, at least not enough to suit his needs.

She'd turned his head, that's all he could say. When he faced front again, Elizabeth was gone. Her, and his ticket to the good life.

But that was in the past. Now, his ideal woman was back, and so was his Plan A.

Jackson threw his arms around Elizabeth, lifting her off her feet, and swinging her in a circle.

She remained stiff.

Oops. He'd forgotten about that stick up her backside. No public displays of affection for this girl. It simply wasn't done.

Gently, he set her down. Placing his hands on her shoulders, he left a respectable distance between their bodies and grinned down at her.

"Sorry about that; I got carried away. It's so good to see you again." He gave her another quick hug. "How have you been? *Where* have you been?"

"Hello, Jackson. I'm well, thank you. I've been in Scotland."

"Holidaying?" Man, wouldn't that be the life?

She shook her head. "I was in school at Glasgow University."

"But you're back now?"

This time, she nodded. "I'm in my final year now."

"Glasgow! Seriously? I've always wanted to visit Scotland. What was it like? Have you got time for a coffee? I'd love to catch up with you."

Without giving her time to object, he linked arms with Elizabeth, guiding her toward the street and Starbucks. As they walked, he chatted, covering up his frantic efforts to remember what Elizabeth's favorite beverage was at the place.

If he got it right, that had to give him brownie points, right?

SETTLED AT THE SMALL, round table, Elizabeth cradled her Cold Brew with Cold Foam, surprised Jackson had remembered her favorite cold drink. The smile he flashed at her suggested he remembered more than just that; the man looked genuinely pleased to see her.

For her part, caution stifled her response.

When she'd first left home for college, Daddy's lectures stayed with her. "Be on your guard. Your name goes before you and people will want a piece of the heiress. Both men, and women. Take care to judge what people are after."

Perhaps good advice, but not conducive to making friendships. That was all right; she wasn't used to having close friends, anyway. Acquaintances, sure. Buds, no.

For a while, she'd thought she'd found something more with Jackson. He didn't seem to care about her money. He paid for everything on their dates, never asking her to foot the bill, never asking about her financial status. He just seemed interested in her.

Until he wasn't. Until something bright and shiny caught his eye—a beautiful woman, fun and outgoing in ways Elizabeth could never hope to be. Plus, she was in an MBA program like Jackson. How could quiet Elizabeth hope to compete? She couldn't, and she wouldn't.

In her family, negative emotions were not expressed. But she must have been especially morose when home one weekend, shortly after she'd seen Jackson around campus with his arm around a stunning redhead. Not usually the prying type, Melody found Elizabeth in the sunroom and asked if something was wrong.

Even knowing she was supposed to say everything was fine, Elizabeth broke protocol and confessed the end of her relationship with Jackson.

Melody's eyes expressed more sympathy than did her words. "That's what young men do—they play the field. Better now than if you'd married the fellow." She turned the page in her magazine before looking up again. "Your father never did like him, you know."

"I know, Mother."

Would he like *anyone* she brought home? Anyone *he* didn't choose?

Now she was back from Scotland, older and wiser. Maybe Jackson was, too.

He certainly seemed interested now; his eyes never once left her face, never roamed the Starbucks coffee shop full of gorgeous co-eds from the nearby campus.

"Tell me all about Scotland," Jackson said.

Elizabeth stirred some of the foam into her coffee. What to say? During a recent dinner party at her parents', a guest had asked the same thing. She'd launched into some of the more fascinating aspects of her courses, her animation at sharing making her forget to study the faces of the listeners. It wouldn't do to bore people at the dining table, but that is exactly what she'd done. Only her mother's muffled throat clearing behind her napkin brought her out of her enthusiasm to notice the politely blank looks on the faces of her mother's guests.

So, what to say to Jackson? Short, amusing anecdotes are always appropriate, her mother had taught her, as long as they raise nothing controversial.

"I worked at a cattery."

Jackson sputtered some of his coffee. Wiping his chin, he checked he'd heard correctly. "You worked at a cathouse?"

She nodded. "They call them catteries in the UK."

"You?" Maybe there was more to this woman than he'd noticed before. "Tell me more about this cattery."

"At first, I just donated to their charity. Seemed like a good cause—getting them off the streets."

"Of course, always a good thing, getting away from that life."

"A woman from my floor in the dormitory worked there and mentioned they needed help, so I went along."

"Help, ah, with rehabilitation?"

"That too, for the traumatized ones. But also, basic day-to-day help. This cattery had two parts—rehab and re-homing, plus a breeding program."

Jackson's brow furrowed. "And *you* were involved in this?"

"Not the breeding program, of course. That was specialized. Did you know that different breeds of cats are raised for different purposes?"

"Are we actually talking cats here, like the furry, four-legged kind?"

Now Elizabeth was confused. "Of course. What did you think I was talking about?"

"Never mind. My mistake. Go on, this is fascinating."

"They also had a boarding program where people could bring their cats when they had to be away. That was my first volunteer job, petting and playing with those cats so they wouldn't be so lonely."

"Petting cats. Well. Who knew?"

"I didn't. Growing up, we never had pets. Daddy was allergic. Mother felt they were too messy to have around the house. Not that she did the cleaning herself, but she felt it wasn't fair to the staff to add to their workload."

"Sounds reasonable."

"What I found out in Scotland is that I must have inherited Daddy's allergies. It took a few weeks to develop, but every time I played with the cats, I got stuffed up and my eyes got red and itchy. It got worse, so the cattery manager switched me to clerical work."

"Interesting." Reaching across the table, Jackson took her hand in his. "Wait until I tell the guys that my girlfriend worked in a cattery."

Elizabeth tried to pull her hand back.

Jackson was having none of that. "Elizabeth? Will you forgive me? I was a stupid kid two years ago. I lost track of what was really important—you."

He raised the back of her hand to his lips. "Can we try again? Will you be my girlfriend?"

Elizabeth looked into the eyes pleading with hers. Could she forgive him that misstep? Melody said it was normal for young men before they settled down. Jackson looked like he saw her, the real Elizabeth, not just the daughter of Winston Abberly. Now was the time to take a chance.

She smiled and nodded.

———

"WHERE'S YOUR GIRLFRIEND?" PAUL asked as he raised his beer.

"Gone to her parents for the weekend. Some kind of fundraiser they're having and demanded her attendance."

"Without you?"

"This time."

Jackson rested his arms on the pub table, checking they didn't stick to any old beer. "It's not exactly a fun time going there for a visit. Quizzing me about my assets and my future. Looking down their noses at me because I wasn't born with a silver spoon."

"How long can you hold out?"

They both knew what Paul was asking.

"I have enough cash to last out this school year, and for a few months after that."

"I thought you were broke when we talked before, didn't even have enough cash to cover your drinks."

"Yeah, things were tight then."

"Your scholarship didn't come through?"

"Scholarship? You've got to be kidding. That was just for Elizabeth's benefit."

"Then how can you be here at Vassar?"

"I probably should have been here all along, or a place like this. I deserved it. My mother was from a wealthy family, one like these." He gestured around the campus. "Her stuck up family disowned her when she insisted on marrying my father, a working-class guy. Another example of blue bloods closing ranks, keeping out the riffraff."

"You ever meet them?"

"Never. When the rich shut you out, when you go against them, it's forever."

"So, how'd you get the money to come to a place like this if it wasn't scholarships?"

"When my parents were killed, I was their only kid, so I sold their house. My old man had a pension, and I had the choice of getting it in monthly payments over twenty years or taking it as a lump sum. I'm not the patient type, willing to settle for paltry amounts trickling to me over decades. So, I went big. With the house sale, and the pension payout, I figured I had enough to get me through four or five years here at Vassar, meet the girl of my dreams and marry her. Then my investment would have paid off."

Paul smirked. "Nice gig if you can get it."

"I think I've got it. Just her parents to get around."

"Do you have to win them over?"

Jackson shook his head.

"Nah, I don't think so. She's their only chick, and they're not about to cut her off, even if she displeases them. I'm working on it, getting her to see how they're trying to control her life, that she can make her own decisions."

"And you're part of her decisions?"

"The most important one. I'll be reeling her in any time soon."

The men clinked glasses.

––––––––––––

"They don't like me, do they?" Jackson asked.

Elizabeth didn't have to guess who he referred to. "It's not that they don't like you, darling, they don't know you."

"Haven't made much of an attempt to get to know me."

He made an effort to soften his voice, to rid it of the petulant little boy angst he felt. Stuck up snobs. Thought he wasn't good enough for their daughter.

Linking her arm through his, Elizabeth continued their stroll. "Doesn't matter. I'm of age, and I get to choose." She resisted crossing her fingers behind her back.

"Just so your father knows that."

"He does, of course he does."

Her tone didn't match the conviction of her words.

Stopping and turning to her, Jackson spoke as if an impulsive thought entered his head. "Let's elope!"

He studied her face carefully to see if he'd timed this right. She might need a little more convincing. "I love you, and you love me."

Elizabeth nodded.

"Your parents don't like me, so they'll put up every blockade then can to stop us from marrying." When she didn't respond, he prodded. "Right?"

"Daddy likes things to be his idea, his way. I'm afraid that would extend to my marrying, as well."

"And your mother—what sort of wedding do you think she'd want for you?" This should set the hook.

Cringing, Elizabeth considered the elaborate, society affair her mother would spend a year planning. It would all be done ways

Melody and her friends would approve of, that would meet their standards. Never had she liked being the center of attention.

"I think I'd dread the wedding," she admitted.

At the look on his face, she hurried to explain. "Not the getting married to you part, but the ceremony my parents would insist on."

"So?"

Elizabeth looked at the diamond on the fourth finger of her left hand. It was nothing like the gem that graced her mother's hand, but who needed that? This one was what Jackson could afford, probably more than his budget allowed, but he'd sacrificed to show his love for her.

That spoke more than any money in a bank account.

"Let's do it."

"How should we tell them?"

Elizabeth twirled the plain gold band on her finger, the one that matched Jackson's wedding band. Normally, she was not a fiddler; her mother would never have stood for that when she was growing up. But whenever the topic of telling her parents came up, she couldn't help herself.

It was a simple ceremony in the living room of the home of the Justice of the Peace. Paul and his girlfriend stood up with them and signed the registry as witnesses. Looking at their signatures, Elizabeth realized that she'd never before heard the woman's last name.

But it was done, and with far, far less fanfare than if her parents had been involved.

She knew how disappointed Melody would be that she'd not gotten to plan an elaborate wedding for her only daughter. Daddy would let his irritation show that he hadn't walked his little girl down the aisle. But, as Jackson pointed out, giving away the bride was an archaic notion that didn't apply to them. Elizabeth was her own woman, doing as she pleased.

True. That was how she wanted to live her life.

But they couldn't keep their marriage a secret forever; her parents would have to know. They'd been legally married for almost a month now. Going home for the weekend and breaking the news at the dinner table held little appeal.

In fact, she'd rather sleep with the cats and risk her allergies than face down her parents.

Jackson understood, thankfully, and he didn't press her on this. But they had to be told, and soon.

"I have an idea," Jackson said.

GRADUATION DAY. MAY 22ND, just five weeks after the other most important day in Elizabeth's life—her wedding.

Jackson's plan was simple. They wouldn't have to do any explaining themselves. Being in public, her parents would never risk a scene. They'd have time to calm down and come to grips with the idea before the four of them met for dinner.

From her seat near the back of the row of graduates, Elizabeth was grateful she could not see her parents' faces. In alphabetical order, students were called up to receive their diplomas; she knew her parents would be perturbed when the As went by, and no Abberly was called.

Once she had the official marriage documents, Elizabeth took them to the registrar's office to have her surname changed to Whitmore.

A faint nudge from the right brought her back to the present. Jackson whispered, "That's you."

She'd missed the officiant calling 'Elizabeth Whitmore'. To her credit, it wasn't easy getting used to a new name.

She rose, showing every bit of poise she'd acquired from finishing school. She made up her mind. She was done hiding.

As she accepted her diploma, she faced where she knew her parents would sit. Yes, there they were. For once, her mother's grace deserted her, and her shock and dismay shone through. Daddy's eyes glared; his arms crossed. Oh, well. Now they knew. Let the fallout happen.

And happen it did.

JACKSON HAD TO SPEND time with her sometime. Wouldn't do for her to get bored and leave him. But it was more fun going out for a drink and a little something more with the boys. Still, when needs must...

Lately, he might have detected a restlessness in Elizabeth. Better lure her back in. Feign interest, and all that.

"Have you always gone by Elizabeth? What did your parents call you when you were a kid?"

Elizabeth frowned. "Elizabeth, of course. That's what they named me."

"They didn't have any cute pet names for you? Something a little less formal? Liz? Lizzie? Beth? Betty?"

"No, they always called me by my proper name. And they called my brother Jonathan."

"Brother? That's the first I've heard of a brother. Where is he?"

His death was not something Elizabeth enjoyed talking about. In her family, it was almost a taboo subject. After the funeral, by tacit consent, they all refrained from saying his name.

"He was three years older than me, almost four. I looked up to him."

She thought back to those years. "Sometimes he tried to ignore me. I guess that was normal. He was twelve, and I was just nine. I couldn't keep up with him in the things he liked to do. But when he paid me some attention, it was nice. I adored him and wanted to please him."

"Did you?"

"Pardon me?"

"Did you please him?"

What an odd question. "I don't know. He treated me okay, at least at far as older brothers go, I believe."

"Where is he now?"

"He...he passed away."

"Cancer?"

"No. There was an incident."

"What happened?"

Incident. Such an innocuous word for those few moments that transformed all their lives.

"We were at the ocean. Daddy rented this cottage." Elizabeth thought back. "Mother called it a cottage, but really it was a house, a pretty pleasant house."

"Yeah, what was it like?"

"It had three bedrooms and a den where daddy worked much of the day. There was a kitchen, and a butler's pantry. Mother used that to get us drinks. Marcia was our cook. She came with us and spent time in the kitchen. She had a small suite off of the kitchen where she stayed."

"Sounds like a nice place."

"It was," Elizabeth agreed. "Smaller than our home, but just right for a summer holiday." She smiled. "We went there three summers in a row. We had some good times there."

"What did you do there?"

"Mostly play with my brother. We didn't really make friends in the area, or my parents didn't. There were a few other kids on the beach some days, but they were mostly either a lot older than us or a lot younger. Our parents didn't encourage us to socialize with others."

"Did you want to find other kids, anyway?"

Elizabeth looked at him quizzically. The thought had never occurred to her.

"No. No, I don't think so. We were used to being on our own or playing with the children of our parents' friends when they arranged play dates for us."

"So, it was just the two of you kids playing?"

"Yes. That day, we went swimming. Marcia was supposed to be watching us from the kitchen window. It was a bay window over the sink and looked out on the ocean."

"Where were your parents?"

"Daddy was working in the den. He rarely took time off from work and always had lots to do."

"And your mother?"

"She was reading a book and napping in a lounge chair on the deck. Jonathan and I played on the beach, and then we got hot. We had on our bathing suits, so we went into the water to cool off."

"Sounds like fun."

Elizabeth closed her eyes. "Yes. Yes, it was. The ocean water at first was freezing on my skin after being overheated on the sand. But almost right away, it felt good.

"Jonathan went in first; he always did that. While I'd stick in my toe, then creep in inch by inch, he took half a dozen lunging steps, then dove right under. None of that slowly getting used to it for him."

"Sounds like my kind of guy."

"Yes, you would have liked him." Her attention turned inward.

Jackson moved to put his arm around her and snuggle on the couch. This was all new information to him, stuff that might come in handy later.

"Go on," he urged. "It might help to talk about it."

"Jonathan was a decent swimmer. Excellent, even. That's why my parents didn't worry about us going into the water on our own. They knew how well Jonathan swam, and that he'd look after me." Her eyes filled, and she blinked several times. "He did. He did look after me."

"What happened?"

"Jonathan went out deeper. I didn't like to go past where I could touch the bottom, but Jonathan never worried about that. He was a fish.

"I tried to keep up with him this time, and so went out deeper than I'd usually ventured. It was okay. I was swimming, and it's easier to float in the salt water than in our pool at home.

"The sun felt good, and it was just the right temperature now that I'd gotten used to the water. I lay on my back floating, just enjoying the feel of the air and the ocean and the sun."

Jackson waited, sure the good stuff was coming soon.

"Then Jonathan shouted. My ears were under the water, so his words came through muffled. I straightened up to tread water so I could hear better. I couldn't see my brother. I spun in the water and couldn't see the shore, either. How had I gotten out so far?

"Then Jonathan's shouts came closer. He was making a lot of splashes as he swam toward me. When he was closer, I could see the muscles in his shoulders straining. I wondered why he was swimming so hard. Then I noticed that although I was just treading water, he was swimming hard. I was still drifting farther away.

"He told me not to worry, that he'd get me. I'd be okay. He started yelling at me to swim to him. I'd never heard him use that tone of voice before. He wasn't teasing and he wasn't mocking. He seemed, well, scared. My big brother didn't get scared."

"What did you do?"

"I started swimming to him as hard as I could; I wasn't a great swimmer." She added, "But I'm better now. I've worked at it so that this would never happen again."

"What happened next?"

"We made some progress in getting closer to one another. Jonathan kept yelling, 'Swim across it. Don't fight the current. Come to me.' Then he kept hollering about riptides. I didn't know what that was.

"Finally, our fingers touched, and he grabbed onto me. He pushed me to the side and yelled to swim as hard as I could. When I hesitated, he said he'd be right behind me. Then he pushed me harder, and I torpedoed through the water. Or that's what it felt like. He said to get to shore and get Dad. When I turned my head to look back at him, he waved his arm and said to go, go fast. He needed me to get Dad."

Elizabeth brushed a tear from her cheek, but others followed its track immediately. "My brother never needed me for anything. I was the one who always needed help. So, this one time he asked me for something, I would do it. I swam as hard as I could. When I had no breath left, I kept going.

"I was fairly close to shore when I heard voices calling my name. When I looked up, Marcia and my mother were there, both wading into the water with their clothes on. They pulled me the rest of the way to the beach. Their faces were all wet. I thought they'd gone under the water, too, but later realized that they were crying.

"Daddy was there. He was launching the canoe and paddling faster than I'd ever seen him move. He hollered at mother to go get help."

She looked at Jackson. "Daddy never raised his voice and definitely not at mother. That's when I knew that something was really wrong. Something bad."

"Was it as bad as you thought?"

Elizabeth nodded. "Worse. Daddy canoed way out, so far that we couldn't see him anymore. Then other boats came, motorboats that sailed back and forth, in and out."

"Do you know what happened?"

"I didn't at the time, but I learned about it later. A riptide came up. They can come out of nowhere. While I was floating on my back, I got caught in one, not even realizing that I was being pulled out to sea. My brother noticed and tried to get me. He did, like he said he would. When he pushed me, he got sucked in the riptide and it must have gotten stronger. It pulled him out to sea quickly. Daddy and the other boats stayed out all night looking. Light beams were all over the water and klaxons sounded for hours, but they never found him."

She reached for a tissue. "That was the last time I saw my brother. The last that anyone saw of him."

THIS EXPLAINED SO MUCH.

Jackson held his softly sobbing wife in his arms. No ugly, gasping crying for his Elizabeth. No, even in her sorrow, she was every inch the lady, keeping up appearances, never breaking protocol.

The knowledge he'd just gained fell into two categories. First, he now understood why Elizabeth upheld her good girl image, and her aversion to ruffling feathers. Guilt. He just had to make sure she switched her allegiance to going along with *him*, rather than her parents.

Second, he realized that the Abberlys needed a son. He was just the fellow to fill that role.

Yes, this had been a fruitful evening, full of knowledge he could use. He made soothing sounds as he gathered his wife closer to his chest.

He smiled.

"OF COURSE, THIS WILL be annulled."

Winston Abberly was the iceberg heading for their marriage ship.

"Sir..." started Jackson.

Elizabeth held up her hand to her husband, then turned to her father. "No, Daddy. It will not."

"I will have this annulled by next week."

"No, Daddy."

"Don't you 'No Daddy' me."

Anticipating her parents' reactions, the young couple had prepared for this. "Daddy, there are grounds for annulment, and none of them apply."

"Have you already looked into it, tried to do it?" Melody asked. "Let your father handle it for you. He'll get it done."

"Mother, we looked into it, knowing that's what Daddy would suggest."

"Mr. and Mrs. Abberly," Jackson boldly intervened. These people had to get used to him sometime, so might as well start now. "An annulment only applies if one spouse was already married to someone else, if one of the pair was under age 18 and didn't have parental consent, if they didn't have the mental capacity to understand marriage, or if they married under duress or fraud."

He smiled kindly at his in-laws. "Clearly, none of those things apply to us." He wrapped an arm around his wife's shoulders.

"Duress or fraud." Winston looked triumphant. "We'll work with that." He turned to Elizabeth. "Obviously, this man forced you, holding something over you."

"No, Daddy."

Glaring at Jackson, Winston continued, as if his daughter hadn't spoken. "What is it you want? How much will it take to make you go away?"

For just a split second, Jackson considered. Just how much would Winston offer him? No, he and Paul had gone over this scenario countless times. Whatever the sum Winston put on the table would pale in comparison to what would be his if he just waited. Elizabeth, after all, was his only child and heir. "Sir, you wound me. It's your daughter I want. She means the world to me."

Or at least the means to get into the world he preferred to live in.

"I give you one week to come to your senses, Elizabeth. If you don't, then you're on your own."

Carefully, Winston placed his napkin on his plate, rose from the table. "Are you coming, my dear?" He held out his arm to his wife, and they left the restaurant.

ELIZABETH, BEING ELIZABETH, HELD it together until they got back to their small apartment. Even then, while tears rolled down her cheeks, she remained in control—no sobbing or wailing for the Abberly's princess.

"That went well," Jackson said. On a scale of one to ten, it had been about a five in his predictions. There had been no welcoming arms, but no talk of disowning or disinheriting Elizabeth. He couldn't expect them to be happy about Elizabeth hooking up with someone not from their elite circle.

This next part required patience. Elizabeth was their lone kitten, and they'd spent their lives sheltering her. That included her lifestyle.

If Jackson read these people right, they'd not be able to stand their daughter living in what to their eyes was squalor. This was a perfectly respectable apartment for a young couple starting out, but not if you're from the uber rich.

To prove to Winston and Melody that he wasn't a gold digger, Jackson pledged to look after Elizabeth, including financially. It would not be fun, but he considered it an investment. If he waited them out, Winston would cough up money so his daughter could live in the style in which she'd grown up.

That style would spread to include her husband, of course.

At the end of the week, there was a phone call from her father's law firm.

"Ms. Abberly," the lawyer began.

"Mrs. Whitmore," Elizabeth corrected him. "That's my name now."

"Mrs. Whitmore, your father has instructed me to ask if you're ready to begin annulment procedures."

"No, I'm not, nor will I ever be. I'm married, whether Daddy likes it or not."

"I understand what you're saying. Your father will not be pleased, though."

"True, and I'm sorry for that, but this is the way it is."

———

IT TOOK ALMOST ANOTHER month before Melody called her daughter.

Gradually, the two women spoke more and more on the phone. At first, Jackson worried that Melody might influence her daughter against him, but he should have had more faith in his bride. She might appear meek, but there was backbone in the girl, and she stood up for him, determined to make this marriage work.

It was kind of neat; he couldn't remember anyone taking his part like this before. Someone who stood up for him, plus came with a wad of cash large enough to last a lifetime. Yep, he really knew how to pick 'em.

Much as Melody disliked the whole idea of Jackson, she didn't want to lose her daughter.

So far, Jackson's go-big-or-go-home strategy worked. He got the girl. Now he needed to secure the money. He'd rather get it *now* than wait until the old man popped off.

While old lady Melody looked like she kowtowed to her husband, she had some power. It was her influence that got the young married couple an invitation for the weekend.

Man, he could get used to a house like this, especially with all the staff to look after it both inside and out. No offence to his wife but cooking and cleaning were not her forte. Any culinary skills she possessed were learned at the elbow of one of their cooks, who didn't mind the lonely little girl hanging around. That is, when her parents didn't know she was in the kitchen, mixing with the staff.

Sure, Elizabeth tried, yeah—but what else did she have to do with her time? Trying to curry favor with the old man, Jackson insisted that his wife stay at home, that *he'd* support her. This could earn his brownie points two ways.

First, being a man after Winston's heart, he'd be the provider for his wife. Second, and this was the one he counted on, Winston would be unimpressed with the lifestyle Jackson's salary afforded the couple. So, he'd either cough up money for them, or offer Jackson a decent job in his company, one befitting the son-in-law and spouse to the heir of the dynasty.

Yep, there was no way this could fail.

ALTHOUGH HE RECEIVED AN air kiss from Melody, Winston ignored Jackson's outstretched hand. Okay. So, this was how the old man wanted to play it. Game on!

Dinner was civilized, with Melody, that mistress of polite conversation. Elizabeth joined in on cue, but her heart wasn't in it. Winston's eyes darted between his daughter and her husband.

A polite time after dessert, Winston offered, "Mr. Whitmore, shall you and I retire to the back patio?"

It was more order than a question.

"I'm sure Matilda can rustle us up some good Scotch." He raised his arm to make it so. The waiting server scurried from the dining room to do his bidding.

LEFT ALONE IN THE dining room, Melody suggested, "Let's go to the sunroom, dear. I have some brandy there."

"Yes, mother."

Seated, and cradling a brandy snifter, Elizabeth said what was on her mind. "What does Daddy want with Jackson? I hope he's polite to him."

"Do you not think your husband can stand up for himself?"

"Of course he can. But he's hampered by trying to get along with my father."

"If he's cowed by Winston, best we find out now. I think he'll like what your father has to say, though."

"Why? He's off this annulment kick? Took him long enough."

"I think your father is resigned that this man is in our lives." Looking over the rim of her snifter, Melody added, "At least for now."

"Mother!"

"We must be realistic, dear."

"Jackson is my husband, and I love him. We're in it together forever."

"Whatever you say, Elizabeth. But would you permit me to say that you seem to have lost that newlywed glow?"

"I'm fine, Mother. I'm happy. It's just..."

"Just what?"

"It's just that the days are long sometimes. This is not how I imagined my life after graduation."

"Married?"

"Being married isn't the problem." She turned to face the older woman directly. "Mother, do you ever get bored?"

"Bored? Nonsense. When would I have the time to be bored?" She studied her only child. "Bored is a state of mind. You can choose to never let yourself be bored."

"But what do you *do* all day? Our place is small, and I clean it in half an hour. Then I can spend another hour looking up recipes, but then what?"

"Why do you think I've always been on so many committees? I have to keep my mind active."

They sipped in silence for a few moments.

"Jackson doesn't want me to work." There. She'd said it.

Melody nodded. "I suspected as much."

"Why? Why would you suspect that? He met me at college and knew I was on a career path."

"Some men are like that. They want to be the providers and have their wife look after the home, even in this generation."

"Mother, you're an intelligent woman. Didn't you ever want to have a career?"

A wistful look came across her mother's face, quickly shuttered. "Maybe, at one time, it crossed my mind, but your father wouldn't have liked that."

"Does what *he* likes take precedence?"

"In many ways, your father's an old-fashioned man. He believed that it was his job to look after his family, to provide for us. That was his role. My role was to make this place into a home."

"But didn't you want more? Couldn't you do both?" Something occurred to her. "Didn't you go to college?"

"I attended Mount Holyoke."

"Did you graduate?"

"I did."

"What in?"

"Art History and Architectural Studies."

"Mother! Why didn't I know about this?"

"You never asked, dear." She waved a hand. "Besides, it's ancient history, and hardly matters now."

"It does! We have similar interests. We could have been talking about this all along."

"I didn't want to encourage you because it might not fit in well with your future. Anyway, your father wouldn't have liked it."

"I don't care what he'd have liked!"

"Please keep your voice down. Remember, this is your father we're talking about, and my husband."

"But, Mother, didn't you miss it? Didn't you resent Daddy for not letting you work in the career you studied for?"

"We all make choices, dear. I made mine. You can't say we haven't had a good life, can you?"

ALTHOUGH THE GROUNDS WERE beautifully landscaped, you could only stare at the scenery for so long.

"Sir," Jackson said, "you look like you have something on your mind." Let's get this over with.

"I do, young man." He inhaled the slightly smoky aroma of the scotch. "So, you think you're going to stay with my daughter?"

"I do, sir. I love her and we're in it for the long haul."

"So you say." He paused. "This," he indicated the house and surrounding acres, "is how she grew up. I can't have a daughter of mine living in a tenement house."

"Sir, I object to that. Where we live is small, but it's pleasant. And it's just for now. I've only been at this job a month; it will take me time to move up and earn a higher salary."

"Yes, well, my Elizabeth should not have to wait for that."

Yes!

"I realize that, but it's the best I can do for now. I'm on a career path."

"A path to what? A hundred grand a year? My daughter is not used to living on an income like that."

Neither was he, but now was not the time to bring that up.

"Here's what I suggest." He turned his direct gaze on Jackson. "There are many companies in my holdings. I've looked at your transcript."

He paused at Jackson's startled look. "Boy, when you have money, you have access to all sorts of things. But back to you. You did all right, respectable in most classes. Good thing you took an MBA."

He rose and stood at the edge of the patio.

"Here's what I propose. I have an opening coming up in one of my companies. It's not an executive position, but it's not entry level, either. The job's in the marketing department—sales. It will require some traveling. Are you opposed to travel?"

"No, sir."

Travel! He'd hardly been out of the state. To see places on someone else's tab, maybe even overseas travel. Hell, yeah, he could do this.

"You might be on the road a bit, flying around. Think you could handle it?"

"Yes, sir."

"We wouldn't want Elizabeth to get lonely while you were away."

"No, we wouldn't want that."

"Good. We're agreed, then."

"Sir?"

"Elizabeth should not be alone while you travel, so she'll move back in with us."

"I'd have to talk to my wife about that before we make any decisions."

"Son, this has been her home all her life. Do you think she enjoys being cooped up in your tiny one-bedroom apartment? Do *you*?"

He had a point. "Not really, sir."

They could live *here*?

"Melody will have a suite in the west wing prepared for Elizabeth." As an afterthought, "and you, of course."

Yes! Whoa, better not appear too hasty.

"About this job. What does it entail? Is there room for advancement, and what is the salary?"

"You don't beat around the bush. First thing I've approved of in you."

Winston swallowed more Scotch before continuing. "I'm big on my staff earning their job titles, working their way up the ranks. With some, I fast-track that, but it pays for managers to understand what those under them do. Am I making myself clear?"

"Yes, sir. Makes total sense, and I wouldn't have it any other way."

Winston looked skeptical. "As for salary, for the first six months, we'll match your salary to what you're currently making."

At Jackson's dour look, he added, "but you'll have no living expenses. After the six months, we'll talk. If your performance is satisfactory and we both agree to continue, the company will pay off your student loans and your salary will rise by 50%. You'll be contacted Monday morning with a job offer. We'll talk again at the end of the first year."

Winston drained his glass of Laphroaig Cairdeas Scotch, set it on the wrought iron table, and went into the house.

———

So, they moved in.

This was the life he'd always dreamed of. It would be perfect if it was just he and Elizabeth. Having to share meals and space with his in-laws, he could do without. But they were old and would not live forever.

Then this mansion would be his.

Thankfully, the job kept him on the road.

A lot.

Maybe more than strictly necessary, but hey, a guy needed to have some fun. Flying first class, renting only the best vehicles, staying in the best hotels—man, a guy could get used to this.

And he was.

Of course, there were obligations—society stuff. These black-tie affairs required the proper clothing. Since he was able to spend all his salary on himself, no problem.

And Elizabeth? Well, she kept off his back. She had her own stuff to do.

Daddy-O allowed her to work, doing some of the interior design for his real estate holdings when something needed to be staged, or for new developments. He paid her decently, too. It was sickening that she made more money than him, but that was temporary.

He'd see to that.

TIME FLIES WHEN YOU'RE having fun.

The next several years flew by, and life was good.

Living in a mansion while footing none of the bills worked for Jackson. Yes, there were social obligations, mostly of the stuffy kind, but they suited his needs as well. Plenty of opportunities for schmoozing as the Abberlys introduced him to all the right people.

Work went well. Slowly, then not so slowly, Jackson rose in the company. When you're the owner's son-in-law, it wasn't hard to get candidates vying for the same job to back off.

Senior management, even those who didn't like him, recommended him. Who wanted to make an enemy of the heir apparent?

Lately, though, he detected a slight cooling from Elizabeth's parents, especially Winston. Although the man had never truly warmed to Jackson, polite toleration reigned. Most of the time.

Disapproval, some of the time.

Once, when he came home in the early hours of the morning, a surprise awaited him. Quickly punching in the code to prevent the alarm from going off, Jackson removed his shoes so their soles wouldn't click on the marble floor. As he silently walked toward the stairway, a glow came from the open door of Winston's office.

"Jackson, would you join me in here a minute?" It was more an order than a question.

Biting back an expletive, Jackson complied. Feigning a relaxed pose, he leaned against the open doorway.

"Good evening, or should I say morning?"

"Let's be blunt, man to man. Gentlemen have things we need to do. Those activities are best kept away from home. This might be a major city, but it's a small town with the circles we keep."

He rose from behind his desk. "Our women are to be protected at all costs. That means financially, and emotionally. If anything gets back to Elizabeth, or you hurt my daughter in any way, I shall have you removed. Do I make myself clear?"

"I don't know what you're getting at. I love my wife and would never hurt her."

Winston's steely gray eyes pierced him. "You travel enough to give you opportunity to indulge in whatever. We never soil our own nest. Understood?"

After that, renovations began. Out of his own pocket, Jackson paid for the addition of a private entrance to the west wing of the mansion, the area he and Elizabeth called home. Now, he could come and go unmonitored.

Or so he believed.

———

THE CEO ANNOUNCED HIS retirement plans.

Yes! Although the man ran just Jackson's company, not the entire Abberly conglomerate, it was a start. That meant Jackson had six months to plan his campaign. He'd risen quickly in the firm, given his name and—he liked to think—his job performance. Taking over the

CEO job meant leapfrogging over two senior managers, but that was doable.

If he played his cards right.

Ostensibly, the board had the final say, but everyone knew that behind the scenes, Winston Abberly had his finger on every senior appointment in each of his companies. Winston couldn't deny his son-in-law the job, could he?

But there was that imperceptible cooling he'd sensed. Time to reel the Abberlys back in.

Time to play his trump card.

"Winston, Melody, we have an announcement to make."

Gathered in the formal dining room at home, Jackson timed this just right. The gazpacho cleared away; the maid set glasses of shrimp cocktail in front of each of them.

Knowing the Abberlys frowned on public displays of affection, Jackson did it anyway, placing an arm around Elizabeth, and a kiss to her temple.

"We're pleased to let you know that you'll be grandparents soon."

Melody's spoon clattered to the charger plate, a major breach of protocol. "Oh, we'd worried it would never happen."

Was the cow questioning his virility?

"Something this important has to be planned," he told her. "We waited until our careers were established. A child is a big deal, you know, and we wanted to be sure he or she would be our main focus."

There. That sounded right, didn't it?

Winston pressed the button discretely located under the table where he presided over dinner. When the maid appeared, he ordered, "Cecile, please bring us some Krug Grande Cuvée Brut Champagne, as well as some sparkling cider for my daughter. We're celebrating."

Questions about Elizabeth's health—fine. How far along she was—three-and-a-half months. The sex?

"We don't know, sir, and prefer not to. We'll love a little girl or boy equally."

Although a boy would fit his plans best. Didn't matter hugely; if they didn't produce a male this time, he'd hold that in reserve for next time.

Instead of retiring to his home office to work, as was his usual habit, Winston invited Jackson to join him in the den. The butler opened the humidor, offering the men their choice of cigars, then switched on the whisper-quiet air cleaning system.

"So, Jackson," Winston said when they were alone. "Big news."

"Yes, sir. We're very pleased."

Winston studied the glowing tip of his cigar. "I hear that you're making a play for Anderson's position when he retires."

"Yes, sir."

"That means pushing two men out of the way."

"I'm aware of that. I wouldn't do it unless I believed I was the best man for the job, the best qualified to run the company, to put it where you'd like it to be."

"That's a tad cocky for a young man who's only been with us a few years."

"I think of it as confident, not cocky. I know how important the company is to this family, and I know what I am capable of."

"I, too, contemplate what you're capable of."

Jackson smiled. That was a compliment, right?

———

THE JOB WAS HIS.

Of course, it had been a no-brainer, but the official appointment cemented both the job and Jackson's importance in the conglomeration. Today, this company.

Tomorrow, who knew?

After expanding this one, he'd move on to one of the Abberly's larger holdings. Before Winston retired, Jackson would have positioned himself as the only likely successor to take over the financial empire.

But it was work, more work than expected.

Not everyone under him showed the loyalty that was his due, and they needed to be dealt with. Winston was not a fan of firing long-term employees, so some finesse was needed to keep his father-in-law from getting his shorts into a wad.

It would take time, but he'd get there.

———

ON THE HOME FRONT, things weren't working out quite as he'd intended either.

Elizabeth and her mother grew closer. Often, when he'd enter a room, their heads would be close together, and they'd stop speaking. When he'd ask what they were talking about, he'd get a vague, "Girl stuff."

At dinner one night, Winston insisted Elizabeth cut back on the number of hours she worked.

Damn! *He* should have been the one to bring that up. Never mind, he could recover from that.

"Good idea, sir. Elizabeth and I talked about that last night. I've been worried about how tired she is of late, and we wondered how to broach this with you." He squeezed his wife's hand. "Her well-being comes first, you know."

Although Elizabeth brought in a nice chunk of change to their joint account, it was obviously charity money her father threw her way.

After all, what did she really do? Pretty up some places before they sold. It's not like *she* actually did any of the work; she directed others to do her bidding. How hard was that?

She didn't have the responsibility on her shoulders that he did he, as CEO of a company. If it was anyone but his wife commanding such a salary for so little, he'd object.

As it was, it helped swell his coffers. Theirs, really, but Elizabeth rarely dipped into it.

That was due to Daddy Dearest.

Old Winston insisted that even if he and Elizabeth had a joint bank account, she must still maintain her own account. Terms of her trust fund, and all that.

So Winston claimed.

Jackson suspected the old man didn't want him getting his hands on Elizabeth's cash. Didn't matter. He'd make tons of his own, and one day, he'd have it all.

But in the meantime, his spidey senses told him things were falling off the rails. With this pregnancy, her parents were pulling hard on all their over-protective measures. Geez. You'd think Elizabeth was the first woman to ever conceive a child.

Slowly, Winston and Melody were drawing their only child into their net, and it was closing with Jackson on the outside.

That would never do.

"Elizabeth, babe, I've got something to discuss with you."

Tell her, in reality—not discuss. Jackson pulled Elizabeth onto the bed beside him and took her hand. "You know how committed I am to your father's companies."

"You've impressed Daddy with your diligence. I've never seen anyone rise in his companies as quickly."

He kissed her fingertips. "I'm doing it all for us—you, me, and our baby." He pressed his other hand to her abdomen.

She rested her head on his shoulder.

Good. This next part would be easier without her looking at him.

"Now that I'm CEO, I've given a lot of thought to this company, and what's best for it. I commissioned researchers, and the results are in. Babe, this company has flat-lined here, but it has huge potential on the west coast."

"You'll expand your marketing?"

"That, too, for sure. But I'd like to move the entire operation out west."

Elizabeth lifted her head. "Won't that mean even more traveling for you?"

He shook his head. "You don't understand. I'd move us, too."

"Us?"

"Yeah. You and me—our family. And I'd like to do it now while you're still feeling well, before the baby's born."

"Leave my parents?"

"Yes. You didn't expect that we'd live with them forever, did you?"

Elizabeth paused. Maybe that's exactly what she had thought.

"I guess not."

"Good. That's settled then. We'll tell your parents at supper tonight."

THIS TIME, JACKSON WAITED until they had cleared the dessert dishes from the dining room table. He cleared his throat.

"I have an announcement to make."

Melody's hand went to her throat. "It's not twins, is it?"

"No, Mother Abberly, nothing like that. Elizabeth and the baby are just fine."

He turned his attention to his father-in-law. "Sir, I'll be moving my company to the west coast."

Winston studied Jackson. "What do you mean? Are you starting a branch office?"

"No, sir. We'll shut down operations here and relocate to San Diego. I have all the research to back up the decision, if you'd like to look at it."

He doubted Winston would; he left management decisions up to each CEO.

"But you have employees here."

"True. They'll all be invited to move with the company, with no loss of salary."

Melody rarely intruded on business discussions, but said, "These employees have homes here, families."

"That's also true. This will be a test of their loyalty to our company. I will reward those who move with us. Those who choose to stay behind—well, that's their choice."

He turned again to Winston. "I trust, sir, that you might make an attempt to make room for them in one of your other companies."

"Are you sure about this, Jackson?"

"Yes, I'm positive it's the best thing for the company. Give it a year, then you'll see just how much more lucrative we are."

"That's a lot of traveling you'd have to do."

Elizabeth explained. "Not really. We'd move, too."

Silence.

Finally, Winston broke the tension. "When do you propose all this will happen?"

"Within the next month or two. I'd like us to get settled in a new place while Elizabeth is still feeling well. Definitely before the baby arrives."

"The baby!" More of a wail than a statement from Melody.

"Mrs. Abberly, I have a favor to ask of you." He looked at Elizabeth, then tucked a strand of hair behind her ear. "Elizabeth and I haven't talked about this yet, but I'm sure she'll agree."

He covered Elizabeth's hand that rested on the table. "Mrs. Abberly, when it's time for the baby to arrive, would you consider coming to stay with us? Please? I know it's a lot to ask, but it would mean the world to Elizabeth, and to me, too.

———

WHEN YOU HAVE MONEY, things happen quickly.

Once Winston realized Jackson and Elizabeth were serious about moving, he took over, at least in their personal affairs. He hired the right people to investigate homes and neighborhoods, then purchased a house for the young couple.

It was nothing like the sprawling abode where Elizabeth grew up, but was a decent-sized, modern home for a young family. He presented a set of keys each to Elizabeth and Jackson.

"A house-warming present for you—a house. It's not like this," he gestured around his own place, "but adequate for the two of you, plus a child, with plenty of room for when your mother and I come to visit."

Elizabeth gave her father a peck on the cheek. "Thank you, Daddy. I was wondering how I'd find time to fly there to hunt for a house."

"There's a link in your email to a virtual walk-around. I insisted it be unfurnished so you can put your own touches on the place."

"I've been looking online at baby furniture. Want to see possibilities I've bookmarked?" Melody led Elizabeth off to her computer in the sunroom.

Left alone, the men eyed each other. "Thank you, sir. That is most generous." Did he think I couldn't provide for my wife? "Not necessary, but nice."

"I want my daughter well-protected."

"As do I, sir, as do I."

Was there more behind Winston's words? Never knew. He was a cagey old bastard; didn't get where he was without some smarts.

But not as smart as me.

Melody ran into Jackson in the upstairs hallway.

"Jackson, I've been meaning to ask something."

"Certainly, Mother Abberly. How may I help you?"

"It's not for me. I've been wondering about Elizabeth and what will happen to her job when you move to California."

"Job? Since she's expecting, her time will be fully occupied with getting ready for the baby, then taking care of our child. But before then, she can have a go at designing the interior of our offices. It shouldn't tire her out too much to arrange a few couches and paintings."

"There's a lot more to what Elizabeth does than move around furniture, you know."

"Of course, I know that. She has a whole degree in this stuff, and she's very talented. I'm proud of the work my wife does."

"Right."

Melody walked off.

Not wanting his daughter to suffer with the masses on a commercial flight while she was pregnant, Winston hired a jet to carry Elizabeth and Jackson to Southern California. Then he booked them a suite for a month at the Fairmont Grand Del Mar in San Diego, so they could be comfortable while they organized their new home.

Suited Jackson. If old Daddy wanted to throw money their way, who was he to stand in his way?

As it happened, it took them only half the month to get their house ready to move in, thanks to Elizabeth. The woman certainly could organize things.

The house was nothing lavish like the mansion, or even the suite within the mansion where they'd spent the last few years. But it was fine. Definitely many steps up from the place where Jackson's parents had raised him.

Besides, it was a house—presentable enough to entertain business clients—and that was all that mattered. One day they'd have something much grander.

Sooner, rather than later, if Jackson had his say.

WORK DIDN'T SETTLE IN quite as well as did their home.

Who knew that some of those executives who refused to uproot their families to move to California were actually doing something? Doing a lot, apparently, to keep operations functioning.

Of course, there would be blips due to the move, but this bad? Everyone wanted a piece of him; no one seemed able to do anything on their own, especially the new hires. It was a mess.

Several times, Jackson was tempted to ask Elizabeth for help. With her calm organizational skills, she might just make a difference. But no, that was not part of the plan. He was the man, protecting and providing for the little woman.

Except, it was her father who'd bought their house and gave his daughter a new SUV so she could get around independently. It was Elizabeth's trust fund that paid for their day-to-day expenses and bills.

That was fine. He had enough on his plate at the office, so if the wifey managed the home front, all was well.

———

ELIZABETH NEARED THE END of her seventh month of pregnancy. She didn't move as fluidly now. She rested. She focused inwardly, rather than doting on her husband.

He'd heard that was typical, and life would return to normal after the birth.

His secretary, Barb, giggled when she heard him say that.

"Sure didn't work that way for my sister and her husband."

"It will for us. Elizabeth is devoted to me."

Again, Barb giggled.

She felt free with her boss, freer than he'd ever let an underling get before. But there was something about Barb....

She was smart. New to the company, she initially feigned ignorance of the Abberly empire; a few internet searches quickly changed that. Hmmm.

Over a FaceTime visit, the Abberlys announced they were coming to San Diego for a visit.

Melody wanted to lay eyes on Elizabeth in person to make sure her pregnancy was going all right. This would just be a five-day visit; they'd return for an extended stay after the birth.

Making sure he was alone, Jackson made a call.

"Paul, this is Jackson."

"Hey, buddy. How's it going out in Lala land?"

"Fine. Look, this morning I FedEx'd a parcel to you. Open it and have it ready at this time tomorrow. I'll call you on it then. I need to pick your brain in confidence."

"Anything special?"

"Yeah, what I need is specialty advice from some of your associates who know how to get things done."

JACKSON HAD A SURPRISE for his in-laws. Several surprises, in fact, but he'd start with this one.

The senior Abberlys flew west by Lear jet. Flying was Winston's passion, an indulgence he allowed himself. He owned two small planes, but neither was large enough to safely wing them west over the Rockies.

An idea stuck in Jackson's mind well over a year ago, but it took time to percolate and solidify. It began with flying lessons. Learning about small planes would help with this plan, plus Winston would think Jackson was trying to emulate his father-in-law, in a hero worship sort of way.

On the third morning of Winston and Melody's visit, Jackson launched the first part of his plan.

"Girls, I have a treat for you." He pulled back his sleeve to check his Rolex. "In about 45 minutes, a limo will pull up out front. It will take you to the top baby stores in San Diego. Since women do not live by shopping alone, I've made you a reservation at The Addison in The Grand Golf Club for lunch. Then the limo will return you here. You, my darling," he gave his wife a squeeze, "will be ready for a nap by then."

"What will you do, dear?" Melody asked her husband.

"Leave that to me; I have a surprise for Winston." Jackson gave his best guileless grin.

"I'm not a fan of surprises."

"You'll like this one, Daddy," Elizabeth assured her father. "Jackson's been working on it for months."

While the women left to get ready for their shopping spree, Jackson grabbed his car keys. "Shall we?"

Winston followed him out. "Planning to show me what you've accomplished at the office?"

"Winston, Winston. All work and no play makes us dull boys. I want to show you what I've been up to."

Twenty minutes later, Jackson pulled into the parking lot of the Montgomery-Gibbs Executive Airport.

"You want me to take you somewhere?" Winston asked.

"Nope. I'm taking *you* somewhere. I'll be right back."

Soon, he returned with the keys to a modern, four-seater Cessna 186 airplane. "I've been taking lessons. Just got checked out on this thing last month."

They only spent an hour in the air, scouting out the sights. Jackson kept looking at his watch.

"You late for something?" Winston asked.

"Ah, no." Jackson tried for a sheepish look. "It's Elizabeth. I want to make sure I'm near home in case she calls me. She tires easily these days. I know she was looking forward to shopping with her mother, but I don't want her overdoing it. I feel like a worrywart, but do you mind if we head back?"

"Can't complain when someone looks out for my daughter."

"The surprise isn't over. I've booked this baby for you and Mrs. Abberly for this afternoon and overnight." Jackson patted the cowling on the plane. "We've made reservations for you tonight at the Sierra Nevada Resort and Spa, including dinner. We thought it would be like a mini holiday for you and missus. Elizabeth picked out the place. There's a small airport just outside of Mammoth where you'll land, and the resort will send a ride for you whenever you call them."

"Jackson, this is a lot." Winston wasn't used to someone else planning his life.

"Indulge us, please, sir. This was your daughter's idea, and she's excited about pleasing you. The plane's booked; all you need to do is let them take a photocopy of your pilot's license."

"In that case, thank you, boy. Very thoughtful."

He pulled a pressed handkerchief from his pocket and blew his nose. Again. "Damned allergies. I'd better take another antihistamine. I don't know what's set them off today."

Jackson did.

Barb might be an amazing administrative assistant, but she had crazy cat lady tendencies. Most days, her clothing sported fine feline hairs. Once she even brought one of her cats to work. It was sick, she said, and would stay in its cage all day.

Two towels covered the mattress in the cat's cage. Not sure at the time how he'd use it, when Barbara left for the break room, he stuffed the towels in a garbage bag, getting himself scratched in the process. They'd remained sealed in bags and a box on the top shelf of his side of their bedroom closet, waiting for the right time.

Once he learned the dates of his in-laws' visit, the plan took shape. While Elizabeth napped in the family room, he spread the towels over the bed sheets and pillowcases.

Yesterday, he slipped out of work, ostensibly to reserve the plane, but while checking it out, he shook those same towels vigorously all over the plane's interior.

———

THEY STOPPED FOR SOME takeout Cuban sandwiches, and at a drug-store for more antihistamines. Back in their kitchen, while the coffee pot did its thing, Jackson got out the plates and a Greek salad he'd put together that morning.

"Can't wait for you to try these new coffee beans we found. Of course, poor Elizabeth doesn't do more than inhale the fumes from my cup, but she's counting down the days before she can enjoy a full cup of her own."

"I enjoy most coffee, as long as it's strong and fresh."

"I guarantee this one will have a little something different."

While his back covered his actions, Jackson poured into Winston's cup several doses of antihistamine dissolved in water that he'd pre-pared before anyone else rose from bed.

By the time their wives returned home, Winston was ready for a nap. "Why don't you go lie down for a few minutes, Jackson suggested. The plane will be ready when you are."

"Think I'll do that. Want to join me, Melody?"

"No thanks. I'll start organizing our purchases while Elizabeth has a rest."

Half an hour later, when Winston rose, the women were still folding and admiring tiny clothes.

"Have a good rest, dear?" Melody asked.

"I would have, if not for these damned allergies. They haven't been this bad in years."

"Sorry, Daddy. While you're gone, we'll make sure to clean your room thoroughly in case there's something in there bothering you."

"About that." He started to suggest maybe they should postpone their trip until he felt better. But looking at his wife's eager face, and his daughter, so pleased with herself, he didn't have the heart. "I'll take another antihistamine, then I'll be fine."

Jackson loaded his in-laws' overnight bags into the back of his Suburban SUV and drove them to the airport. While Winston presented his pilot's license at the office and signed off on the plane, Jackson offered to do the dirty work.

"It's hot out. You and the missus stay in the air-conditioned vehicle while I do the outside walk around for you."

Under Winston's watchful eye, Jackson made an exaggerated show of carefully inspecting all the points required in a plane's pre-takeoff walk around. Turning his back so Winston couldn't see, Jackson loosened, then removed the clamps holding the rubber fuel hoses aft of the right and left door posts.

Rummaging in his pockets, he then pulled out a pocketknife. With a flick, he turned on the mini laser light. Showing it to Winston with a grin, he pretended to shine the light into the undercarriage, inspecting whatever was within reach.

Pressing a button on the knife, a thin, razor-sharp blade protruded. Honed to a fine point, Jackson used it to prick little holes along the fuel lines. For good measure, in a couple places, he gouged larger holes, watching to see how quickly the drips spread. Not bad, but maybe not enough.

He made several larger gashes in areas where the aviation fuel would puddle inside the cowling and not show outside the plane before takeoff. Just what he needed was for some other pilot to spot the pooling fuel prior to Winston taking off.

"All clear, sir," he told Winston, as he held the door for his mother-in-law.

"What's that smell, dear?" Melody asked.

"Can't smell a thing. My nose is stuffed up."

"Probably the aviation crew spilled a little fuel when they filled up the plane. Happens all the time," said Jackson. "You won't notice once you're in the cabin."

He reached into the back seat of his SUV. "Here, I know those seats aren't always the softest, so I brought you some towels to sit on during the flight. I'll spread them out for you."

The cat towels in place, he turned to Winston. "If you'll humor me, sir, I know this is old hat to you, but it's still new to me."

Taking a deep breath and reciting, as if from memory, he said, "This Cessna 182 SkyLand cruises at 180 miles, and burns 11 gallons an hour. It holds 55 gallons of av fuel, and is full, so it has a range of just over a thousand miles. It's 351 miles from here to Mammoth Lake, so you should be in good shape."

"Well done, boy." Winston sneezed. "Damn this nose of mine."

From his pocket, Jackson pulled out a fresh package of antihistamine tablets and two bottles of water. "Better take one now before you get too stuffed up. Maybe two would do the trick."

"Thanks, son. Thoughtful of you."

"I've done my best to think of everything."

***

"Would you mind if I had a little nap, dear?" Melody asked. "Elizabeth might be the one who's eight months pregnant, but she wore me out this morning."

Melody settled herself more comfortably in the right-hand seat of the plane. She noticed how her husband stretched and twisted his neck.

"Head rest not comfy for you? Here, I'll fold one of Jackson's towels and put it behind your head."

She fussed with getting it just right. "That's better. Now I'll shut my eyes for just a bit."

"Go right ahead, dear." He sneezed. "I'm going to take some water and another of these antihistamines. I'll wake you up if anything exciting happens."

This was their standard joke. Not a fan of small aircraft, Melody usually slept during their little jaunts, confident that Winston would handle anything that cropped up.

With his wife snoozing beside him, Winston relaxed into his flying. In a plane, he felt free, as if when he took off, he left the cares of the world behind him.

If he could only breathe better, and wasn't so sleepy, he'd enjoy this more. Correcting for the wind, and setting the trim, he switched the plane's settings to autopilot. It was straight flying for the next hour, with a head wind. He'd take in the passing scenery...

Winston came awake with a start.

Instantly, he scanned his gauges, but all looked well at a quick glance. He'd never before nodded off while in control of a plane. Better take it off autopilot and concentrate on his job. A sharp look to the right showed him his wife hadn't noticed his little nap.

How long had he been out? Couldn't have been more than a minute or so. He frowned when he spied his fuel gauge. Less than a quarter of a tank. He could have sworn it was full when they'd taken off. And hadn't Jackson mentioned the tank being filled?

Something wasn't right.

Why was he sweating so heavily? The air conditioning was on, and Melody looked comfortable.

He yanked the towel from behind his neck and mopped his face with it. Why was his heart pounding? He was on high blood pressure pills. Weren't they supposed to control such things? He couldn't think straight, couldn't get control over his mind.

He sneezed four times in quick succession. Then his nose ran. He leaned forward to fish the now well-used handkerchief out of his back pocket.

Slumping, his weight pushed down on the yoke, altering the attitude of the ailerons, sending the plane into a dive.

Hours and hours of flight experience had him recovering from the incipient spin by steadily pulling back on the yoke. Flying straight and level again, he once more mopped his head and face with the towel. The rivulets of sweat rolled down his face, unimpaired. Another bout of sneezing attacked him.

Reaching into the cup holder, Winston downed two more antihistamine pills he'd placed there, along with a swallow of water. At the rate he was losing perspiration, these two bottles of water wouldn't have him breaking even in the hydration department.

Maybe water was what he needed. Couldn't dehydration affect your heart rate? He thought he'd read that somewhere. He'd try anything to get his stupid heart to quit pounding.

He looked over at Melody, warmth filling him. Such a loving, trusting woman. He thought back over the good times they'd had together. There had been bad times, too, times when he'd neglected her for his business, times when their grief nearly tore them apart.

He rarely allowed himself to think about those dark days when they lost Jonathan. Jonathan. His son and heir. The fearless kid who'd tackle anything. The boy who would grow to be a man and work alongside his dad.

Winston fought to keep his eyelids open. Images of Jonathan assailed him.

Times when the boy stood in the doorway to his dad's office with a baseball and glove in hand, wanting to play catch. How many times had he said, "Sorry son. I need to finish this work, but I'll be out to play with you later."

But later never came.

He shut his eyes on the memory and slumped forward, pressing down and to the right on the yoke.

MELODY SLOWLY OPENED HER eyes. Something about the movement of the plane felt different and woke her. Were they there already, and about to land?

Glancing out her window, the brown and reds of the Sierra Nevada Mountains greeted her. Close. Much too close.

"Winston?" No answer. "Winston!"

She tore her gaze away from the approaching mountain to look at her husband. He wouldn't try to scare her, would he?

Winston's hands were loose at his sides, his head turned toward her, eyes closed, and his body pushing down on the yoke.

She screamed at him, pushed on his shoulder, but all she succeeded in doing was moving the yoke under the weight of his slumped body. Had he had a heart attack?

Oh, God! What to do, what to do?

Okay. Winston had gone over this with her. She knew the rudimentary tricks of flying a plane. She needed to get control of it before they crashed.

Taking a deep breath, she placed both hands on the yoke, but she couldn't pull it up against the weight of Winston's body.

Letting go, she shoved on Winston until he slumped against the far door, leaving the yoke mostly unencumbered.

Taking hold again, she pulled back on the yoke slowly, although every single atom inside her urged her to just yank on the thing as hard as she could. Avionics didn't work that way, Winston had instructed her. Small, firm corrections worked better.

Okay, okay, it was working. Slowly, the view through the front screen changed from solid red-brown mountains to a patch of blue, then more and more blue.

She let out the breath she'd been holding. Yes! Sky! They were no longer plummeting toward a crash with the earth.

Let's get some distance between this plane and the ground so she could think of what to do, and rouse Winston so he could get them safely on the ground.

She continued to pull back until all she could see outside was blue, blessed blue with wisps of white clouds. Her shoulders relaxed. Crisis averted.

Shaking her left hand to release its cramp from gripping the yoke so tightly, she reached for her husband, trying to shake him awake. She opened her mouth to holler at him when the plane's stall warning blared.

She knew what that meant. She'd never been in a plane when one sounded; Winston practiced his stalls and spins and spiral dives when she wasn't around.

That sound meant the pilot had to do something and right away, or bad things would happen. Exactly which bad things she didn't know. But the screeching decibels of the wild blaring didn't go away.

Then it did. With a gentle motion, the nose of the plane stopped its climb. For a few seconds it hung, suspended in silence, almost at peace.

Then the nose tipped, first into a gentle dive, and then plunged straight down.

"Nooooo!"

She knew what had happened. She'd pulled the nose up too high, removing the vital flow of air over the wings that kept them aloft. Now the plane was in a stall, heading for the ground, no longer able to resist gravity.

"Winston, wake up! Get us out of this!" Twisting in her seat, she wrenched her husband's arm.

In her panic, her left foot connected with the rudder pedal, stomping on it. Now the nose pointed not just straight down, but spun to the left, at first in a gentle circle, then faster and faster. Not just a stall. Now they were in a spin.

G-forces pushed her into her seat, swallowing her screams. The lazy circles accelerated, as did the speed at which the mountain rushed up to meet them.

All she could do was check that their seat belts were on, mere seconds away from impact. Too little, too late.

She laughed.

JACKSON AND ELIZABETH SNUGGLED together on the couch, her head on his chest, his arms around her, hands on her abdomen, awed at the rippling movements that came from her distended belly.

Neither paid much attention to the movie on the television.

Elizabeth yawned and stretched. "You know, I probably shouldn't say this, but great as it is to have Mother and Daddy here for a visit, it's nice with just the two of us."

"My feelings exactly."

The sound of Jackson's cell phone woke them from their doze. "Excuse me. I think I left it on the kitchen counter."

"Mr. Whitmore, this is Amelia from The Addison. Would you like me to still hold the dinner reservation you made for Mr. and Mrs. Abberly? It's almost 10 o'clock, there are no other guests, and we'd like to let the staff go home."

"What? They didn't show up yet? They should have been there hours ago."

"Yes, their reservation was for 6:30."

"Perhaps they ordered room service instead."

"No sir, they haven't checked into their suite, either. I checked."

"Is there another restaurant on the premises? Perhaps they got mixed up."

"There is a bar. Are they the partying type? It's on the wild side in there, a young crowd."

"No, that isn't them at all."

"Is there another resort nearby?"

"No sir, nothing of this calibre, just a couple small motels."

"Jackson?" Elizabeth stood with one hand on the doorframe to the kitchen, the other rubbing her stomach. "What is it?"

"That was the resort. Your parents haven't checked in yet, and they skipped dinner."

"That's not like them." When had Winston not rigidly held to a plan? "Do you think something's happened?"

"Your dad's an experienced pilot. The weather's fine, and they had plenty of time to get there in daylight."

He kissed his wife's forehead. "You go get ready for bed, and I'll look into this. We'll have it cleared up soon."

The small airport at Mammoth Lakes was not staffed at night. A call to the front desk of the resort confirmed that Mr. and Mrs. Abberly had not checked in, although their room was being held, since it was paid in advance.

It took a while to rouse anyone, but The Montgomery-Gibbs Executive Airport, although at first reluctant to divulge any information, finally confirmed that Winston's Cessna had not touched down there since this morning.

Time for the big guns. Not 911, though.

Jackson looked up the number for the SDPD. "I'm not sure if this is an emergency, but I'm concerned that my in-laws aren't where they are supposed to be."

Once the dispatch operator understood that a plane was involved, one flying in the mountains that hadn't arrived when expected, action started. "One of our officers will get back to you."

Within an hour, two officers rang the bell on the Whitmore's' front door. Sitting stiffly in the living room, the two men took notes, then left. Elizabeth, in her robe and slippers, leaned against Jackson.

"Don't worry, honey. You dad's a competent man. He can handle anything. Maybe there was a mechanical problem, and he had to touch down. Pilots practice that all the time. Search and rescue will find them."

AND THEY DID.

Hours had passed, though, since the small plane veered far off its flight path. It was almost daylight when a helicopter saw the tendrils of smoke. The flames had long since died out.

Because of the mountainous terrain, the chopper landed several miles away. While the pilot remained with the machine, his partner hiked to the crash site.

Radioing back, he relayed that indeed, it was a small plane, although the call letters were obliterated. Hard to tell how many bodies were inside; the flames had engulfed the aircraft, leaving little other than twisted metal, embers, and smoke.

They wouldn't know more until they recovered the black box.

The recovery took time, but once daylight arrived, rescuers combed the area. Parts of the plane scattered on impact, but the bodies remained with the cabin section. Identities would be confirmed using dental records, but with confirmation that this was the plane the Abberlys were in, it was safe to assume this was the couple searchers were looking for.

The same officers came to the house to deliver the news to Jackson and Elizabeth, with assurances that the pair would not have suffered. They died immediately under the force of the impact.

Elizabeth collapsed; Jackson was there to catch her. Her usual stoicism gave way to wracking sobs.

"I tried. I tried so hard to make it up so them. I knew I never could, but I tried. I made them lose their son, and now they're gone, too. There's only me."

"Shh, darling. You're not alone. You have me to lean on. I'll take care of you."

"It's all my fault," she wailed. "They're dead, and again, it's my fault. I should never have planned that trip for them."

Jackson turned Elizabeth to face him. With hands on her shoulders, he said, "Elizabeth, listen to me. I can tell you for certain this accident was not your fault. Not one little bit." Then he gathered her close. "Officers, may I ask if you'd see yourselves out? We'll be in touch."

It was hours later when the pains began.

———

"BUT I HAVE ANOTHER month to go," protested Elizabeth. "This can't be true labor."

"Tell that to the baby," said the obstetrician. "He says it's time."

"Isn't there something you can do to slow things down?" Jackson asked. "Wouldn't it be better for the baby to wait the full nine months?"

"Babies survive these days at just five months."

"I don't want my child to just survive," Jackson said. "I want him to be healthy and ready to thrive."

"I understand your worries, but your baby's the one in charge here—not me, you, or the mother."

Jackson motioned for the doctor to follow him out of the labor room into the hallway.

"My wife has just received devastating news. She's an only child, and yesterday her parents died in a plane crash. She is distraught, understandably. Could grief have brought on early labor?"

Tired from pregnancy, weakened by the crushing grief of losing her parents, Elizabeth did not fare well. At first refusing all analgesics, it soon became apparent to those attending the birth that the young woman had had all she could take.

She drifted in and out of consciousness. Jackson gave consent for an epidural-spinal block, but the contractions took more out of Elizabeth than she had to give. Her body agreed, and the contractions dimmed in both frequency and intensity.

Things became critical, with the baby's head already engaged, and a barely conscious mother.

"Mr. Whitmore, we need you to make some decisions." The obstetrician laid out the options, including what might happen if they allowed things to progress naturally.

"Are you saying my wife could die?"

"Yes."

What would that mean, especially coming so close on the heels of her parents' deaths? Of course, Elizabeth's fate could not be placed at his feet; there were enough medical professionals around to attest to that. He had copies of their wills in his desk at home; he was Elizabeth's sole heir. She was her parents' heir.

Still, it was one thing to get people out of the way who didn't like him and stood in his way. But Elizabeth? What had she ever done to him?

He had another question. "And the baby?"

The answer was the child's life was also in danger. The child. His son. A piece of him to live on. Whitmore genes that would rule the former Abberly (not Whitmore) empire. His son deserved a chance at life.

He decided. "Let's do the C-section. Please, anything to save their lives. My parents are dead. My in-laws just died. I can't lose any more of my family."

TIMOTHY WINSTON JACKSON WHITMORE entered the world almost exactly 24 hours after they received the news of his grandparents' deaths. Placed on his mother's chest, the silent infant scanned the skin and objects closest to him.

His mother still slept through the anesthetic; later, that would be used to explain the lack of bonding, the lack of eye contact infant Timothy shared with those in his environment.

As a baby, he nursed and slept, not seeming too fussed over either. He was a remarkably content child, able to amuse himself with his own hands, endlessly passing his fingers in front of his face.

His parents bragged about what a self-possessed child he was, never overly demanding, patiently waiting until someone offered him food, but rarely crying to be fed or changed. The exception to his serenity was noise. Loud noises, and unexpected sounds startled him, rocking his world until the room filled with his inconsolable screams.

Elizabeth and Jackson learned to keep things quiet around their home. Not a problem. Elizabeth was raised that way, and Jackson was rarely home, anyway.

The baby thrived physically, and met all developmental milestones, with one exception. A major exception.

Although positive they had an extremely intelligent son, Timothy remained silent. None of that typical baby babbling, no mimicking sounds his parents made, no single words by his first birthday.

Nor his second.

Elizabeth got on Jackson's nerves. She started saying stupid things, pointing out problems with their son. Things she thought he should be doing or shouldn't be doing, comparing him to other kids and dumb things like that.

He was *not* like other kids. He was a Whitmore.

Then other people started noticing things.

Of course, in his position, he needed to entertain; it was expected. When they entertained guests, there were only so many times you could tell people that the child was shy, that he was going through a stage. When that same excuse went on for years, people noticed.

The kid remained silent. While other toddlers loved roughhousing with their daddies, Timothy made it clear he hated it. He might not speak, but the kid sure could scream. And those screams went on and on for hours. Enough to ensure Jackson didn't venture near the kid again for a long time.

From time to time, Elizabeth made noises about there being something different about Timothy.

"There is nothing wrong with my son!" he told her. "My son is *not* an imbecile. We're both Vassar graduates. The kid has good genes. I don't want to hear any more about this nonsense."

A MAN NEEDED A son, a son to be proud of. It was becoming clearer to Jackson that Timothy might not be the son he had in mind.

Then the seizures started. At first, brief and rare, then more intense, and frequent. The kid looked like an idiot during them. Frothing at the mouth, the whole bit. And he'd piss himself. The kid was four. Who still wore diapers when they were almost ready to go to school?

And endless rounds of medical appointments. Elizabeth ragged on him about coming with them, but geez, a guy had to work.

It became easier to spend more and more time away from home. Besides, when he was there, Elizabeth spent all her time fussing with the kid, almost ignoring her husband.

What did she expect? Of course, he'd find solace elsewhere. And fun.

A guy needed fun in his life.

HIS HOME LIFE WAS not the only thing not working according to plan.

From his grave, Winston Abberly taunted him. Rather than inheriting the coveted CEO position of Abberly Enterprises, Jackson maintained control over just the company Winston already let him have. The will sewed everything up tighter than any lawyer Jackson hired could untie.

Upon Winston's death, the management of his empire was taken over by the board Winston had set up for just such an eventuality. His wife, and on her passing, his daughter received a monthly income. Sure, it was a nice sum, but was meted out in dabs at set intervals. No access to the vast fortune the company sat on.

Even more insulting was the knowledge that Jackson was not mentioned in Winston's will. Nor in Melody's, not one word.

It was as if he didn't exist, as if they didn't recognize his potential. Another example of the elite closing ranks around their own, refusing admittance to those of humbler birth, no matter what their merit.

To top it off, the home they lived in was in Winston's name—Winston's and Elizabeth's. When the old man died, the house became solely Elizabeth's. Sure, she said it didn't matter, that what was hers was his, and it was their home together. Right.

Upon Elizabeth's fortieth birthday, she had the option to take over managing her father's enterprises or leave it in the hands of the current controllers.

That was a while off, but his wife showed no interest in being more involved in her father's companies. That was fine, but *he* could.

She resisted his hints about approaching the board to insist that Jackson play a more active role. No matter how many times he offered to step in to relieve her of some of the corporate weight on her back, she'd insist that it was no work at all. She only had to meet with the board a few times a year.

No, her focus remained on their son, fussing, and pampering the kid, making him into a right mommy's boy. The kid would be better off away from his fawning mother; then Jackson could make a man out of him.

***

ONE THING ELIZABETH LEARNED from her father was to keep her house in order—physically and financially. Just as her parents kept updated wills, so did Jackson and Elizabeth. They were each other's heirs.

If anything happened to Elizabeth, everything she owned passed to Jackson.

He could do so much more with the assets than Elizabeth ever would. He could make the company zing.

Or not, if he chose.

Liquidating companies would provide him with the luxury few people ever dreamed of. With that amount of money, he could do anything, go anywhere, and never worry about a thing.

What stood in his way?

Elizabeth.

He could fix that....

MEET SHARON A MITCHELL

Dr. Sharon A. Mitchell lives on a farm, with her nearest neighbor several miles away. Doesn't that seem like the ideal setting to spark the imagination? She takes long walks with her hundred-pound German Shepherd dogs, Pickles, and Dill. (Don't blame her - she didn't name them).

When a Plan Comes Together is prequel to the psychological thriller *GONE*, which begins where this story leaves off.

Sharon's working on her eighth novel for the psychological thriller series When Bad Things Happen series. They are all available on KU, plus *GONE* is free in Amazon Prime.

Care for a free short story from this series? Get it at <u>sharonmitchellauthor.com.</u>

Dr. Mitchell has also written six novels, each featuring an autistic child or young adult. Two nonfiction books accompany that autism series.

Sharon's been a teacher, counselor, psychologist and consultant for decades and continues to teach university classes to soon-to-be teachers and administrators.

To see all of her books, visit sharonmitchellauthor.com. Sharon loves to hear from readers and responds to each message. Contact her at sharon@sharonmitchellauthor.com.

THANK YOU FOR READING

We hope you enjoyed reading the stories in *Breakneck*.

We invite you to seek out more of our work and encourage you to get in touch via the information included at the end of each story.

Most of all, we wish you the best in all your reading experiences and hope to see you again soon!

www.ingramcontent.com/pod-product-compliance
Lightning Source LLC
Chambersburg PA
CBHW022005050726
47499CB00002BA/312